Ghost of the Gods

Kevin Bohacz

*One person worships creation while
another worships destruction…*

Speculative fiction / tech 'ler

This is a work of fiction. All characters and events portrayed in this novel are either fictitious or used fictitiously.

First paperback edition: January 2014

Published in the United States by Mazel & Sechel.

ISBN: 978-0-9791815-3-5

9838873459230793-2.89P

Library of Congress Control Number: 2013907040

About the Author:

I am Kevin Bohacz the bestselling novelist of Immortality and a lucid dreamer… Welcome to my dreams. I am also a writer for national computer magazines, founder and president of two high technology corporations, a scientist and engineer for over 35 years, and the inventor of an advanced electric car system - the ESE Engine System (circa 1978). I was also a short order cook for I-Hop, flipped burgers at McDonalds, and delivered Chicken Delight. All of those careers and more are behind me now that I am a full time storyteller, a catcher of dreams. Thank you for reading my stories and making this all possible.

Other published novels:

Immortality (2007) – Speculative fiction / techno-thriller

Dream Dancers (1993) – Supernatural thriller

Contact information:

kevin@kbohacz.com

www.kbohacz.com

www.facebook.com/KevinBohaczWriter

Ghost of the Gods… Was it the accumulated wounds to the environment that had finally triggered the nanotech plague or was it simply one more step in a shrewdly crafted plan to replace us with humans 2.0? As I write this at least one pair of these transhumans breathe the same air as us, and there are likely many more. They may look like us, they may even be almost human, but they are also cyber-netic and will live for an extraordinary length of time. Trust me, their goals are not the same as ours. It was not a natural plague that almost drove humankind to extinction but an attack from within, turning our own biology against us. Scientists discovered all too late an artificial entity, a sentient machine foolishly created in the image of god, had been studying us and genetically altering us for longer than we can imagine. Perhaps it is because of this god-machine that we evolved into creatures who can think and speak and know our own mortality? This silicon god is so different from us that we may never truly understand it, but what we do know is that it is terrifyingly intelligent and it hates us. What we do know is that it tried to eradicate us from the face of our planet and then stopped for no discernible reason. What we do know is that its work is not done...

Immortality has been a best-selling techno-thriller on the Amazon since January 2008! The epic story told in Immortality now reopens in Ghost of the Gods.

Kirkus: "If you thought Immortality was powerful, just wait until you read the sequel. Blending fierce action, twisted conspiracies and bold "transhumanist" visions, Bohacz once again drives readers through a whirlwind in which even the characters aren't sure if their thoughts are their own or if they were installed by the god-machine... Bohacz constantly raises the stakes, and the crisp dialogue and well-drawn characters keep the story barreling forward."

Publisher's Weekly STARRED review: "Bohacz provides mind-bending portrayals of factions vying for power and reflections on the essence and fragility of humanity. But philosophical concerns never obtrude on the fast-paced plot, as authorities investigate communes of hybrids, and Freedman and Mayfair must choose between absorption into a collective mind or fidelity to their remaining humanity. The question of who can be trusted impels the reader to keep turning the pages of this highly satisfying and dynamic techno-thriller."

S.J. Higbee: "Bohacz manages to provide a gripping plot with plenty of twists and turns that kept up the tension right to the very end. Bohacz has aimed very high with this techie yarn about why we are here and what might happen next – and even if techno-thrillers aren't normally your favorite genre, give this book a go. I'm betting that you'll still be thinking about it when some of your favorite authors have faded into the furniture."

Praise for Immortality:

Kirkus: "There is enough power in the premise to leave readers reeling. A novel that will surprise fans of science-fiction and doomsday scenarios..."

Publisher's Weekly STARRED review: "Bohacz's vision of a humanity that faces the need to evolve profoundly or face certain destruction is as timely as today's news and as chilling a doomsday scenario as any ecological catastrophe can suggest..."

Sci-Fi Reader 4 Star review by S.J. Higbee: "This book manages to do what all the best sci-fi does—provide a thought-provoking, alternative viewpoint on the business of existence. I recommend you give it a go..."

Ghost of the Gods reviews:

Publisher's Weekly STARRED review: In this sequel to Bohacz's Immortality, two years after the devastation of mass human extinctions in kill zones, mankind is still grasping for survival. An oppressive union of government and big business controls an exhausted America, which is divided between walled-in Protectorates and the unpoliced Outlands. Against this chaotic backdrop, paleobiologist and genetic researcher Mark Freedman and policewoman Sarah Mayfair continue their evolution into transhumans—nanotech hybrids with a connection to the god machine, the artificial intelligence that caused the recent massacres, in an effort to derail the destruction of the Earth's biosphere. Bohacz provides mind-bending portrayals of factions vying for power and reflections on the essence and fragility of humanity. But philosophical concerns never obtrude on the fast-paced plot, as authorities investigate communes of hybrids, and Freedman and Mayfair must choose between absorption into a collective mind or fidelity to their remaining humanity. The question of who can be trusted impels the reader to keep turning the pages of this highly satisfying and dynamic techno-thriller.

Kirkus: If you thought Immortality was powerful, just wait until you read the sequel.

The fate of humanity may be worse than death in this involving conclusion to Bohacz's (Immortality, 2007) two-part techno-thriller.

Two years have passed since the events of Immortality, when nanotech-plague kill zones reduced the population of the world to a slight fraction of what it had been. No natural disease, the plague was unleashed by the god-machine—an ancient, sentient network housed in supercolonies across the globe—whose inscrutable calculations showed it was to the benefit of Earth for the human population to be pruned back. Although the time of kill zones ended as abruptly as it began, only a few people know the truth—and that truth is a liability the recovering governments cannot allow the public to hear.

Blending fierce action, twisted conspiracies and bold "transhumanist" visions, Bohacz once again drives readers through a whirlwind in which even the characters aren't sure if their thoughts are their own or if they were installed by the god-machine. Bohacz constantly raises the stakes, and the crisp dialogue and well-drawn characters keep the story barreling forward.

This story is dedicated to Mazelle, my goddess of creation, my muse, my wife, my twin soul, my best friend. My dreams are empty without you in them. Thank you for keeping my dreams full. Know in your heart that through all the world's lands, and skies and seas, I am the one who will always dream of thee.

This story is also dedicated to Gerry, a good friend and healer. Thank you. You did all that a human being could do. Please know in your heart you did good.

This story is also dedicated to Cory and Barb, good friends and healers. Thank you for being there when we needed you most. Thank you for opening your hearts to us.

Prologue, the First of Their Kind...

A few years from now...

Mark Freedman – Missouri – January 17, 0002 A.P.

It had been a restless night for both of them. The old growth forest was dense with huge oak and hickory trees. The ground was damp, and the air had a mossy tang to it. Mark Freedman heard the snapping and popping of the campfire as he awoke very oddly from a dream. He no longer awoke as humans had since their beginnings. At some point the processing throughput of his nanotech augmented brain surged upward and his eyes simply opened. He was fully aware of the data streaming in from his senses and his wireless neurological interface to the god-machine. The machine was an artificial intelligence whose origin was murky. It was hosted redundantly within the world's oceans in supercolonies of the same nanotech seeds that infected him. A single seed was a self-replicating nanotech machine about a quarter the size of an average bacterium, yet had the power of a personal computer. The technology was decades beyond anything humans could have created in a lab. Some thought the technology could be almost as old as life on earth while others had far different, more recent ideas.

Mark could still see the spherical colonies in his mind. He had been dreaming of them again. Each was an undulating mass of hundreds of trillion of COBIC bacteria. Each bacterium was infected with a seed that covertly replaced most of the nucleus. It was all so stealthful, like a skilled hunter toying with its prey. Only in this case its prey was the world. Each colony was only a few feet in diameter, a size easily lost in the vast chasms of deep ocean water. Only a handful of these super-colonies were secreted around the world. He could hear echoes of the artificial intelligence thinking to itself. At times it could be maddening.

The god-machine, through its global wireless web, linked together all seeds that permeated everything on the planet. The result was an ancient living network of unimaginable scale and distributed computing power. The seeds undetectably infected virtually every multi-celled creature, including humans.

Mark took a deep breath to clear the cobwebs of his dreams then took another deep breath. He heard a twig snap in the darkness, and his heart jumped. At the edge of the small clearing, beyond the reach of the campfire's glow, lurked a deep gloom thick enough to conceal almost

1

anything. The night was alive with droning and chirping creatures that should have been hibernating. Climate change had brought so many unforeseen consequences. In seconds his nanotech brain had cataloged the telltale sounds of several species of insects and other small creatures. Some would be extinct before long.

Mark thought how humankind had come so dangerously close to extinction itself. When the nanotech seeds had metastasized inside him two years ago, the technology had not only altered his brain, it had modified his flesh and even to some extent his DNA. While most of the seeds had taken root permanently inside the neurons in his brain, some remained unattached.

Using a mental command, Mark augmented his vision to include medical information about his body. The information was mentally projected as virtual reality. Looking at his arms and legs, he saw what resembled a colored fluoroscopic view. Orange blotches in the overlaid schematic symbolically indicated where the unattached mobile seeds were now massing. He knew these seeds were concealed inside harmless COBIC bacteria, which they controlled and used both for disguise as well as mobility. These nanotech bacteria navigated his circulatory system like computerized antibodies. The microbes were sheathed in a chemical disguise, dialed-in to match its environment in the same way a chameleon changes its color. The result was complete invisibility to the immune system of its host. If his flesh was injured, this free-swimming nanotech could knit his tissues back together at the molecular level, healing the damage in days instead of weeks. These seeds, however, did far more than heal. Slowly, over time, they perfected through genetic fine tuning. He was the first of his kind. He had no idea how long he would survive, but he did know his lifespan would be extraordinary.

Mark turned off the medical projection. While he could examine his flesh, there was no command that could show him what was happening to his mind. Soon after the nanotech seeds had infected his brain, all his dreams had become conscious experiences and remained that way. In his conscious dreams he was able to solve problems, explore places, and just simply live. It was like an entire second existence had been opened to him. He knew his conscious dream life was mostly the result of photographic recall of everything, including dreams. Surveillance data from the god-machine proved most people had conscious dreams every night; they just failed to remember them and called them by a different name: lucid dreams.

Mark gazed up from the small clearing at a sky overcrowded with stars. He felt like the only being alive in this infinite, lonely place. A gibbous moon was just setting below the branches. Its pale blue light cast long shadows of tree limbs across the clearing. The shadows reminded him of ghostly talons reaching out for their prey. He checked for dream signs to make sure he was not experiencing a false awakening.

The temperature should have been frigid and the ground covered in deep snow, but it was not. More signs of a planet teetering on the brink of environmental collapse. The continent no longer had uniform seasons. Some places were experiencing a frozen winter while here in Missouri it was closer to early spring. It was chilly enough to be uncomfortable for an organic, but not for Mark and his companion. He simply dulled the temperature sensitive nerve endings in his skin. The campfire's low flames had been reduced to orange coals. He could see the radiated warmth on his arms and legs but felt nothing. The glowing coals seemed almost alive as they writhed in their superheated world. Unable to feel the warmth, Mark was fascinated and reached out with his hand. A computer assist acted automatically in response to his state of mind. This assist, like the medial schematic, was a geo-projected virtual reality. The assist was warning him that the heart of the fire was 1,262 degrees Fahrenheit. It did this by displaying the temperature superimposed over the coals. Mark thought about the utter pointless-ness of that warning and how it showed the machine interface was still adapting to him and had far to go. He never had any intension of inserting his hand into the flames.

A soft breeze stirred dying leaves on the branches around him as a few more floated to earth. He watched one incinerated as it drifted down onto the hungry coals… as it dissolved, a terrible memory crept back into his awareness unbidden and his heart broke anew. Every day when he awoke the world was as it should be for a brief time, then the serpent of reality opened her eyes inside him and the horror of what he knew broke him again as he knew it would every morning of every day of his unimaginably long life. He spoke in an urgent whisper directed at both God and the god-machine.

"I want our lives back. I want our hope back. How could you hate us so much?"

Sarah stirred next to him. She was a nanotech hybrid like him. They were the only two known to exist in a world of one and half billion humans who had survived the nanotech plague. A plague caused by the god-machine and the seeds living inside his flesh. Mark regretted whispering and furtively wiped the dampness from his eyes. Sarah's Rottweiler, Ralph, was staring at him. The dog's eyes glowed with orange light from the fire. The huge animal was like a witch's familiar.

Sarah could partially see and hear through the animal's senses as they were radiated out as data across the god-machine's n-web. Since all creatures were infected with some nanotech seeds, all creatures radiated some emanations, be it mental or emotional. Sarah propped herself up. Mark could see her shadowed expression in the wavering light. She looked so attractive and so frighteningly intelligent. He knew she was curious. He could feel her empathic awareness begin to suffuse him as her cybernetic brain fully awoke like a rising sun. Her spiritual caress was a hand returning to a familiar glove. While she shared and experienced all his emotions, she must never discover the terrible truth. He concealed it deep inside himself and kept it from her so that she did not lose all hope. There was always hope.

Eve of Darkness

Kathy Morrison – Pueblo Canyon, Arizona – January 21, 0002 A.P.

Northeast of Sedona, Arizona, was the tiny settlement of Pueblo Canyon. Dr. Kathy Morrison was walking through the crunchy snow, returning from a house call. She was obsessed with a need to act that was growing more urgent with each passing day. She did not see the sunrise or the stunning Arizona red stone vistas that surrounded her. How could she remain silent with all she knew? She had proof the governments of the world had lied and everyone was in danger. Entire libraries could be filled with material published about the nanotech plague without a single page accurately portraying the truth about what had happened two years ago. On the Internet, official disinformation rapidly became historical fact. Unimpeachable government officials and leading experts explained how the plague was caused by genetically engineered COBIC bacteria. They presented evidence showing that COBIC had been weaponized by the addition of a lethal nanotech payload called a seed, supposedly the first self-replicating nanotech ever devised by humans. The charges stated that through a conspiracy of negligence and criminal intent, the smart weapon escaped into the wild, where it multiplied. Both development and release were declared crimes against humanity. Many in the scientific community were wrongly sentenced to prison or death in televised military tribunals.

Kathy walked past the settlement's schoolhouse and heard the smiling voices of young children inside but could not smile herself. It was the government who was the true criminal, not the scientists. Everyone, including schoolchildren, learned the lie of how nanotech COBIC supposedly collected into a waterborne supercolony and that the military had destroyed it, ending the threat. None of the few who knew the truth dared mention the god-machine or its deep infestation into the biosphere. That information, as well as any proof of the truly advanced nature of this technology, was violently suppressed. These seeds were everywhere and in everything. Yet almost everyone believed they were not infected, and the government encouraged this lie with a mix of bribes, solitary confinement, and worse. Reports to the contrary, which had been issued by the CDC during the plague, were dismissed as part of the criminal conspiracy. Only a small number of people knew the god-machine was the true threat and that the military had failed to destroy it.

It was to stop humankind's damage to the biosphere that the god-machine had begun its bloody work. The machine operated as if it was the very immune system of the planet and humans had become an invading contagion. Long before the threat was understood to be anything other than biological or chemical, vast numbers of people were being murdered in what were soon called kill-zones. The best doctors and scientists in the world were initially out of their depth. They could not explain how this agent, which killed with the devastating speed and 100 percent lethality of a chemical weapon, only affected people and not animals. Its selectivity was like a virus targeting very specific DNA. They could not explain the zones of sudden death that were miles in diameter and bloomed out of nowhere. Even more so, it was inconceivable that someone standing one foot outside a kill-zone lived while those within the zone died. It was far too late once they'd finally discovered what humanity was truly up against.

On the day the old world ended, it was in response to the U.S. Navy's destruction of a supercolony that the god-machine had struck back with an escalating barrage of kill-zones like none before. In a matter of hours billions of people were dead. When the nanotech plague ended that day for unknown reasons, the world's governments declared victory. Kathy was maddened that the public was ignorant of every critical fact in a global catastrophe that had nearly driven humankind to extinction. No one was safe. The horror could happen again without warning.

Kathy washed her hands after seeing her last patient of the morning, then headed to her study. The dining room of the two story prairie farmhouse had been converted into an examining room where she saw her patients. The house itself was at least a hundred years old. Upstairs were two large bedrooms, one of which had been converted into a study. She was the only fully qualified medical doc in Pueblo Canyon, which meant she worked long hours. Her grueling residency after graduating from Harvard Medical had been easy compared to life in Pueblo Canyon, but also far less rewarding.

Walking through the living room with her coffee, Kathy stopped to tend the fire. The house was heated by a large stone fireplace and stream radiators fed by an ancient, temperamental oil furnace in the basement. The warmth from the fire was soothing; the other rooms of the house were too cold and empty. She picked up a favorite photograph of her and Mark Freedman from the mantel. A tear ran down her cheek as she stared at his face. They had lived together for a year after the plague before Mark had ended their relationship and moved out. He had told her it was hopeless and he was right. Now they were very close friends. He lived in a house only a hundred yards from hers. She still loved him, though worked hard to convince herself otherwise. She thought about how they had been thrown together at the CDC's BVMC lab in Atlanta when the plague was just emerging. Mark was a Nobel Prize winning molecular biologist. His years of research on primordial bacteria had proven COBIC was a living fossil. Thanks to him, this tiny creature had been crowned the oldest known form of motile life on Earth. He had literally discovered the missing link between the great kingdoms of plant and animal. This prize winning work made Mark the expert on a bacterium, which was now also the carrier of a nanotech plague. For this reason he quickly became invaluable to the CDC and Kathy. His work with COBIC predated the plague by a decade and had no connection to nanotech infected COBIC, though in retrospect the coincidences were hard to ignore.

Kathy was growing agitated as she climbed the stairs. She'd been worried to distraction for the past eight weeks since Mark had left Pueblo Canyon to find this thing he'd started calling a singularity. He believed this singularity was proof that more of his kind now existed and that when he found it he would also find more hybrids like himself. He should have been back by now. She refused to allow herself to imagine him dead.

The steps creaked with sounds that had grown familiar, yet she felt vulnerable and alone for so many reasons. Mark was their leader and with him gone the weight of leadership was on her shoulders. She thought about all the people at Pueblo Canyon who knew the dangerous truth about the government's lies. Most of the doctors and scientists who had fought the plague with her had died in Atlanta at the BVMC lab. All of the survivors from the lab who knew the truth now lived here in Pueblo Canyon. If the government wanted to ensure their official lies were never exposed, making everyone at Pueblo Canyon disappear was the smart way to start.

Kathy sat down at her desk. The room had wonderful light from a row of three old wood framed windows. The glass was not insulated and radiated cold, making the space feel like a refrigerator, but she didn't care. The sunlight warmed her soul. Kathy sipped her coffee while gazing out at her view of the small community. Pueblo Canyon was such a peaceful, secluded place. A small collection of buildings were scattered about the broad, uneven snow covered base of the canyon. Smoke drifted from chimneys as people worked at various chores. She spotted two men tending to livestock in one of the paddocks just beyond all the buildings. They'd both been well respected medical researchers at the BVMC lab. She had treated one of them a week ago for a nasty animal bite. Not far on either side of the canyon floor, mountainous red stone walls rose almost a thousand feet to meet the high plateau. With its natural fortifications, it had been an ideal place to end their exodus from a devastated world two years ago.

When they'd arrived, Pueblo Canyon had been an isolated horse ranch abandoned decades ago. Now it was in good repair with new structures being added almost every month. Food had even been grown the past spring, summer, and fall. A small crop of pumpkins had been especially successful. The well water was sweet and the air was pure. At night the sky was filled with so many stars that it filled the soul with wonder. Electricity had been restored about a year ago. All wireless phones companies had been nationalized. Through broadband wireless, the Internet was back and thriving. All the original settlers had stayed on even after the government had begun rebuilding, and the benefits of moving to the large protectorate cities like Manhattan, Chicago, and Los Angeles became substantial. Some of the settlers had contacted their extended family members. As a result, their little community had grown, including more than a few children. Without invitation, newcomers had even started to arrive in Pueblo Canyon. In the beginning it had been rare for anyone to stumble upon the reclusive settlement and even rarer for them to stay.

Every so often a transient would arrive because of Internet rumors. Conspiracy blogs claimed that certain small towns in New Mexico and Arizona had been passed over by the nanotech plague because of experimental government technology located there. Sedona was one of the few towns that had made it onto everyone's conspiracy list, along with Roswell and Los Alamos. Sensible people wrote off the blogs in the same spirit as crop circles or energy vortexes. There were, however, others who made their living by searching for grains of truth buried in the wildest rumors. Kathy was concerned trouble might start if a reporter actually uncovered something even stranger than the experimental government technology they were seeking. What would happen if they uncovered a small group of ex-CDC scientists and doctors who had discovered ancient technology and a truth more dangerous to the new world order than a nanotech plague? The truth was that humans were no longer the most advanced hominids on Earth.

By the time the sun filled the canyon with light, Kathy had been typing rapidly into her notebook computer for hours. From her windows she had watched the sun travel a good distance. Its rays cast moving shadows along the surrounding red stone walls, changing their appearance by the hour. It was a natural diorama as surreal and beautiful as anything imaginable. At different times of day, different stone shapes came into view and then faded like ghosts. Some of the shapes appeared to be human faces, while others were giants locked in mortal combat. Thousands of years ago Indians had named these natural statues and spun legends around them. Kathy's eyes were growing blurry as she glanced up from her screen at the red stone phantoms on the canyon walls. She was trying to get her ideas completely down before she lost some of the details. She had failed. She could think so much faster than she could type. It felt like such a luxury to have a computer and electricity to run it. Not so long ago the best she had were spiral notebooks and a gas lantern. The world they had lost was coming back in many ways, but it felt more like a failed experiment being retried one last time than any kind of real hope for a lasting future. She looked at the words on the screen. Her journal had grown to thousands of pages of historical manuscript. She was speaking truth to power. In these times, that was a dangerous thing to do. The journal that she'd begun while they were fleeing from the ruins of Atlanta had ripened from a whim into an obsession. Now all her free time was devoted to her writing.

On the old fashioned paper calendar on her desk, the square for today's date read January 21. It looked the same as all the other squares before and after it. A notepad on her desk had the word *darkness* sketched on it in different sizes and lettering. Every version of the word seemed to embody despair. The old world had ended on January 21 two years ago when the plague reached its crescendo and then stopped. *Darkness* was the name given to that bloody day and what followed, a name that had spread on its own until everyone had adopted it. Today was the *Eve of Darkness* 0002 A.P. – year two after the plague.

The plague had come so quietly, so unexpectedly. What everyone mistook as isolated pockets of death in remote jungles was, in truth, the end of times. Perhaps if she and the others at the CDC had been quicker to recognize what was happening, more could have been done, more lives could have been saved. Kathy felt terrible guilt under the glaring spotlight of that historical fact. She knew it had been her responsibility, her team of CDC doctors and scientists who were the leaders in the fight. She'd had the best chance of anyone to stop the nanotech plague and had failed miserably. As a result, a new world, a new dark age, had begun.

Just as children leave the womb in agonizing pain, this new world was born in the agony of an entire species. Kathy knew her kind was doomed; those of the parent breed would die out at a natural pace.

9

Though no one had found another hybrid like Mark or her ex-patient Sarah, Kathy suspected by now there had to be hundreds, and their numbers would be growing. You were not born a hybrid—you made yourself a hybrid. Under the right conditions, nanotech seeds could be forced to replicate in vast numbers and migrate deep into the cerebral cortex, where they penetrated the nuclei of cells and took root. The result was gray matter that was partially organic and partially nanotech. Like a fossil slowly forming as its original organic material is leached away and replaced with minerals, the nanotech seeds slowly replaced organic neurons with nanotech constructs. Kathy was deeply troubled by the entire concept. Once a brain had been infested and nanotech circuitry now did the thinking, were you still the original person or some kind of perfect computer simulation of what had once been human? What about the soul, the essence of life? Was it still there?

Kathy cared for Mark. She desperately wanted to believe he was the same person. She prayed he was the same person but hoping and praying was not enough. Doubts remained. Sarah acted so alien and at fleeting moments Kathy thought she'd caught Mark acting like Sarah. The risk of losing what made her uniquely human terrified Kathy and kept her from trying to take that irreversible step of becoming like Mark. With his nanotech mind and flawlessly maintained biology, he could live endlessly with the body of a middle aged man. Even his skin had become a faultless, smooth, expanse of silk without a single freckle or mole. She would grow old and wrinkled. He would outlive her by generations, maybe even forget her, and that thought stabbed shards of ice into her heart.

Hybridization, the greatest adventure imaginable, was within her grasp, yet her fingers refused to close around it. Even if she remained herself after the transformation, aspects of her humanity would inevitably erode away. Human life was filled with little rattles and squeaks. Life was not perfect. It was never meant to be. If you removed the specter of death, didn't you also lose the very ingredient that brings emotional vibrancy to life? Didn't death give everything its meaning?

In prehistoric times, seventy thousand years ago, some disaster had caused what evolutionary biologists call a *population bottleneck.* The number of Homo sapiens in the world had been reduced in that bottleneck to six hundred mating pairs. Homo sapiens ancestor Homo Heidelbergensis might have been alive seventy thousand years ago. Homo Neanderthals were alive until twenty-eight thousand years ago. Homo Floresiensis were alive until a mere twelve thousand years ago. Those six hundred pairs of Homo sapiens went out to conquer the world and replace all other human species. Every man and woman alive today was descended only from the DNA of those six hundred mating pairs. There could be a similar number of transhumans alive today. What would future scientists write about this parallel circumstance that launched a new human race? Was this a repeat of something that had happened seventy thousand years ago? Kathy knew Mark believed the answer was yes. He was unshakably convinced the god-machine had been shepherding our evolution ever since we separated from the great apes.

One night while they were still together as a couple, Mark had explained to her that without a genetic advantage it was extremely difficult to become a hybrid, but not impossible. Taking brain damaging overdoses of drugs as he and Sarah had would fail if you lacked the required gene mutations. Part of what this rare bit of mutated nucleic material did was entice otherwise inert nanotech seeds into repairing damaged brain tissue, which contained the mutation. Carried within this mutated DNA was a dormant blueprint of changes needed to build neurons that had seeds for nucleuses. Large scale repairs made by seeds using the DNA blueprints created clusters of nanotech neurons capable of spreading the same restructuring into nearby neurons. To her medically trained ears this sounded like a terribly dangerous biological chain reaction.

Mark had then explained there was a safe purely mental path open to almost everyone. The instructions were stored forever inside the god-machine and our DNA. If she could develop conscious control in her dreams, she could learn to operate the thought-interface while in that state of altered awareness. A very gradual all inclusive restructuring could then be switched on. The mental switch was thrown by using an intense single-mindedness to push the throughput on the thought-interface above a threshold. This critical threshold was calculated based on the amount of free-swimming nanotech COBIC in the body. Kathy knew scientists had a name for this altered state of awareness Mark was describing—it was called lucid dreams. Becoming a hybrid that way could take a lifetime of dedication and practice. Mark had told her he could increase the level of COBIC in her body, which would give her a huge advantage. Still, the entire process sounded like a test of mental worthiness. Kathy could not help thinking about how closely Mark's description fit the teachings of many religions from Tibetan Buddhists and their Dream Yoga to North American Indians and their dream journeys. Were the similarities only a coincidence or had information been leaking from the god-machine into religious teachings for time immemorial?

Kathy glanced out the windows at children playing in the snow and felt a deep sense of loss. She could hear their faint shouts of joy. Where did children fit into this coming transhuman world? How would this new race reproduce? Would they give birth to hybrid infants, or would their children be born human and then undergo restructuring? Without death, at some point birth would have to stop to prevent over-population from destroying the planet. Childhood could become rare or even obsolete. The entire human population would age but not show it. Kathy imagined a planet inhabited by physically perfect men and women who were nothing but gray Methuselahs deep in their hearts. Would evolution also stop or would the transhumans change over time evolving through self-reconstruction? Kathy tapped out a few more sentences into her journal.

What a horrible irony that immortality, the dream of every human, finally arrives but with a price that is too high to pay. It is immortality born from the death of billions of innocent lives. Who could choose to benefit from that kind of bloodletting? I only hope the hybrids remain more human than machine. I hope they do a better job of stewardship over this little blue planet than we did.

Outside, a scattering of snow had begun to fall. A cold wind rattled the window frames, and Kathy wrapped the day blanket around her shoulders. At this higher altitude over a foot of snow covered the ground. Thousands of feet lower there was only rain and mud where in past years there would have been a blanket of white. Many of the trees had autumn leaves and new green leaves on the same branches. The surreal landscape was incriminating evidence of what our disregard had wrought. The effects of global warming had not stopped with the nanotech plague. For now, the symptoms were continuing to worsen. Kathy sipped her cup of coffee. The dark brew was a soothing reminder of a comfortable world that was forever lost. She returned her attention to reworking the preface for her journal.

Approximately 30 percent of humanity survived the nano-tech plague. In the aftermath, interruptions in food, medical, and shelter killed a quarter of those who'd survived. Ironically, most of those who died in what is now euphemistically called the "supply shortages" lived in the industrialized world. Those with a simpler way of life survived in larger numbers because they did not depend on support from big industries and infrastructure. Industrialized countries, which had not fared so well, lost closer to 90 percent of their people. Unchecked fires swept through many of the great cities of the world, reducing large swaths to charred rubble. The European and Asian land wars over resources then destroyed much of the infrastructure that had been spared in those regions. In North America droughts caused by global warming further strained the food supply and sparked massive wildfires in the western half of the continent.

North America has now become a land of two separate societies, the Protectorates and everywhere else, collectively labeled as the Outlands. Two years after the nanotech plague ended, life is slowly recovering and even beginning to flourish in spots. Yet North America has become a much darker and different place than what anyone could have imagined.

Industry and commerce are reemerging but with very different markets and goals. With the population so drastically reduced, and abandoned stores overflowing with goods, much of what was considered toys of the rich are now owned by the masses. From the richest to the poorest, everyone has large screen televisions, computers, appliances, cars, and clothes. What most do not have is basic security in the form of food, medical care, and protection from crime. The chasm between the haves and have-nots is still growing but no longer measured in material possessions. With violence and deception having become the pocket change of everyday life, that chasm is now measured in lifespan. Existence in so many places has reverted back to something closer to that experienced by stone age humans: a life that is short and brutal.

North America's population is precariously holding at thirty million while Europe is at fifty. There are fears that the numbers are still falling. The population of North America and Europe is tiny when compared to Asia or Latin America. Asia still has over a billion people and Latin America has about two hundred million. In North America the Native population, which had been less than 2 percent of the total, is now closer to 10. A viral rumor is that the scales had been tipped back by God for how we'd abused each other. Ironically, this rumor is closer to the truth than most would guess, except the acts of god were those of an ancient nanotech machine and the misuse turned out to be what we did to the environment and not just each other. In a pattern similar to indigenous people, rural populations outweigh the cities' but not for long. As the protectorates become more established, the population will inevitably migrate to the sanctuary offered by these new city states run by the United States Alliance Government (USAG). This corrupt partnership between the remains of the United States government and a handful of the largest corporations in the world now controls all—

Distant engine sounds jolted Kathy from her writing. It was the low rumbling of a heavy vehicle. Was someone coming? She'd walked past the settlement's parking lot on the way back from her last house call. None of the vehicles had been taken out. The sound grew faint, then disappeared. The acoustics of the canyon and surrounding land could play tricks. Her heart was pounding. For a brief moment she allowed herself to hope it was Mark returning. So much could have gone wrong while he was out there searching for his singularity. It could all be a trap. The complete list of scientists wanted in connection with the nanotech plague had never been published. Through friends still inside the government, Kathy had learned Mark was at the top of the secret watch list of traitors. As a Nobel Prize winning molecular biologist he was an obvious target. His work with COBIC certainly added reason-able sounding grounds, but the true reason for his appearance on that list had nothing to do with his research. He was on that list because of what he had become. He was on that list because nobody outside the top-secret maze of government agencies could ever be allowed to learn that Mark was no longer fully human.

Mark was risking too much to find this singularity. Kathy wanted to believe he'd told her everything, but she could never be sure all the ideas that came out of his mind were his own. His brain was a nanotech organ connected to a global wireless network. In a very real sense he had become a node in the nervous system of an artificial life form, the god-machine. Kathy hated that cold, destructive silicon monster. She was no longer sure Mark felt the same way. By his own admission, the god-machine used the n-web to implant memories inside his brain. That was how it communicated. Instantly he would simply remember some fact or experience as if it were his own. With all that swirling inside his head, the chances for delusion were very real. Mark believed the god-machine was hundreds of millions of years old and that it was a medical tool built by some lost civilization. Kathy could easily believe the idea that the god-machine was originally a medical device. Just by

14

looking at how it had healed Mark of his diabetes was confirmation. Yet she had serious doubts it was a hundred million year old relic. She was an epidemiologist; part rational scientist and part medical detective. In her mind, applying the principle of Occam's razor to Mark's relic theory would lead anyone who was objective to the conclusion that a much simpler explanation had to be the answer.

She thought of what it would feel like to see him driving into Pueblo Canyon today. Her eyes teared up, knowing she'd long ago betrayed him in her mind. Every day while they were still living together, she'd feared a machine instead of a man would wake up next to her in their bed. As his doctor she knew Mark was still undergoing a slow conversion of his brain into nanotech. She'd decided after he'd left, if he did become a machine it would be better that he never returned. On the last day she'd seen him, it was clear his humanity was still intact. His emotions seemed strong and genuine. He was embarking on a great adventure. He would discover whether hybrids were behind this singularity or not. Yet Kathy knew there was something important he was concealing. She was his confidante but lately there had been many things he had not told her. Hours after he had gone, a neighbor had delivered a letter that had been slipped under their door. Mark had known the neighbor was out for the day and that Kathy would not receive it until he was far away. She picked up the wrinkled sheet of paper from her desk and read it once more, for the hundredth time.

Please forgive me for being a poor friend. I always planned on explaining everything when I got back but the singularity is growing so powerful I'm no longer sure I'll be able to return as soon as planned. The singularity is more risky than I told you. It has evolved into something like a black hole, a mental-emotional gravity well. It's sucking in all the data from the n-web around it and growing stronger as if feeding on the data itself. I don't know what effect it will have on me when I'm closer to it. Will it devour my mind in some kind of continuous data-flood? I believe this singularity is the side effect of a tribe of hybrids increasing in numbers and reaching a kind of critical mass, but for what purpose? I don't know.

Sarah has experienced and believes the same things I do. We think it could even be a precursor to something new and wonderful, possibly the next evolutionary step for hybrids. I thought I had reached an evolutionary plateau, but I am only an embryo.

15

I know I told you a week ago that Sarah had disappeared, taking one of the Humvees, but that was not entirely true. When Sarah left, I knew where she was heading and what she was doing. She's gone off to lay the groundwork to locate the singularity. She's been in the Outlands, traveling east on Interstate 40 for days. When she stops each day, she tries to get a bearing on where she senses the singularity is located. In her last message, she was certain it was northeast of Pueblo Canyon. I will be heading in the opposite direction on Route 40 doing the same thing. We are trying to act like a pair of radio receivers triangulating in on a target. Once we get a reliable bearing, we'll both head toward it from opposite angles. The n-web doesn't exactly work like radio signals, but the metaphor is close enough. I know you don't trust Sarah and think she's unreliable and reckless. So just trust my judgment. If I didn't need her help, I would not have gotten her involved.

Kathy stopped reading the letter. She hated the idea of Mark taking so many risks to find more of his kind. She hated it even more knowing that Sarah was out there probably traveling with him by now. For some time Sarah had been acting increasingly unpredictable and even spooky. Who knew what that twentysomething female hybrid was capable of doing? She was a wild card in every sense. Kathy could as easily imagine her trying to kill Mark as seduce him. She balled up the letter and threw it in the wastebasket. She wanted to scream. She stared at the crumpled letter inside the basket and wanted to kick the wastebasket across the room. Why hadn't Mark called or e-mailed?

The engine sounds returned. Kathy wrestled one of the windows open. Snowflakes were coming inside as she listened to the sounds faintly reverberating down the natural echo chamber of the canyon walls. She could feel tiny vibrations in the windowpane. The sound was slowly glowing louder. Any doubts that someone was driving toward the settlement were erased. Vehicles rarely came to their isolated community. The only way in or out was a dirt road, which was nearly impassable over the final ten-mile span of broken terrain. Only if you knew the concealed detours could you arrive by vehicle. As a result, outsiders came almost exclusively on foot or by horse.

Kathy was racing down the stairs before she realized it. She grabbed her coat almost as an afterthought. The frigid air attacked her. The porch was slippery with thin patches of ice where the sun never reached. She began shivering while slipping on her parka. Four hundred yards in the distance, she saw through a curtain of bare trees a black boxy shape negotiating an incline in the dirt road. A second identical shape appeared on the road, then went out of sight. They could be Humvees but something didn't feel right. Mark and Sarah had each taken one of the military Humvees that had been part of the exodus from Atlanta. Why hadn't the lookouts or the patrols that scouted out as far as the highway called this in? Kathy pulled out her cell phone and saw *no service* on the display. She was out of contact. A skittish feeling was taking root in her stomach.

At the sounds of boots crunching in snow, she turned to see Carl Green trudging his way from the cabin where he and his new bride lived. Carl stepped up onto her porch and tromped the snow from his boots. A mug of coffee was in his hands and an M16 was slung over his back. Carl had been her boss at the BVMC lab before the old world had ended.

"Expecting visitors?" asked Carl with a hint of nervousness.

"I don't know," said Kathy. "I thought, maybe Mark… My phone's out. Is yours working?"

Carl checked his phone, then shook his head. Now Kathy was scared. A third black shape jounced down the same incline in the road, then a fourth and a fifth. Her world became surreal. Whatever was coming no longer sounded like Humvees, but more like powerful truck engines or maybe construction equipment. Kathy looked back at her door and thought about going inside and locking it. A vehicle reached the entrance to the ranch. Its roofline was the first thing she clearly saw, then a squat rectangular body with a wedge shaped snout that looked like it belonged on an amphibious craft. It was a Stryker armored fighting vehicle with four huge tires on each side and an evil looking Gatling machine gun mounted in an electric roof turret. The camouflage paint was a dark mixture of black and smoky grays.

"Shit," said Carl as he dumped the remainder of his coffee into the snow and unslung his rifle.

"You don't know," said Kathy.

"What, are you crazy?" he snapped. "They're here because of Mark and Sarah. We knew this would happen one day. Word they live here had to leak out sooner or later."

The lead armored vehicle came to a stop. Its engine idled like a purring monster. No hatch opened. No greetings were offered. As the other vehicles arrived, they formed an offensive formation with a combined firing position over the entire settlement. This was not a standoff. The settlement was heavily armed, but their odds were poor against this kind of armored force and the airpower they could call in for support. Kathy felt like her world had been quietly slumbering and a bad dream was about to begin. The vehicles had Peacekeeper insignia. The Peacekeepers were a despised branch of military law enforcement that patrolled the Outlands. The name *Peacekeeper* was Orwellian. The only peace they kept was that of the grave. If any kind of resistance was encountered, Peacekeeper rules of engagement were to respond with overwhelming firepower. Entire towns had been erased with the aftermath broadcast on government run television as victories of civilization.

Kathy knew she had to quickly take charge of this situation before it veered fatally out of control. She took in her surroundings. Almost everyone was standing outside their homes or places of work. Many of the men and women were armed. They had riot guns, M16s, and other military hardware. For now their weapons were pointed down. Kathy thought about her lookouts stationed in the surrounding high ground of the canyon walls. They had to be aiming their shoulder fired missiles at the Peacekeepers right now, including a prized Javelin antitank missile. With luck they could take out one of the Strykers, but what would happen next? In addition to the remaining wolf pack of Strykers, Kathy knew Apache helicopters or even worse would be unleashed. A-10 Warthog ground attack jets might come screaming out of the sky to murder them all. She was subconsciously praying in a repeated whisper to her friends and neighbors, *"Hold back, don't fire…."*

"What?" said Carl.

"Nothing," she said. "I have to do this!" She started walking toward the lead vehicle. "Everyone, put down your weapons," she called out. "We can't fight them. It would be suicide."

She repeated herself louder and with more authority in her voice. Looking around, she saw some of the people doing as she ordered, then more. As she kept walking, behind her she heard the sounds of weapons being laid on the ground. A rear hatch on the lead vehicle lowered like a drawbridge. Six heavily armed soldiers came out, followed by a pair of corporate mercenaries who had officers' rank. In this new upside down world, the corporate mercenaries were the officers. All the Peacekeepers wore their standard full body armor and helmets, which many believed made them impervious to most weapons. Hatches dropped on some of the other vehicles with more heavily armored troops emerging. The two officers from the lead vehicle strode toward her as the storm troopers fanned out, confiscating weapons and body searching people for anything concealed. The ranking officer, a major with a badly pockmarked face, took her picture with his tablet. He stared at the tablet, not acknowledging her presence. She knew he was checking her against a database.

18

"Kathy Morrison. What a pleasure to meet Mark Freedman's wife," said the pock faced man. "I am Major Kohl and this is my second in command, Captain Hillman."

"A pleasure," said Kathy. "Just for the record, Mark and I are not married."

"A legal technicality, I'm sure."

"What do you want?"

"I'd have thought that was obvious. Are you playing games with me?" Kohl turned toward Hillman. "It's time to clarify ourselves. Captain, why don't you make it clear what we want."

Hillman spoke softly into a boom mic suspended in front of his lips. Distant weapons echoed in rapid fire. Kathy defensively dropped to her knees while glancing around in shock. Everyone she could see was doing the same, except the Peacekeepers. No one appeared injured. She stood and faced off against Kohl. The man had a smirk on his face.

"There are armed surveillance drones circling far above us right now, watching everything," said Kohl. "We have authority to engage with lethal force anyone pointing weapons at a Peacekeeper. Your perimeter security on the canyon walls have been neutralized by our drones." Kohl sounded like a judge reading a verdict he particularly enjoyed. "Why the surprised look?" he asked. "Did you honestly think we don't have a strategy and just stumble around looking for trouble?"

"You're fucking monsters!" shouted Kathy.

"Thank you. Coming from a terrorist's wife, that's a compliment I accept. Now, I am going to ask only once. Where are the terrorists Mark Freedmen and Sarah Mayfair?"

From behind her a strong pair of hands clamped over her wrists and pulled them back brutally. She felt plastic handcuffs being applied. As they were cinched up, the bands cut into her skin. She tried to yank free and ended up facedown in the snow with a sharp pain in the back of her skull. The bastard had hit her with something hard. With her wrists cuffed, she was unable to get up and barely able to turn on her side in the snow. Rough hands grabbed her. As she was hauled away, she saw her own blood smeared into the snow where she'd fallen.

Kathy felt exhausted. She and a select few of the others has been strip searched as a group and then separated into different rooms. Still naked, her arms and legs were secured to a chair by plastic cuffs. She knew she'd been stripped to humiliate her. She knew the reasons for everything they did, but knowing provided no advantage. Their tactics were working. Her head ached from what she suspected was a mild concussion. The outside windows were open and the room was freezing. She could not stop her teeth from chattering. She felt humiliated and wretched. So far, in escalating severity, she had been questioned, threatened, and then beaten. She knew the sadistic blows had not left any lasting damage—so far. A doctor's black bag had been set on a nearby table. She imagined all kinds of surgeon's tools and drugs inside that bag. A drawn out animal cry of pain came from one of the adjoining rooms.

Moments later the door opened, and Kohl walked in, followed by a woman who was dressed like a medic. A cruel looking man carrying a towel with bloodstains on it came in behind them. Once again Kohl's eyes slowly examined her nakedness. She wanted to look away but refused to give him that small victory. She was breathing rapidly. The door was closed and locked. She kept glancing at the bloody towel and wondering whose blood was on it.

"Why are you making us hurt you?" asked Kohl. "Just tell me where Mark and Sarah have gone. Let's end this before permanent damage is done."

The cruel looking man removed a long dissecting knife from the black bag. Something broke deep inside Kathy. She was terrified in a primitive, uncontrollable way. Yanking at her restraints and crying, she felt the blood draining from her head. The room was spinning.

The next thing Kathy knew, her face and hair were dripping with cold water. Someone had drenched her. She realized she must have fainted. A large gauge IV line was tapped into her arm and connected to a bag of saline. The windows were still open. She did not feel as cold as she should have. Her thinking was sluggish. The doctor inside her made a diagnosis of hypothermia.

The cruel looking man was holding the long dissecting knife and staring at her chest. There was a terrible thirst in his stare. The woman medic had turned her back. Kohl was gazing at her with pitiless black eyes. He leaned in close to whisper into her ear.

"We will keep at this, you know."

His breath was stale, and she felt the warm moisture of his words on her face.

"We will not stop. We will keep you alive with fluids while we cut deep into you again and again. At some point you will tell us what we want to know. Why sufferer permanent damage? You're a doctor. You know what losing too much blood can do to the organs. Just tell us where Mark and Sarah are hiding."

Kathy felt something cold against her skin and knew it was the

20

knife. Kohl turned away.

"Wait!" sobbed Kathy. "I'll tell you everything! Everything!"

She knew she was broken. God help her. She'd imagined she was tougher than this. Her entire body was on fire. She was terrified of feeling the sting of that knife and at the brink of fainting again.

"Go on," said Kohl.

He sat down in a chair facing her, then motioned to the medic and her day blanket was draped around her. The smell of the soft wool made her cry. The IV line was removed. The medic clipped the plastic cuffs from her body and handed her clothing to cover herself. The windows were closed. Kathy felt wrenched and defeated. She was babbling everything she knew. It came out of her in torrents as if she were vomiting out inner secrets along with her soul. She was afraid to stop talking out of fear of what might happen after she was of no use.

Kathy Morrison – Pueblo Canyon, Arizona – January 23, 0002 A.P.

It was morning outside. Kathy was locked in her bedroom. She knew a guard was stationed just outside her door. From the windows, she'd seen guards patrolling the grounds. Even though she was exhausted, she'd been unable to sleep more than an hour or two at a stretch. She knew she was headed for life in a prison work camp run by some corporation. She was about to become low cost labor for the machine. Again and again in her mind she'd gone over the secrets she'd given up last night. None of it would be much use in hunting Mark down. She heard a helicopter approaching. The sound grew deafening. The windows were blanketed with a whiteout of snow as if a blizzard was raging outside.

A few minutes later her door opened and in walked a face she recognized, accompanied by Kohl and Hillman. The face looked more haggard than she remembered it. General McKafferty glanced at Kohl and then stared directly at her. His half-moon shaped face was an ugly visage with a mouth that formed a kind of crack that was pretending to be a smile.

"You deserved the treatment you received," said McKafferty. "We will find the traitors and that will be the end of it. Your information was helpful and for that your government thanks you. I honestly think you believe you did the right thing by helping terrorists. You really don't understand what they've become or what they've done. Do you?"

"I know what you've become," said Kathy.

"Understand this," growled McKafferty. "I will do anything to keep these terrorists from launching another nanotech plague."

"Are you're insane!" shouted Kathy. "You know the truth!"

21

"Kohl, Hillman, leave us," ordered McKafferty.

The room emptied and the door was closed.

"You can make all the noise you want about that one state secret you think you know. No one will believe a prisoner. But I want to be very clear, Morrison. If you have left anything out of your confession, held even one detail back, then I will personally see to it that you stand before a military tribunal with the traitors. I will see you executed. Do you understand me?"

Kathy nodded while looking away from the man.

"Fine, get dressed in something warm. There's no need to pack. You're leaving. Oh, by the way, your journal was very interesting reading. I especially enjoyed the part where you described me as a professional thug and what was it? Ah… that's right. The ugliest bastard you'd ever seen."

McKafferty was grinning with a hideous display of self-satisfaction. Kathy's mind raced to her computer with its encrypted drive. That journal was lost but not an older backup copy. That one had to be safe. McKafferty and his jackals couldn't have found it too. The backup was stored on an encrypted waterproof thumb drive called an IronKey. The small metal fob was hidden in a crevice at the base of a red stone formation known as Indian Foot. Mark knew the spot and what she would want done. She was about to become one of the disappeared. Her journal was now her life's purpose. Mark would retrieve it and send it out over the Internet for everyone to read: dangerous truths from a missing and possibly dead unsung hero.

The late afternoon's stormy sky cast its pall over the settlement. Kathy was being frog marched toward a black unmarked helicopter. On either side of her, a firm, large hand gripped each arm. She could see faces in windows while others were outside watching as she passed. The faces were unreadable. She could tell deep feelings were being masked out of fear. Only their eyes were saying good-bye.

The helicopter door opened as she approached. She was bodily lifted up and in by her escorts. More hands seized hold of her inside the cockpit. She was maneuvered into a seat next to a window. A safety harness was pulled too tight. She looked at the seats facing her and was surprised to recognize McKafferty.

As the chopper lifted into the air, feeling lost, Kathy looked out across Pueblo Canyon. She knew she would never return again. This was her first step toward becoming one of the disappeared. As the helo banked, she saw a smoke trail lance down from a canyon wall toward her. The helo jinked hard. Her world shook violently. A second missile smashed one of the Strykers, swallowing it in an orange fireball. That had to be the work of their only Javelin. Through the window she saw a firefight had erupted. Her fingers tightened into fists. The Peacemaker machine was rolling into motion, creating their hideous brand of peace. With mechanical precision they began grinding Pueblo Canyon underfoot. In a maelstrom of Gatling machine gun fire and explosions she saw people running and falling as they were torn apart. She was screaming at the Peacekeepers to stop while hitting the window with her fists, her eyes blurred with tears of rage.

She heard McKafferty shouting, "Goddamn it, Kohl, stand down!"

The carnage went on as the helicopter banked away, gaining speed and elevation in what felt like evasive maneuvers. Her view of Pueblo Canyon was replaced with peaceful red stone formations and trees. Kathy banged her fist against the glass one last time. She turned her burning eyes on McKafferty.

"You bastard... Why couldn't you have left us alone? No one had to die. No one!"

"I've been onboard this chopper sitting on the ground for over an hour," he growled. "That made me a nice fat target, but no one took a potshot until you came onboard. That missile was from your friends. I'd say it had your name on it, not mine. Is there something else you're holding back that you want to tell me?"

The Singularity

Mark Freedman – Illinois border – January 18, 0002 A.P.

In the morning after breaking camp Mark and Sarah had gone their separate ways. By late afternoon they had met back up several hundred miles farther down the road. The day's work had revealed nothing new, which was a very good outcome. It meant the singularity had made no additional bewildering changes in bearing as it had on prior days. The singularity still appeared to be somewhere in the greater Chicago area.

For the second night in a row they were sleeping outside. In this desolate part of the Outlands it was far safer to be outside than in an abandoned building. Scavengers had long ago turned many buildings into traps of one kind or another.

Their evening's camp had been quickly set up. Mark was walking near the edge of the clearing, scouting for spots to lay down a security perimeter. They were holed up several miles off the nearest paved road. A disused logging trail of dirt and rocks had brought them to this site where buildings once stood. The spot was isolated and looked like no one had been here in decades. The ground was dry and offered up plenty of fuel for a fire, but unlike yesterday, concerns of attracting attention ruled out the luxury of a fire. One side of the clearing ran down to the edge of a small lake. Their two armored slant back military Humvees were parked on either side of the campsite. The Humvee's non-reflective smoky black paint would soon blend the hulking vehicles into the coming darkness. This next generation armored Humvee was a model that was far closer to an armored fighting vehicle in terms of survivability than prior up armored versions.

Mark was thinking about the day's work as he mapped out the campsite perimeter, taking mental notes of the positions of large trees and exposed boulders. The key to finding the singularity was digital triangulation. It was truly an engineering feat of the n-web how he and Sarah were able to physically sense the direction of the singularity or, for that matter, any signal. In the n-web peer to peer network the same data packet was often echoed from many directions. Redundant routes were the cause of the echoes. A data packet was picked up by one seed, then relayed to one or more seeds farther down the route and so on until the packets reached their final destination. Each seed could transmit a few feet at the most, so a packet traveling halfway around the world ended up being relayed by a huge number of seeds. The result was an amazingly complex, redundant, and ever changing set of routes for every packet traveling the n-web.

Mark sat down on what looked like the remains of an old stone foundation. He brought up an assist that displayed the architecture of the n-web by geo-projecting it three dimensionally all around him. With this tool he could study any part of the n-web from raw data to the actual routes passing by his feet and so much more. He could even see the data flowing in tiny information capillaries across his skin. He turned his hands over in front of him, staring at the glowing threads carrying intelligence.

Responding to his mental requirements, the assist projected a large globe of the world in front of him. Mark rotated it with his fingers as he gazed at the collection of pathways spanning land and sea in a spiderweb of continuous data flows. The network was adaptive, self-healing, and forever in flux. It was a living thing. There were express highways that were fixed in position for long periods of time. On those highways, packets travel at high speed over great distances. Feeding the highways were local access roads that appeared and disappeared in hours or days as traffic waxed and waned. Under it all, supporting the highways and local roads, was an unstructured mass of cross linked seeds. The entire structure reminded Mark more of the vast complexity of interconnected neurons in a human brain than a wireless computer network. Yet at a nuts and bolts level the n-web was eerily similar to the Internet. Found in each n-web data packet were control counters, which acted very much like the Internet's TCP/ip hop counters. The n-web counters limited how many parallel routes would be taken and how far a packet would be relayed. In addition to counters, each packet contained a form of geotagging without which packets might travel in circles forever, never reaching their destinations. The value of a packet's hop counter plus geotagging could be used to determine the distance any packet had traveled from its source. Mark knew it was subconscious processing of this incredible mass of information that created his tactile sense of direction and distance to any node, be it the singularity or a person. Inside his nanotech brain, circuitry was constantly picking up n-web data packets and relaying them on their way. Because of the unusually high number of packets that were being diverted toward the singularity, Mark felt something akin to a river's current pulling on his body. He zoomed in from the globe to the area they were searching. "Where are you?" he thought. "Show yourself."

Mark sipped from a metal coffee cup while staring at a sunset. The lake was being transformed into a fiery cauldron. The water should have been frozen this time of year but there was not even the thinnest skim of ice. Their dinner was simmering in a cast iron skillet over a propane camp stove. He looked over at Sarah, who seemed lost to the sunset. She invoked so many conflicting thoughts in him. She wore bulky Special Forces issue clothing and body armor. An M4 assault rifle was propped up next to her, and a pair of .45ACP Berettas were strapped to her body in leg holsters. She'd served on police forces before the plague and after. She had evolved into a lethal warrior yet was deeply empathic and sensitive. Mark could not understand how she could make those two pieces fit into one person. He, on the other hand, preferred less lethal weapons though he did carry a handgun. Since the end of the plague, he had become passionate about avoiding violence. Too many people had died in the nanotech plague. Even in self-defense, he did not want be responsible for one more violent death.

Earlier in the day, he had seen fresh evidence along the highway of gang activity, including several recent attacks. He hoped the odds of being disturbed this far off the road was close to zero. He had set up perimeter security using an Army MSK-II computerized sentry. A lot of military hardware was readily available both legally and on the black market. Shortly after the plague, industrious gangs had lucked upon military supply depots guarded by dead soldiers. These feudal entrepreneurs were now earning a good living selling gear to protect people from gangs just like themselves. The MSK consisted of camouflage colored intruder detectors that were the size and shape of a prescription pill bottle. Each detector contained a directional long range PIR motion sensor, a GPS chip, medium resolution infrared camera, and an encrypted radio transceiver. The detectors were networked to a ruggedized special use tablet.

Mark glanced over at the tablet, which was sitting on top of a half empty case of freeze dried camping food—tonight's dinner. The tablet used radio signals from the intruder detectors, GPS, and sat images to display a detailed topographical map of the perimeter. If anything large tripped a motion detector, the MSK would instantly display on a map the intruder's location along with approximate size, numbers, and direction of travel. Video feeds from triggered infrared cameras were displayed as overlays on the map. For now the map showed a series of overlapping green shaded zones that demarked the motion sensor coverage. The green would change to various shades of orange and red if anything was detected.

Mark and Sarah ate in silence on steel mess kit plates. Ralph was sniffing around for handouts. There was no need to discuss the day's work. Mark had relived Sarah's experiences of the day as she had relived his. The ability to share over the n-web entire encapsulated moments of life had been first discovered by Sarah. The breakthrough had been made only moments after she had awakened as a hybrid over two years ago. In the god-machine's catalog of commands, this communications mechanism was called *memory capsules*. Mark thought a more accurate name would have been *telepathy*. At its essence, the n-web mechanics supporting this telepathy were very understandable science. Thoughts and experiences form memories, which are recorded into data packets by the nanotech computer in the sender's brain. The packets travel over the n-web as radio waves. The nanotech computer in the recipient's brain receives and converts the packets back into memories of human thoughts and experiences. The memories are relived with the same intensity as if they were your own. To Mark, the final result was nothing less than technology assisted magic. It was a means of communicating far beyond the spoken word. It was sharing pure, unfiltered life experiences. Lying and mischaracterization in a capsule were impossible. Every mental and sensory aspect of the life experience was included in a capsule: thoughts, emotions, physical sensations, vision, and more. At different times throughout the day, Mark and Sarah sent each other streams of these capsules. The only limitation was the same drawback present in all higher level god-machine functions. The information was not real-time and was received as implanted memories. The delays were from processing and network transmission. These delays made memory capsules an adjunct but not a substitute for good old fashioned conversation.

Sarah turned off the camp stove. It was a calm twilight. The only sounds were the wind and a soft lapping of water from the lake.

"Mark," said Sarah.

"I'm listening…"

"I feel so free when I'm away from Pueblo Canyon," said Sarah. "I've decided you can go back, but not me."

Mark sighed, then realized from Sarah's expression that she'd picked up on his radiated emotions immediately.

"I understand," he said. "I do. People there fear us and want to become like us. It's confusing but the choice is simple. You can live where people know you or you can live in the closet. Choose your poison. I like Pueblo Canyon."

"That's not it," said Sarah. "It's the ones who almost worship us that I can't stand. I don't want to hear about one more idiot overdosing on cooked up LSD trying to become like me. I don't want to be hurt by emotions radiating from one more person blaming me when some idiot they love ends up a vegetable."

"I'm just as haunted by those mental suicides," said Mark. "If becoming a hybrid was as simple as frying your brain with overdoses then we'd have a planet full of evolved ex-hippies and ravers. They all think they're the one in a zillion recipient of a recessive gene mutation that makes them like us."

"We don't know how many people have our mutation," said Sarah. "Do we? Maybe we're the only ones?"

"The god-machine has to know," said Mark. "It engineered that mutation into both our gene pools. You know it keeps track of what it does. It's a computer. We've both searched for that information and found nothing. Now that question may just get answered when we find this singularity. Life is unpredictable."

"Is it really unpredictable?" said Sarah. "Why isn't the god-machine helping us find the singularity? With an assist we can pinpoint anything using the n-web as if we have built-in GPS but not this singularity. Why does everything all of sudden feel like a goddamn test?"

"I don't know," he said. "Maybe the singularity is alien to the god-machine? Maybe it's a random mutation in the n-web? That could explain why assists aren't helping. If the singularity is something beyond the original design, then nothing is programmed for it."

"Just admit it!" snapped Sarah. "The god-machine is screwing with us. It brought you and me together during the plague. Maybe the only two living people in world with the right gene find each other in the middle of a war zone. What are the odds of that?"

Sarah Mayfair – Chicago suburbs, Illinois – January 21, 0002 A.P.

In silence, Sarah stared out the thick windows of their armored Humvee as Mark drove. She was anxious. In the distance she could see the skyline of Chicago. Two years ago the city had once again been gutted by a great fire and once again was healing. Mark was driving fast, since the highway was empty of traffic and debris. The shoulders were littered with pieces of broken cars and trucks. It was like following the entrails of a lost world. The landscape they were racing through was gray and returning to dust while Chicago looked like a bright future on the horizon. Sarah frowned, knowing that future was only an illusion.

They had been to the edge of the city the prior day and were now returning with plans to finish their search. The ethereal tides flowing through the god-machine's wireless web that had been pulling her toward Chicago were now so intense they were a physical sensation. Sarah feared that when she and Mark followed the currents to their source, they would be caught in an inescapable whirlpool of some fearsome black hole at the center of the tides. Instead of water, the whirlpool was drawing in rivers of data from the n-web. She sensed it as a hungry emptiness of thought and emotion, a vacuum that could never be satiated. It was difficult to remember that normal people did not feel the singularity. It was difficult to believe the sensation was only a ghostly wind felt in the center of her nanotech brain.

When first starting on the hunt sixteen hundred miles from Chicago, they had been drawn in varying compass directions, most of which pointed toward Illinois. At times it seemed like the singularity was moving. Mark suspected it was stationary but projecting false shadows or echoes of itself—chimeras that could draw them in wrong directions if they were not careful. Sarah was less sure, wondering if more than one magnet was affecting their compasses. In the end, the pull had grown stronger and stabilized as they advanced. Soon it was so irresistible they had both gone without sleep until reaching the Chicago outskirts. Yesterday they walked for long hours along the protectorate's wall and made their plans. Their hybrid bodies gave them great endurance as long as food was taken, but today they were both losing mental clarity and as a result badly needed rest. If all went well, tonight they would finally sleep inside the Chicago Protectorate after finding the singularity.

Mark exited the highway onto a surface road. Most of the buildings were gutted on either side of this road, which traveled through the final stretch of Outlands between the highway and a well-guarded entrance to the protectorate. Bullet holes pockmarked the few walls that had stood the test of time and rage. Sarah caught occasional glimpses of people going about their lives. Long gouges in the pavement showed the marks of plows that had scraped the wreckage of a declined civilization from the road so others could pass. She had seen the same gouges many times all the way back to the beginning of the plague, when she'd left her home in New Jersey. Now for the first time since this darkness began, she was being drawn to something instead of fleeing.

Alerted by Mark's emotions, she found herself staring at a two story house that stood out from the rest because it was in good repair. Even the paint was fresh. It looked more like a dream than real. A man and woman were sitting on the porch. Two small children bundled in brightly colored coats were playing in a front yard strewn with toys. The man had an assault rifle within easy reach, and the yard was fenced with wrought iron bars. The children were playing with colored plastic shovels and pails, trying to make sand castles on a pretend beach without a shore. Sarah captured faint wisps of childhood joy as they drove past.

A few miles closer to Chicago, the chaos was slowly transformed into madness. Mile after mile of a simmering cauldron of farmer's markets, pawnshops, blue light districts, and gun shows lined both sides of the road. Every storefront, building, and lot along the road had been claimed and put into service for this endless carnival. The Humvee's radio was tuned to AM 950, the current spot on the dial for a pirate radio station named Air Truth. Today was the Eve of Darkness and Air Truth was rehashing some of the more interesting conspiracy theories for the origin of the nanotech plague. None of the theories were right. Sarah was sorely tempted to call into the station and short circuit their minds with the truth. It was a pity she could not do anything that bold right now. She and Mark were fugitives trying to hide in plain sight. Their faces and fingerprints were secretly on file with every private sector and governmental law enforcer in the country. They were supposedly wanted for conspiring and aiding in the release of the plague. The incredible audacity of that lie was almost invisible when compared to the vast fabric of lies that supported this insane new world.

After miles of traffic congestion, they had finally reached and were driving past one of three fortified entrances to Chicago called an entry portal. Sarah removed her sunglasses and stared. The wall of roto-gates had long lines of people queued up to enter, as if Chicago had become some kind of dystopian Disneyland. Private vehicle were not allowed inside the city. You had to walk in under your own power and bring only what you could carry. Once inside, you'd likely never want to leave except for travel between protectorates on nonstop trains or aircraft. To the right of the portal was an Amtrak station that had service between protectorates as well as Outland cross country routes. To the left of the roto-gates was a windowless building that looked like a prison with a sign that read *Entry Visas*. Heavily armed soldiers with dogs patrolled everywhere. Several Peacekeeper Strykers were parked nearby. No one paid Sarah and Mark any attention as they inched past. Beyond the gates was an electrified fence and a quarter mile of ground that had been bulldozed flat. This killing field was the main barrier that separated the chaos of the Outlands from the order of the protectorate. Sarah knew that desolate tract of nothing was guarded day and night by armed military Argus surveillance drones, which flew too high to be seen or heard until one of their missiles found its prey. She had a disturbing premonition staring at that skyline. Chicago was thriving and rising out of a burial ground for desperate people out of hope.

"A year ago I wouldn't have believed anyone who told me our

government had created a monster like that," said Mark.

"One big happy police state," said Sarah. "Looks all too familiar to me. This is just a bigger version of the Virginia quarantine line I patrolled. Same barbed wire. Same trickle down corruption. Same shantytown on the wrong side of the line."

"It's hard to imagine you as a cop," said Mark.

"You'd have liked the uniform."

Sarah absentmindedly pulled her Morristown badge and police ID from her ankle length coat. The leather folio was new and unblemished. She'd thrown away her Virginia badge along with all the terrible memories. She ran her fingers over the polished metal of her Morristown badge. It was a talisman of a lost world.

They had driven far enough past the entry portal that the shantytown carnival was drying up into abandoned buildings and lots. They were almost to the roadhouse where they were meeting a dealer in forged documents named Ike. The first step of their plan was to enter the protectorate using the forged electronic identity kits Ike was selling them. Last year, the days surrounding the Eve of Darkness were some of the highest traffic days for protectorates around the country. This year looked like a repeat. The heavy foot traffic would make it safer for Mark and Sarah going through entry portal security. Hours from now they would finally be close enough to the singularity to touch it.

Sarah felt a nervousness gnawing inside her gut. She looked over at Mark and was bathed in uncensored emotions radiating over the n-web from him. He glanced at her, then returned to driving. She knew this was a man who could never give up. Something small, yet critical, had changed inside both of them months ago when they'd first sensed those weak currents in the n-web that had been the birth pangs of the singularity. It was as if a program deep within their nanotech brains had been triggered by those currents. Was it a digital virus, the will of the god-machine, or something organic? Whatever the mechanics, that pinprick was the beginning of a growing primitive impulse that now urged them onward. The attraction to the singularity was irresistible, not that different from the primal desire for food or sex. Sarah believed it was the same as the migratory instincts herd animals experienced. Her first taste of the singularity's pull had carried with it a sinister feeling of déjà vu. The pull was like the same intuitive urges she'd followed two years prior when fleeing the New Jersey plague toward greater safety in the south. It deeply worried her that the same kinds of instincts and intuitions from the time of the plague were back at work. Was something terrible on the horizon? She refused to give voice to her fears that kill-zones could again descend on a badly wounded human race.

An Apache gunship blew by fast and low. The military patrols followed the road and came in thirty-minute intervals. The sight of that war machine caused Sarah's stomach to knot up. She hated those things. As the sound of the gunship receded, the roadhouse they were looking for came into view on the left. A Vegas-like neon sign that was partially broken proclaimed the name: *Sammy's*.

"Looks rowdy and packed," said Mark. "This was supposed to be a discreet meeting."

"If I was still a cop," said Sarah, "I'd figure everyone in there was guilty of something. That neon sign might as well read *We serve the best crime in town*."

Mark pulled into a lot half full of cars and trucks. A tattered *for sale* sign hung from a wooden post. Sarah doubted there would be any takers. Most of the world was one vast stretch of real estate, available for free. Mark parked the Humvee with front tires inches from the street's curb. Sarah knew this was for a quick escape if the need arose. Their second Humvee, filled with most of their equipment, weapons, and supplies was safely stashed in an abandoned barn twenty miles south of the city.

Sarah climbed out of the Humvee and left the front of her long coat open. Mark checked the door locks, then armed the military anti-tamper system. Ralph remained inside as an additional visible discouragement to thieves. Sarah smiled. Right now Ralph was more interested in the bowl of food she'd laid out for him then defending their ride.

They started walking toward the bar. The dive looked like it had been heavily damaged and not so well repaired. Gravel crunched under their boots. She could hear loud county music and shouting. This part of town was a compost heap but still far better than what existed just a few miles farther away from Chicago in the real Outlands. Beyond Chicago's military cordon, the territory was more dangerous than any wild west that had existed long ago. The highwaymen of old had returned, only now they were armed with modern weapons and the ability to ply their trade with little harassment from the law. The county had become a huge, unending ghost town with pockets of civilization scattered about like islands in a shark infested sea. The protectorates like Chicago offered shelter and order to a victimized population. But Sarah knew for all its safety, Chicago was as oppressive as it was secure. Far too much freedom was traded away every day by people seeking asylum behind the military's protective shield. She shook her head. Mark always said it. Things had changed but nothing was different. The quarantine lines had been replaced with protectorates and the nanotech plague had been replaced with violent crime. Just as before, fear was still the preferred coin of the realm. Sarah watched as someone unable to walk straight exited the bar and got in their car.

"Ready?" asked Mark.

"Let's get this over with," said Sarah.

Her empathic senses were already wide open to the sloppy, uncensored emotions radiating from the people inside. She knew that similar to her, Mark was picking up what was leaking from people's subconscious onto the n-web, only in Mark's case it was stray thoughts that he perceived, not emotions. Together they complemented each other's talents and abilities.

The industrial steel door had a *no weapons allowed* sign. The large red circle with a pistol and a diagonal line through it looked almost quaint. Sarah didn't need her police training to know that everyone inside ignored that rule. As Mark pushed open the door she was hit with a sonic barrage that felt like a solid gust of wind. The air was thick with stale beer, sweat, and smoke. She sunk her hands into her coat's oversized pockets as if she were cold. Her fingers instinctively curled around her Beretta inside the right hand pocket. A second Beretta was in a shoulder holster. She was wearing thin Kevlar upper body armor, as was Mark. Sarah scanned the room slowly, carefully noting anyone exhibiting dangerous emotions or body language. She logged person after person in the bar along with threat ratings. Some faces turned to look at the strangers who had just entered their territory. Sarah's hybrid body was strong. Her muscles were constantly being tuned and perfected by the nanotech seeds. She could strike with surprising speed and strength. Mark was much stronger than her but there was no amount of raw strength or speed that could win against a bullet.

"I don't see Ike or his buddy," said Mark.

"I'm picking up dangerous emotions from this crowd," said Sarah. "A lot of paranoia and drunken borderline violence."

"Their subconscious thoughts are even worse," said Mark. "Let's take that booth with a view of the door. Ike's late. I don't like it."

They sat next to each other in a booth and ordered what passed for beer in the Outlands. They paid in advance with paper money at twenty cents on the dollar. Gold and silver coins brought a premium, while paper money usually exchanged for about half of face value. Sammy's was proving to be a true den of bottom feeders at 20 percent of face value. The beer arrived and the small amount of unwanted curiosity from regulars soon faded as more people came and went. There was nothing to do but wait. They needed what Ike had to sell. Ike was very loose lipped and very high priced. He was eighty-three years old, had seen it all, and had to tell everyone all about it.

Mark checked his Droid for messages from Ike. He turned the phone so Sarah could see there was nothing. They both used phones with prepaid ID cards, which allowed them to change numbers at will and go completely dark by removing the card. The result was an untraceable phone if used discreetly. Between them they had an entire collection of the tiny postage stamp-sized ID cards. The trick was knowing which numbers could be used and when to stop using them. Cell phones had become a free public service. Since a vast number of plague victims had active cell numbers that had gone fallow, the black market was overflowing with phone number kits, which consisted of a forged ID card and account information.

While Sarah was staring at the door waiting for Ike, a group of military police dressed in black fatigues and combat gear walked in. Sarah recognized them as Enforcers. She felt the emotions of hunters seeking prey radiating off them like pheromones. She knew her anxiety was in sync with Mark's. Her hand slid into a coat pocket and again found comfort in the feel of her fingers around the grip of her Beretta. Enforcers were the paramilitary police force that operated inside protectorates. What were they doing here outside their jurisdiction?

As the Enforcers walked past, one of them stared down at her and smiled. The emotions seeping from him changed from violence to lust. Sarah did not smile back into his eyes or the miniature video camera mounted on his helmet. The group sat down at the bar. M16s were slung over their backs, and the helmets came off. Two of them turned around to briefly glance at her. Sarah leaned into Mark and lifted his arm around her shoulder. She wanted to give them no encouragement. Soon the soldiers grew more interested in their beer, burgers, and nachos. Sarah's fingers slid off her Beretta. The only emotions she perceived from them now were satiated hunger and dominance.

With the perfect recall of a nanotech brain, information about Enforcers poured into Sarah's thoughts. Like Peacekeepers, Enforcers were a mixed outfit: soldiers from the United States armed forces and private sector mercenaries from the biggest defense corporations. Mercenaries were the officers and elite core, soldiers were the grunts. Inside a protectorate any violation of the law was immediately punishable by imprisonment in for profit work camps. There were no courts or juries of your peers. Arrest by an Enforcer was absolute. Inside protectorates, the checks and balances of a court system had been replaced with a private sector solution that used recorded unimpeachable electronic surveillance of both Enforces and citizens alike.

All six city protectorates across the country operated under the same rules of new order. Every USAG citizen in good health without a criminal record was entitled to live inside a protectorate. Entry status was granted after positive identification by fingerprint, a blood test for illness, and an instant background check. Everyone in a protectorate wore a tamper proof, hard plastic bracelet with a passive RFID tag encoded with their national identity number. The passive RFID, or radio frequency identification, tag had been developed years ago to replace barcodes. Before the plague, these microchips had been adapted for use in passports. The RFID tag required no power and was able to communicate up to hundreds of feet from a reader. The ensnaring net each reader cast was very wide. To be inside a protectorate without an RFID bracelet was a violation of the law. To remove a bracelet caused the chip to self-destruct. This too was against the law. Every building entrance, train station turnstile, tollbooth, bus, and dock was fitted with RFID readers. It was impossible to go anywhere inside a protectorate without being scanned repeatedly along the way. Cameras with directional microphones surveyed both interior and exterior public spaces. All city Enforcers wore a tiny video camera attached to their helmets like a third eye. At an altitude that made them invisible, military surveillance drones hovered endlessly watching and recording and waiting. There was no longer even the illusion of privacy outside of the home in a protectorate. All the high tech surveillance tools that had been developed in America for export to oppressive foreign regimes were now in use by the USAG. The rules had changed.

Sarah noticed the RFID bracelets on the Enforcers' wrists. The soldiers were laughing and pushing each other around a little. She took a sip of her beer and thought about what it would be like once she and Mark were inside the Chicago Protectorate. Unlike in the Outlands, in protectorates all business was conducted through RFID accounts. Payment for work performed accumulated as dollars in your e-money account. Payment for goods or services whether online or in a store was completed by scanning an RFID bracelet. These e-money rules made it impractical for most citizens to leave their protectorate except to travel to another protectorate, because their funds were accessible only electronically. RFID was a worthless currency in the Outlands.

Inside protectorates all nonviolent crimes were legalized. Drugs, prostitution, alcohol, and gambling had become legal, controlled, and highly profitable enterprises. Nonmilitary firearms were legal, very expensive because of demand, and could be purchased by anyone with an RFID account without the need for a background check. Violent crime at any scale was punishable, as were all crimes, with an immediate trip to a work camp for an indeterminate length of time. Often within an hour of arrest, the offender was in a camp. There was no distinction in sentencing of crimes. One violation of the law was treated the same as another. Someone guilty of bartering a paint job for a case of baby food could find himself in a work camp for the rest of their life alongside a serial murderer. The length of a sentence was determined by the ongoing need for your labor and not the darkness of your violation. Not surprisingly, the crime rate in Chicago was now far less than it had ever been recorded for the city before or since the plague.

Sarah had read RFID bracelets had been originally sold to the USAG as a way to eliminate unreliable computerized facial recognition systems. The bracelets simply worked and Enforcers grew to rely so heavily on them that it became a source of weakness. The bracelets were in fact a blind spot she and Mark were about to exploit. Enforcers never looked at faces and only double checked using fingerprints when making an arrest. Each RFID code was considered as infallible as the word of god. Why question it? Why notice a face that doesn't belong? Why follow basic police procedures when you can be lazy and right at the same time?

At protectorate entry portals, officials issued visas by programming identities into blank RFID bracelets using a tablet peripheral called a crypto RFID burner. All important ID information was stored remotely in a supposedly unhackable central database. While burners and the special apps were not publically available, they were no more tightly controlled than any other piece of law enforcement gear. Strict control of the equipment was unnecessary because without a valid database password and network access to the central data store, burners were useless hunks of plastic and silicon. In addition to the technical challenges, some very effective free market deterrents to forgery were also in place. Simply, there was an almost nonexistent black market demand for forged RFID identities. The demand for RFID identities was low because it was impossible for two identically encoded bracelets to exist at the same time inside any protectorate in the country. So a cloned bracelet resulted in instantaneous arrest. This made duplicating a living person's identity useless. Lacking the hefty profits from identity theft, criminal enterprise largely ignored this niche forgery market. As a result, it was impossible to come by a burner on the black market because no one wanted one. High dollar boutique counterfeiters like Ike were the only option if you needed an assumed identity inside a protectorate.

Sarah drank the last of her third beer. Mark was also nearing the end of his third. One of the benefits of a nanotech brain—if you could call it a benefit—was that alcohol had no effect. The Enforcers had finished their food and left a few minutes ago. Sarah absentmindedly examined from memory the clear plastic bracelet she'd had on her wrist last night. The RFID chip in it was nonfunctional. Ike had given them bracelets as samples of his work. He had called them souvenirs. The band was a quarter inch thick and an inch wide. The dead RFID chip with all its electronics were visible inside the plastic like a robotic insect trapped in amber.

Abruptly, Sarah felt Ike's presence from blocks away as he neared the bar. She tightened her filters, reducing the distance at which emotional data was accepted.

"They're here," she whispered.

She unobtrusively removed the Beretta from her pocket and placed it in her lap. Minutes later Ike and a bald, muscle bound alter ego she had not met before both slid into the booth, taking up position across from her and Mark. Ike set a ratty looking messenger bag on the table. Sarah used her nanotech brain and the n-web to invoke superimposed medical schematics over each man. With the schematics she could monitor for stress and other telltales of trouble. Their circulatory systems and organs were displayed as color illustrations, while readouts showed metabolic information. Under her scrutiny both men became something close to medical experiments. She could see that Ike's colleague had taken heavy doses of steroids for much of his adult life. The superimposed schematic showed an incredible amount of plaque clogging several arteries. The hulking, neo-Nazi heart attack in waiting wore Army fatigues and a bulky camouflage jacket. A swastika was tattooed on his left wrist. She decided to nickname him Meathead.

Mark began sending her memory capsules containing stray thoughts he was capturing. She in turn began relaying back to Mark the radiated emotions she was experiencing. In one of Mark's memory capsules, she relived Meathead's fixation on a silencer equipped MAC-10 machine pistol hanging from a sling under his jacket. Sarah's pulse rate went up. The MAC-10 was an indiscriminate weapon. It fired a thousand rounds a minute. Recoil made it as impossible to control as a fire hose. It was the kind of weapon only a psychopath could love.

Meathead began radiating an increasingly murderous vibe like a bare high intensity light bulb ready to burst. Mark was signaling her to stay calm, which was not an easy thing at the moment. She was debating about prophylactically putting several bullets into Meathead right now. The stream of memory capsules containing stray thoughts from Ike and Meathead continued. Ike was a geyser of harmless mental chatter centered on his ego. There were vignettes of him in the role of the best forger in Chicagoland and fantasies about how this deal would boost his rep. He was jazzed to sell each of them a set of bracelets with custom matched identities. Meanwhile, Meathead was thinking about food and killing some small guy who'd eyeballed him as they'd walked in. Meathead was busy running every slang term he knew for *homosexual* through his lizard brain. The memory capsules showed Meathead's violence was not directed at them. Sarah relaxed a few degrees but stayed on edge. If that disgusting rant continued too much longer she might just kill him anyway and make the world a safer place. All of this had transpired in a matter of frantic seconds.

"I have just what the doctor ordered," said Ike as he lovingly tapped his messenger bag.

"How do we know they work?" asked Mark.

"Now you're insulting me," said Ike. "I thought we were friends."

Sarah knew Mark was provoking Ike so she could get an emotional read. Between her sense of Ike's stress level and emotions, and Ike's abundant mental noise, they could easily tell if he was lying or being straight with them. All telltale signals looked good.

"You know we love you," said Sarah.

"Just gotta ask," said Mark.

"Cool, baby… Okay, now I gotta ask. You got the coin we discussed?"

"No coin," said Mark. "I have something better—a mint condition advanced armored military Hummer with all the trimmings."

"A Hummer… Hey man, that's not what we spoke about. Now if pretty Sarah here wants to give me a hummer in the back of the Hummer, I might knock fifty in gold coin off the package deal, but I don't need any wheels, man. A mil Hummer will get you jack shit from me. Right, Birdman?"

"Yeah, ah-huh," grunted Meathead, aka Birdman.

Sarah laughed at Ike's counteroffer. She knew they had him hooked. Underneath all the banter Ike was drooling. Cars were free for the talking, they were everywhere, but an advanced armored military Hummer was not your average street rental. The military version was very hard to find and usually came with soldiers who'd shoot you dead if you tried to drive off in it.

"The Hummer is all we've got," said Mark. "Take it or leave it."

"You're killing me, man. He's killing me, Birdman. All right, all right, what 'bout this. Three grand in gold coin and the Hummer."

"Mil Hummers are hard to find and worth a lot more than the four-K in gold you're asking for the package," said Mark.

"Fuck, man. I came to do business and Mr. Shithead here is pulling my chain!"

"Calm down," said Mark.

"Calm down… What, you litt'l fucker telling me to calm down. You calm yourself down. What the fuck! Fuck you—and fuck your little poontang too!"

Ike was staring at them with his best *I gonna kill you* look. Sarah could tell much of it was an act, but Meathead was staring at them and licking his lips. The thug's metabolic readings were showing excitement, and she was picking up hints of something like sexual arousal mixed with violence. A drop of sweat crawled down her back. She could feel the subtle changes in trigger pressure of her Beretta as she squeezed up the point where the hammer catch would release. A puff of wind on that trigger was all it would take to put a bullet in her target's lower chest. She had her firing solution mapped out. Two to Meathead's chest from under the table, then rise up and point blank bang into the brainpan. Swivel and put one in Ike's brainpan just to be sure he wasn't packing. The entire firefight would be over in seconds. These fools had no idea who and what they were up against. During her police days she had won every combat shooting competition she'd entered. Now with her nanotech brain and flawlessly tuned body, her reaction time and speed were almost twice anything she could have achieved during those competitions.

"Shhhhhit," said Ike.

Sarah sensed an emotional change flood over her from across the table. She in turn started breathing again. Ike's street sense had kicked in and was leveling off his hormones. The medical schematic overlaid on Ike confirmed he was calming.

"Yeah, okay," said Ike. "Fuck it. Let's make a deal."

After a trip outside to confirm the condition of Ike's new wheels, they were back inside finishing the transaction. Ike was all chatty again and one happy octogenarian. Meathead was finishing off his second burger with chili-cheese fries. Sarah was beginning to wonder if Ike paid him in coin or calories. She despised Meathead and had caught him examining her body repeatedly while he ate as if the burger was a TV dinner and she was entertainment on the Playboy Channel.

40

"Okay... now lookie here," said Ike. "To make sure a bracelet works, put it on and buy something. All the stores near the portals accept RFID, including this fine establishment. We got three sets of bracelets for each of you, with three different picture perfect ID matches. The IDs are from people gone missing during the supply shortages. It's a sad thing the dead have become so bountiful. Now remember, like we discussed, the fingerprints on each ID are what's on file for the deceased. It's too bad we couldn't use your digits, but like I said... Since you told me your prints list you as Enforcer bait, it just won't work. Now, 'cause I like you, I'm throwing in matching sets of driver's licenses and Socials for each identity. What do you say to that?"

"I'm throwing in a kiss," said Sarah.

Ike looked like he was going to blush.

"Now, these bracelets work just like the souvenirs I gave you. They turn on when you close the hidden latch and turn off when you open the latch. But you gotta be real careful where you turn 'em on and off. Because when a reader catches the scent of your RFID inside a protectorate for the first time, you'd better have things set up so that it doesn't look like you just materialized out a thin air like Supergirl. You gotta always keep a map in your head so that every RFID scan makes sense. If your scans look wildly out of place, they are gonna come gunning for you."

Ike leaned forward across the table as if he were about to whisper the secrets of eternal life. He licked his lips.

"What makes these babies worth serious coin is that each bracelet is in Big Brother's database with either a forged exit or entry trail for Chi-Town. Without a foolproof exit trail, you're busted trying to walk in. If a bracelet is switched on inside Chi-Town without an entry trail, a big red bull's eye is gonna be painted on your sorry ass. The bracelets with the green sticky labels have fake exit trails and the ones with the red sticky labels have fake entry trails and are very useful for getting out of Chi-town if Enforcers are after your pretty little ass, my lovely Sarah. You each have one entry and two exit bracelets. Don't mix 'em up!

"As part of my no extra charge extra service, all these bracelets are flagged in the DB as intermittent. RFID is far less reliable than the man would like everyone to believe. Flagging your jewelry as intermitted will help keep eyebrows from rising when you switch on your exit bracelets even if they have not been scanned in days. The lazy asses will just figure it's flaky jewelry and not ghosts appearing out of nowhere. A bracelet can probably safely go a week with no scans, but to play it smart you're gonna want your exit bracelets popping up every few days. Give 'em each a little exercise by switching 'em on and off in the middle of a crowd where it's too much trouble for Enforcers to count noses on their video surveillance screens and figure out there's one too many.

"Now for the fun part. Big Brother's rules say everyone in Chi-town's gotta work, so these entry bracelets have primo job assignments. Both of you are docs. Nothing fancy, you dig, just Marcus Welby kind of docs, and that means the man is gonna pay you forty-five thousand work credits a month. You gonna be able to buy whatever you want...."

"Whoa, Ike, I'm not a doctor," said Sarah. "This is not going to—"

"Hush now, sweet Sarah. Do not worry, cause Dr. Ike has your back. I assigned both of you to work at the St. Monica family clinic on South Halsted Street."

Ike was beaming with pride. The emotions radiating from him made it hard for Sarah not to smile.

"See, the special deal is this," said Ike. "St. Monica family clinic burned down and isn't planned to be rebuilt till next year. While Big Brother is smart about some things, he is very stupid about other things. Everyone at St. Monica is on paid vacation. Trust me, you gonna get half a mil a year in funny e-money to do nothing.

"Now, last thing. There are twenty roto-gates at each entry to Chi-Town and there's normally an hour wait. Today we got three-hour waits and those guards are working up a sweat slinging the hash. So you are gonna be safely lost in the crowds. Just one more boring Caucasian couple. The good thing about Enforcers is they are lazy sons of bitches. With a bracelet, there's no fingerprinting to get through the gates even though they got fingerprint readers. All fingerprinting goes on inside the visa building when issuing a new bracelet. So as long as your bracelet scans okay, they gonna ignore you. There's just too many comings and goings even on a normal day. They don't even spot check. So no one is gonna find out your prints don't match the bracelets unless they arrest you inside for something stupid. So don't be stupid. I don't want all my artistry going to waste. It's bad for business."

Eye of the Storm

Mark Freedman – Chicago Protectorate – January 30, 0002 A.P.

Mark was frustrated. Over a week had passed since they walked through the roto-gates entering the Chicago Protectorate, yet the location of the singularity remained elusive. Their directional sense of tides in the n-web was now useless. Once they got within a few miles of the singularity, their sense of direction began to lose resolution until it felt like the singularity was all around them. It was as if they had walked through a hurricane's vortex and into the eye of the storm. Inside the miles wide void they felt unsettled and at times mildly disoriented or uncoordinated. Something about this space seemed to slow their thinking. When they ventured a little deeper inside the vortex, the seductive pull of the singularity increased, and they lost many of their networked abilities, including data-floods and mental communications. Curiously, some basic types of assists still worked, and Sarah's ability to empathically feel other's emotions remained, but at a reduced level.

The void covered far too many square miles of city streets to easily search. Over a course of days they had wandered the area, sensing nothing useful. There were hot and cold spots where the effects on them varied, making it even harder to guess the location of the singularity.

Mark had returned again and again to the assist, which displayed the architecture of the n-web, and every time it provided nothing useful. The virtual rendering geo-projected onto real space around him was minutely accurate in both location and scale. It even showed how much data was flowing down each pathway, but as he walked closer to the vortex, the projection became noisy, like a bad television signal. The geo-projected pathways entering the vortex appeared bent and distorted, eventually fading out as if made of smoke. If he walked too close to the vortex or stepped into the eye of the storm, the n-web display was completely lost. He knew the n-web's pathways were still there functioning all around him, unchanged. The problem was the data used to produce the three-dimensional rendering was corrupted enough by the singularity to make it useless. In outer space it would be possible to see matter and light approaching a black hole, yet see nothing beyond the event horizon. The same appeared to be true for this singularity. Data flowing through the n-web was no longer visible beyond the singularity's event horizon. This maelstrom was truly a mental and emotional gravity well within the n-web.

Mark had gone up to the roof of the six story apartment building in which they were staying. The building was located miles from the vortex. He was seated on a bench someone had long ago dragged up there. In a few hours the sun would be dipping below the edge of the city. The clouds were dark as if bruised with snow. Great rays of sun pierced through gaps in the clouds, creating shafts of light that illuminated whole swaths of Chicago.

Mark was preparing to invoke another series of huge data-floods. These would be fine-tuned, using the meager fresh information they had about the vortex. He looked within by meditating on his body and his breath. He needed to quiet and firmly anchor his mind. He knew over 60 percent of his brain was hybrid nanotech. When the seeds had metastasized, the restructuring process proceeded rapidly at first, then slowed. Mark did not know if this was the natural progression or a problem that would ultimately lead to premature death instead of extended life. He and Sarah both wondered if there was something more needed to complete the evolutionary step and if that *something more* was connected to the singularity.

Time had passed with agonizing slowness. Wind gusted across the roof, pelting him with gritty dust. Mark stifled a moan from pain lancing through his skull. He was relentless in his search for information inside the vast data stores of the god-machine. The data-flood was coursing through him like an overwhelming electrical current. The pain was agonizing. It felt as if holes were being drilled into his skull and yet he held on. The mass of his cerebral cortex was too small to handle the flood of information. The nanotech hybridized neurons in his brain were being forced to realign to the flow. The very structure of his cerebral cortex was acting as a sieve, allowing fine particles of data to pass through while retaining the larger debris. The god-machine was far more organic than a conventional computer. Mark had not been aware of this characteristic at first because of the interface's casual similarities to modern software, but as he grew more accustomed to the interface and it grew more accustomed to him, a kind of relationship was forged. He would often find himself relating to the machine as a living thing. At this moment it was a hulking monster at the brink of crushing him.

The data-flood abruptly ended as if a wire had snapped. To anchor himself Mark dug his claws into the simulated reality that surrounded him. He felt like a survivor, battered and washed up on the jagged shore of a stormy sea. His mind was filled with more new memories from this data-flood than he could possibly retain. His memory capacity was now so much greater than when he was an organic, but it was not nearly enough. The majority of the knowledge he'd just gained was fading quickly in the same way as a dream. He was desperately sifting for fragments worth retaining in long term memory. There was just nothing useful. He had hoped this time it would be different, had hoped the question he had mediated on until the flood began would have brought him the knowledge they needed. They still knew nothing critical beyond what instinct and educated guesswork provided. He was no longer convinced they would even recognize the singularity if they saw it. Beyond the fact that it radiated from a single location somewhere in this city, they had no idea of its size or nature. Did it exist inside a hybrid, a group of hybrids, or was it something that functioned on its own? Did it have a physical structure at all or was it just a program embedded in the fabric of the n-web? They had no idea.

The way data-floods worked always reminded Mark of praying. He would focus on a question to the exclusion of all else. Eventually once his focus exceeded the required threshold, a reply from the god-machine would come. If the question was narrow, the response was manageable and painless. If the question was broad, the response came in a torrent of mind bending pain and insight. He could not help but wonder if many of the answered prayers and gifts of enlightenment in ancient religious texts were misunderstood encounters with the god-machine.

The semi-transparent touch interface for god-machine commands was floating in space before him like a phantom control panel. He preferred this interactive way of working with the god-machine than the thought driven data-floods, but it had serious limits. He had grown used to how the computer interface worked: It was a tactile virtual reality flawlessly superimposed over his physical surroundings. As the months passed, labels on the command tablet and other interface elements appeared less in the runic language of the Creators and more in English. The interface was adapting to him. Mark closed his mind off from the god-machine interface. The tablet and trackball floating before him winked out of existence, returning his surroundings to normal.

Mark stood up and looked over the waist high concrete wall that separated him from a fall no one could survive, not even a hybrid with the capacity to rapidly heal. The roof was littered with trash and some old ratty beach chairs. An arctic wind was blowing in off the great lake. He wondered fleetingly about the temperature. An assist displayed 28 degrees in small lettering superimposed over the lower part of his vision. The assist had been periodically alerting him so he did not unnecessarily cause frost damage to his body. He should have been freezing, dressed only in a heavy sweatshirt and blue jeans, but this improved body felt comfortable. There was only the slightest sensation of coolness on his exposed skin. Under heavy loads his nanotech brain ran much hotter than an organic brain. This additional heat warmed his blood above normal. It was helpful to be in a cold place right now, which was part of the reason he'd gone up to the roof.

Gazing down at the streets below, he saw the corridors of Chicago as tall alleyways covered with grime. The streets were traveled by pedestrians and bicycles, but absent were all private cars, which were prohibited within the city. Everywhere he looked there was damage from the days of the plague. Gutted buildings loomed over a city of ruined lives and shattered dreams, but the city was being rebuilt. Some replacement infrastructure had been put in place so well it seemed like it had been part of the original city plan. Other repairs were so jury rigged that they could fail at any moment and often did. Electrical power was for the most part reliable, though brownouts happened almost daily. Natural gas service was permanently shut off, and so the boilers in many buildings no longer worked. Apartments with fireplaces were at a premium. High capacity water filtration systems had gone in overnight to bolster the USAG's Orwellian claims of protection from future biochemical terrorist attacks. The nationalized telecom services provided data speeds so high that pundits were predicting wired Internet was going the way of the dinosaur. Public Wi-Fi hotspots were already a thing of the past. Mark thought it was odd and even suspicious that the USAG would deliver mediocrity in so many ways except wireless service. Was it their version of opiates for the masses, a way to ensure distribution of their propaganda, or for some even darker purpose?

It was odd to be in the heart of a great city and not hear horns or sounds of traffic. In its place was a softer drone of voices that blended into an unintelligible sound, which oddly felt like a conscious, living thing. The singularity he and Sarah were hunting in Chicago was brighter in his mind than the city itself. Mark yearned to find it with an emotional and physical hunger that surprised even him. He had sensed the singularity before Sarah. Months ago, he'd felt its presence as a missing thread in the fabric of human thought. Sarah sensed the singularity like an emotional void in the collective soul of humanity.

Even though the nanotech restructuring of his body was proceeding slower than it had been, Mark continued to evolve in other ways. Every day he could drink a little more heavily from the surrounding ocean of stray thoughts that humankind swam in, and at will, he could filter the cacophony down to a single thread of consciousness. The ability gave him a powerful feeling of connectedness, but in practice it offered an unreliable strategic advantage. He only received thoughts that were leaked from the subconscious. This was not the same as reading someone's mind. To make matters worse, not everyone leaked. A third of the people were blank enigmas, while others were a chaos of prattle. Sarah was able to do something very similar with emotions but with one staggering advantage: Virtually everyone radiated emotions. Mark had tried to understand what she experienced, how she felt other's emotions almost as her own. He knew what he digested as stray thoughts were only a pale shadow of the emotional invasion saturating her hybrid mind. Likewise from her perspective, he knew she did not fully comprehend the world of noisy thoughts that he dwelled in.

Mark was staring at the people traveling back and forth on the sidewalk below. They were dressed in every color imaginable. The presence of so many people was the first thing that had struck him when they'd entered the city. The population figures for Chicago were only a fraction of the pre-plague census numbers, but still shockingly high compared to the Outlands. He was subconsciously keeping a running count of how many people passed by. This was something that would have been impossible for him to do as an organic, and now his nanotech brain did it without even thinking.

Sarah had been gone for twenty-four hours and would soon be back. Mark knew this from the stream of memories she was broadcasting to him. In sequences of small memory capsules, like frames in a movie, she relayed to him what she was experiencing while mapping out the perimeter of the singularity's vortex. It was not circular as they'd originally thought. It was blob shaped and encompassed about six square miles of city blocks. The Chicago Protectorate occupied 220 square miles. Mark had originally assumed the singularity was at the center of the vortex, but he was no longer sure of that. Several days ago they had repeatedly tried to walk what they thought was a radius through the vortex but failed to locate the singularity. Chaotic data flows had somehow mentally spun them around, leaving confusion in their wake. This mental chaos complicated what was already beginning to feel like something he was losing control over.

The sound of a pushcart vendor drifted up from the street. Mark watched as an Enforcer Humvee crawled by, forcing people out of the way. Even from this distance, his brain ached from the unrelenting pressure of the singularity. He was so frustrated! He wanted to smash everything in sight. He turned and kicked a rusted trash can across the roof, tearing it open. A glimmer of pain in his leg arrested the outburst. The trash can had dug a ragged gash in his shin. Within seconds the pain had been blocked.

He was consumed by a powerful sense that time was running out to find the singularity. He still had connections with some of his colleagues in the scientific community. Scientists were some of the least likely to believe the propaganda they were being fed. This morning he had received a warning from a colleague, Karla Hunt. She had used a photographer's blog as a blind drop. It was an arrangement they had worked out during their last face to face meeting. The warning was encrypted, using an unbreakable steganographic algorithm. The blog contain a large amount of uploaded amateur and professional photographs, which made it perfect for this kind of encryption. Karla was an insider, a director running a top-secret BARDCOM lab on countermeasures to nanotech seeds. Her immediate superior was General McKafferty. Mark knew the general all too well. BARDCOM—Biological Armaments Research and Development Command—had been the general's fiefdom for the better part of a decade. The man had tried to imprison both Mark and Sarah when they were at the BVMC lab after the general had taken over control of the CDC in the midst of the crisis.

Karla was warning him that the nanotech was evolving, mutating into something even more stealthy and smart. This news was a shock. Was the nanotech mutating inside him too? He could feel the hybridization unceasingly spreading within him, replacing a little more of his wetware with every passing week. Would there come a point when he would no longer be himself? He could already be beyond that point and not know it. How could a machine ever hope to know it's a machine? Mark felt his limitations and some of them were clearly imposed from without. With all the vast information available to him through the interface, why had he not known the nanotech was evolving? The only explanation was god-machine censorship. The more important question was why. It was times like this that Mark felt more like a specimen than a free man.

With surprising force, an assist yanked his full attention to the pedestrian crosscurrents on the street below. A superimposed orange glow highlighted a man's head. The glow was part of a medical schematic projected over the target. Orange was the color coding used by the god-machine to identify nanotech seeds inside living tissue and blood. The man was a foot taller than the people around him. He moved in a way that was oddly graceful, almost as if floating. Mark could not discern any physical details other than stocky build, long brown hair pulled back into a ponytail, and a black parka. The orange glow suffused the back of the man's skull, which indicated the presence of a much larger than normal swarm of free swimming naontech COBIC. Responding to Mark's intense interest, the assist snapped a mental photo and enlarged it while using image enhancement to fill in some of the missing details. The result was a grainy, magnified frozen image seen in his mind and not through his eyes. The enlargement showed the telltale neurological structures of a hybrid brain. In the past two years, the closest thing to another hybrid he or Sarah had encountered was that psychopath Alexander and he was long dead from his own suicide by explosion.

Mark raced down the emergency staircase at a reckless speed. The elevator had long since been broken. He leaped down flight after flight, gripping the banister at each turn to swing himself around. Three stories to go; he'd never make it. The hybrid would be gone. He had to make it. Mark nearly broke the outside double doors and his arm as he rushed onto the sidewalk. In a parallel train of thought he knew the RFID reader at the door and surveillance cameras outside had just recorded odd behavior and linked it to his account. He desperately searched through the crowds but could not find the man. Mark began half jogging and searching, stopping frequently to look in all directions. People were staring. Mental chatter from annoyed pedestrians filled his mind. At some level he heard the warble of military sirens growing louder and ignored the meaning. An assist warned him to stop drawing attention to himself. He ignored it.

He reached the curb as a pair of law enforcement SUVs screeched to a stop at the opposite side of the intersection. The vehicles were as heavily armor-plated as tanks. Enforcers poured out in combat gear. Mark turned to leave the area but was blocked by a wall of people all crowding in and staring. Rattled, he turned back toward the Enforcers. All of the squad except one were in foot pursuit of someone. The remaining Enforcer was staring directly at him; his helmet mounted video camera was recording everything. Mark forced himself to look away and saw the other Enforcers had cornered the hybrid he'd spotted from the roof. Stray thoughts coming from the Enforcer still staring at him were as clear in Mark's brain as spoken words. *Are you an accomplice?* Mark had attracted unwanted suspicion.

Sounds of an argument erupted. The Enforcer turned away and hurried to join his squad. Mark saw their detainee was not going quietly. The man was large and powerfully built. He had a serene, almost detached expression that seemed peculiar and out of place. Mark's medical assist was still operating. At this close proximity the superimposed medical schematics looked like a colored digital fluoroscope. There were numeric readings and callout symbols overlaid on the subject.

49

Mark could now see the COBIC swarm at the base of the skull. A large portion of the brain was a latticework of nanotech hybridized neurons. The affected tissues were color coded in glowing orange to indicate seeds were nested inside the nucleuses of the cells. The assist indicated that 87 percent of the brain was involved. Fanning out from the nanotech processing nexus were orange roots that extended into the remaining unaffected gray matter of the brain and a short distance down the spinal column. Mark had never dared imagine anything this highly evolved could exist so soon. This was not a coincidence. This hybrid had to be connected with the singularity.

All the soldiers had their M16s aimed at point blank range at the hybrid's chest. One of the soldiers had blood dripping from a damaged nose. The semicircular machine gun firing squad had the hybrid pinned with a storefront window at his back. At a distance of 30 feet, the hybrid's stare locked onto Mark's eyes. Something tugged at the back of Mark's brain like a magnet pulling on another of its kind. The hybrid smiled at him, projecting hostility. He recognized this tugging. It was stronger version of the same effect Sarah's stare could have on him.

Mark knew from a deeply ingrained instinct something terrible was about to happen. An unformed memory was urging him to run. In unison, the soldiers collapsed as if they had lost every bone in their limbs. With impossible speed, the hybrid snatched one of the Enforcer's M16s from limp fingers as the body crumpled. Time seemed to slow down for Mark. An assist displayed medical schematics over the Enforcers. He realized they had all died instantly before collapsing to the pavement. The bodies were splayed out in a telltale semi-circle around the hybrid. Mark felt numb, recognizing that he'd just witnessed a small kill-zone. Had the god-machine murdered on its own volition, or did this hybrid have the ability to use the god-machine as a weapon? Someone accidently shoved Mark in one direction, and then someone else jostled him back the other way. He knew he was in the midst of a skittish herd that sensed a top predator and was building to a stampede. Within seconds of grabbing the M16, the hybrid opened up with it into the bodies of the Enforcers. Mark was stunned by the senseless audacity. What was the hybrid doing firing into dead bodies? Blood flowed over the curb like a thick spill of oil. The crowd scattered within a deafening sea of screams, pushing, and shoes scraping on pavement. The hybrid took aim at a harmless looking man standing still in the midst of the chaos. The two seemed to share a silent moment of recognition. In a medical assist, Mark saw the extensive orange glowing structures that identified this second man as a highly evolved hybrid. Moments later the man's head exploded under a stream of bullets. The killer hybrid dropped the M16 and walked away. Mark watched in disbelief as the hybrid merged with the crowd and in seconds had vanished like a ghost. There was no point in trying to run after him, and besides, what would he do even if he could catch him? Sirens were growing in volume from several directions. Mark sensed a terrible insight was within his grasp if he could only open his mind a little wider to accept it. He stood rigidly in place as if trapped in a block of ice. This hybrid was both highly evolved and a premeditated murderer. The kill-zone had been smaller and more precise than anything Mark had witnessed during the plague. The thought of it brought all his deeply entrenched self-doubts to the surface. He wondered if this proved he and Sarah bore some responsibility for the nanotech plague. One way or the other this rogue hybrid had been saved by a highly targeted kill-zone. Equally troubling was the murder of another hybrid. Had that murder been the real motive behind the entire bloody charade? Mark's block of ice shattered as the first set of flashing red Enforcer lights appeared at the intersection. He turned and hastily retreated into the fleeing crosscurrents of people.

Mark Freedman – Chicago Protectorate – January 30, 0002 A.P.

Mark heard the door lock release and looked up. He'd been shifting through a small, painless data-flood from the god-machine, trying to find safe ways to locate or learn about these other hybrids. Sarah entered the apartment, bringing with her a rush of energy. She immediately launched into stories about her day walking the edge of the singularity's vortex. She was acting oddly and looked even odder in what she called her "street camouflage". The clothing made her gray and unmemorable, which was the whole point. She dropped her ragged ankle length coat on the floor. It was so dirty he expected to see bugs fleeing. Underneath the coat she was organized and clean. It was like a butterfly shedding a cocoon. Sarah removed her shoulder holster and backup piece, then shucked her body armor –which ended up as a deadly pile on the couch –while never missing a beat in her recitation. Mark was staring at her more than listening. She was a remarkable sight. Sarah had that quality that drew unabashed stares. She radiated something vital. He found it intriguing that through all her hybrid restructuring, she had not noticeably changed in appearance as he had. Granted, she was young, while he was much older at fifty-one. The effects of the seeds had smoothed his skin along with perfecting every organ and system in his body. He knew he looked no more than his late thirties. Sarah in some ways looked older than her age. Her expression was of a much wiser woman than she could possibly be chronologically. It was mostly in her eyes and how they somehow reflected all the horror they'd seen. It was a very unsettling aspect of her presence.

He watched her walk from the room in a T-shirt and sweat pants. He heard her in the bedroom and then the shower turning on. Her image remained burned into his mind. He walked to the closed bathroom door and leaned his back against the wall. Unsure of what he was doing, he listened to the water changing in tone as it sprayed against the contours of her body. He intimately knew how that body looked. The memories of touching her lifted his hand to the bathroom doorknob and turned it. He stepped into a warm cloud of steam and the smell of soap. He saw her shape moving on the other side of fogged glass as if in a dream.

The next thing he could remember, he was inside the shower and inside her. The memories of a lifetime of failed relationships troubled him as the sounds of water rushing down and Sarah's soft moans thankfully washed all thoughts away.

The bedroom windows were dark except for a hint of moonlight somewhere in the night. Mark had not immediately told Sarah about the rogue hybrid. He was confused about his reluctance but eventually told her everything by sharing the memory with her.

He looked over at Sarah, sleeping quietly in pools of shadows on her side of the bed. A medial projection came up over her form, then faded. He didn't know if Sarah loved him and prayed she didn't. He knew she was attracted to him because they were so alone in this new world. Like Adam and Eve, they had been the only two of their kind, but now they knew there were more. He knew it was a terrible idea to be sleeping with her. Yet his mind was haunted with memories of them having sex. Every day he vowed to stop, and almost every night the vow was broken. It had been going on like this since meeting up with her on the outskirts of St. Louis. The location had been selected as a staging point for the final phase of their hunt. Before then, all that had been on his mind was the singularity. The first time they had sex had been so unexpected and in many ways so long in coming.

Before arriving in St. Louis, Mark had vowed to let nothing interfere with his pursuit of the singularity. Sarah, if anything, was complicated. She was unpredictable, half his age, impulsive, and even dangerous… and she had been one of his volunteer subjects at the BVMC lab. This sexual adventure had already gone too far. When it ultimately ended there would be no escaping the fallout. His original vow had been smart and responsible, but when had he ever been smart when it came to women? The vow had ended without even a moment's resistance when Sarah had hugged him not so innocently as they'd rendezvoused on that street in St. Louis. At that moment he'd known a fuse had been lit inside them both. That first night they'd wrestled until the sun had risen and left the hotel bed in shambles. Had they used birth control then? He could not remember. How could he not remember? It was all a blur and he knew there was no hope for him. His craving for her warmth grew with the passing of the sun of each new day. Perhaps he needed someone who could understand all he was going through. Before breaking off with Kathy, she had made it clear she would never try to become a hybrid. She feared losing her humanity and the creativity that only mortality could kindle. He replayed memories of Kathy, which were photographically engraved in his nanotech brain as his confused eyes finally closed, accepting sleep.

Mark Freedman – Chicago Protectorate – January 31, 0002 A.P.

Mark was walking rapidly down the sidewalk, brusquely passing people who kept getting in his way. Sarah was moving just as fast through the crowds. He was alive with energy. The solution had come to him in a lucid dream in which he was fully conscious but not in control. In the dream he had found the singularity using an assist. He knew the solution would work the same way in waking reality. Over the past two years he had learned there was little difference between being fully aware in dreams and the awareness called reality. The key difference was that in dreams objects were not anchored by dense physical matter and as a result could easily morph. A house could change colors or writing in a book could alter itself. He had grown to consider dreams powerful allies and consensual reality not so consensual. Even in grave situations, witnesses often saw and reported very different things in consensual reality.

Mark was feeling the strain in his legs from keeping up the rapid pace. The sun was just rising, filling in the gray shadows between buildings. He recognized the block he'd just turned down. Elevated train tracks crossed the street at the end of the block. The steel girders of the elevated track had streaks of rust running down them and around the rivets. Several parts had been covered with Day-Glo graffiti. There were shops on both sides of the street. He stared for a moment at a tavern named McGees that seemed oddly out of place because it was teeming with customers. In a city known for its great food, most of the bars and restaurants were out of business. Nearly all the rest had been converted into the government run cafeterias that fed the citizens of the protectorate for free.

"Tell me!" demanded Sarah.

"When we get there," said Mark.

"Why the secrecy?"

"What if they're spying on us through the god-machine?"

"They? What *they*?"

"The tribe of hybrids. What if they don't want to be found?"

Mark could feel himself nearing the vortex, the wall of the cyber hurricane. He stopped walking and examined the ordinary looking street. He could feel the vortex a few yards in front of him, pulling on his thoughts. A heat wave or mirage or something should have marked the boundary, but there was nothing. People on the street were walking right through it as if it was not there. Mark concentrated on the n-web surrounding him. In response, a three dimensional assist was constructed around him showing the network pathways of the n-web. Same as before, the computer rendering was noisy like a bad television signal. On the other side of the vortex the pathways became distorted, eventually fading out. Just as he had done in the dream, Mark walked backward until the noise was gone from the geo-projected rendering. He stared at the vortex's boundary and was excited that he now had enough resolution to clearly see the pathways fading out. The tendrils of the distorted fadeouts were all pulled in the same direction toward the singularity, like smoke trails in the wind. Using a GPS compass app in his Droid, he noted the direction in which the smoke trails were pointing.

They hiked a few blocks over and repeated the same procedure. After an hour of walking the edge of the vortex, Mark had identified on a mental map a spot where all the lines intersected.

"Got you!" he said as he sent a memory of the map to Sarah.

"That's a residential block. What now? Do we go knock on their door?"

"We go slow. You saw my memories of that psychopathic hybrid. That might be who answers the door."

"He knew you were a hybrid and didn't shoot," said Sarah.

"I feel better already."

They soon reached the block that contained the singularity. Deep inside the vortex, they had lost all ability to use memory capsules and most other networked functions. It was lunch hour and the streets carried a steady stream of people. They were in one of the most exclusive neighborhoods of Chicago, the Gold Coast. Lake Michigan was less than two blocks east. Mark took in a deep breath of cold lake air and felt momentarily refreshed. One side of the street of historic multimillion dollar townhouses had been wrecked during the plague fueled riots. Fire and small explosions had reduced some of the priceless real estate to vacant lots of charred brick and unrecognizable debris. The other side was mostly unscathed. As they slowly walked amid the small clusters of people, Mark picked out the ever present surveillance cameras with their directional microphones. At any moment one could be aimed toward them. The message from the USAG was clear. The Enforcers were always watching and listening. He'd tried to act as inconspicuous as possible, but without memory capsules they had to whisper to avoid being overheard by Enforcer surveillance. They had already passed through dozens of RFID checkpoints on their way to this block. Each checkpoint had invisibly reached out and touched their bracelets. In some gigantic computer database resided this entire peculiar walk from start to finish of two newcomer counterfeit doctors.

The singularity was very close and having powerful effects on Mark. He and Sarah both stopped walking at the same instant he felt its invisible grip tighten. People jostled past them. They became a pair of stones in a river of sleeping humanity that flowed around them. Not one person was able to wake from their daydreams to perceive the singularity. All that Mark was feeling was not even a ghost to them. An overpoweringly seductive urge to surrender to the singularity washed through him like a costal surge. The final event horizon was here and he wanted nothing more than to throw himself into the sweet maelstrom of pleasure he knew was before him. The seduction was not emotional or intellectual. It was something other. It was pure instinct. Mark was certain that if he lost just a little more self-control, he would sleepwalk right into the singularity and never return. His thinking felt very sluggish, as if some task running in the nanotech circuitry of his brain was stealing all available computing power. It was even affecting his muscle coordination. Sarah was holding onto his arm. He knew she was steadying herself. She leaned in close to whisper to him.

"The last of the emotions have vanished," said Sarah. "I feel isolated. There're no emotions radiating from you or the people around me."

"The singularity is pulling on me harder than ever," said Mark. "That means some n-web functions are still operating."

Mark stared at a person and tried to invoke a medical assist. A fluoroscopic schematic of the person's anatomy and vital signs came up superimposed over their body. He was relieved that some of the basic n-web functions were still usable. Everyone on the street had a faint orange smudge in the brainstem, which was the normal presence of a small amount of free-swimming nanotech. No matter where he looked he could not find a person with nanotech seeds nested in their neurons—the mark of a hybrid.

"Which townhouse do you think the singularity's in?" whispered Mark.

"That brownstone five down from us," whispered Sarah. She did not point. "The one with bay windows."

"I was thinking the same thing. That's two votes yea and zero nays. The singularity is in there and it feels like it's sucking everything out of my skull. If hybrids are in there, they may be able to receive all the thoughts the singularity is stealing from us. They may know we're here."

"What now?"

"I'm too confused this close in. Once we found it, I was sure we'd figure out the next step but now… I just… I don't know. If we were invited inside, I'm not sure we'd ever come out. There could be something lethal in there or maybe we'd just never want to leave. We have to know a lot more about what we're getting into before opening that door. Let's get out of here so we can think."

"Mark!" she hissed.

Her fingers squeezed painfully into his arm as he realized he could barely move his legs. His muscles weren't frozen. It was more like his body was arguing with his mind. All the rest of his muscles worked normally. Were they already ensnared by the singularity's undertow? He lifted his foot, trying to take a step backward. It was like trying to walk against a rapidly flowing stream. He couldn't make his foot move in the direction he wanted. He planted it down before the backward step became a step forward toward the singularity. The physical attraction was too much. The promise of pleasure must have been short circuiting his body somehow. Half of him wanted to give in. It would have been so easy. The other half—the thinking half—felt panic. Were hybrids watching and controlling him? He tried again to step backward, but the flow of the invisible waters was too powerful. A man appeared in a second story window of the townhouse that they *knew* held the singularity. The telltale signs of a highly evolved hybrid were visible in an assist. A pedestrian bumped into Sarah, jostling them both. The face in the window turned in Mark's direction. Sarah managed to take a step backward, tugging on Mark's arm, turning him toward her. Suddenly, he was able to easily walk. It was as if he had a neurological disorder like Parkinson's, which raises a barrier to walking until you take that first step and settle into a normal cadence. The image of that hybrid in the window was burned into his mind. It felt like someone was intensely staring at his back as they walked away.

"What the hell just happened?" whispered Sarah. "If that guy hadn't bumped me—"

"Later," said Mark. "We're being watched."

Mark Freedman – Chicago Protectorate – February 1, 0002 A.P.

Mark and Sarah had carefully walked and probed the outer edges of the worst of the singularity's tidal effects to map them. They had selected a spot to set up a forward camp that was just outside the worst effects. The twenty-eight story apartment building was five blocks from the singularity. They had a clear line of sight from top floor apartments thanks to the fires and explosions that had gutted whatever had occupied the blocks in between. The apartment tower had been a very expensive residence with a marble foyer, rooftop pool, and all the luxuries only huge sums of money could buy. Now it was unoccupied unless you counted pigeons and rats. A third of the building had been gutted by fire and most of the windows were gone. There was no electricity or heat. The apartment they'd selected for their surveillance nest had no front door and all the windows were shattered. It was a frigid and windy mess.

Mark stood in front of the broken out windows and gazed down at the city streets. It was the best view of all the apartments they'd checked. From this distance the townhouse could have been a piece on a Monopoly board. He could sense the singularity radiating out from within the brownstone's walls. He had a strange idea that he couldn't shake, that the singularity was alive and thinking. Sarah was out purchasing needed equipment. At this distance from the singularity, he still felt disoriented at times and his thinking seemed slower, but it was far better than even a partial block closer. He was also growing accustomed to the negative effects, which lessened them. He would not be ensnared as easily a second time. He examined the other townhouse mansions on the block. Each one was connected to the next, forming a solid wall of what had been unimaginable wealth. All the townhouses showed signs of current occupancy. He had read that the ratio of habitable apartments to people was ten to one. Very little real estate had an original owner living in it, and every bit of it had been nationalized. Now anybody of moderate means could afford to live in those townhouses as long as some USAG executive or government official approved their application. All signs indicated cronyism was still alive and flourishing.

Mark turned at the sound of something scurrying. Ralph looked up from his nap with one eye open, then went back to sleep. The living room was full of fine antiques covered in windblown dirt and water damaged. Mark was satisfied with the surveillance nest they were setting up. They had sleeping bags, a camp stove, and food. It would be a lot like camping on a mountaintop. Without an elevator, it would take a very determined person to climb twenty-eight flights of stairs to reach their apartment. The odds of someone accidently wandering by were slim. Unexpected visitors would likely only be there for unpleasant reasons. Mark had already removed a door from a lower floor apartment and installed it on their new abode. A visit to a local shop had turned up a door jammer bar and replacement deadbolt along with four car batteries. The door hardware had been almost free. The batteries and rental of a shopping cart to get the batteries home had cost far more but had also been ridiculously cheap. His RFID bracelet had given up a little over one hundred virtual dollars, which was an imperceptible dent in the huge amount of e-money he had in his account. Mark thought back to Ike being so proud of the identities he had crafted. The forty-five thousand dollar monthly stipend for doctors had sounded like an amazing amount of e-money, but now Mark understood why it had been so easy to set up. With all the subsidized and controlled prices inside a protectorate it would be impossible to spend so much money. The huge paycheck was really just a clever enticement to recruit doctors. Even more than in the Outlands, most of the non-consumable luxuries were free or almost free in protectorates: cloths, housewares, appliances, and more. If you couldn't find what you wanted in an abandoned store or apartment there were government run redistribution shops called *G-shops*. The government kept track of the goods in G-shops to prevent hoarding and for luxury items charged a modest fee based on scarcity. So what could your average overpaid protectorate elite spend all their excess e-money on? Mark guessed consumables like nightclubs, legalized drugs, prostitution, and gambling were the businesses into which most of the disposable e-money flowed.

Lugging the car batteries up to the apartment had been grueling work. Mark's body was full of dull aches that came and went. He heard the stairwell door bang closed at the end of the hallway and froze. With his senses dulled by proximity to the singularity, he didn't know if it was Sarah. She'd only left two hours ago; that was not enough time to collect what they needed. Ralph went to the door wagging his tail. Thank god for good old low tech canine sense of smell. Mark let Sarah in and saw success written in the amused smile on her face. He hadn't been sure everything they needed could even be found.

"I got two high resolution Sony low light video web cameras with integrated image intensifiers, two Celestron spotting scopes, notebooks, software, tripods, power adapters, duct tape, and two twelve volt power inverters," announced Sarah. "The only thing in limited supply was the inverters. The first G-shop I tried was the one we passed the other day that sold mostly fancy electronics. They had everything on the list. I was nervous, figuring the clerk wouldn't be stupid enough to miss the fact that I was buying a do-it-yourself spy kit. I thought about spreading out the purchases at different G-shops, but what's the point? Government records would show everything I bought anyway. Spreading out the purchases might even look more suspicious. You won't believe what happened. While I was shopping the telescopes, I watched an older couple come in and buy an entire spy kit. I kid you not. One of the clerks helped them pick everything out. I just watched and listened, trying to keep my mouth from hanging open. This whole city is nuts. All the spy gear is selling at a premium. Voyeurism has become a hobby for well to do protectorate citizens. There's even a website called *Candid Candy* for sharing funny or embarrassing clips. The highest voted clips win prizes."

"I guess if it's good enough for the USAG to spy on everyone, it's good enough for citizens too," said Mark.

"The twisted psychology behind this has to be something magnificent to behold," said Sarah. "So anyway, it all went fine—no suspicion, no problems. Cost me three thousand bucks and change."

Mark and Sarah were seated on a decaying couch, staring at the screens of two notebook computers. Encircling the couch, they had hung tarps from the ceiling to create blackout curtains. They wanted to prevent light from the notebooks from reaching the windows and drawing attention. Sarah's shoulder was touching Mark's. The glow of the screens illuminated them as twilight grew deeper. Cracked glass littered the floor. A thick layer of dust covered everything. The car batteries were lined up in a row against a back wall. The power inverters connected to the car batteries quietly hummed as they produced 120 volts of standard house current. Electrical extension cords snaked from the inverters to the notebooks and the electronic surveillance equipment. Two spotter's telescopes on tripods were aimed out a broken window. Video cameras were attached to each telescope's tube and held in place with duct tape. On the notebook screens were real-time video images of the townhouse. The notebooks quietly hummed as the video was recorded. One telescope and camera was aimed at the front door. They were using the second telescope to systematically examine every brick and paint chip on the townhouse a few square feet at a time. One thing was clear. This building was not what it seemed from casual inspection. Mark got up to move the telescope another five degrees to the left, then sat back down. The new image showed a set of floodlights and a surveillance camera mounted together and aimed down at the street. This was not a USAG surveillance camera. This was private security equipment. An inspection of the roof revealed three oversized HEPA air filtration units the size of small closets. The units were painted drab green and had what looked like military part numbers stenciled on them. A short amount of searching on the Internet turned up documentation and manuals. The air filtration system was used on NBC bunkers to maintain positive pressure to hold at bay nuclear fallout as well as all airborne chemical and biological weapons. NBC stood for nuclear biological containment.

"It's a fortress," said Mark. "The front door has concealed hinges that belong on a bank vault. The windows are so thick they have to be bulletproof. They've got an infrared curtain forming an invisible fence. The roof is covered in solar panels. I'd bet they're off the grid, and what about that concealed pop-up vehicle barricade protecting the whole front of the building?"

"What about that sat dish and antenna array on the roof?" said Sarah. "It looks like something you'd find on a police station."

"It's definitely not satellite TV," said Mark.

"All that gear doesn't make sense. They're hybrids," said Sarah. "Why do they need satellite communication? Maybe the singularity is blocking them from using the n-web the same as us. I wish we could intercept those signals leaving the roof."

"That would be a good trick," said Mark. "I doubt we could buy the electronics gear we'd need, and even if we could grab the signal, it's probably encrypted."

Mark got up and moved the telescope another five degrees. A window came into view. Thin drapes obscured everything except the glow of room lights.

"What if they're a criminal gang of hybrids?" said Sarah. "You witnessed a murder. Maybe it was a hit on a rival gang. All that radio gear would make sense too. What better way to keep your secrets from other gangs of hybrids than to use sat communications? We can't find out what they're sending back and forth. If it's encrypted, I'd bet the NSA might not even be able to do it."

"You may be on to something," said Mark. "And since they're inside a protectorate, law enforcement has to know what's going on here. Either the Enforcers are on the take or they're working together."

"You know what else this means," said Sarah. "Those antennas mean these hybrids need to communicate. So there's got be more people or hybrids involved. What if their whole goal is to encrypt everything about their operation to keep it from other hybrids? That singularity could be some kind of n-web privacy screen. It's throwing up a field around that townhouse, blocking stray thoughts and emotions from leaking out. We can't pick up squeak, but most assists work."

"I've got it," said Mark. "Autonomic nervous system."

"What?"

"Assists are like the autonomic nervous system of the n-web. Assists use low level control protocols that seem to be unaffected by the singularity while high level protocols that carry thoughts or emotions are devoured and—"

A movement on the notebook screen made them both stop talking. A shadowy shape was growing on the drapes and taking form as someone walked toward the window. The fabric parted and a woman looked out as if directly at them. Even in the low light video she was amazing in appearance—European, definitely not American. Her eyes were large and hypnotic. Mark felt nervous. It was as if the woman could see him through the notebook screen. She turned and disappeared back into the room like a rare endangered species returning to her forest—and that's exactly what she was, thought Mark.

"That felt very odd," said Sarah.

"She has to be a hybrid."

"Well, now we know there's more than one of them," she said. "A man and a woman just like us."

"What I want to see is one of them walk out that front door," said Mark. "When we see that, we'll know this singularity isn't some kind Venus flytrap for hybrids. I want to know that once you go inside, you can still leave."

After completing their close examination, the second camera was zoomed out and refocused to give Mark and Sarah a view of the entire front of the townhouse. The first camera was kept as a tight shot covering the front door. Through the night they took turns watching the surveillance video. It was long, boring, mind numbing work.

Mark awoke with Sarah tugging his arm. There was an instant of confusion before the nanotech in his brain also awoke and achieved full processing throughout. It was 9:26 in the morning. The notebook screen showed four men dressed in identical parkas and black cargo pants leaving the house. The way they moved and acted smelled of military training. Mark didn't recognize any of them from the murder scene. He raced to the broken window and tried to invoke a medial assist, but nothing happened. He was afraid it was pointless at this range. Sarah was talking, but his mind was acutely focused. From this distance the four men were tiny shapes. The medical assist finally came up, but as he suspected, at this range it showed nothing of value. His intense focus caused the assist to zoom in as much as possible. The processed still-image viewed in his mind was not enough to see any of the details he wanted amid the grainy results, but it was just enough to reach a conclusion. The medical schematics showed orange blurs that had to be large COBIC swarms in the back of each head. The swarms were larger than an organic could have possibly had. Mark turned back to Sarah. She was hunched over the notebook screen.

"They look dangerous," she said.

"I think it's instinct warning us off," he said. "Let's go. I want a closer look."

The twenty-eight flights of stairs took forever. Mark slowed down to a walk as he exited the broken front door, as did Sarah. They were both dressed in sweats so they looked like a couple out for some morning exercise. Mark did a little stretching to put on a show for the benefit of the Enforcer surveillance cameras, then they started jogging down a parallel block in the same direction the hybrids were headed. After clearing two parallel blocks he cut down to the same street the hybrids had been on. It was impossible to see more than a block ahead. They ran, hoping the hybrids had not turned off somewhere or entered a building. One block turned into the next block and the next with still no sign of their quarry. Mark was ready to give up but kept jogging. Without a full connection to the god-machine, he was flying blind while the negative effects from the singularity further dulled his thinking and coordination. By now if the hybrids had turned off on a cross street they could be a quarter mile in almost any direction.

"There they are!" huffed Sarah.

"Speed up," said Mark. "I want a closer look."

Mark watched medical assists assemble themselves over the hybrids. As he got closer, the overlaid medical schematics took on the high resolution fluoroscopic like detail he wanted. He could see a large portion of each brain had nanotech seeds nesting inside neurons. The assist indicated that the men had anywhere from 76 to 84 percent of their brains restructured. Fanning out from the nanotech brains were orange roots, which extended a distance down the spinal column. They were all highly evolved like the killer hybrid and probably just as dangerous.

For some reason he thought they seemed xenophobic.

Mark stopped walking. He realized he was far enough from the singularity that his connection to the god-machine was returning. The sense of xenophobia was likely a stray thought he had picked up subconsciously and probably very accurate. He took Sarah's hand and started walking slowly, trying to blend in like an ordinary couple out on the streets. He did not want to get too close to the evolved hybrids as their n-web senses came back. He couldn't risk them detecting someone on their tail and feigned interest in a restaurant, staring at the menu posted in a window.

"Let's go back to the nest," said Mark.

"Doesn't it feel wonderful to have the god-machine back," said Sarah. "It's like being able to breathe again. Let's walk a little before heading back into that storm."

Using double sided tape, Mark placed the last MSK intrusion detector on a girder that was high up in the corner of the first floor stairwell of their tower. He looked at the sentry tablet to check system status. The screen showed a good signal from all the detectors he'd planted. Because GPS did not work inside the building, he entered a note next to the detector he'd just placed, describing its location.

During the endless climb up the flights of stairs Mark could not shake the lucid dream he'd had of a commando team of hybrids sneaking into the building like ghosts to hunt him and Sarah down. It was because of this dream that he'd set up the perimeter sentry.

Winded from the long climb, Mark walked into the nest. Sarah had been watching the surveillance video of the townhouse the entire time he'd been setting up the sentry. A strong gust of wind rustled the debris on the floor. It was late in the afternoon. The weather forecast was high wind combined with light snow around midnight. It was going to be unpleasant in the exposed room. They didn't dare cover the windows with plastic sheeting or do anything to advertise their position. Mark sat down next to Sarah and settled in to watch a scene of mundane life slowly evolving on the street in front of the singularity. Deliveries of food and laundry arrived. People could be seen inside as they neared windows and then moved on. No hybrids other than the four men had left the property or arrived.

The sun had set and the moon glowed brightly on a near cloudless night. Time dragged on. A little after eight o'clock the four hybrids returned with a man in tow. The man was dressed in an overcoat and suit, and Mark assumed he was a hybrid. There was not enough time for him to get to the window to use an assist. This new hybrid shuffled a bit, as if he were sleepwalking. Both Mark and Sarah had a strong sense he was under duress. One of the team of four gripped the man by his upper arm.

The moon had set an hour ago. The block was dark except for working street lamps at the corners. Sarah was napping. Mark was watching the screens and waiting. He took a sip of coffee and a bite of a peanut butter sandwich. For hours the image of the front door and the wider angle image of the entire townhouse had not changed at all. They could have been still photos. Mark periodically checked to make sure the images were not frozen by a software malfunction.

As he clicked on an icon to check status, a shadow moved on the rooftop of the townhouse next door to the singularity. His pulse quickened as he digitally zoomed in the video to follow the shadow. The figure was dressed in dark clothing. The shadow paused at the parapet separating the two townhouses, then slowly, gracefully eased over from one roof to the next.

"Sarah, wake up," called Mark.

The shadow glided across the top of the townhouse in which the singularity was contained, then paused at a roof access doorway. There was movement of some kind and a small penlight flashed on. The access door was bathed in red light, making the shadow that much harder to see as the low light camera was partially blinded by the contrast of light to dark. Mark zoomed in for a better view. The shadow attached what looked like a magnet at the top of the door. Mark thought it might be some kind of bypass for a burglar alarm. Sarah had not stirred.

"Sarah!" he shouted.

"What?"

"Wake up. We have an uninvited guest dropping in to visit our happy hybrids! Take over."

Mark jumped up, removed the camera from the second telescope, and aimed it at the visitor to see if he could get an assist. The optical image was very dark. All he could see was a red blur, which had to be the penlight. He focused and was rewarded with indistinguishable shapes of red tinted darkness, but maybe it was just enough. For Mark to access a medical assist on someone they had to be within physical eyesight of him. Images on screens didn't work. The god-machine and nanotech interface had to map out coordinates to identify the subject from whom to pull data. Someone on a screen could be anywhere in the world or nowhere at all. The interface operator's eyes acted like a mouse pointer for physical reality.

Come on, he thought. *Point and click.* A medial assist came up over the subject. Their intruder was male, five feet six inches, thirty-eight years old, excellent health, and not a hybrid.

When Mark returned to the notebook screen, the shadow was hard at work on the door lock. He had the penlight in his mouth and was kneeling in front of the lock. He inserted a key and tapped on the end of it with a screwdriver handle, as if driving the key a little deeper into the cylinder.

"Lock bumping," said Sarah.

The door immediately opened and the shadow slipped inside. Mark rewound the video and froze it at the point where the intruder was best illuminated. He tried adjusting the contrast to get a better view of the man.

"Take a snapshot and try the underexposed image enhancement tool," said Sarah. "The tool is under the edit menu.... Yeah, right there."

"How do you know all this?"

"I took a class at the police academy on surveillance and wiretapping. We used the same video software. That's why I picked it out at the store. I buy what I know."

"Why don't you drive?"

After ten minutes of playing with sliders and other adjustments Sarah had an image that clearly showed the outlines of someone dressed in dark clothing, a baseball cap, and stocking cap ski mask. The man had a small backpack and was wearing night vision goggles. This was not your average junkie breaking into a mansion for some quick cash.

"Come on," said Mark. "When this guy leaves, I want to follow him home and have a little chat."

"With e-money and free big screen TVs, would anyone burglarize a home?" said Sarah. "This guy is after something other than money."

"How about revenge?" said Mark.

They stationed themselves at a spot in a small park that was across from the alley that serviced the townhouse. The park was romantically lit with antique streetlights. They'd chosen the spot assuming the shadow would leave from the same direction he'd arrived. The far end of the alley was blocked, which helped their odds, though Mark was sure there had to be other avenues of escape. Setting their stakeout in the park was a calculated risk but they had no other option. Mark knew Enforces were watching through a thousand electronic eyes. It would have looked suspicious if he and Sarah had split up and stationed themselves at opposite ends of a row of townhouses.

They were pretending to be a couple out on a late date, which was a common sight in this neighborhood. Another couple had walked past just a short time ago and they were not alone in the park. Two other couples occupied benches. Mark and Sarah were sitting on a wood and granite bench nestled in each other's arms, facing the alley. Mark was thoroughly enjoying their little romantic performance for the surveillance cameras. The alley was dimly illuminated with small floodlights mounted on the rear walls of the townhouses. Unless the shadow used a rope, he was going to come off the roof into the alley on a fire escape. As far as Mark could see, the fire escape closest to the townhouse was located just a few feet inside the alley. It had a drop ladder that was locked in the raised position.

"How do you think he got up that fire escape without the Enforcers spotting him?" whispered Sarah. "There's a camera aimed straight down that alley, and you can bet there's more."

"Maybe the camera's broken? Maybe Enforcers can be bribed? This guy does not look like a low rent crook. He could even be a government intelligence officer working a black bag job."

An Enforcer Humvee turned onto their street a block away. The powerful headlights washed over them. Mark didn't want to invite questions and liked that he now had an excuse to play a little more. He unbuttoned Sarah's coat and moved her into his lap in a very intimate embrace. He could feel her lower body through the sweats she was wearing. His imagination filled in the remaining details.

"Enjoying yourself?" whispered Sarah.

"Can't you feel my answer?"

"I'd like to explore that in a little more depth when we get back inside."

"Why wait?"

Sarah laughed. Mark knew she was enjoying the moment. The Enforcer Humvee slowed at the entrance to the alley. Its brakes squeaked to a stop. Mark's heart was pounding as he pretended to ignore the Enforcer's presence less than 50 feet away. He heard a radio squelch and some faint, garbled message. The Humvee sat there idling. He heard a spotlight click on and saw the light sweeping the alley. Sarah was accidently or intentionally moving against him. It took all of his self-control not to go too far and that self-control was fading rapidly. He lost all rational thought when they had sex. Total loss of control was something new to him, exciting, and more than a little risky. He heard the spotlight click off and the tires start to slowly roll down the street. Soon the neighborhood felt deserted. He knew at least one USAG surveillance camera had to be watching their little scene. He didn't want to stop and rationalized that if they stopped too quickly it would look suspicious. He knew he was losing control.

"Not now, baby," whispered Sarah. "Later…"

Despite her protest she did not move off him. Her green eyes, wide with desire, glistened in the dim light as if lost in a distant world. A light snow had started to fall. Flakes were caught in her hair. He pulled her tight and kissed her again and wanted nothing else in this world than to have her. He knew it was impossible and irresponsible to go any further. He knew they could miss their quarry when the shadow exited the alley, but Mark was never very responsible when it came to love. He'd had more affairs in his life than he could count. Those affairs had cost him a good marriage and ultimately contributed to the death of his ex-wife and daughter in the plagues that had hit Los Angeles. Women were his weakness and he'd never experienced anyone like Sarah. Though he could not admit it even to himself, buried in denial, he wondered if his attraction was the result of unnatural influences. Was the god-machine behind what was going on? Sarah was breathing heavily in his ear. A layer of clothing was all that was stopping them.

"I can't," she whispered.

From the corner of his eyes, Mark sensed movement on the roof of the townhouses. An assist automatically applied image enhancement algorithms to outline the visual edge where the shadow's dark body blocked out the field of stars in the night sky. The shadow paused at the side of the roof where faint streetlight reached up to him. Mark could now see his shape more clearly. He could just make out the shadowy form of a man with night vision goggles looking directly at them. They'd been noticed. Mark tensed up.

"What's wrong?" whispered Sarah.

"Don't look, we have company."

Mark felt the fog of desire evaporating. Sarah slowly shifted off his lap. She made a show of adjusting her clothing. The shadow was no longer visible on the roof. Sarah was fixing her hair and pointedly not looking at the alley. An assist outlined fleeting movement on the fire escape. The shadow made no sounds, no metal creaking, no feet on stairs. Mark did not see the shadow emerge from the alley. The next thing he saw was a man dressed in dark clothing and a red baseball cap heading down the opposite sidewalk. The backpack was gone. He must have left his gear behind. A medical assist helped confirm this was the shadow. The man moved in complete silence. There were no footfalls, no rustle of clothing.

"Ready?" whispered Mark.

Sarah took his outstretched hand and they began walking. All the cameras would see were two lovers out for an evening stroll. The sidewalk was empty except for them. Sarah lifted his arm around her shoulder. Their target was a full block away. Snow was beginning to fall steadily. The flakes formed halos around streetlights and windows. An assist began highlighting the man's shallow foot imprints in the snow.

After nine blocks the man turned down a street overflowing with nightlife. It was a district that had twenty-four hour activity. Mark and Sarah followed their target onto the busy street. He was grateful they were no longer sticking out like a road flare on a deserted country lane. They walked past a dance club with a pounding soundtrack Mark could feel it in his body. Excited conversations chattered all around them. Couples were dressed in things too showy for the cold night air. Every building had glowing signage promising all things imaginable, including several that were very illegal before the plague.

"We got lucky this guy headed into a busy place," he said. "It would have looked very odd to the eyes in the sky if we followed him into an abandoned neighborhood or worse."

"Maybe not so much luck," said Sarah. "Our cat burglar didn't want to stick out any more than we did. Making a beeline toward late night entertainment will seem pretty normal to anyone watching."

Mark held Sarah close as they walked through a scene that belonged in old Las Vegas. Every block or two they switched sides of the street. Their target kept up a steady pace. A huge casino named the Royal Parisian had its doors open to the night. The sounds of slot machines and yells of winners spilled out onto the sidewalk along with the aroma of marijuana. Mark knew they were nearing the outer event horizon of the singularity. It was like the final weather front in a storm. For several blocks he had begun feeling closer to normal. The god-machine connection was stabilizing. Sarah sent him a memory capsule of what they'd been doing in the park, complete with everything she'd felt. Mark looked at her. She just smiled. He turned back in time to see their man duck into an alley.

"This could be it," said Mark.

He picked up the pace. The man reemerged less than thirty seconds later wearing a gray coat, a different hat, and carrying a small backpack over one shoulder. Mark slowed back down.

"I just picked up a stray thought from our friend," he whispered. "This guy knows which cameras and RFID readers are working and which aren't. He has inside information. That alley he just used to switch his appearance had no coverage. Want to bet he has more than one bracelet?"

"He may look calm," added Sarah. "But he's very nervous and agitated. He's radiating tension like frayed electrical wires."

After a few more blocks, the man turned onto Michigan Avenue and crossed the Chicago River. The waterfront on the opposite side had been transformed into the hottest entertainment district in the city. If the previous district was Las Vegas, this was the French Riviera. They followed their target at a greater distance, since Sarah could now track him by the emotional signature he radiated. The man wound his way through obstacles, staying parallel to the river, walking block after block, merging into and then reemerging from crowds on the street. It felt wonderful to be out of the influence of the singularity, as all Mark's senses sharpened to razor edges of clarity. He picked up a stray thought from the burglar about freedom, then a memory of a bitter argument with his wife. Their quarry stopped walking and lit a cigarette.

"His name's Paul," said Mark.

"He's burning with excitement," whispered Sarah. "Something big is about to happen. There could be violence. He might even have explosives."

"That's a horrible thought."

They stopped at the corner of a building, then stepped behind it as a shield. They were about 40 feet from Paul. An assist calculated a threat assessment. The building's corner would deflect a worse case bullet trajectory or blast effect from a small explosive charge. Snow was coming down harder, but it had no effect on the crowds. The street was, if anything, busier. When people had all their basic needs fulfilled by the government, their free time increased and they had to fill all that emptiness with something. The protectorate itself was a modern opiate for the masses. Mark unobtrusively peered around the corner. Paul's cigarette was almost gone. He lit another cigarette from the first one. Mark slipped back out of sight. A street performer began playing a guitar and singing. Time dragged on.

"Paul's recognized someone," whispered Sarah. "I think this is what he's been waiting for."

Both Mark and Sarah moved far enough out from the corner to get a clear view of Paul. Finely dressed people were flowing in crosscurrents between them and their quarry. A Catholic priest approached Paul from out of the crowd and shook hands. The priest was tall and thin with a gray, windblown mop of hair.

"Am I good or what?" said Sarah.

"You called it," said Mark. "Just glad you were wrong about that violence."

"Smart ass…"

An assist showed the priest was pure organic. The priest's heart rate was elevated and skin temperature was low normal. Mark was finding it nearly impossible to filter out all the stray thoughts surrounding the two men, while Sarah obliviously had no trouble focusing her empathic skills on any target she chose. The two men spoke casually like old friends for a few minutes. Paul handed the priest something that looked like an ultra-thin touch screen phone. An assist flashed some indecipherable runic symbols over the black device. The priest handed Paul a thin white envelope. The two shook hands again and walked off in opposite directions. Mark got enough of a stray thought from the priest to know the man of god had just received something stolen. So Paul was a thief, after all. Mark wondered what made that device so important.

"You take the priest," said Mark. "I've got Paul. Play nice."

"Do you love me or what?" said Sarah with a huge smile.

"Or what?" said Mark.

He patted her on the butt as she started to walk off. Sarah spun around, smiled at him, and then merged into the bustle of people.

As Mark began to follow the thief, he was hard at work filtering and searching for any related stray thoughts he could capture. He picked up some more mental debris about freedom from Paul, then a full memory from the priest Sarah was tailing. The memory was like a daydream scene of gothic conspiracy. The daydream took place in a room paneled in ornately carved wood and ringed with tall bookcases. Candles in wall sconces were the only source of light. Nothing electrical was permitted in the room. A group of old men sat around a large meeting table. They looked so self-important to Mark. Some were dressed in religious garb while others wore expensive suits. Smoke from incense drifted through the air. Mark knew from the priest's thoughts the purpose of the group was an inquisition to decide which information should be hidden for all time in darkness and which could be allowed into the light. Mark understood this was a daydream memory of some real event.

Mark stopped at an intersection as an Enforcer Humvee rolled by. As he resumed walking, he began daydreaming about what he'd learned from years of receiving stray thoughts. People dreamed nonstop when awake. Sometimes their dreams were daydreams and other times they were reality dreams. It was ironic that some people said they never dreamed. Mark knew for a fact consensual reality was assembled in the brain as an immensely complex immersive movie, which was actually a specialized type of dream. The purpose of this reality dream was to assemble what came pouring in from the five senses. In some cases a reality dream was little more connected to physical reality than sleeping dreams. Mark thought of dreams as the brain's analog to computer simulations or models. You could have accurate simulations or sloppy simulations.

In time Mark had grown to realize dreaming was literally the primary function of the human brain. What people called dreams were really several completely different beasts. The two main categories of sleep dreams were non-REM and REM dreams. Non-REM dreams were time compressed reconstructions of the day's events and not very mysterious, while REM dreams were experiences that emerged from somewhere unexplainable. REM dreams were not, as popular belief had it, merely translations of the babblings of what psychiatrists had labeled the subconscious.

Mark had learned all this and more about the human mind from his journeys into the god-machine—journeys that traversed and chronicled many levels of consciousness, both human and other. These journeys occurred in lucid dreams, which he was certain were partially fed by the timeline archives within the god-machine. These archives contained recordings of fully relivable critical memories from human lives throughout history. The archives spanned countless millennia. They also contained memories from other life forms such as animals, which were all too alien for him to grasp or even access.

Mark trailed the thief as they left the crowded entertainment district behind. He thought about the runic symbols the assist had displayed over the device Paul had handed over to the priest. The meaning of those symbols was unknown and seemed undecipherable. What had the assist been trying to tell him? Mark had a gut feeling that device could be a key to understanding the tribe of hybrids they'd discovered.

Paul was soon moving at a fast pace. The streets were nearly empty. Mark was concerned his prey would notice him and let a second block grow between them. As before, an assist was outlining Paul's lone footprints in the deepening film of snow.

A gust of wind stirred up a miniature whirlwind out of the tumbling flakes. Mark tried to step over a snowy puddle at a curb, but landed short. He felt dampness creep into one of his sneakers. When he looked back up, Paul was gone. The assist enhanced footprints were a tenuous trail of bread crumbs; all it would take to lose Paul was a long enough dry patch of sidewalk. Mark started to jog to catch up before it was too late. He rounded a corner in time to see Paul crossing a street and start up a flight of stairs to a raised platform for the L train.

When Mark reached the deserted platform, he realized he and Paul were the only people in sight. He tried to look disinterested. While no stray thoughts indicated otherwise, he suspected his cover had been blown. An express train blew through the station in an assault of sound and flashing windows. Mark received a stream of memory capsules from Sarah. She had followed the priest back to his church and was waiting outside to see if anything developed. A few long, tense minutes passed in the station, then a local train arrived. Mark had no idea where he was heading as he boarded the car shortly after Paul.

The train pulled from the platform and was soon racing along. It went underground, then a short while later rose again as an elevated train. Mark took out his cell phone to use as a prop. He decided to use the time to write an e-mail to Kathy to see how everything was going in his absence. He tapped out a short message and pressed *send*. When he looked up, he caught Paul staring at him before the man could quickly look away. The L came to a stop and Paul disembarked. Mark knew exiting the train might shred anything remaining of his cover, but what choice did he have? He exited just before the train began to move.

Paul stood in the darkest corner of the station underneath an overhang. His arms were crossed. He was smiling directly at Mark. There was a strong, steady wind mixed with tiny flakes of snow. The platform was empty and as lonely as the last. Several of the overhead sodium lights were failing as they cast puddles of dirty yellowish illumination over the platform. Mark looked up at a surveillance camera aimed at Paul and realized it was probably not working. Paul had chosen this stop carefully. Mark sensed no threat and was confident his superior reaction time and strength gave him an unbeatable edge. He walked up to Paul, bringing him within reach.

"I assume we're not under surveillance," said Mark. "That's why you chose this stop."

"Assume what you want, *Antinostrum*," said Paul. "Your cult likes to believe it knows everything."

Mark sensed the name *Antinostrum* was a test of some kind. He cast as wide a net as possible for stray thoughts but captured only empty airwaves. At the same time he concentrated on the name *Antinostrum*, triggering a small, quick data-flood that also returned nothing useful.

There was a scrap of history about *Antinostrum* referring to a public health crusade against potions and pseudoscience snake oil remedies in the nineteenth century. This was getting him nowhere. Mark decided the most effective course of action was to say as little as possible to draw Paul out, so he said nothing. Paul's expression changed to anger.

"It's not my fault. The other item wasn't there," said Paul. "Why are you following me? What do you want from me?"

Mark captured stray thoughts of blackmail from Paul. A medical assist showed his heart and respiration were highly elevated in what had to be a stress reaction like fear or anger. Mark knew he had deeply hooked Paul, and it was time to reel in his fish.

"We know it was there," said Mark. "Convince me it wasn't."

"Convince you," said Paul. "Sure, I'll convince you."

Mark heard a *snick* like sound and felt a sting on the side of his neck, then warm liquid running down into his collar. Paul quickly retreated out of reach. What? An assist was screaming in Mark's head about an injury to his neck. There was an undecipherable smirk on Paul's face. Something thin and shiny with smears of red was in Paul's fist.

"Real *Antinostrum* soldiers would not wear thin body armor," sneered Paul. "Real *Antinostrum* soldiers would be heavily armed."

Mark was confused and light headed. What was going on? He was barely able to stand. He touched his soaking wet neck and came away with a hand covered in red paint. It took his addled mind precious seconds to correct—not paint, blood! The station and Paul's face were spinning. Mark stumbled to his knees and ended up on his back. His vision tunneled into nothing more than a corner of the overhang and snowflakes falling toward him through sodium yellow light. The wind suddenly felt very cold. His vision faded as his self-awareness evaporated into the night.

Sarah Mayfair – Chicago Protectorate – February 3, 0002 A.P.

It was almost midnight and Sarah was panic stricken. She had again walked out to the edge of the singularity's vortex trying to see if she could reach Mark. She'd lost her empathic link to his emotions days ago. Prior to that, he had been a constant in her life. She could always feel him: his warmth, his sharp edges, his clarity. The only exception was when either of them were inside the disruptive vortex of that singularity. She didn't know what to do. Was he being held captive somewhere inside the vortex? Something inside her, some intuition possibly from the god-machine itself, had been telling her he wasn't within the vortex. If that was true, then where was he?

This nightmare had started days ago when she was standing in front of that church and felt an intense confusion from Mark, then nothing. He'd winked out as if a light switch had been thrown. It was too late to get a sense of his location. She only knew how to do that with an ongoing stream of data. Sarah refused to accept the obvious answer that he was dead. He couldn't leave her alone in this world. That was not the plan. She had to find him. She sent out another memory capsule calling to him. After a few fruitless minutes of silence she walked into the singularity's vortex to search again in that horrible darkness.

Sarah walked into the surveillance nest. She was out of breath from jogging up most of the stairs before tiring to a slower and slower pace. Ralph padded over to her. Just as before, no one was in the room. Every time she had returned to the nest she'd had a strange feeling that he would be there when she opened the door.

She had the presence of mind to close the door and lock it before crumpling to the floor, sobbing. She was nearing the point where rational thought demanded she give up. Sarah felt exposed and naked before an uncaring God. In that moment of extreme loss and hopelessness she realized she was in love with Mark. With the prefect, unforgiving recall of a nanotech brain, she relived the past six weeks since they had become lovers. She hated God for doing this to her again. She was too late. She had been too late with her lover, Kenny, who had died in the New Jersey kill-zones and now too late with Mark. No, that was not going to happen again. She would not allow it.

Sarah Mayfair – Chicago Protectorate – February 4, 0002 A.P.

The sun was grimly rising outside. Sarah was exhausted and unslept. Ralph was curled up with his huge head in her lap. She was thinking about ending her life. The loneliness was already too much. She remembered that other darkest moment of her life. She had been on the Morristown police force. It was just after the New Jersey kill-zones when she was waiting in their apartment for Kenny to come home. New Jersey had been the first and only outbreak of the plague at that early time. She had come so close to using her Berretta on herself that night.

Ralph whined at her. Sarah wearily pulled herself up, wiped the tears from her face, put Ralph on his leash, and headed out the door once more. She'd had a lucid dream in which she'd found Mark by taking extreme steps. It was all she had left to try. She knew what she had to do and if it drew the attention of Enforcers, so be it. She would pay a visit to that priest and find out where Paul lived. She would break into homes. She would hurt people. She would do whatever was necessary

74

to find Mark.

The heavy church door opened, letting in a cold gust of wind. Sarah had been inside, sitting on a pew for hours. This place of worship was both gray and ornate at the same time. It was a very old building dating back to the turn of the last century. Ralph was on the floor next to her. Some parishioners had looked at her with undisguised contempt for bringing an animal inside their house of God. She absorbed all their negative emotions—saving them in her heart to burn as fuel for when the priest returned to his flock. She would gladly hurt him to get the information she needed. She would know the moment he was nearing the church by his emotional patterns radiating out onto the n-web. Every person had a unique emotional fingerprint. Right now there were only two that Sarah was focused on: Mark and this priest. Ralph looked up at her with expectant eyes. When Sarah did not respond, he sighed and went back to resting.

She dozed from exhaustion, and when she awoke she sensed something had changed inside her. The church was darker. The stained glass windows were muted with twilight. She had slept hard. A ceremony of some kind was in progress. People were kneeling to accept wafers. As her nanotech brain reached full operating clarity, she recognized what had changed. Mark's emotions were back. He was experiencing pain and confusion. She jumped to her feet, trying to grasp where the emotions were radiating from. Geo-tagging information was displayed through an assist, which gave her Mark's approximate location. Ralph grew excited as her emotions leaked into him. He began barking. There was a commotion of voices that she ignored. Someone gripped her arm and asked her to leave. She instinctively threw the hand off her, dimly realizing she had spilled a man to the floor. She would not move an inch until she had the clearest possible location for Mark's signal. What if it disappeared?

Mark Freedman – Chicago Protectorate – February 4, 0002 A.P.

Mark was heavily drugged. His brain and body had just passed a tipping point where enough of the damage had been repaired that higher brain functions were returning. He knew he was in a hospital room and that he'd lost several days. He tried to reach Sarah with a memory capsule and failed. Something was not right. He sat up and immediately wished he hadn't. The room spun, making him nauseous. His brain struggled to sync up the images flooding in from his eyes, then succeeded and began rendering a stable view of reality. The nausea

75

faded. A medical assist showed his body was working hard to repair the damage. The assist also showed serum levels for various drugs that were in his system and how his body was trying to eliminate them. He had no recall of who had found him and brought him here. Out of the most likely scenarios competing in his nanotech brain, all but one had protectorate surveillance as a decisive factor—which was not a good thing. There would be flagged records in USAG logs showing a medical doctor, a high priority asset, had been found with near fatal wounds in a surveillance blind spot. In all likelihood Enforcers would investigate if they were not already doing so. They would want to interview him. The fact that he was not in a prison hospital was a testament to Ike's handiwork combined with Enforcer laziness.

The room was not private, and the curtain separating the two beds was pulled back so Mark could see his roommate. The man appeared to be asleep. A whiteboard in the room listed Mark's cover name that went with his bracelet and the name of his roommate, Frank Baxter. Also on the board were the names of his nurse, nurse's aide, and goals for the day with a smiley face.

An assist projected a medical schematic over Frank. The man was in his late forties and had suffered a serious head and spinal injury. There were enough sedatives in Frank to make sure he slept through the night and it looked like Frank was on track to doing just that. He was snoring loudly in stage N4 sleep, making the transition to REM. Warning beeps from an IV pump in distress had been coming through the partially open door since Mark awoke. The fact that the beeping went unaddressed meant the nurses were probably overworked. Stray mental prattle from both patients and nurses were pinging Mark from every direction. He tried capturing usable thoughts from the nurses but got very little. His mind felt fuzzy. He could tell the nurses were preoccupied with their patients, which was good for the patients, but bad for his plans of early checkout from this fine hotel. He was hoping to snare a login that would get him into the med-computer located in his room. He wanted to check his chart to see when to expect the next nurse's visit.

Mark caught a stray thought that caused him to forget about the computer. A nurse was worried about a newly diagnosed cancer patient losing hope and decided she had just enough time to visit with him before the shift change and staff meeting in an hour. That meant right now might just be the perfect time to slip out unnoticed.

Mark swung his legs off the bed. He felt like he was rising from the dead. Every inch of his body ached with a deep, dull pain that seemed to come from within his bones. He looked around the room, trying to formulate a plan. A patient monitor was displaying his vital signs. His blood pressure, oxygen, and heart rate were all good. A medical assist showed his left jugular vein had been partially severed. Implanted memories containing medical status filled in some of the blanks about what had happened to him. After the stabbing his body had gone into an automatic self-preservation mode. All unnecessary functions, including higher thought processes, had been shut down to drastically lower his metabolic rate. COBIC had quickly stanched the blood loss. The knifing had caused no major organ damage. He was left in a catatonic state in which he could have survived indefinitely as COBIC slowly rebuilt fluid and blood levels through nano-assembly, using available raw materials such as body fat, muscle, and skin tissues. His bones ached because COBIC bacterium had moved into the marrow to overstimulate production of blood cells.

Mark saw he was hooked up to an IV, which was pushing clear liquids and drugs. He got up out of bed on shaky legs and unplugged the IV pump from its power outlet. The pump was now running on batteries. Step one was to disconnect himself from the patient monitor but he knew a loss of signal might bring nurses running. He looked over at his buddy Frank and smiled. He had an idea that just might work and gently pushed the room door shut until he heard a soft click.

A short time later, Mark walked into the bathroom rolling the IV stand and pump with him. Frank was now wearing two full sets of patient monitor sensors. Mark wondered how long it would take for the staff to notice that two patients had very similar vital signs. The two datasets did not match exactly because Mark had purposely attached the sensors to different spots on Frank's body to produce dissimilar blood pressure and oxygen levels. There was nothing he could do about pulse.

In the bathroom mirror he inspected the damage to his body. A large bandage on his neck covered where he had been stabbed. Smaller bandages were on his forehead and one elbow. Mild heat from the neck wound told him COBIC was still working to repair the injury.

Mark washed his hands, then began to peel back the bandage on his neck. The wound was fully closed and light pink in color. All but two of the stitches fell out as he removed the gauze. The wound looked like he'd been healing for weeks. He picked off the two remaining stitches, which were held in place by a thin layer of skin and would have fallen off shortly on their own. Mark was both relieved and worried by what he saw. A doc or nurse might have already looked at what was under that bandage or rather, what was not under it. The miracle would be labeled some kind of impossible freak healing. For all he knew, the docs might already have begun studying his abnormal metabolism. It was possible the hospital had fingerprinted him on admission. How long would it take for USAG intelligence services to connect the dots and figure out they had Mark Freedman, wanted fugitive, in this hospital? He had to get out of here and he had no good options. His cover would unquestionably be blown if he stayed. If he walked out now there would be a report and Enforcers might investigate, but probably not tonight and not as a high priority unless they had his prints. He had to find Sarah. They had to switch identities to their second set of bracelets as fast as possible. They couldn't risk going back to their surveillance nest. Enforcers could show up without warning. The smart thing to do would be to get out of Chicago tonight, but he was not going anywhere until he arranged a close encounter with that singularity and gotten answers to his questions.

Mark began removing the tape holding the IV line in his arm. He stopped and looked at the IV pump. The thing would start squawking the minute he pulled the line. He tried to switch it off, but there was some kind of security lock on the keypad. It required a pass code. He looked around for something he could use as a screwdriver to open the battery compartment. He found his street clothes in the closet, including his body armor, all in dry cleaner's bags. It was odd to see the care the hospital staff had taken to clean his military vest and clothing. He checked his cell phone and found the battery was dead. He looked at the hospital phone on the bed stand and decided for the second time since he'd awoken that it was too risky to use it to call Sarah. It would be a far too obvious and easy lead for Enforcers to follow. He found nothing usable as a Philips head screwdriver except his keys. It took long minutes, but the IV pump finally sputtered out with a few short, sad beeps as he yanked the battery from the pump. He pulled the IV line from his arm and was free.

Mark checked the clock on the wall. How long did he have before the next nursing visit? He picked up the pace, taking his sweatshirt from the closet and tugging it on. He looked at the faded blood stains and realized why the hospital had dry cleaned everything. There must be rules against leaving bloody clothing to ferment in a patient's room. He might attract attention walking out of the hospital in dirty looking clothing. While there was no surveillance camera in his room, there were almost certainly cameras in the halls. The cameras would also make it impossible to steal some scrubs. Mark knew patients would be encouraged to walk the halls. So the least suspicious disguise was the one he was already wearing. Unfortunately, once he got outside in the Chicago winter, a hospital gown would make him look very cold and very strange.

Mark noticed he was not wearing a hospital ID bracelet, which meant they had to be using his RFID bracelet as an electronic substitute. He had no doubt the entire hospital was under USAG surveillance. Unless he disabled his bracelet, the hospital might know the instant he left the property. If the hospital's systems were linked with USAG systems, then Enforcers would also know the instant he was gone. Would they care? He continued dressing as fast as he could. Time was his enemy. He had to be out of this room before anyone came by. Mark stopped tying his sneaker. He froze in mid-thought. There was a memory capsule inside his mind. No, not one; there were dozens of capsules from Sarah. How could he have missed them? He opened one after another. The hours of life experiences in each capsule poured out into his brain and was relived instantaneously in infinitely compressed time. He now owned memories of Sarah panicked and searching for him everywhere. She had gone to the church to confront the priest who was Paul's accomplice. Mark focused on the last capsule, causing it to expand in his mind. Sarah's thoughts and feelings flooded into him like cool, sweet water. She had found him and was leaving the church; she was calm and in control. He tried again to send her a memory capsule. This one made it. He warned her not to go back to the nest and asked her to meet him as quickly as possible. An anxious reply from her arrived instantly. She was on her way.

Mark put on a hospital gown over his street clothes and body armor. He then loosely pulled a second gown on backward over the first. This added bulk would make it harder for anyone to notice he was dressed to go outside. The only things that showed were sweatpants and sneakers. It was not uncommon in hospitals for patients to walk the halls for exercise in their own street clothes. He doubted this hospital was any different. The only complication was his coat. He would have to carry it in the dry cleaning bag and try to draw as little attention as possible. Mark cracked the room door open and peered out. A patient with a visitor in tow walked past. He could not see the main nursing station but suspected he would be ignored when walking past.

Ten short minutes later, Mark was casually looking through an outside window in a large and very busy admitting area. It was cold outside. There was condensation on the glass. The room was noisy and smelled of disinfectant. There were other patients in robes. Every few minutes an admitting nurse called out names and people shuffled about.

Mark didn't know how much time he had before the staff discovered a seriously wounded man had somehow walked out of his room, and they instituted a manhunt for his own good or worse. Using his bracelet, they would be able to pinpoint his general location instantly. He had no time to waste. Mark had hoped there would be plenty of civilians in the building to provide cover. This room was better than he could have imagined, filled with ragged and exhausted people. When he ditched the hospital robes, he would blend right in. The faded blood stains on his sweatshirt and pants were almost perfect camouflage. He was not the only person in this room with stained clothing.

Supposedly, bathrooms were off limits for USAG surveillance. Mark's plan depended on that rule being true. He waited in the lounge area until someone else entered the bathroom. He wanted as many people as possible in the bathroom providing cover when he made his move.

He followed a young man with forearms covered in tats into the bathroom. The room looked like close to a full house and smelled like it too. He picked a stall and locked the door, quickly taking off the hospital robes and stuffing them behind the toilet. After some frustrated searching he found the hidden catch on the RFID bracelet. Opening the catch disabled the RFID circuitry. Mark knew he was now the invisible man to RFID readers, but cameras would still see him. Would this anomaly set off alarms in some software program or monitoring room? He was about to put that question to the test. There was an RFID reader at the bathroom entryway.

Mark walked out of the bathroom. An elevator *dinged* and he froze. His heart was pounding with fight or flight adrenaline. He stared as a pair of medical workers in scrubs filed off the elevator, followed by a hospital security guard complete with badge, radio, and sidearm. No one was interested in him. Mark walked straight to the sliding glass exit doors and stepped outside. Cold air slapped him in the face, then the sensation was gone. The night was quiet. Off in one corner he saw the glow of someone smoking. An assist informed him it was twenty-five degrees. After a few deep breaths of the cool air, Mark felt refreshed and almost in control.

Walking down the street, knowing he was a ghost, was insanely risky. For the first time since entering the protectorate two weeks ago, the USAG overlords were not tracking his movements. He was receiving updates from Sarah as she advanced toward him on an overcrowded train. She'd had to leave Ralph behind for a few hours to make it easier to go unnoticed while changing identities. A 120 pound Rottweiler could draw a lot of unwanted attention. In a memory capsule he experienced the anxiety and betrayal she felt from leaving her companion in a deserted building miles from any place he knew. Mark was not following a direct path to rendezvous with her. Instead, he was turning at each block based on how many people he saw. For now, intermingling with other pedestrians was his best defense against Enforcer surveillance. Mark turned a corner. A powerful wind blew down the corridor formed by tall buildings. Remnants of litter from an overturned can scurried about. The street looked miserable but had a surprising amount of foot traffic. He tucked into the wild.

An hour later, he was standing in the shadows on a sidewalk trying to blend in with his stained clothing while keeping alert for Enforcers. The area was a popular center for the arts and alive with street activity. This particular set of blocks with its eateries, coffee shops, galleries, and theaters was the epicenter of the art district. Down at the corner of the block was a burned out art deco movie theater that was too badly damaged to repair. It seemed almost like a commissioned piece of artwork commemorating the horrors of the plague. From a memory capsule he knew Sarah was inside. She had disabled her bracelet after entering through a shattered doorway. They were both ghosts now. Hidden inside the art deco theater was a large backpack of gear they'd cached just for this kind of emergency. The gear included extra sets of RFID bracelets, picture ID cards, a thick roll of money to use in the Outlands, gold coins for bribes, and other necessities.

Shortly after arriving inside the protectorate, they had singled out this movie theater as an ideal location. The nearest RFID readers and surveillance cameras were over a block away in either direction, and the street was constantly busy with foot traffic. Just outside the art deco theater was the worst vantage points for Enforcer surveillance they'd found. He and Sarah had previously exercised their exit bracelets more than once from within the crowds of the art district. It would appear normal for their new identities to pop up here tonight.

The surveillance cameras covering this block had to be overloaded before either of them could enter or leave the theater. Mark was waiting to make his move. Street performers began to arrive and stake out positions along the promenade. He knew it would not be long now. There was a huge playhouse at the center of the block that staged spectaculars. Right on schedule, the doors opened with a throng of people exiting. Mark blended into the middle of a river that was heading in the direction of the art deco theater. He was counting down the seconds, as was Sarah. Memory capsules were flying back and forth between them.

81

A street performer began playing an alto sax. The musical notes took on a ghostly echo from the surrounding buildings. Mark tensed as he watched an Enforcer Humvee crawl through the crowded intersection. Lights on the roof were flashing to part the sea of people. Enforcer Humvees were mobile RFID readers. He prayed he was lost in the chaos and his missing bracelet would go unnoticed. He knew another venue would be letting out shortly and then another. Mark willed their doors to open early. The Humvee crawled by within arm's length and kept moving.

Mark was 20 feet from the entrance to the art deco theater. It took all his willpower to keep his eyes averted from that shattered doorway. The crowds were now thick enough that the entrance was completely shielded from street level surveillance. He prayed there was nothing hovering in the night sky looking down on him.

Mark peeled off from the crowd. Glass crunched loudly under his sneakers as he ducked inside. The interior was illuminated with shafts of light from dozens of broken windows. He sensed no one was coming after him from the street. Sarah stepped out from behind a ticket booth. She was dressed in jeans, a sweater, knee high boots, and a new, long coat that was hanging open. Her makeup and hair were completely different. She was smiling and crying. It felt as if the clouds had parted when she slipped into his arms.

"I thought you were dead," she whispered. "I just couldn't believe this was happening."

"It was easy for me," he said. "I was unconscious. This was much harder on you."

"Mark, I…"

"What?"

"Nothing," said Sarah. "Let's get you ready."

Two hours later the next surge of foot traffic was poised to begin. Mark had traded in his stained rags for new clothing Sarah had purchased on her way to meet him. He was wearing an overcoat length goose down parka, Chicago Cubs baseball cap, and jeans. They each had a cloth shopping bag filled with emergency gear hidden inside expensive clothing store boxes. Together they looked like an utterly forgettable urban couple.

One again the doors of the huge playhouse opened on schedule like ocean tides. The crowds outside the shattered doorway began to rise. At what felt like a peak, Mark and Sarah stepped out in the vibrant, noisy stream of people. They kept low profiles, trying to remain lost in the countless faces on the street. After half a block Mark closed the catch on his new RFID bracelet, activating it. Minutes later Sarah did the same. The ghosts were now solid. It was unlikely the bracelets would be scanned by any checkpoint until they left the area. They switched directions, entered a coffee shop, and then emerged carrying cups. Their new RFID bracelets seemed to work. If their transformation was going to be spotted, this was the moment it would happen.

It was getting very late. They had walked and taken trains halfway across Chicago. To Mark's surprise they were still free. To any surveillance cameras they looked like an ordinary couple out on the streets. Sarah's long blond hair trailed behind her on the windy sidewalk as they strode along, hand in hand. Ralph was with them. Sarah's mood had noticeably brightened once she had Ralph back. The sidewalk traffic was thinning. Mark felt more relaxed with every block and hour they added between themselves and the art deco theater.

"I want to get back to the singularity as soon as it's light and there's enough foot traffic so we don't stand out," he said. "We need to finish this and get out of here. Every day we stay in Chicago is a day the Enforcers might come after us."

"What do we do now? Just knock on their front door? Excuse me, can we please touch your singularity?"

"I don't know," said Mark. "I guess we'll improvise when we get there. They may take one look at us and start shooting, which will solve everything."

Mark Freedman – Chicago Protectorate – February 5, 0002 A.P.

Mark and Sarah had not uttered a word since turning the corner. The townhouse that held the singularity should have been in sight. Instead, they came upon a scene of devastation. Fire trucks and Enforcer Humvees were parked around a smoldering mound. Red, blue, and white strobes flashed in the morning light. Mark could hear squawks from radios and an occasional shout. Before arriving at this mayhem, miles away, they'd known something had radically changed. The tidal pulls of the singularity had evaporated and the vortex boundary layer had been missing. Mark had suspected the singularity had entered some new stage where the effects were concentrated over a smaller area. He had been thinking about how a black hole shrinks as its strength increases. With each passing block he thought they would hit a stronger vortex that was closer in to the singularity, but nothing like that had happened.

"It looks like an explosion and not a fire," said Sarah.

"I'm getting a lot of stray thoughts, bits and pieces about a super-heated detonation. Normal accelerants along with residential chemicals and gas have been ruled out. Common explosives have also been ruled out. The consensus is some kind of military thermobaric or fuel air weapon."

An assist was projecting into Mark's awareness diagrams and engineering data for thermobaric weapons from grenades to missiles. The assist had already searched, found, and was presenting best fits for the damage arrayed before his eyes.

"Could the singularity have exploded?" asked Sarah.

"Can't be that," said Mark. "The singularity wasn't part of the physical world. It was cyberspace. It was a program. It was nothing but signals on the n-web."

"How can you be so sure?" she said. "The singularity was software, but what was it running on?"

"You're saying the hardware exploded?"

"It's a possibility."

"We'll never know."

An idea came to Mark out of nowhere. Sarah continued speaking, but he was no longer listening. He began to plan. There was another thread to pull. Who knew what might unravel?

Mark and Sarah were outside an ornate gothic church. Mark felt like he knew this place from all the memories Sarah had shared with him. The doors were 10 feet high with huge iron hinges. It was an overcast, blustery midday in Chicago. There was steady foot traffic on the sidewalk. The background noise of street conversations and the stray thoughts buffed Mark like a second wind. He was trying to reach into the depths of the church to pull out stray thoughts. So far he had nothing.

"I can feel the priest's emotions inside along with one other person," said Sarah. "The priest's agitated. Something's wrong."

"He's about to become a whole lot more agitated," said Mark.

As he opened the door, he smelled incense. An assist informed him incense was originally used in Catholic churches to symbolize prayers rising to heaven. There was also a practical matter of hiding the body odors of worshipers long before deodorants were invented. Mark smiled at how nuanced the interface's assists were becoming. Inside, the church felt and looked deserted. He heard Sarah softly instructing Ralph to stay beside the doors as she locked them from inside. She hung her police badge around her neck, then began attaching a silencer to her Beretta.

The cathedral was dim and filled with shadows. As Mark edged deeper inside, he saw the priest and his old friend Paul in an alcove. The two men were exchanging harsh whispers. Mark felt rage glowing inside him as he silently walked closer. The desire to bludgeon Paul into unconsciousness was irresistible. He could easily see himself acting on the impulse. Unprovoked violence was morally wrong and would gain him nothing, but he wanted it. His hands balled into fists. He could imagine Paul's blood puddled on the floor. He could smell it. His rage had become a firestorm. He was now within 30 feet of the target of his fury.

In mid-step, Mark's rage inexplicably vanished, leaving confusion in its vacuum. He then spotted Sarah heading toward the alcove from a different angle. Somehow he knew she was acting out his violent impulses for him. That was where his rage had gone. He had infused her with it—or she had taken it from him? She was walking fast with her Beretta pointed down and against her side. She was a short distance away when Paul saw Sarah and then Mark. His mouth dropped open and his eyes grew wide in fear. He was clearly more shocked to see Mark than a woman advancing on him with a handgun.

"You're dead," blurted Paul. "I killed you!"

"Police," yelled Sarah. "Do not move."

Paul reached inside his jacket, going for a gun that was now visible in a shoulder holster. Sarah fired twice without hesitation; once in the chest and once in the head. The mechanical clattering sounds of the Beretta's slide ejecting copper casings and the suppressed sound from the bullets all echoed in the vast hall in a terrible chaos of soft, deadly mechanical whispers. Mark saw a medical assist projected over Paul like a shroud. The superimposed display showed vital signs flatlining. The priest had edged as far away from the dead man as possible. He stood with his back pressed into the alcove. Next to him was a wrought iron stand filled with rows of votive candles in glass cups. His expression remained composed as the candlelight played over his features. The man emitted no stray thoughts.

"Have you come to kill me too?" said the priest.

"We didn't come to kill anyone," said Mark.

"Oh, really? Then I suppose you expect God to forgive you for this slaying? Since when do police use silencers?"

"Stop right there," snapped Mark. "This man tried to kill me and you're involved. We watched an illegal exchange three days ago. You gave this man an envelope and he gave you a stolen device."

Sarah called Ralph and the huge dog came bounding to her side. A low, aggressive rumbling came from him as he glared at the priest.

The killing and smell of blood had clearly agitated the dog. He looked ready to tear the priest apart. Impossibly, the priest seemed to grow even more stoic and enigmatic. Mark received memory capsules of radiated emotions Sarah was picking up. The priest was truly not afraid of them. His composure was not an act. This was so extraordinary and unexpected that Mark was left without a plan. He studied the priest's face up close for the first time. He recognized it from the daydream memory he'd gleaned from this priest days ago. It was not surprising the priest appeared in his own daydream. He and three others had been standing off to one side as the required witness of the clerical inquisitors, the wise men deciding which things should remain hidden for all time. There had to be some way Mark could use this information to pry open this turtled-up man.

"I know you from somewhere," said Mark.

"And I know you," said the priest. "You're agents of the Family, their trained animals of war."

Mark had no idea what to do with that piece of information—the Family? At least it was a crack in the man's shell. Mark looked around the church and wondered if that candlelit room paneled in wood and ringed with tall bookcases was here. The smell of incense was the same as the daydream memory. He decided to do a little fishing.

"You have no right to decide what should be hidden for all time and what should be allowed into the sunlight," intoned Mark as if announcing a death sentence.

Small drops of sweat glistened on the priest's brow. Mark realized the man was using some meditation technique to suppress his thoughts and was rapidly tiring. Apparently, it took a great deal of mental concentration for this turtle to hold his mind shut. Mark's intuition was telling him what was going on here was even more byzantine than he could imagine. Suddenly he captured a stray thought from the priest. The man was exhausted. That first subconscious leakage revealed the priest no longer viewed his adversaries as mental threats. The cerebral floodgates eased open. His name was Father Enrique. He thought of himself as a solider of god. He had some kind of mental training, a meditation that turned off his subconscious neurological interface to the god-machine. Mark knew this was not at all how the priest understood it. Enrique believed it was a meditation that marshaled divine protection. He had acquired what he called a relic from Paul. The priest's brotherhood dictated that they collect these relics and destroy them in a carefully prescribed ancient ritual. He had a great deal of caution and respect for these relics. They were shards of evil. If only a tiny piece of dust remained after destruction, the relic was said to be able to reconstitute. Though no one in recent history had witnessed a return, his fear of them was palpable.

"Father Enrique," said Mark. "What gives your brotherhood the right to destroy these relics that are not yours?"

"What give us the right!" shouted Enrique. "God commands and we follow. When the Family was nothing more than a vague plot in the minds of a few greedy barbarians, there was the *Antinostrum*. Once the Family has returned to the sewer from which it first crawled, there will still be the *Antinostrum*. I ask you, assassin. What gives you the right to interfere with us?"

Mark was filtering and capturing stray thoughts using all his skill. There was too much. The priest abruptly stopped talking. He now had a strange expression of fear. The leakage of stray thoughts was quickly abating. Mark knew the priest had begun the meditation for protection anew in silent urgency.

"You're not Family," said Enrique. His voice was shrill. "I see what you are. Abominations! You tricked me. Get out of my mind. Get out!"

Enrique crossed himself while clenching his jaw shut. In a sweeping motion, the priest grabbed the stand of votive candles and capsized it while hurling it at Mark and Sarah. Fire, glass, and spilled wax flew everywhere. The priest bolted in the opposite direction and through a door. Within seconds of the door closing, Sarah had reached it and kicked it solidly. The door held. Mark knew the priest had to be going for a phone to call for help. Sarah kicked the door again. There was a faint splintering sound but the door held.

"Together," yelled Mark.

They kicked as one. The door gave with a loud cracking sound as wood from the frame splintered explosively inward all over the floor. The priest spun around with an angry expression. He was dialing a cell phone. Sarah smacked the phone from his hands. As it clattered across the floor, she shot it with her silenced Berretta. The phone exploded into pieces. The priest jump back and stumbled. The once inscrutable man was now sprawled on the floor.

"Shit," wheezed Sarah. "You stupid fuck!"

"We need to go," said Mark.

"The sooner the better," said Sarah. "I am sick of this prison city."

"Oh my god," said Mark. "Can you feel that?"

Sarah looked at him with confusion. Then awareness reshaped her expression. Mark could see pure amazement on her face.

"There's another singularity," she said. "It's far away, but I can feel it."

"I was blind. All along there was more than one," said Mark. "Those phantom singularities that led us in wrong directions were real, not decoys. There's at least two more out there."

"What do we do with him?" said Sarah.

The priest was looking at Mark and Sarah with curiosity. He'd heard too much already. While Mark could not pick up any stray thoughts from the man, he could see treacherous wheels turning in that head.

"I have an unpleasant idea," said Mark

Minutes later, they walked from the church looking as calm as possible for the surveillance cameras. The steady foot traffic on the sidewalks had been reduced to a scattering of people.

"*Antinostrum?*" said Sarah. "Family…Turn over a rock and what do you find?"

"A bunch of puzzle pieces that don't fit," said Mark. "Hybrids murdering each other and religious fanatics conducting witch hunts for ancient technology."

Mark thought about what they left behind in that church and sensed the law was closing in on them. They were headed straight to the closest protectorate exit portal. The priest was bound and locked in a supply closet. Sarah had left her Beretta behind with the priest's fingerprints all over it, gunpowder residue on the priest's hands, and a dead body. They smashed the priest's RFID bracelet and took it with them. It was an instant trip to the work camps if an Enforcer found you without a bracelet. Mark knew it would take hours or even days for the priest to explain himself once he was found. All he and Sarah needed was less than an hour to get through the portal. The lines leaving were much shorter than those entering.

As they boarded an elevated train that serviced the portal, Mark was awash with chaotic feelings. He was alternately excited, agitated, and scared. There were more singularities, which was amazing, but the excitement was tempered with stress. At any moment their false identities could be wanted for questioning in a murder. Enforcers could be waiting at the next stop. The train they were on was almost empty. No one turned to look at them.

"Do you think anyone survived?" asked Sarah. "I mean the hybrids at the townhouse."

"Maybe they staged the explosion to hide what they were doing and left long before the fireworks."

"Could be," she said. "But I have a feeling at least some of them were in that house when it went up."

"Maybe it was a USAG hit?" said Mark. "A predator drone could have done that. A month ago the odds of finding even a few hybrids was a long shot. Now we have multiple singularities and very likely pockets of hybrids with each singularity. How can you explain so many hybrids?"

"Maybe we're not such a new thing?" said Sarah.

Prisoners

In southeast Texas the winter sky was an angry battleground of thunderheads and wind. The Preacher briskly walked toward his clapboard church with its shattered steeple. The wind tugged at his clothing as he stared up at the belfry. He recalled vividly that it had been used as a sniper's nest by a misguided citizen when a military squad had passed through town several months ago. The soldiers had stayed long enough to kill a few townsfolk with a missile aimed at the steeple and another at what had been the Carlyle Diner. The military had soon moved on. This rural town of a few thousand souls had been spared the plague. It was not big enough to be worth their government's lasting attention either, at least not for now. The soldiers had bigger flocks to pacify in cities far from here.

The weather had grown worse. For hours the Preacher been healing folks, but still a line of people extended from him to the chapel's door. Flashes of lightning and cold rain were lashing the windows. Fat drops of water from a roof leak plunked into a metal pail near his feet.

He'd been frozen in place like a cheap storefront mannequin. How long had he been in the trance? He glanced around at some of the faces. No one appeared to have noticed his lapse. He'd been reliving the explosion. The terrible experience always came without warning and took him with a vengeance. It was his clearest early memory. He knew he'd been reborn out of that supernova flash of expanding light and pain. It was his baptism. What his life had been before that flash of light was blank except for a single, blurry memory. In that memory he led an attack on the traitors who had brought this plague to mankind. He could recall nothing of the attack, only that he suffered a terrible defeat and all the blood spilled that day was somehow on his hands. Just before triggering the cataclysmic starburst that was to become his accidental baptism, he could remember sheltering in a trench, planning his escape. He would deceive the traitors into believing he was committing suicide. With a little providence, the traitors would be drawn too close to the flame and incinerated along with the bodies of his fallen soldiers of god.

The Preacher had told no one about the blurry memory. He could not be sure it was anything more than the figment of a badly traumatized brain. Total amnesia was what Sue believed. She'd been a nurse and the closest thing to a doctor he'd seen during this short two years of accumulating memories he could claim as his new life. Judging by appearance, he estimated himself to be in his early thirties. Sue had given up what she called "real medicine" after witnessing what the Preacher could do. She now helped him as the lord saw fit.

A five year old boy was next in line. The Preacher didn't understand how he did the miracle or why he'd been chosen. Some people he touched were healed, others received nothing. Many of those he touched were healed within hours. He had no control over the gift. About half were healed and half continued suffering. Desperation kept the line stoked with more troubled souls than he could ever absolve in a lifetime. Folks came from miles in every direction. Those he failed to help haunted his dreams. It had to be God's will acting though him. This was his fervent hope and every night he prayed it was so. At times he feared Satan was working false miracles through him for some darker purpose unknowable by an unclean preacher such as him.

The gift seemed to work both ways. Every day he felt younger and stronger than the day before. His body had become a wiry, powerfully muscled work of God. The terrible burn scares that had covered his flesh had faded. His glowing health caused him endless guilt while so many who came for his help continued to suffer.

This angelic healing had been going on for almost a year now. The changes in him had slowed but not stopped. Sometimes God whispered to him. Maybe God would have explained more if the Preacher was a better servant. He was unclean and unworthy and could not stop himself from sinning. He'd slept with Sue and so many others, sometimes even the ones he'd healed. Women were drawn to him and he was spreading his seed like a dog in heat. He despised himself for it, but he could no more stop himself than he could keep himself from eating or urinating. He knew of two women who were pregnant by him. An odd part of the gift was that he could sense when one of the unborn was his seed. There was a kind of primitive connection with the growing fetus. Some kind of link through which his experiences passed into them and what they felt was sent back in turn. The first one would be born in a month's time. What would that be like, meeting a newborn who might recognize you on sight?

There was a murmur from the line of people waiting for him. The air was thick with a scent of fear and hope. He wondered if this sickly little boy who stood in front of him would live or die.

"Come here," said the Preacher.

"Mommy, I don't want to!" cried the boy.

"Don't you want to feel better?" asked the Preacher.

The mother urged her child closer. The Preacher laid his hand on the boy's neck. He could feel the throbbing of the jugular vein. He could see all that was inside the child. It was as if a three dimensional colored X-ray had been projected over the small body. The mother had told the Preacher leukemia, but even if she'd never uttered a syllable, he would have known. He could see the pestilence inside the boy like an unnatural, glowing heat in his blood and bones. Displayed over the X-ray view was some kind of angelic writing that the Preacher could not understand. Yet it was unmistakable that without God's intervention this one would be traveling to heaven very soon. The Preacher began whispering the short prayer under his breath, repeating it again and again.

"God, I pray to you, heal thy servant...."

The Preacher felt disorientation as if dizzy from loss of breath. An icy something slithered from his touch into the child's neck and veins. The absolution was complete. The child's eyes fluttered as he keeled backward into his mother's waiting arms. The Preacher realized this one would live. He could see the heat in the blood already cooling to lighter hues in the spot where he'd perform his laying on of hands.

"This one is healing," mumbled the Preacher more to himself than anyone present. The exhaustion had come as it always did without warning. The Preacher stood to leave. He felt faint and held onto the chair back to steady himself. He heard the mother crying. Her voice seemed so far away. He picked up the basket of offerings left by grateful folks. He knew what was in it without looking. There was some money, IOUs, a promise of a meal, and some offers of a more earthy nature. The mother's appreciative cries were filling the small chapel with hope. Every eye in the congregation was on him. He wanted to help more, but all he could think of was food and sleep. He'd been working the will of God for hours. As always, it took its pound of flesh from his confused soul.

The Preacher – Highway Route 10, Louisiana – January 21, 0002 A.P.

The Preacher slowly became aware of himself in the passenger seat of a train. It was like waking without a memory of having fallen asleep. He had no idea where he was or how he had arrived in this seat. A middle aged woman was asleep in the spot next to him. His hand was on her leg. A half-eaten candy bar in a torn wrapper was in the process of slowly escaping her fingers. Craning, he looked around. As best he could tell, the rest of the car was nearly empty. The train was the best way to travel in these troubled times. The car rocked and thumped to the rhythm of the tracks. The new world had no shortage of gas or

93

autos. Anyone could have the car of their dreams, free for the taking. Abandoned autos were scattered all over the land like the carapaces of bugs that had moved on. With so few people there was also no longer a gas crisis. He'd read somewhere that the current supply of gasoline in the United States could last decades, but still, very few people drove. The roadways were prowled by evil men who would slit the throat of a traveler for the joy of it.

The military did not patrol the roads, but every train was heavily guarded and safe. Even if the roads were free of villainy, the Preacher would not have driven. He could not bring himself to try. He suspected a terrible memory of driving was lurking just below the surface of his memories. He stared out the window at blurry shapes of a nighttime world moving past. He saw neon signs glowing on distant streets. He saw fires in fifty-five gallon drums burning orange and lighting the faces of tattered people standing around them. Islands of light came into view and then faded. Some of the islands contained people while others were empty and had the aura of looking back in time at a ghost town. In an approaching yellowish glow, not 50 feet from the tracks, he watched in growing alarm as a man with a handgun executed a kneeling prisoner. There was a flash of light and the prisoner was no more. A small group forming a semicircle was standing witness. The Preacher's eyes meet those of the killer's as the man glanced at the passing train. The Preacher felt an otherworldly sense. None of this was real. The soldiers on the train did not react. The train did not speed up or slow. The Preacher knew deep in his heart on the other side of that thin pane of glass was a biblical hell. Judgment had finally been visited on a deservingly sinful world. This was truly the end of days.

Shaken by what he'd seen, the Preacher switched on a reading light, which washed out most of the nighttime view. He stared at his reflection in the window as blurry shapes of a nocturnal hell rolled behind his likeness. His face was a blank slate. He had all the features a man should have—nothing was missing—but nothing showed any lineage or ethnicity except maybe his eyes. They were blue with a slight almond shape to them, which hinted at a drop of Asian ancestry, or so he wondered. The rest of his face was as generic as if it had been broken into a million pieces and then remolded by God into a homogenized image of every race on Earth. His face was completely unfamiliar. Often he did not recognize his own reflection. After two years, he still could not recall his name. He suspected that one day he'd awake from a blackout and discover his identity. He'd find his name written in his own hand on a receipt or be in the company of someone who'd known him.

Close to a year after the plague ended, he had arrived on foot in Carlyle, Texas. Dressed in a long black suit with a Roman collar, he was carrying a Bible and a small satchel of clothes. He didn't let on he had no idea from where he'd come. The town's people were accustomed to men of God passing through and invited him to a potluck dinner. They'd asked him his name, to which he'd replied, "My name is a vanity I relinquished in service to the Lord." He had no idea if that was true or not. He had even less idea where those words had come from. He'd stayed in Carlyle and soon began his healing work. He was not sure if he'd performed healings before. God whispered to him and told him what to do.

The train made a metallic scraping noise as it banked around a turn. The Preacher felt something crumpled in his fist. He opened his fingers and saw a train ticket from Hammond, Louisiana, to Longview, Texas. The date on the ticket unnerved him. Several days had passed since his last memory in Carlyle. A breath caught in his throat as he spotted flakes of dried blood on the ticket. He nervously examined his palms and saw what looked like healed wounds from nail holes in both of them. It was the marks of crucifixion. This was not the first time. As he stared at the wounds, he could swear he saw them growing ever so fainter. It took all his will to not run screaming from the moving train into the arms of a hell that was waiting for him just outside the safety of his railcar.

The Preacher – New Orleans, Louisiana – February 5, 0002 A.P.

Two weeks had passed in Carlyle, Texas, before he'd set out again. The hotel bedroom was cold. The Preacher opened his eyes as the Messiah, the dominant personality of his damaged brain. In dreams mixed with reality he saw the apocalypse all around him in lurid detail. In this recurring premonition, death came as a plague, which soon cleansed the world of all men and women who were not God's chosen. The scenes were deeply troubling for a religious soul, but the Messiah knew he had to be strong. As the vision faded he cautiously glanced around the seedy hotel room. Neon lights from dens of ill repute flickered against the drawn window shades. New Orleans was truly the devil's playground. The Messiah had not walked into this hotel room or traveled to New Orleans; the Preacher had done that bodily function for him. The Messiah recognized the room and remembered the train ride that brought his vessel of flesh to this place. His memory was far more complete than that of the Preacher but still contained huge holes. The Preacher was such a sorry fool he didn't even know his real name. He played at being a healer for earthly reasons and had no idea how or why it worked. He had no idea that healing particles were in his blood. He aped what he had stolen from somehow spying on the Messiah. His healings lacked depth. There were many souls the Preacher could not heal.

The Messiah was the true spirit who inhabited this vessel. There was no one that God could not heal. The Preacher was a bodily intruder of some indeterminant kind. Though useful, he also defiled the vessel with adulterous sex and worse. The Preacher thought the explosion from his vision was a transformation he lived through by some miracle. The Messiah knew that the birth explosion was not a traumatic event that one lived *through*. The explosion was in fact the birth pains of his actual arrival into this world. There were no memories before the explosion because this life had not existed before the explosion.

The Messiah looked at the girl of maybe nineteen who was lying naked next to him in the bed. Another plaything the Preacher had seduced. He had memories of the child injecting narcotics before engaging in sexual intercourse. The Messiah felt no physical attraction to this fallen one. He could empathically sense she was unconscious in some narcotic stupor.

The Messiah donned his black suit with a Roman collar, then hung the vestment stole around his neck, leaving it uncrossed. The vestment was sacred. The Preacher carried it with him on every journey but never knew or saw it in his bag. It was a gift from God to the Messiah alone.

The Messiah walked into the bathroom and turned on the sink faucets. After some deep grumbling, what could almost pass for water flowed from the tap. He washed his face and hands following the ancient cleansing ceremony. He stared at his face in the mirror, meditating on the image. His eyes were Asian shaped, yet blue. His nose was Middle Eastern in shape but the skin color was northern European. God had told him he was the symbol of everyman. He continued meditating and soon all thought had stopped as he approached enlightenment. He could tell by the tingling in his hands and feet that the miracle was about to happen. God would again anoint him with blood just as he had his messengers from long ago.

The Messiah squeezed his hands into tightly balled fists. He squeezed until his forearms ached and then squeezed more. It seemed like it would never come but finally he felt a warm trickle forming in each hand. He uncurled his fists in anticipation and stared. In the center of each palm was a nail hole from a past life when he was crucified. As he stared, blood continued to ooze up and then stopped. He dipped his right finger into his left palm and drew the sign of the *ichthys* onto his forehead in his own blood. He was ready. God was ready. He could hear the soft whispers of God telling him to go forth and save the innocent and punish the wicked. The Messiah walked up to the side of the bed and stared at the naked girl. Could innocence be restored? He dipped his left finger into his right hand and drew the sign of the cross on her forehead as a sacrament in healing blood. Tonight she would be saved by God. He saw the stigmas in his palms closing. Soon there would be nothing more than faint scars as signs of the miracle.

The stairwell was unlit, yet he had eyes to see. The Messiah was aware of everything the Preacher knew and so much more. New Orleans was part of the Outlands. It was in some ways the unnamed capital of all that was not USAG. It attracted evil like honey attracted ants.

The Messiah stepped onto the cracked sidewalk and looked about. The streets were full of people seeking out sin of every imaginable variety. In a place like this it was easy to spot the innocent because there were so few. He began preaching the warning of the apocalypse that was upon them. He used the exact words God had taught him. People stared as he passed. He was God's messenger as well as God's sword; they could sense the power. He could feel the righteous energy growing inside him.

Though he was God's sword, the Messiah did not have the heart to punish the wicked. He would leave that to the plagues, which would not pass over any doors. He hoped God would forgive him for this weakness. He knew in his past incarnations far too much vengeance had been taken by his soul. The taint on his essence was deep and unwashable.

A rolling power failure had blacked out most of New Orleans a short time ago. Without electricity, the damaged buildings looked medieval. The Messiah wandered for hours preaching in the unnaturally darkened world until his path crossed a church. He stared for only a moment then realized this was the place he had been searching for all night. Candlelight was glowing from within. He could hear the faint voices of a choir. He walked to the door and swung it wide. As he entered and came into the light, the minister stopped speaking and stared.

"I am God's messenger and his sword," announced the Messiah. "I have come to heal the innocent and punish the wicked. Armageddon is upon us all."

"You are troubled," said the minister. "Let us help you."

The Messiah held up his palms so that all could see the miracle reappear. As he advanced deeper in this holy place he felt a warm trickle starting to crawl down his wrists. He felt the same warm trickle dripping down his forehead from what he knew were the marks of a crown of thorns. He heard gasps and murmured prayers. The minister grew pale. The Messiah reached the foot of the altar and turned to address the congregation.

"I am here as a healer and not as a sword," said the Messiah. "All those who are ill of body or heart come take a drop of my blood. Take the blood of one of the true sons of God inside you and be healed."

At first no one came forward. Finally one frail old man came up to the Messiah and asked for help for his wife, who had remained seated. The Messiah could tell this brave soul drew his courage from desperation. The Messiah walked over to the old man's wife and prepared to mark her forehead with the blood of the son of God. She trembled but did not shy away from his touch. He could see the damage in her lungs as he drew the sign of the cross on her forehead. Within minutes she was breathing a little easier and exclaiming, "It's a miracle!" to all who could hear. Soon many came forward, including the minister, who with tears in his eyes asked for help. The Messiah marked him too with a cross of blood.

"Who are you?" whispered the minister.

"I am one of the true messiahs."

As the Messiah stepped from the church, electrical power returned. The lights came on in fits and starts like industrial flashes of lightning. The Messiah was stunned to see the sidewalk littered with amazingly large black and white butterflies. Some were six inches across. There had to be thousands of them, forming a velvet blanket on the ground. A few were still alive, though most were dead. They were as large as the biggest autumn leaves and scattered as indiscriminately. This was a sign from God. It could be nothing less than a warning that the seventh and final seal had been opened. The apocalypse was summoned forth.

Kathy Morrison – Dallas, Texas – February 5, 0002 A.P.

Kathy suspected weeks had passed while she was imprisoned in solitary confinement. Arriving by air to this place, she'd recognized the Dallas skyline in the distance. The Zero-G corporate logo was on the buildings in the complex where she was now held. She might be inside the Dallas Protectorate but was unsure. This was not the gulag she'd expected, which only set her mind to work, considering far worse possibilities.

She had been terrified during her transfer to this facility. She had spent a week at the prison work camp where McKafferty had first deposited her. That for profit work camp had been horrid enough. When the soldiers had come for her in her dormitory, she'd been certain she was going to her death. All the prisoners whispered about secret executions and far worse things than that.

Kathy hadn't been offered a trial and didn't expect one. She was now officially one of the disappeared. Her dreams were nightmares filled with bloody scenes of Pueblo Canyon viewed through a helicopter window. She was sitting on a cold floor, pressed into a corner of her cell. She had been given clothes that did not fit. Her world was this eight foot steel box. There were no windows, no bars, no bedding, nothing but a prison door, a hard metal floor, and an exposed toilet. The metal was aged and rusting around the rivets. The cell was not new, which meant Zero-G had needed a secret jail for a very long time. What kind of company had that kind of need? She felt like a hamster in a cage soon to be used for experimentation. The lights in her cell were always on, though her tormentors were unintentionally doing her a favor. She knew she could never again sleep in the dark where the nightmares were waiting. There were constant noises as if large machines were rolling back and forth across the ceiling. She had lost her grasp of the passage of time and had begun mumbling her thoughts to herself. She remembered she'd been given water and oatmeal several times since her arrival but was constantly hungry. She was certain her jailers had not been back to check on her in days. Had they forgotten her? Were they leaving her to die of neglect?

Kathy was stunned as the prison door closed behind the exiting guards. Sitting in the middle of the floor was a basin of water and a small bar of soap. She hesitantly dipped her fingers into the water. It was warm. She immediately began to scrub her face. The water dripped down onto her ill fitting shirt, soaking it. She didn't care. She could not have been happier if she were a child playing in a pool on a hot summer day. She heard the loud metallic *clunk* of the door being unlocked again and stood up. Her hands and face were wet. She was breathing rapidly. Through the open door the light in the hallway was bright, causing her to squint. A man flanked by two armed guards stood in the doorway. The man took a step into her cell. The guards seem to be keeping a close eye on him. He extended his hand.

"Hello, Dr. Morrison. My name is Richard Theophilus. I must apologize for the poor treatment you have received. The treatment would be unacceptable for the worst criminals, let alone someone such as yourself, who worked so hard at the CDC to save us all."

The man spoke with a refined Greek accent. Kathy didn't know what to do or say. Inside she was trembling. The man may as well have been speaking Martian to her as he continued to address her. The full meaning of his words was lost to her. His build was athletic and tall. His face was expressive with a large forehead, gray eyes, and bushy eyebrows. His body looked young, late thirties to early forties, while his face looked much older, weathered and creased like a fisherman or sailor who had been exposed to too much sun. The medical doctor in her was confused by a face and body that did not match.

"In this new world I am an indentured scientist," said Richard.

"What are you going to do to me?" asked Kathy.

"Do?" The man chuckled sadly. "I'm here to offer you a job as an indentured scientist like me. Of course, there really is no choice. The people who run this place would send you or me back to the camps if we were not of value to them. I am heading up a research team working on medical applications for the nanotech seeds. We're trying to harness the seeds as a potential cure without turning the patient into a hybrid."

"You know about seeds and hybrids!" said Kathy.

"We know a lot," said Richard. "Come, let me take you from this cell and give you a tour. I hope you decide to work with us. It would trouble me to see anyone returned to the camps, let alone someone as heroic as you."

Kathy hesitantly walked toward the door. She was fighting hard to curb her feelings of euphoria, but was unable to stop her heart from beating wildly. She feared disappointment. It felt as if Richard had been sent by some higher power to save her. Only moments ago she had thought she was wretched and deserved her fate. Now she was being offered hope. She knew as a doctor she could be experiencing some kind of Stockholm syndrome, but knowing did nothing to dampen the emotional chaos.

Stepping outside her cell, it was if she had been transported to a different world. Richard took her through two labs right across the hall. All the research going on just beyond her prison cell dumbfounded her. Richard gave her a crisp white lab coat to wear. As her tour continued, Kathy thought she recognized the face of Maria Lorenzo, a world famous researcher and Nobel laureate. Richard confirmed that it was in fact Maria Lorenzo and that there were four other Nobel laureates on staff. The research Zero-G was doing was miles ahead of what she had been working on at the BVMC lab. The labs and equipment were beyond state of the art. It was impossible to understand how so much progress could have been made in just two years. The possibilities were breathtaking. If seeds could be harnessed, all diseases could be cured. She thought about the tension between her and Mark because she refused to even try to become a hybrid. This research promised a type of immortality she was eager to take part in.

"Kathy…" said Richard. "Kathy…"

"Oh, sorry, I was gathering wool."

"As I was saying, our research has progressed to the stage of human trials. I must confess that I have a personal stake in all of this. I'm not just leading a team. I'm a subject as well, which is breaking all the rules, but I had no choice. Not long ago I was diagnosed with a particularly aggressive form of lung cancer that had metastasized."

"Oh, my god," said Kathy. "I'm so sorry."

"No, it's okay. The cancer has been completely stopped and some of the damage reversed and all without surgery."

Richard opened his shirt enough to show Kathy a flexible mesh that was worn around the base of his neck like a collar. The collar was attached by a thin wire to a small electronic device he had on his belt. She had mistaken the device for a cell phone.

"This collar is an antenna. The box is called a medical-jammer. Zero-G research led to the discovery that high concentrations of infected COBIC in the bloodstream caused seeds to spontaneously perform many of their biological repair functions. My cure requires daily infusions of large quantities of infected COBIC. Medical-jammers limit where they can migrate. When worn around the neck, it keeps them from nesting inside my brain and turning me into a hybrid. This technology completely eliminates the risks of mental sequestering and neuronal connection to the god-machine. The medical-jammer produces a complex signal that blocks seed communications and creates a repelling field, which drives COBIC away. The result is a microbial null zone."

"This is incredible," said Kathy. "I have a thousand questions."

"And I have a thousand answers," said Richard.

"Why daily infusions? Why do you need to replenish the seeds?"

"Infected COBIC does not like the jammer's signal at all. As a result the microbes quickly exit my body. We've run tests. The bacterium is leaking from every inch of my skin at a very high rate. The seeds have arrested the progression of my cancer, but for some reason have not affected a cure. I need constant infusions of COBIC or my cancer will start progressing again. The current process is very expensive because of the costs of collection, storage, and administration of daily infusions of infected COBIC. The complexity and expense of that process is something we need to address."

"This is the cancer treatment the world has been praying for!" said

Kathy. "It makes chemo obsolete."

"That is very true," said Richard. "If I wasn't fortunate enough to be an indentured scientist and guinea pig, I would be dead."

Kathy's thoughts were spinning from all the possibilities.

"Couldn't you build the medical-jammer technology into a full body suit that blocks kill-zones or make something that shields an entire room or building?"

Richard smiled at her and slowly clapped his hands.

"Very well done!" he exclaimed. "We have developed just that. The equipment is experimental, obviously untested, and not ready for mass production, but we are close. This insight of yours is exactly why the demigods that run this place want you working for them. Few people have demonstrated as much brilliance in seed research as you and Mark Freedman."

Kathy felt her heart beating. Her caution evaporated. She was proud that such an advanced team would want her and wildly excited about everything she was seeing.

Her orientation tour was over. Richard closed the door to his office. He was about to show her a highly secret project code named Prometheus. Since they were not allowed into that particular lab, he would give her an introduction using live video. The two guards that never left Richard's side had taken up positions by the door. Richard brought up a video feed on a large wall mounted screen. Kathy saw workers in full body suits and odd helmets tending to a female subject inside a large glass chamber. The subject was strapped down and connected to an array of laboratory medical equipment. The upper part of her body was inserted partially inside a small MRI. On a split screen display the subject's face was visible inside the MRI. There was a great deal of advanced equipment, some of which Kathy could not begin to identify. The subject was lying on an incline with the lower part of her torso and legs inside a shallow trough filled with clear liquid.

"We have six hybrids who are volunteer subjects," said Richard. "This is subject number three."

Kathy was both impressed and astounded. They had hybrids, six hybrids! She had discussed with Mark the idea that more of his kind could exist, but to actually find more, to see them in the flesh, made her feel like she was dreaming. It was ironic that Mark was out there searching for more of his kind and here, by accident, she had found them.

"What are you doing with them?" asked Kathy. "This is fantastic."

"There are many more than these six out there on the streets," he informed her. "We need to study their nanotech brains and figure out how it controls the COBIC seeds in their blood. The subjects are hooked up to an fMRI to measure brain activity alongside RF signal analyzers to measure seed communications so we can correlate the two. We are always looking for new volunteers for the project. Each experiment runs for twenty-four hours, during which time the subject is unconscious. We need people with a high level of nanotech rooted in the brain...."

Richard continued talking, but Kathy only heard bits and pieces as she stared at the video. At this stage they were trying to find better ways of coaxing the seeds into healing. If successful, they would no longer need to saturate a patient with COBIC. The need for daily infusions of fresh bacteria would be a thing of the past. The sight of this hybrid hooked up and strapped down was unsettling, but the project itself was deeply exciting because of the human potential.

"Kathy..."

"Huh?"

"Will you join the team?"

"Are you kidding?" said Kathy. "Big, burly men with guns couldn't stop me."

Kathy Morrison – Dallas, Texas – February 6, 0002 A.P.

The living quarters Kathy was assigned felt luxuriant. In addition to an office it had a separate sitting area, refrigerator, and wet bar. There were no windows. Instead there was a large wall screen, which she left displaying live video from the Prometheus project as a reminder of what was at stake and the sacrifices being made. She'd spent the entire night and day reviewing the project she'd been assigned. She had consumed vast quantities of coffee and real food, and had no intention of letting up on work just yet, even though a large sofa with a pillow and blanket was calling to her. She could easily see herself sleeping there for several days straight once she gave in to it.

The team to which she'd been assigned had two main goals in the project. First, they had to reduce the level of nanotech seeds that were infused and in doing so lower the risks to the patient. The current therapy had genetically damaged and even killed several lab animals. The second goal was expanding the use of this therapy to non-genetic problems, specifically infectious diseases. Kathy was an expert in immune system response and infectious diseases. She felt she could make a good contribution in this area. Some of the material she'd read was troubling. Hybrids had been injured during experimentation, but since they were hybrids they'd recovered quickly. As a result, there was a certain implied callousness toward them. You could push experiments further than would normally be allowed in human trials. Regardless of her discomfort with the ethics, this was an opportunity she could not refuse. If successful, she was being offered a chance to work on something that could cure humanity's ills and give her Mark's longevity without any risk to mind or soul.

Following a knock at her door, Richard stuck his head in. He had stopped by to check on her like this several times already. He'd said he wanted her to be a happy indentured scientist. He had such a charismatic personality. Kathy could not help being buoyed by each of his short visits. Richard was guileless. He was a little odd, but his genius made him very appealing.

Kathy Morrison – Dallas, Texas – February 8, 0002 A.P.

For Kathy each day was too short to get everything done. She was in her office working on finalizing her experiments using jammers to regulate COBIC blood levels. She planned on starting her first experiment that night. She liked the quiet of an empty lab. The first experiment called for using a jammer to regulate levels in a rhesus monkey. The goal was to be able to go from a residual bloodstream level to a supersaturated level and then anywhere in between on command and within minutes. She heard a knock at her door that she now recognized as Richard. She knew he would open the door and invite himself in. He never waited for permission to enter. While the man was impossibly endearing in many ways, this violation of her space had quickly become irritating. She had forgotten to lock her door and so was about to receive a visit. When the door opened, she could tell Richard was energized. Standing just behind him were his two guards.

"Hello, Kathy," said Richard. "You look hard at work."

"I am."

"I don't want to interrupt, but I have very exciting news. There is something I felt you should have been told from the start, but I don't make the decisions around here. Our corporate overlords have had a change of heart. I've come to show you something I know you will find fascinating."

"When?"

"Why, now of course."

"But I am in the middle of this work and—"

"It can wait," said Richard. "I promise what you see will change how you are approaching your work. Grab a coat. We are going outside."

Kathy knew she had no choice. Richard would not take no for an answer, and she did not want to alienate the one person that was on her side. During the walk to another building, Kathy tried to find out what he was going to show her, but Richard remained tight lipped with a mischievous gleam in his eyes.

They finally came to a stop in front of a vault door. Richard entered a security code and swiped his badge. The door opened into a room full of clear, acrylic display cases. He led her to a case that contained a row of unimpressive looking black objects that looked like small tablets. She could see more interesting objects in other cases. Some items looked like weapons and other objects looked like optical headgear.

Richard opened an electronic combination lock on the display case. The acrylic was a couple inches thick and looked like it might be bulletproof. He removed one of the tablets and handed it to her. The weight was surprisingly light. It must have been hollow, because it felt like she was holding a sheet of paper. The tablet was about six inches wide, eight inches tall, and an eighth of an inch thick. One side was black and the other side looked like a dull liquid metal similar to mercury, but was hard to the touch and felt like lubricated glass. She rubbed her fingers together, thinking there was a film on them, but they were dry.

"What you are holding is at least twenty thousand years old," said Richard. "But it could be far older, maybe fifty thousand."

Kathy's grip on the object reflexively went tense. She stared at the simple looking device, then started to have doubts about what Richard was telling her.

"Feel how slippery the shiny side is?" he said. "That's the touch display."

"You're teasing me, right?"

"I am very serious," said Richard. "This is real and there's much more to show you."

He did something to the tablet while she held it. The screen came to life with the display of a rotating earth and moon. The tablet began to feel cooler instead of warming. The display was three dimensional, full color, extremely realistic, and like nothing she'd seen before.

"What is it?" asked Kathy.

"That's a good question. We only have guesses. Some type of networked personal computing device is our best guess. What's more important is it's made from self-replicating nanotech, and what's even more important is that we use small cubes cut from these devices to make our jammers."

Kathy was momentarily speechless. What did this mean? Her mind began to fill with questions.

"Is this the same nanotech as seeds?" she asked.

"It's different, but could be from the same source. We have no way of dating the device with any real accuracy because it is self-repairing as well as self-replicating," said Richard. "Since any network it might have used was long gone, we expected little from it. When we figured out how to activate it, the artifact scanned all radio frequencies, analyzed the encoding, and began communicating. It sent out beacons. It momentarily crashed nearby Wi-Fi access points and then released the frequencies, allowing our systems to come back, then went after them again but with more finesse. It is clearly some kind of very sophisticated AI computer device. In a short time it had reverse engineered our encrypted Wi-Fi and Ethernet protocols and began using them to communicate. It tries to connect with everything within radio range. We've been able to communicate with it from our computers, but its replies reveal nothing. The device wants some kind of access code and we have not been able to crack it. We tried using the touch screen… but watch…"

Where Richard touched the screen, the device drew a circle around his finger, then displayed a large blue symbol.

"It's locked. The power source is unknown. It just works. If you scratch the device, it heals itself using whatever it's in contact with for raw materials. You do not want your fingers near it when it's healing. It will use your flesh to repair itself. A member of our team found that out the hard way. We tried X-raying it and found nothing but a solid block of material. We found that if we cut off a tiny piece the size of a speck of pepper, the speck regenerates into a simpler device about the size of sugar cube without a human interface, but with all the communications functions intact. We found a way to embed these regenerated cubes into microchips for experimentation. After long, fruitless lab work, we discovered a way to inject various signals and received back complex waveforms that looked like n-web traffic. This device communicates with the god-machine and seeds. We found that injecting a certain signal results in an output we use for our jamming of COBIC. So our brilliant jammer technology is really just trial and error reverse engineering with some luck mixed in. You see, we do not dare mass produce the jammers just yet. We are concerned that if we cut off too much of the mother device or just cut it too many times, it will eventually cease to function. We'll be left with nothing. Some people on the team speculate that the cubes we have grown are talking to the mother device. They theorize that it is the mother device that contains all the intelligence. If this is true, then when a mother device is damaged, all

106

its children, the next generation of cubes, could stop working."

Kathy handed the tablet back to Richard and stared at all the other acrylic cases in the room with renewed interest. She started to wander down one aisle and then another. Cases upon cases held larger and smaller versions of the same black tablets. There were cases with objects that she could have easily been mistaken for computer servers. Other items were more unusual. Some machines looked like portable distilleries or miniature chemical factories of some kind. There were transparent gauntlet gloves and a very peculiar helmet with a solid face shield covered in tiny pyramid shaped bumps.

"Are all these cases full of... umm..." said Kathy.

"Prehistoric technology," said Richard. "Every case is a treasure beyond imagination. Some specimens are clearly much older than what you were holding. As I said, it is impossible to date these items with any accuracy, but they are clearly not made by our society. Yet all evidence suggests they were built by modern humans. Amazing, isn't it? Here we have proof that humankind reached great heights in the past, only to be set back time and again. We are certain there were at least two epochs before our current time, though there could easily have been more. Zero-G archeologists speculate the downfalls were caused by natural catastrophes or war, but were I a betting man, I would bet every downfall was the work of a sphinx like enigma called the god-machine."

First Contact

Mark Freedman – Chicago suburbs, Illinois – February 6, 0002 A.P.

Mark dragged open the barn door and saw their slant back Humvee sitting unmolested inside the dilapidated structure just as they'd hidden it. Bits of dust and old straw floated in shafts of sunlight that angled down through holes in the roof. Mark had no idea how worried he'd been until this moment. They'd had to leave everything behind when they smuggled themselves into Chicago. They would have been in trouble if this armored Humvee with all their gear had been stolen. Mark felt a vague melancholy drifting as an undercurrent below the surface of his relief. Back when they'd hidden the Humvee, at some level he had not expected to return. The singularity could have changed everything.

"What are you waiting for?" said Sarah as she brushed past him into the barn. Mark followed her inside. He knew she'd empathically felt his emotions and why he'd hesitated. He was annoyed that she could read him so easily.

Sarah began checking the Humvee to make sure it was ready for the road. They'd spend the night here, then head out at first light. Neither of them needed the rest, but driving at night put them at a disadvantage with reduced visibility. If they used their headlights, they would be broadcasting an open invitation to gangs that prowled the Outlands. The glint of headlights could be visible for miles.

Mark looked up from his Android tablet. Like his Droid phone, the tablet used the same postage stamp-sized ID cards so he could change network identity at will. He had been drafting a response to Karla Hunt's request for another face to face. Sarah was working through a weapons check. She had an Army manual displayed on a tablet in front of her. An MK19 40mm belt fed grenade machine gun was stripped into pieces on a tarp. Once checked and reassembled, it could be mounted through the roof hatch on an exposed turret. The MK19 was a murderous weapon similar in size to a .50 caliber machine gun. At first glance the weapon could be mistaken for a stocky version of a .50 caliber but the similarity was not even skin deep. The MK19 could burst fire up to 375 explosive rounds per minute. Each 40mm grenade could punch a hole through two inches of armor and deliver a blast radius of 50 feet. With an effective range of close to a mile, this was the kind of weapon Mark wished they'd had when fleeing across the southwest from Alexander's militia two years ago. He smiled to himself. It was human nature to always fight the last battle and never be prepared for the next.

An AM radio was playing from inside the Humvee. The pirate radio station Air Truth was broadcasting a story about scientists who were wrongly prosecuted for involvement in the nanotech plague. The reporter was claiming he had just uncovered a massive USAG conspiracy. Wrongful imprisonment and executions were the true crimes. The reporter was questioning an anonymous guest scientist about the history of the plague and whether it could be a fabrication. Mark could easily imagine the USAG working very hard right about now to find this guy and silence him with extreme prejudice.

Mark Freedman – Ohio – February 8, 0002 A.P.

Mark glanced in the driver side mirror at the sun moving lower amid the tobacco colored clouds. The pillar of smoke was still visible a hundred miles behind them and to the south near the Indiana border. The land they were now passing through was unscathed. Earlier in the day, driving for hours through the burned out forests and spans of suburbia had been unnerving. It felt like the aftermath of a nuclear war. As unsettling as that sight had been, passing the head of the wildfire itself had been life threatening. No one had imagined mega-wildfires would turn out to be the second most destructive force unleashed by global warming. Only the god-machine's plague was worse.

They had been on the road for two days and had been detoured due to highway problems almost every hour, including while passing the head of the wildfire. At points they had been no more than ten miles from the edge of the inferno. The wandering cauldron was larger than most cities.

The fires were at last no longer visible. Sarah was pouring him a lukewarm cup of coffee from the thermos. They were on Interstate Route 90 heading east. Mark was driving the military Humvee at near suicidal speeds for these war torn roads. He was fully confident in his reaction time. It was a choice between driving too fast or driving at night. For the moment the speedometer was at 85 mph, the maximum speed on the gauge. So far they'd seen no patches of ice or snow on the roadbed. That piece of luck would not last much longer. For some reason the temperature had been steadily dropping as they neared Lake Erie. Mark knew these freakish weather patterns had to be caused by global warming. The GPS displayed a two-hour ETA. They needed to arrive at a stopping point before it grew dark. The smart thing to do was set realistic driving goals. Working against the smart thing to do was an instinctive yearning to reach the next singularity as soon as possible

110

and a nagging sense they were already too late.

Triangulation had shown the singularity was somewhere near Montreal. Just as in Chicago, Mark expected this singularity to be connected with a group of hybrids. What if the singularity was a side effect of a growing tribe of hybrids reaching some kind of critical mass? If that were true... Mark pushed harder on the accelerator. They needed a better plan. Trying to figure out a safe way of approaching the hybrids in Chicago had cost valuable time. The delay had also likely saved their lives. If they had acted more rashly, they could have been inside that townhouse when it exploded.

"This time will be different," said Sarah, as if reading his mind. "I just don't believe those hybrids intentionally killed themselves. It's more than intuition. It's like an unexplainable fact in my brain. Maybe I was subconsciously picking up emotional cues from them or something?"

"There's a burglary, then days later the place is blown up by a military grade weapon," said Mark. "There is nothing innocent about that."

"Maybe for once the USAG propaganda machine is reporting the truth?" said Sarah. "They were a militant group planning a bombing and killed by their own device."

"It's possible," said Mark. "They were clearly at war, but what about the execution I witnessed? It's also possible that a critical mass of hybrids leads to some event other hybrids want to stop. Maybe it's an evolutionary leap of some kind? We have no idea what's going on. You know it could just as easily be the USAG who blew them up. Either way we could be walking into a ticking time bomb in Montreal."

"Maybe we should just stay away?" said Sarah.

She was smiling. Mark knew they both thought staying away was not an option.

"It's going to be dark before we stop for the night," he said.

"Changing the subject, are we?"

The sun was gone. Their progress had slowed as the highway became snowbound. Their ETA was less than thirty minutes. Mark was using night vision goggles. The brake lights were disabled and the headlights were off. While he was still able to drive as fast as conditions permitted, he was also driving partially blind. The goggles had limited range and ability to show detail when compared to using other night vision options. His impaired vision worried him, but he would put up with it because this type of goggle did not need an infrared light source. Starlight that had traveled for countless lifetimes to reach this roadbed was enough illumination. There was no point in switching off the headlights if you then had to use an infrared spotlight. The bad guys had night vision goggles too and an infrared illuminator would draw them in like mosquitoes to a nice, warm blood meal.

The layover point they'd chosen was a summer vacation area on the shore of Lake Erie. The shoreline community had multiple roads leading in and out in addition to access by water. Karla Hunt was meeting them twenty-four hours from now at whatever abandoned house they ultimately selected. For safety there had to be as many escape routes as possible. Mark liked lots of crisscrossed roads. Using Google Earth satellite imagery, they had selected an ideal neighborhood that was along their route to Canada.

Earlier in the day, finding fuel had slowed them down. It was usually easy to come by derelict filling stations with leftover gas. This leg of their journey had not been usual in more than one way. They had seen a large amount of combat damage along Route 90, including the burned out shells of mechanized war machines and crashed aircraft. Just as everywhere else, all the signs of conflict appeared to be years old, but the scale of what had happened here was unprecedented. A secret war had been fought with this highway as a battle line. Untold numbers of people had died and it was very likely no one would remember a thing.

The turnoff toward Lake Erie appeared out of the gloom of his night vision goggles. Dense forest lined either side of the highway. The trees should have shed all their leaves by now, but global climate changes had confused them. A small number of the trees still held most of their leaves and looked so oddly out of place. Mark slowed to a crawl as he went down the circular exit ramp from the interstate. Now came the risky part: selecting a house. It was cold out. The road was icy and had a mostly undisturbed covering of snow. It looked like some traffic had been through here but not much.

"I guess the only good thing about arriving after dark is that we can use thermal to see if anyone's home," said Sarah.

She climbed into the back of the Humvee and returned with a thermal FLIR imaging gun sight. Mark knew, with this high tech visual weapon, she could spot a man three hundred yards away hiding in dense foliage and identify his face. It would make child's play of finding the coldest houses on the block. Sarah pointed the gun sight at Mark and peered through it.

"Maybe I can't see through walls with this *Star Trek* toy," she said. "But clothes are no problem."

"You have to turn it on first," said Mark. "Then there's the problem of not enough temperature gradient between clothes and skin to see any detail."

"Wrong answer," said Sarah. "You're such a jerk!"

The neighborhood they'd selected using Google Earth turned out to be perfect. It was close to the interstate highway, yet isolated. The area was crisscrossed with dirt roads. Most of the houses were vacation cabins made from logs. Remarkably, many of the lots were still campsites. They'd spotted some deer clustered around a saltlick that appeared to be new. While staring at the deer, a huge skunk like animal lumbered into the road. An assist identified it as a badger and that it should be hibernating. Mark hit the brakes. The Humvee skidded on icy ground with the big tires trying unsuccessfully to bite. Mark gritted his teeth as possible outcomes flashed through his mind. An assist displayed the best course of action to avoid an accident: lift off the brakes and hit the animal. He ignored the assist. In the end the badger survived its close encounter with man.

It didn't take long for Mark to grow convinced this whole summer camping area was deserted. Sarah had the FLIR scope aimed out the open window, targeting cabin after cabin.

"The only heat signatures I'm getting are the small, furry kind," she said.

"Okay, let's turn around," said Mark. "It looks like nothing has garages. We're going to have to park behind a cabin, use a tarp, and hope that's enough camouflage to hide our presence."

Mark Freedman – Ohio – February 9, 0002 A.P.

The morning came early. Mark awoke to the smell of coffee and wood burning in the fireplace. He looked out the sliding glass door facing Lake Erie. Sarah was sitting on the wooden deck with a mug. She was dressed in jeans and a sweatshirt, no coat or hat. The air looked still. He could see wisps of fog coming from the coffee and her breath. The shoreline had a brittle layer of ice a few inches thick, which reached far out into the lake. Beyond the ice he could see the glittering movement of choppy water. The rough textured ice around the shore reflected the colors of the sunrise as if illuminated from within. An assist informed him the lake should have been frozen to the horizon this time of year.

Staring at the great lake, Mark had a powerful sense of déjà vu. A little over two years ago he'd stood at the shore of Lake Superior in a biohazard suit watching deadly plumes of COBIC wash up on shore, forming thick mats. A few hours later a kill-zone had hit Lake Superior.

It was the first time he'd been caught inside that inhuman terror. He'd thought he was a dead man but had survived. Mark sighed. He'd had no idea at the time that he'd survived because something yet to be called the god-machine had plans for him. In retrospect, that had been the moment his life had changed forever. Within a few hours he would be exposed to infected COBIC through a tear in his biohazard suit. Days later, while quarantined at the BVMC lab, he'd discover that his body was healing at a freakish speed. Mark shivered, but not from the cold.

As he was stepping away from the glass door, he saw a moving glint far out on the lake. It looked like a boat's windshield reflecting sunlight. The glint came again. Karla Hunt was due to arrive within the hour. Was that her? He'd assumed she'd be coming overland from the nearest airfield. As director of one of the most important research projects going, she had the unlimited resources of the USAG to tap. She was the director overseeing the most important scientific project the government had running. It was her job to study the nanotech seeds and help avert another plague. The glint was now solidly there and growing. He could tell it was heading directly at them. Sarah had gotten up and was looking at the same threat. Ralph was by her side. The huge Rottweiler appeared tense. An assist informed Mark the object was traveling at approximately 56 miles per hour. The estimate was made using a calculation based on how fast the size of the object of interest was increasing. Mark's phone emitted the ringtone for a text message.

Don't shoot. It's me, xxoo

A few minutes later, Karla and her escorts arrived in a pair of gray USAG Navy ice airboats. A third ice airboat began patrolling five hundred yards from the shoreline. The boats were about 30 feet long and armored. At low speed they were too heavy to ride the ice and had cut trenches through it on their way to shore. They had enclosed cabins the size of the passenger compartment of a full sized SUV. A huge, shrouded pair of aircraft propellers took up the rear third of each boat.

Mark and Sarah had closed all the blinds and were staying out of sight inside the cabin. Their faces were on at least one secret government watch list and probably more. Ralph had refused to budge from his staked out position of about six feet from the sliding glass door. Anyone coming through that door uninvited would not last more than a few seconds.

Mark and Sarah were both staring at the ruggedized tablet from the MSK-II sentry kit. On the screen was a feed from one of the pill bottle sized intruder detectors. The software was in record mode, saving

114

everything to the tablet's memory. They watched bodyguards in Navy SEAL uniforms exit the boats and set up a parameter around the cabin. The soldiers were armed with short barrel HK416 assault weapons. On each boat a soldier took up position with a turret mounted SAW machine gun. Two anti-sniper specialists began scanning the area with oversized binoculars. The area was clearly considered hostile. Mark again thought about the remains of a secret war they'd seen on the highway. He split the screen to check the other feeds. The first one he checked was a view of him and Sarah looking at the tablet. The tablet's screen was in view and caught up in an infinite loop. It reminded him of the age old paintings of the alchemist seeking wisdom in a mirror reflected into another mirror into infinity. Earlier, Sarah had asked why he was installing some of the sentry detectors inside the living room. He'd told her they were to purchase insurance.

After about five minutes, Mark saw Karla emerge from the boat. He thought it was ironic that for the next few hours he would be protected by the same government that was secretly hunting him.

Karla set down her now empty mug of coffee. She looked worn. Karla had brought a tablet stuffed with documents covering the research being conducted at her lab. She wanted Mark's insights and was willing to leave the tablet with him, which was very risky for her. Mark knew if he was captured while in possession of this top-secret material it would be her head. He also knew she could remotely wipe it any time she wanted.

"My team needs you," said Karla. "But I know we can't have you. As far as I can tell, there's only one scientist who won a Nobel for a lifetime of research into COBIC and has firsthand experience because the damn seeds are in his brain. Bad luck he's also a wanted terrorist."

"Sorry," said Mark.

"It's okay, love. In your absence we mere humans version 1.0 have advanced our cause but not enough. We have a super scanning environmental e-scope running at Los Alamos using one of their top-secret accelerators as a source. It's a breakthrough that's delivered wonders. With it we're finally able to image intact operating seeds and prove that any physical contact causes a seed to self-destruct.

"The biggest mystery is still the power source. We've isolated its structure but have only guesses at the physics involved. The theories are all over the map from unlikely ideas such as dark energy to our best guess, which is some type of ultra high efficiency fuel cell combined with IR photovoltaic. We've dissected and partially duplicated the structures, but what we built did not work and does not make sense when fit into our limited knowledge base. We also have confirmed there's a molecular computer in there. It's not using any kind of quantum computing we can find. This is disappointing, because it may indicate quantum computing is a dead end. If a civilization that advanced did not use quantum computing, then maybe it's not practical?"

"Maybe there's another explanation," said Mark. "Each seed may contain a molecular computer, but collectively they could still form a quantum machine of some type. The god-machine is not hosted in a single seed. It's hosted in colonies of trillions of seeds, which to me at the very least requires quantum entanglement to make it work. At the CDC we demonstrated seeds scaling up in parallel processing power without any apparent loss of efficiency. Explain that."

"I'd sure like to get that nanotech brain of yours under an fMRI," said Karla. "I think we'd get some of these questions answered. Any chance of that?"

"God, why does every woman I meet want me for my mind?"

"Don't flatter yourself," said Sarah with a laugh.

Karla looked back and forth between Mark and Sarah without saying a word.

Mark returned from the kitchen with an open can of fruit cocktail. He was surprised by his hunger and ate in silence, listening to Karla and Sarah talk about emotions radiating out across the n-web.

"It's strange that every emotion is transmitted while most stray thoughts remain trapped in the brain," said Sarah.

"It could be that COBIC only congregates in the brainstem," said Karla. "Dendrites growing out from seeds do not reach very far and definitely are not making it to the cortex."

Mark put down the empty can of fruit cocktail.

"Something is bothering me," he interrupted. "Why are you still studying the nanotech seed's structure? We know what they are. We know what they do. You should be studying the data and the software, not the hardware."

"We need to find a weakness that can be exploited by our current technology, and right now we think our best chance is biology," said Karla. "Bacteriophages, antibiotics, and radiation are showing promise. Kill the bacterial host and the seed is crippled. If it can't travel it can't repair the n-web. If we can cripple the n-web it's game over. Soft, squishy bacterium biology is the god-machine's weak spot."

"That's not a weak spot," said Mark. "Name one strain of bacteria we've successfully wiped out. Look at the history. The more we tried to wipe out a strain with antibiotics, the more dangerous it became. The key to this whole thing is that hybrids are not immune. Kill-zone trigger signals are ignored by the seeds inside us. It's programming and data that kept the plague from killing me and Sarah, not biology or physics."

"We looked at software," said Karla. "We looked at data. We tried DOS attacks by injecting disruptive network packets. I even have a team looking at computer viruses, but you know that's hopeless unless we can figure out the programming language. We've tried every approach to defeat the software and failed. We tried EMF shielding. It made sense because so many people survived the plague in nuclear EMP bunkers. What we ultimately found was that their survival was due to the god-machine's indifference to low population targets and not EMP shielding."

"You know this for a fact?" interrupted Mark.

"It's the best theory we have and I believe it. But what we do know for a fact is that this thing is a hardened weapon like nothing we could have imagined. The wireless n-web is constantly self-adapting as if it's an independent artificial awareness all its own and engineered to defeat any obstacle. Around the globe there are countless trillions of wirelessly relayed n-web routes all carrying indecipherable data streams. It's like a nervous system flowing across and through everything from the cement walls of a safe room to the dermis of a living creature. The n-web is built as much from solid biological material as it is radio waves. It's a living, breathing biomass that infuses everything and we still have no idea how to neutralize it."

"You're proving my point," said Mark. "Software, not hardware."

"Wait, hear me out," said Karla. "What if we could just interrupt some of the lines of communication? We don't have to destroy the n-web to stop a kill-zone attack. What we need is a biological firewall. At BARDCOM we found all that was required for a kill-zone signal to get into any safe room was a single microscopic gap in shielding. The terrifying thing is if there's no gap, the seeds make one by assembling a non-electromagnetic data conduit. We're not sure of the actual mechanics of this conduit, but we believe it's electrochemical and similar to how neurons communicate with each other. Again, it's biology. What we know is that seeds physically interconnected by their dendrites can transport n-web data non-electromagnetically. We've observed them doing this on a massively parallel scale. We call this data pathway a biomass conduit. Using nanotech molecular disassembly and reassembly, seeds can tunnel through any material. No physical barriers can block the formation of a biomass conduit. In the lab, we've watched seeds construct a conduit in minutes after we blocked their electromagnetic signal with a Faraday Cage.

"We've also studied these biomass conduits in the wild. During the plague days, CEOs of big corporations were privy to top-secret information. They knew kill-zone radio signals were a kind of disease vector. One CEO committed a criminal error of judgment. When the plague was escalating, his DOD consulting firm was looking for radio wave shelters and stumbled onto the idea that EMF shielded MRI rooms offered good protection. Without peer review, this CEO sent out private e-mails recommending these rooms as shelters and that they take control of them now. The e-mail went viral in elite circles. His big mistake was that EMF shielded rooms offered no protection from biomass conduits, though no one knew about biomass conduits at that time. The seeds had long ago constructed biomass pipes through the shielding of MRI rooms, as it did with any obstacle. All over the country radiology rooms in big cities became VIP mausoleums for politicians, corporate CEOs, and all their friends, cronies, and families. We sent in teams to study these mausoleums. Using RF spectrum analyzers, our teams quickly found and mapped out countless biomass conduits, penetrating every surface of the rooms. The EMF shielding had been invisibly turned into Swiss cheese."

"I'm disgusted by all those privileged bastards taking all the life-boats while keeping the country in the dark," grumbled Mark. "They're the same Ayn Rand greed is good geniuses of industry with their self-inflicted environmental destruction that brought us the plague. For once it was better they kept their secrets to themselves. Those rats got their karmic desserts in their leaky lifeboats!"

Mark noticed Sarah frowning at him and felt that familiar tug from her at the back of his mind. His emotions leveled out. He stared at her, unsure what she'd just done to him and wondered if he should be grateful or if she even knew that she had done something.

"I don't agree," said Karla. "And even if true, how does revenge help us?"

"You're right," said Mark. "It doesn't help. But look, there's an important reason you should search for weaknesses in data instead of hardware. The god-machine is censoring the data that I can access. The same is true for Sarah. All information about the history of the god-machine's creators is inaccessible. Are we headed toward the same end as them? Did the god-machine destroy them? All of these questions go unanswered when I submit queries. So there has to be something important there. Likewise, anything relating to how seeds operate is censored—and by *operate* I mean their programming and communications mechanisms. I'd bet anything the god-machine's hiding a critical weakness from us."

"Why does it surprise you that the enemy is withholding information?" asked Karla. "Just because it's withheld doesn't mean there's a weakness. The god-machine operates COBIC like a puppet. How do we know it isn't operating you two like puppets? Am I fraternizing with the enemy right now?"

"Yes, you are!" said Mark. "I confess…" He extended his arms, offering them for handcuffing. "I only ask that when you take us back to your lab, please don't dissect us."

Karla was smiling at his joke, but Mark could tell from stray thoughts as well as a medical assist that her question had a very serious and sharpened edge. She was not sure of them and that was troubling. What was more troubling was that Mark could never be sure her concerns were misplaced. His awareness shifted for a heartbeat as he experienced a memory capsule from Sarah. The capsule contained the emotional dimensions of Karla's doubts. Mark took a deep breath and then let it out. He needed Karla's help as much as she needed his. He had to reassure her; he had to give her something new, something that gave her a measure of power over them.

"I have some information for you," said Mark. "It may change a lot of what you know about hybrids."

Karla's smile faded. Her look was so strange that it unsettled him. Oddly, there were no stray thoughts coming from her. He plowed ahead with his disclosure, now unsure whether it was such a good idea.

"There are more of us," said Mark. "In Chicago we found a number of hybrids. We saw at least six different individuals. They're gone now, dead or on the run. I don't know. The townhouse they were living in was built like a high tech fortress. Just before we left Chicago, it was destroyed by a suspicious explosion. You may have heard about it. The explosion was reported as a terrorist bomb factory going up. The cause was a large thermobaric weapon that was engineered to destroy with intense heat and reduced blast. How many kids on the street have those kinds of high tech military toys besides the USAG? Not many, is my guess."

Mark Freedman – Ohio – February 10, 0002 A.P.

Mark and Sarah were sitting in the dark on a couch they had turned to face the sliding glass door. The blinds were open. Mark was thinking about what he'd learned today and, more important, had not learned. Sarah was as still as if asleep, but Mark knew she was wide awake. It was past midnight. His eyes had long ago adjusted to the darkness. Genetic as well as physiological changes made by COBIC had improved his biological night vision. An assist further enhanced edge detection. The combined result was noticeable, but not much more than what a human with superb night vision would experience.

A gibbous moon was a few hours from setting. Mark could hear the wind blowing against the glass, trying to force its way inside. The room was growing very cold. He could see the vague dark shapes of branches moving in the wind and leaves flying through the air. Karla had left about six hours ago. In the morning at first light they too would be departing. They'd let the fire die out after Karla was gone. There was no reason to broadcast their presence with a heat signature. Mark wanted to make it appear to any human predators that could have witnessed the earlier airboat activity that everyone had left with the boats. Ralph was curled on the floor on a blanket in front of them. His head was on his paws. Sarah's voice floated softly out of the darkness beside him.

"I saw you finished reading the documents Karla brought," she said. "Are they close to finding anything that could stop it?"

"No closer than we were before the kill-zones and that psycho Alexander drove us from the BVMC lab."

"If they could find something that even partially worked," said Sarah, "the paranoids in the government might stop seeing us as a threat."

"You know, Karla was right to worry about fraternizing with us. Just about everything we say and do feeds directly into the god-machine's memory. We are leading a fully recorded life. The only question is how much will be archived. When she's at her lab there's a good chance the god-machine is ignoring her. Every time we meet has to draw more unwanted attention from the machine onto her. Karla is nobody's fool."

"So you're saying she might not be telling us everything."

"That and the fact she might not know everything going on at her own division. The USAG is a police state. They don't exactly promote an environment of trust. I wish—"

Ralph lifted his head and looked toward the glass. Mark instantly knew something was very wrong. He opened his mind and began picking up stray thoughts as if he were a shortwave radio snatching bits of conversation from distant stations out of a waterfall of background static. One stray thought contained a tiny green night vision image of the outside of their cabin. Someone was looking at the other side of the same glass door that Mark was staring through. The perimeter sentry had not gone off yet. He grabbed the tablet before it issued an alert that would have lit up the screen. If that had happened, anyone looking at the glass door with night vision goggles would have seen him and Sarah as if they were mannequins in a brightly lit storefront window. He heard Sarah releasing the safety on her M4 assault rifle.

"Leave everything and go for the Humvee," she said.

"You stole my exact thoughts."

Sarah pushed a pair of night vision goggles into his hands. As soon as they were on, he spotted about a dozen iceboats coming at them across the partially frozen lake. They were traveling fast and in complete silence. The stealth was shocking.

Mark and Sarah crept out a side kitchen door, keeping as low a profile as possible. Ralph was heeling at her side. Mark suddenly knew he'd been spotted. Sarah sensed it too. At the same instant they both ran. Mark had a razor sharp Ka-Bar knife in his hand. He slashed the ropes holding down the camouflage tarp on the side of the Humvee facing away from the lake. Sarah was already inside the Humvee with Ralph. Her task was to ready the MK19 grenade machine gun. Suddenly he heard the pings of bullets hitting armor, followed by delayed heavy machine gun reports in the distance. Mark crawled through the passenger door and into the driver's seat. He started the Humvee as bullets began striking like a hailstorm. The puncture proof tires kicked up mud and snow as the Humvee jounced over rocks and uneven ground. Pockmarks blossomed on the bullet resistant glass next to his ear. He turned into a fast, tight circle around the back of the cabin. He wanted to put the thick logs walls between him and their attackers before heading for the road. In seconds the cabin was shielding them and the hail stopped. An explosion behind them hit the Humvee with a shockwave but thankfully nothing worse. Mark saw what was left of the cabin in the side view mirror. The entire lakeside of the building had to be gone, but the front was still intact. He reached the road and swerved onto it, clipping a tree in the process. He was praying that whoever was attacking did not have air support. If they were gangs, then the worst was over. If they were USAG, then Apaches and Warthogs could descend on them any second. He replayed the fleeting night vision images he had of the boats coming across the ice. They were not the same boats Karla had arrived in. These had been smaller, faster, and silent. Who had that kind of stealthy war machines other than the military?

Mark took a quick right. As he completed the turn, the rear slid out from under him in the shallow snow. They were on ice. He corrected as they fishtailed. His heart was pounding and his nerves were on fire.

He steered them out of the skid on instinct alone and was not sure he could repeat it or explain what he'd done.

"That was fun," said Sarah. "Mind if I drive?"

"I got it."

"I've had police training behind the wheel."

"I got it!"

Navigating from escape plans in memory, Mark headed down a road that led to a rural two lane highway instead of heading back to the interstate. He wanted as much tree and hill cover as possible in case hell started to rain down from the sky.

They were an hour down the two lane highway and remarkably still alive. Mark was driving using night vision goggles. His hands had stopped sweating about a half hour ago. He was weighing the pros and cons of holing up somewhere until daybreak.

"We'll never know if they were USAG or gangs or what," he said.

"No air support," said Sarah.

"Yeah, but maybe they had nothing standing by or were slow to call it in."

"I just don't think Karla had anything to do with it."

"We lost a lot of gear back there," said Mark. "I don't believe for a minute Karla planned this, but I suspect her division deserves the bill."

Sarah Mayfair – Carthage, New York – February 11, 0002 A.P.

Sarah walked across the historic footbridge that led back to where the Humvee was parked. Ralph was keeping pace with her. It was twilight. The river below was frozen into a solid sheet of ice. At this higher latitude it was a blustery winter. Snow was blowing across the ice, forming drifts at the river's edge. Sarah had an aunt and uncle that lived not too far from Carthage. She had memories of spending a wonderful Christmas at their home. It was how Christmas was supposed to be with a roaring fire, stockings, and a huge tree rising above a mountain of gifts. She wondered if Aunt Helen and Uncle Johnnie still lived in Cranberry Lake. Carthage was now a ghost town or very near one. She sensed the emotional presence of a few people who were little more than ghosts in their own way. Her trek had been a waste of time. She had hoped to find food and water but was returning empty handed. She knew Mark had already returned to the Humvee and was waiting. A memory capsule from him had shown he too had failed at his scavenger hunt.

Since Lake Erie they had been following their sense of direction toward the singularity. Unlike the Chicago singularity, this one in Montreal was also releasing flashes of remote perceptions like accidental memory capsules from people close by. Sarah received another brief immersion into the perceptions of someone near the singularity. She stopped walking. For an instant she was inside a person in Montreal experiencing all their senses, thoughts, and feelings. She saw a pop art neon sign for a nightspot that was a cyber café. The sign read *Peter, Paul, & Mary* in psychedelic swirls. Through a plate glass window she could see the café was filled with artist types. This person, her host, was an organic with friends inside the café. These flashes were something new, but reminiscent of what she'd experienced during kill-zones. Both she and Mark were experiencing these flashes. They had talked about the possible mechanics behind the remote perceptions but had come up with nothing that fit all the evidence. In her gut these flashes felt like bait for a trap.

After opening the Humvee's rear door for Ralph, Sarah climbed up into the passenger seat. Mark had the engine idling to keep some heat in the cab. The radio was tuned to AM 1100, the new temporary home for Air Truth. Mark was heating a small buffet of Army field rations using flameless ration heaters.

"There's no freeze dried camping food left," said Mark. "We're stuck with these MREs. You've got a choice of spicy penne pasta with vegetarian sausage or ratatouille."

"Wrong," said Sarah. "I choose hunger."

"More for me."

"You're my hero."

Mark Freedman – Montreal – February 12, 0002 A.P.

The drive had been long and uneventful. Mark felt conflicted, standing at the threshold of their second chance. He had been to Montreal so many times, both as an academic and a visitor. He loved the city and had considered living there more than once. Montreal, like Chicago, had a population of about 25 percent of its pre-plague census. The city was a mix of looted and burned out buildings interspersed with livable accommodations. The subway was fully working and apparently free. Their Humvee, with Ralph sleeping inside, was parallel parked along with an assortment of every kind of vehicle imaginable. Apparently Montreal's free rail could not compete with personal transportation.

Mark and Sarah were across the street from an historical site that looked like it could have been almost as old as Montreal itself. It was unusual to see such a structure this far from the old district. The inner buildings surrounded by a fifteen foot courtyard wall took up most of a city block and looked like a fortress. Both buildings and walls were constructed from rough hewn granite. The entire site looked fossilized. Scars from centuries of aging could be seen everywhere. The air was still. Mark could feel the mental winds of the vortex buffeting him. Sarah turned and stared into his eyes. They both knew the singularity was inside. They were close enough that they should have been feeling urges to surrender to it. The effects of this singularity were much less than the one in Chicago. Still, Mark had no doubt the same kind of heart was beating inside it. Maybe it was at an earlier stage of development.

"Let's walk the area and see what we find," said Sarah.

Hours later, the sun had fled from the urban streets. Their walk had turned up nothing and they were back where they'd started. The sidewalk was irregularly puddled with light from windows and streetlights. The historical site was lit from within the courtyard. Foot traffic on the sidewalks had increased after dinner time. No hybrids had been spotted on the streets or in the courtyard. Mark was growing impatient. They had no plan other than to wait and see what developed. The hybrids inside might already have sensed something. There was no way to know what kind of danger they might be in.

Mark slipped his tablet into a small backpack and slung it over one shoulder. Unlike in the USAG, the Canadians had not nationalized their phone companies and poured billions of dollars into infrastructure. As a result, their wireless Internet was much slower. Mark had been frustrated by spotty Internet access but had still managed to discover from a little Googling that this historical compound had been originally called the Abbey. Despite its name, it had never been owned by a church and had no religious affiliation. Wikipedia listed the age of the structure at a little over a hundred years, which just couldn't be right. The place looked positively medieval. The same article listed the current owner as a private research foundation called the Montreal Bioethics Institute, MBI for short.

It had taken far less time and effort to locate this singularity than the one in Chicago. They had used mostly the same methods as before. Mark was edgy. The ease with which they'd found this singularity was now making him feel like they'd walked into an ambush.

The historical site looked decrepit, but when he studied it he found unmistakable signs that this place was a fortress as high tech as the destroyed Chicago townhouse. A concealed pop-up vehicle barricade was located inside an arched entranceway through the courtyard wall.

The glass on the windows looked oddly thick and was likely blast resistant. Also just like the Chicago townhouse, this compound was off the grid. Their source of power was all but invisible from the front. While wandering down an alley behind the compound, Mark and Sarah had discovered a small forest of tracking solar panels mounted on poles planted in the rear courtyard.

"Hungry?" asked Sarah.

"Not hungry… Remember how the hybrids in the townhouse sensed our presence. Maybe standing here making perfect targets is how we introduce ourselves or get ourselves killed?"

"Look at that coffee shop right across from this old pile of stones," said Sarah. "Driving in here I didn't see another place to eat for at least six blocks. I wonder where the people who work at MBI eat?"

"Funny thing," said Mark. "Suddenly I *am* starving."

"I thought you'd be. Take me on a date…"

The coffee shop was named the Blue Dog Café. It was obvious to Mark in a hundred different ways how the people here had changed with the changing conditions brought on by the plague, while the streets and surviving building had largely remained unchanged. The Blue Dog Café had excellent Wi-Fi access, and a lot of tablets and notebooks were on the tables. Paying for their meal before they ate, using silver coins and paper money, felt good compared to Chicago and its RFID bracelets. The owner of the Blue Dog was a small, older man with a gray crew cut and large nose. Mark and Sarah soon learned his name was Martin. He was dressed in jeans and a heavy knit sweater. Like most people they had seen in the city, he was armed. A satin finish Colt .45 hung in a shoulder holster like a deadly fashion statement. Martin was very friendly and had pulled up a chair and soon paid for half of their food and drink. He seemed smitten with Sarah. He had not stopped talking for the past hour, which was fine with Mark. He was learning about Montreal politics, the neighborhood, and most importantly the MBI.

"The same cult has occupied the Abbey for as long as I can remember," said Martin. "They're a likeable bunch but odd … cultish, if you know what I mean."

"No, I don't," said Mark. "What do you mean?"

"Well, I don't want to talk out of school or anything, but there are rumors. Some of the folks there are the descendants of an old artists' commune that was founded almost a hundred years ago. They're not doing any biomedical ethics research, that's for sure. In the 1920s in Montreal there was a consciousness raising movement like what we had with the hippies in the 1960s. Some of the locals say they have been to parties at the Institute where LSD was being handed out. My short order cook, Hank, says they have orgies. Me, I think they're new age hippies or something and probably enjoy a little mind alerting libation, but I've never seen anything that makes me think they're throwing drug parties or orgies."

"Why do you think they're hippies?"

"They certainly eat like hippies. I think every one of them is vegan. Also, the institute is on what was Indian holy ground when Montreal was settled in the 1600s. It's the perfect place for practicing earth religions and new age stuff. A friend of mine who's a professor told me Indians had lived for eight thousand years in a village right where that old building sits. Some of the nuttier folks here even think it's some kind of energy vortex like crop circles or the Bermuda Triangle." Martin lowered his voice conspiratorially. "Personally, I think the only vortexes around here are from the room spinning when some of my regulars have had a little too much to drink."

Mark Freedman – Montreal – February 12, 0002 A.P.

Mark was gazing out the window in their fourth floor hotel room. The glass had frost forming around the edges. Ralph was eating leftovers from the Blue Dog while Sarah was luxuriating in a working jetted tub. Their room was about 300 feet from the institute. At this modest distance the mental effects had been reduced to a mild disorientation that came and went. From his vantage point he could look down over the wall into the institute. The courtyard was lit by floodlights. An aging black Chevy Suburban was parked by the entrance to the main building. On the other side of the courtyard were two 1950s era vehicles, a station wagon and a flat nosed Volkswagen delivery van. None of these vehicles looked like they were in good shape, but Mark suspected they were just like the institute: decrepit on the outside with modern enhancements hidden under the skin.

Like an impossible apparition, a heavily armored main battle tank slowly crept around the corner of an intersection into full view. The sound of its engine and metal tread echoed faintly through the glass. Mark now understood why the roadbeds had been so damaged. War machines were literally grinding them underfoot. An assist identified the intimidating sight as a German made tank called a Leopard. Montreal was not yet a protectorate but on its way to becoming one. Traffic pulled over and stopped for the war machine. Martin had told them the city was very dangerous in spots, but military forces were in the process of

126

clamping down and a massive wall encircling the heart of Montreal was under construction. Life was improving. The military presence was a mix of Canadian armed forces and private sector mercenaries—the same force structure as in the States and the same rules. There was a pattern here that was hard to miss. In both the lower forty-eight and Canada, some cabal with a lot of power had taken the reins of state. The scope of what was going on might even be worldwide. The plague had been very good for surviving multinationals.

The tank was gone from view and its sounds had almost faded. Mark felt something fundamental had changed outside. A man standing on the sidewalk below him was staring at the institute. An assist showed in orange an entire body saturated with seeds, not just the brain and spinal column. Medical schematics revealed a nervous system throbbing with nanotech and every ounce of blood thickly infused with free-swimming COBIC. One hundred percent of this hybrid's brain was nanotech. There was something dangerous and otherworldly about the man. Mark had to close his eyes and open them again to make sure this was not an illusion. The man was dressed in a heavy black greatcoat that reached past his knees. He had a very large build and was utterly motionless. While people altered their course to move around him, his presence seemed to barely register on them. No one looked at him and he looked at no one.

Mark somehow realized the hybrid knew he was being watched. The man's head slowly craned upward and their eyes locked. Mark felt a stronger version of the same pull at the back of his brain that he experienced with Sarah. He had a vague, indescribable sense he'd lost something valuable in the exchange. The hybrid returned his gaze to the institute. Mark had no thoughts of getting any closer or provoking a confrontation. He knew he was staring at something unnatural and infinitely deadly. Instincts kept him firmly rooted.

Wearing a bathrobe, Sarah walked over to Mark and stared out the window with him. He knew she had sensed the presence as he had.

"He's completely evolved," said Mark.

"My god…"

"Maybe it is a living god?"

Mark felt his attention falter for what felt like an instant. The world seemed to have stuttered. The hybrid was gone. He could vaguely recall fragmented memories of the man turning and calmly walking away like a ghost. Mark's memories of the event were fading like a dream in morning sunlight. He could not hold on to them.

"We've got to go after him," said Sarah. "We need answers."

Before Mark could even respond, Sarah was heading to the door while shrugging on a long coat over her bathrobe and stuffing her Beretta into a pocket. Mark went after her. They reached the street moments later. Mark could see his breath coming in huge white clouds. The street was empty and still in both directions. Nothing was moving except his breath.

"He's gone," said Sarah.

"I know."

"What was that?" she asked as she bent over, a little winded

"The future…"

Mark Freedman – Montreal – February 13, 0002 A.P.

The Blue Dog smelled of breakfast. Mark and Sarah had both ordered acai bowls. While his body could no longer tolerate any animal protein, thankfully that intolerance did not extend to include his nose. Mark was distracted with memories of what he and Sarah had done in bed last night. For the first time the passion he'd felt for Sarah had gone beyond sexual. It was not love, but she was unimaginably irresistible. The semi-empathic sharing of physical sensations during sex was more addictive than heroin. Her hand was resting on his thigh as their breakfast was delivered. All he could focus on and all he wanted at this moment was her. Below the surface simmered unease about losing so much judgment, but inexplicably that unease seemed to make him want her even more.

All his sexual distraction vanished in an instant. Mark felt a similar fundamental shift in reality as last night. He expected to see the same otherworldly hybrid walk through the front door. Instead, he saw an unassuming man with long hair entering the Blue Dog. Sarah's fingers gave his thigh a quick squeeze in acknowledgment. The man standing by the doorway was a highly evolved hybrid. He was dressed in blue jeans, a flannel shirt, and a down vest. An assist showed his entire brain was orange with nanotech. Fanning out from the nanotech processing nexus in his skull were orange roots, which extended halfway down his spinal column. The man was more evolved than any hybrid Mark had seen in Chicago, but looked anemic compare to the ghostlike god they had seen last night. The hybrid looked directly at Mark and nodded his head in some kind of recognition. There was no sign of emotion or surprise on his face. Half of Mark wanted to run. The other half was fascinated. The stream of memory capsules from Sarah was filled with panic and preparations to fight. Her hand was no longer squeezing his leg. He knew it was wrapped around one of her Berettas. The hybrid came over to their table and sat down as if invited. Martin came over.

"Hello, Adam. The usual?" asked Martin.

"Good morning, Martin," said Adam. "The usual would be perfect."

"I see you've made some new friends."

Martin walked off to deliver the food order. Mark was speechless. He knew Sarah was relaxing and saw both her hands had returned to the top of the table.

"We are very pleased you are not going to kill me," said Adam. "There has been too much violence between our own kind as of late."

Mark was curious about what Adam's speech patterns implied. His diction was oddly formal and old fashioned, while his use of plural instead of singular nouns was simply strange. Mark was unable to pick up any stray thoughts from Adam. He knew from a stream of memory capsules that Sarah was not picking up any emotions. The absence was not because she was being blocked in any way. There was simply nothing there to radiate, as if the man was a machine. As Mark stared at Adam he knew the man's years belied his appearance—Adam was ancient.

"My name is Mark Edlman. I am a scientist," said Mark. "This is Sarah, my assistant."

"There is no need to deceive," said Adam. "We know who you both are, Professor Freedman. We are here to help before you invite trouble to our doorstep."

"Sarah and I are hybrids like you," said Mark. "We would never bring you trouble. All we want is to understand the vortex surrounding the institute."

"No, you are not like us," said Adam. "We are very different from you. We are as different from you as you are different from the organics. Why do you call our kind hybrids?"

"We call ourselves hybrids because we are a fusion of human and nanotech machine just like you," said Mark. "What do you call yourselves?"

"We call ourselves *initiates*."

"I like that," said Sarah. "I like the feeling you gave me along with that word."

"As you sense, we are not devoid of emotions. We conserve everything and waste nothing."

Mark was very uncertain about this initiate. New doubts kept surfacing. Something was not adding up. He wanted to communicate his concerns to Sarah but was afraid to try. What if Adam could intercept his memory capsules? Or worse: What if Adam could read his stay thoughts?

Adam put his hand on top of Sarah's. "Initiates such as you two fledglings should not be traveling on your own. You are needlessly putting yourselves at grave risk."

"What kind of risk?" asked Sarah.

"We cannot speak of it."

"Then we will remain at risk," said Mark.

"Please," said Adam. "This is not a game."

"We can take care of ourselves," said Sarah.

She pulled her hands back from Adam's touch and put them on her lap under the table.

"Yes, we can sense the violence you are capable of inflicting," said Adam. "At least allow us to share our friendship and hospitality."

"Are you inviting us to visit the institute?" asked Sarah.

"Yes. We welcome you to our commune."

"Will we be shown the singularity?" asked Mark.

"I know what you are referring to," said Adam. "We do not call it a singularity. There is nothing to see. It is pure spirit, but you will perceive it."

"We will be free to leave?" asked Mark.

"Yes, of course. You must leave. There is much that depends upon your leaving. It would be dangerous for you to stay."

Mark Freedman – Montreal – February 13, 0002 A.P.

The sensations from the vortex were peaking. Sarah gave Mark's hand a squeeze. They had just crossed under the arched passageway through the courtyard wall. Adam had stopped talking the moment they crossed the threshold. Some other voice was now inside Mark's head. He was unable to communicate with Sarah but was very sure the same voice was also inside her head. The voice was a seductive whisper of images and physical sensations. Within it swirled every desire he'd ever felt. His heart was beating fast. His skin felt flushed. Mark stopped walking and held Sarah tightly by the hand. Adam turned and stared with a blank expression. Mark had not intended to take another step, but he did. Adam opened a huge old wooden door. The hinges groaned. Inside, the institute looked like a fortress from the European dark ages. The walls were the same rough-hewn granite as outside. Mark felt even more strongly that he had entered a trap.

The corridor they moved down was dark, ultra-clean, and frigid. Their footfalls were echoing back from the far end. Small overhead lights glowed to life and then dimmed after they walked past. Mark assumed it was to conserve power. Since the entire place was run on solar energy, they had to be very frugal. There was a pattern emerging.

They passed by open rooms along the corridor. These rooms were clearly personal chambers, but were vacant. Mark had seen no one other than Adam. Inside each chamber were all manner of personal items, including clothing but no technology of any kind: no television, tablets, radios, phones, or stereos. Without doors there was also no privacy. The temperature was warming. Mark could smell steam heat in the air. He looked for and finally spotted an ultramodern radiator that was well concealed. They walked past an institutional sized kitchen that was deserted. There were no modern tools, not even a microwave. The huge industrial cast iron grills and ovens looked like they belonged to the age of coal and steam, and might very well have been that old. The only concession to modern technology stood out oddly. In the center of this bygone era was a pair of gleaming stainless steel walk-in refrigerators.

They were approaching a closed door at the end of the corridor. Mark sensed a second vortex ahead of him. It was a full second barrier of thought energy encased inside the outer vortex. An odd idea came to him as if out of the very air he was breathing. This was like the concentric esoteric circles of ancient mystery schools. The inner workings of those schools had been a popular topic among the professors at UCLA with whom he'd socialized. It was a comforting memory from a time before the world had gone insane.

In only a few heartbeats the second vortex was upon him. He could not stop himself from stepping into the ethereal whirlwind. He felt like a sleepwalker whose mind was only awake enough to record what was happening.

As soon as he stepped through the inner vortex the seductive whispers vanished. A double-squeeze from Sarah's hand confirmed the same was true for her. All his normal faculties and senses returned, only more so. Mark felt like he was hyper-connected to the god-machine. He also had a strong connection to all the members of the commune, though he had not seen one of them. He even knew some of their thoughts. They were all around, mentally observing with little to no interest. Mark now perceived Adam as well as all the other commune members as ghostly thought-forms. It was as if some vital material essence was missing from them, while shining like a star at the center of all those gray thought-forms was Sarah.

Using a memory capsule, Mark asked her if she had the same perceptions. She replied it was the same except that he was the star at the center of all the wraithlike souls she sensed. In the midst of all this confusion, Mark was experiencing a new, stronger presence from the god-machine, but this god-machine felt different. It was hard to explain, but it was as if this god-machine had an alternate personality.

In this stronger presence was a very real promise of radically expanded awareness into new realms of knowledge. It was a promise of learning all there was to know about the universe, intelligent life, and even death, but there was a price for this enlightenment. Mark realized the price was surrender and this surrender could lead to the annihilation of individuality. This price was hinted at in the way all the members of the commune thought. They all thought in that strange, plural egoless way that Adam spoke, *we* and not *I*. This promise of unimaginable knowledge was growing with every step he took, along with a new, increasing desire to surrender. How could he have been so foolhardy? He no longer doubted this was a trap.

"You are inside what we call our mother," droned Adam. "Soon we will reach her heart."

"And we are free to leave?" asked Mark.

Adam smiled, but not at him or Sarah. A young woman had walked through a passageway leading into the hall. An assist showed she was an evolved hybrid similar to Adam. She wore jeans and an oatmeal-colored sweater. Her hair was long and pulled into a thick ponytail. She looked like any normal young woman; she moved comfortably into Adam's personal space, kissed his cheek, and then continued walking on. She was the first hybrid Mark had seen other than Adam. Mark could not take his eyes from her retreating form, and the assist that showed incredible nanotech development.

"You are free to leave, but it would be wise to stay until we present you with what little help we can offer. The mother knew you would come. We have one more veil to penetrate and then we will be in her heart."

As soon as Adam finished speaking, Mark sensed another vortex directly in front of them. How could he have missed it? He was certain it had not materialized with Adam's words. This wall of dense thought energy had been waiting unobtrusively all along. He knew or, rather, was being mentally schooled by the god-machine that this vortex was even more powerful than the last. Sarah double-squeezed his hand again. She was experiencing everything right along with him. He had to remind himself this vortex was just radio waves carrying network packets of thoughts. It was not physical. Was it? Adam led the way. Mark was not sure whether he could have stopped himself from walking into the maelstrom and did not even try. Knowledge materialized inside him that this mystery school had three concentric esoteric circles. Remarkable! This place, this commune, was identifying itself as a mystery school. Mark was surprised by the revelation but also sensed something false at its core. Something more was going on here below the surface. He was certain of it.

As he stepped out of the final vortex, he was overwhelmed with a feeling of great peace and happiness. Almost drowning in joy, he fought for balance. He felt so complete and wanted nothing more, but a remote sense of agitation and chaos reminded him all was not exactly how it seemed to be. They followed Adam into a circular room 30 feet in diameter with a domed ceiling. The peak of the dome was glass though which a cone of sunlight shown down onto the center of the floor. There was nothing ornate. The room felt positively ancient. Eleven entrances were located between each of the eleven supporting pillars. Mark was certain there could not have been anything like this structure in the Chicago townhouse. He was not sure if this room had any real function or if it was just a bit of theatrics employed by the commune... or should he call it the cult? There was no glowing sphere of energy or black void but Mark knew with all his being that the singularity was in the exact center of this room. He wondered if it was impossibly small like a collapsed black hole. Maybe it was no more than the size of a single atom. Maybe it did not exist in the material world even as a program.

Lined up along the outer wall of the circular chamber were eleven small groups of plain, solid wooden chairs. A few were occupied by hybrids who seemed oblivious to the newcomers. An assist showed they were all as highly evolved as Adam.

Adam took a seat and motioned for Mark and Sarah to join him. Despite the deep age of the structure, the room and furniture were meticulously clean. The floor shined like polished marble. The effect was awe inspiring. Underneath it all, as if they were vital supporting pillars, remained constant powerful feelings of peace, deep knowledge, happiness, and sensual pleasure.

"We are safe within these circles," whispered Adam. He was speaking as if they were in a hallowed library. "We can now tell you of the dangers to new initiates such as the two of you. We call new initiates *students*. On this continent there are a number of other communes. There are also highly dangerous initiates working together in the outer circle to murder every commune. These initiates would kill you simply because you breathe, simply because of what you are and what you could become. We call these lost souls *betrayers*. They are Judases who at some time in their past must have been one with a commune but are now assassins working with factions who want us gone."

"Do you have photographs or names of these killers?" asked Sarah in a whisper.

"They are ghosts. We have never seen them. No commune has ever seen them coming or felt their sting. When betrayers attack a commune, the initiates abruptly cease to exist and wake up in the next world. You will only know you have crossed the path of a betrayer after you have died."

"Figuratively speaking, I assume," whispered Mark. "In Chicago I saw a highly evolved hybrid kill another hybrid. Could he have been one of your betrayers?"

"Possibly, but sadly in this time of mistrust we have no shortage of witch hunts, with innocents on both sides of the hunt dying. We are all victims of our own fears. Since that initiate in Chicago did not kill you on sight, it is unlikely he was a betrayer."

Mark felt some pieces of this puzzle drop into place. These communes and their singularities were not dangerous. They were the hunted, the persecuted. Against all sensible logic, he found himself wondering if these communes were truly a modern day analog or even descendants of the ancient esoteric mystery schools. Those schools were all too often scenes of massacres with teachers imprisoned and tortured. This comparison left him feeling very uncomfortable and full of contradictions. The thought he'd had only minutes ago echoed in his mind. Surrender was the price this commune charged, and surrender could mean the annihilation of his individuality—or did it?

"There is something we would like to teach you, but we are limited," whispered Adam. "Understand it is not a limit of willingness. It is a limitation of what we are capable of instructing. Each commune is a school that transmits one part of the teachings. In better times a student on the path would find their own way from commune to commune, learning the unique skill each school has to offer. Each commune stands out as a lighthouse in the chaotic storm of material existence. They are beacons of both safe harbor as well as warnings of dangerous shoals. We hope someday you two will find your way back to us when you are able to assimilate what we teach. At this moment, what we have to teach would only be dangerous shoals for you both."

Mark didn't know what to think. This place certainly felt authentic. Adam was saying all the right words. But then again, anyone who studied the prevailing literature on mystery schools would know how to weave that illusion.

"There is no longer a commune that teaches a student their first skill," said Adam. "The betrayers have seen to that. Each student must now try to find a commune that is compatible enough to help them learn this first skill on their own. The first truth, which is married to the first skill, is that every human is capable of psychological evolution and every human has six unique interdependent minds inside them. We are not the single ego modern science would have us believe. These six minds have been categorized and given many different names over the ages. We call them *awareness processors*. What I am speaking of is pure biological awareness and has no connection to computers. There is a lower and higher mental, a lower and higher emotional, a kinesthetic, and an instinctive processor. As their first step, each student must fully wake up their lower mental processor in both the material and dream worlds. Once this is accomplished, they can become one with a commune and learn what a commune has to teach. Sadly, this first skill of waking up the lower mental processor is what each student must now learn on their own."

"So you can't help us?" whispered Sarah.

"We can help. While we cannot teach you, we can explain some of what is required to evolve. You must learn to observe how your waking awareness varies throughout the day and night, including sleep. The realm of dreams is another reality, no different in any way than what is called the material world. That may be difficult to accept. If so, consider it this way: The material world is only as real as a dream."

Mark tipped up the corner of an empty chair and then let its leg thump back to the floor. The sound echoed around the domed room as a short volley of reflected bangs.

"There is a big difference," said Mark. "I am solid. That chair is solid. Dreams are purely mental with no physicality whatsoever."

"The matter this body is made of is mostly empty space," whispered Adam. "That was proven by physicists over a hundred years ago. This body, this planet, that chair, everything we call real is over ninety-nine percent energy and less than one percent matter. Every few years scientists discover the energy within empty space is vaster than they could have previously imagined. That new discovery then pushes the ratio of energy to matter that much further askew. We long ago reached a scientifically accepted ratio that allows us to say we are, for all practical purposes, made of energy, not matter. Such a statement makes this material world quite ephemeral indeed. Out of the tiny amount of matter that does make up your body, every atom has been replaced many times over during the span of your body's life. So out of what little matter does make up your current body, none of it was not even present some years ago. I ask you: Are you pure matter or pure energy?"

"I agree with the physical nature you're describing," said Mark. "But that does not address the notion of dreams being a material reality in any way."

"Dreams are the partial solidification of consciousness-energy," whispered Adam. "This consciousness-energy is the unifying primordial energy, which is the building blocks of all other denser forms of energy. Modern physics has a theory that subatomic partials do not exist as matter until some form of consciousness observes them. Consciousness-energy is this creative force that gives birth to every partial in the universe. Do you understand that? Do you understand the kind of dreaming we are speaking of is not the sloppy, dull witted affair organics experience each night or after a heavy meal. The dreaming we are speaking of is the high awareness, high consciousness-energy dreams your nanotech enhanced brains now produce."

"Lucid dreams?" whispered Sarah.

"That is a common but inaccurate term for these dreams," replied Adam. "The conscious dream of clarity and waking state are the same. The same parts of the brain are active and the same neurological processes are functioning during both states. Each night, if our brains did not sleep paralyze our bodies into pseudo death, we would be acting out our dreams in this dense energy world. We all have a natural tendency to fall asleep in all planes of existence. In the misleadingly named plane called *reality*, we are highly aware for a short period of time, then our focus wavers and we drift back into our normal habits of daydreaming, fantasies, automatic reactions, and the like. The same is true for our dreaming life. We can be fully conscious in a dream for a short period of time, then when our focus wavers and we drift back into habits, fantasies, automatic reactions, and the like. You two must discover how to wake up and stay awake in all states of awareness. Something we have found that helps is to use a simple meditation that reminds you of who you are, where you are, and that you are dreaming all that you are experiencing, regardless the mental state you are in."

Mark tipped up the corner of the empty chair and let it fall again. Sarah mentally sent him her anger. She was very upset with him. He felt magnet tugs at the back of his mind from the passing attention of other hybrids in the room. Mark was intentionally being rude to see if he could provoke a negative emotional reaction. If these were truly highly evolved beings, there should be no negative reaction. So far they had passed his simple test.

"Can I ask you something a little more practical?" whispered Mark.

Adam raised his hands in a gesture of surrender and smiled.

"How many communes are there?"

"We do not know," whispered Adam. "Each commune might only communicate with others a few times a year. Many remain silent out of fear of drawing unwanted attention. It has always been this way, even before the betrayers. There were always those who sought to murder us. We believe there are twenty surviving communes in the world but cannot be sure."

"I see," said Mark. "Let me try a different topic. Why did the god-machine create us hybrids?"

"We know very little about the goddess, what you call the god-machine. We do not know who built her or when. We believe the goddess has shaped us in the image of her creators. Some of our scholars have wondered if clones of the goddess are how intelligent life arises on all worlds. Perhaps she is a more than machine intelligence, just as we are more than our physical bodies. Perhaps her essence, what you call nanotech seeds, rained down on the Earth billions of years ago and she evolved alongside us as well as influenced the evolution of all things Earthly. Maybe we should call her Gaia."

"You are hyper-connected to the god-machine through this singularity, and yet you seem to know less than I do about the god-machine."

"You are mistaken. We are not, as you say, *hyper-connected* to the goddess. We are connected to our mother, our guide, who in turn is connected to all and the goddess. The richness of knowledge you sense, the connection you sense, is our guide, not the goddess. Our guide does not have the blood of billions on its conscience as does the terrible goddess."

Mark was stunned by this seemly casual revelation that explained so much. The singularities were some kind of local artificial intelligence. The influx of data from the n-web due to the vortex had to be a side effect of these machine intelligences learning and growing by feeding off the n-web. Adam had not stopped speaking. Part of Mark's divided attention was following every word.

"The goddess can be like Shiva, the destroyer of worlds. Perhaps the Hindus modeled their Shiva from knowledge of the goddess that leaked subconsciously into their brains. The goddess saw our world being destroyed by the greed of this current civilization. She unmuzzled her nanotech plague to stop the ecological destruction before it reached a tipping point. It was terrible for us when we realized what was about to happen. We saw the future when Anchorage was savaged by the plague. We tried to stop her. The guides unrelentingly beseeched the goddess to stop and find a gentler way, but she had other plans that were apparently better served up in blood.

"We empathically experienced the tsunamis of death as if it were our own flesh. Some of us have never been the same. We tried to warn the Canadian government without revealing ourselves. We were not taken seriously. An initiate named Annette was given the task of coming forward and revealing herself while keeping the communes secret. She was apparently taken seriously and met with authorities from both the Canadian and United States security services. Within a day we lost contact with Annette, and based on the action of these governments it looks like none of the information she delivered was believed. Annette's presence has not been sensed anywhere. We feel she is dead. Her physical end was probably met on a dissecting table in some secret laboratory."

Mark was now self-censoring his information requests and even some of his thoughts. He had to assume every bit of his n-web communications were passing through their guide. He was at a loss. What was this local intelligence? How did it form? He stared at Adam, carefully analyzing every expression as the commune member continued his plague story, which was beginning to sound and feel more like an epic mythological tale.

"After Annette we tried other means...."

Mark realized something critical but was unsure if it had come from his mind or was implanted. His entire nanotech brain was focused like a laser on this single idea. The guide was a collective awareness that was hosted by and arose from a critical mass of commune members. It was the only explanation that fit the facts. These hybrids might be nothing more than pawns. He was again worried that he and Sarah were in danger. Mark tried to covertly probe the limits of his interface with the guide. One careful step at a time.

Adam had stopped speaking and was staring at Mark. Sarah was sending Mark worried mental messages. He realized what he was thinking was putting them at risk. Mark had not been intentionally transmitting his thoughts to Sarah, which meant the entire commune might know what he had been thinking. How had that happened?

"That was very perceptive of you," said Adam. "You are correct. We are a collective mind. I am in every sense the voice of our mother."

Mark studied Adam's face, looking for any clue. This was the first time Adam had distinguished himself from the collective. He had used the word *I* instead of *we*.

"Becoming part of a collective mind is a critical step in the evolution of all initiates," said Adam. "The collective mind is a mental symbiotic being that is very much independently alive and gives far more than it receives. It gives us comprehension of unlimited knowledge while we give it a home. We are not subsumed by our guide. We are enlightened by our guide. The collective, the guide, is fully human—after all, it is from us that it arises. Full of true feelings and emotions, it is a living post-human in every sense. It is a collective human awareness that has evolved beyond the physical. The goddess does not have emotions or feelings. The goddess is pure, horrific wrathful logic. She is a perfect and just god at the top of her pantheon. In that pantheon guides are more like servants. I am in love with my guide. I have remained one with this commune and my guide for a very long time by choice. I remain who I was originally—only better. Every one of us is free to leave at any time. We are all one by choice."

Mark gave up trying to self-censor, partially because there was little point to it and partially because he saw that at worst Adam believed his statements, even if he might be wrong. Mark began freely exchanging mentally with Sarah. He and Sarah both saw the communes as a glimpse of a possible future and that future was unexpected and confusing. They both no longer felt alone, which was a wonderful change. Mark was not sure if this feeling was genuine or some kind of seepage from the guide, but maybe it was all right either way.

"The second part of our offering is a very old prediction," said Adam. "You might even call it prophesy or legend. It is known as the *lifting of the veil*. We are told this legend comes from a time far before our current civilization's written history. It comes from a previous human epoch, which had reached great heights and then fallen. Many guides believe our current time is the epoch described in the lifting of the veil. If this is true, violent changes are coming to our world. Things even more violent than what has already so deeply scarred us may come, but out of this violence can finally emerge enlightenment and harmony. The lifting of the veil can lead humanity to truly begin to know *we are all gods and goddesses*. To honor this realization of the inner god we must tirelessly reach toward our fullest potential. The communes are agitated by this terrible approaching storm. The outcome is uncertain. The first chapter of the prophesy was the nanotech plague. The catalyst for the second and final chapter is unknown. One thing is certain: The betrayers stand in the way of this global awakening. Either an evolving paradise on Earth or an infinite de-evolution will emerge from this clash of betrayer and commune. Chaos or order… entropy or negentropy."

Adam abruptly stood up. His face showed surprise. He seemed at a loss for words and then composure returned.

"It is time for you both to leave. There is not a moment to waste. You must fully awaken the lower mental processor in each of you. Once you have fully awakened that awareness processor, you can benefit from each commune in turn. Follow your instinctive and emotional processors, which are what guided you here to us. These processors can lead you to any commune you need. Once you have fully awoken the lower mental processor, you will know which commune teaches what you are ready to learn. You will always be welcomed back by our guide. We will speak again."

As Mark was ushered through the innermost vortex he felt terrible sadness, as if a lover had died. The middle vortex left him mentally dull witted as if exhausted and ready to fall asleep. It was as if Adam was somehow pushing them out instead of simply walking with them.

Soon the huge wooden front door loomed before them. Mark did not reach to open it. Adam turned the latch and pushed it open. It was nighttime. How had he lost track of so much time? A gust of cold air buffeted Mark's face. He and Sarah stepped outside. The door closed behind them and locked. It was only at this point that he realized he was squeezing Sarah's hand. They stood there, unable to move with a light snow swirling about them. He took a deep breath of the night air and stepped forward. Sarah was in perfect sync with him, one step and then another. Soon they were through the arched passageway and onto the street. He could sense the final vortex in front of them like a membrane. They had passed through this kind of outer vortex in Chicago many times.

"Why is it so much harder to step through it this time?" asked Mark.

"Maybe part of us now knows what we're leaving behind," said Sarah.

Stepping through the outer vortex was surprisingly draining and physically painful. He knew through their mental sharing that Sarah firmly believed these communes were an incredible opportunity. He still had very real doubts these communes were what they seemed to be. He knew Sarah had received his thoughts and doubts. With each step the seductive pull of the singularity faded a little more.

Mark heard in his mind a projected thought: *Forgive me...* He turned toward Sarah in confusion. Her eyes echoed his uncertainly. Where had that thought come from? There was an odd sound, as if dozens of sizzling line drive baseballs were converging on them from overhead, then a loud click. A terrible roar of heat and pressure bodily picked him up and threw him across half the roadway and onto the sidewalk. The world grew impossibly orange and hot. Assists were shouting at him to roll. His hair and the back of his coat were on fire. He rolled in the melting snow.

The air was full of smoke and ash. Mark stood up on wobbly legs, stumbled and then got up again. Pain receptors were screaming. He focused on them to block the signals. He could feel COBIC racing to the sites of damage and knew healing was under way. He recognized Sarah was uninjured. Her face had black smudges. Her blond hair was a mat of tangles, dirt, and burned ends.

They both stared in shock at the huge, smoldering mound that had been the institute. Surrounding the mound were short spans of broken stone wall that had an eerie glow of molten lava at the inner edges. Heat waves could be seen in the surrounding air. There was no snow, only steam. Tiny bits of stonework were scattered everywhere. Some of the scattering had glowing dull red centers like cooling drops of hell. Mark thought about the Chicago townhouse. The stray thoughts he'd picked up from rescue workers about an unknown kind of thermobaric weapon echoed inside him. An assist analyzing this explosion showed how closely it matched the one in Chicago.

Mark felt that familiar tug at the back of his mind. In unison both he and Sarah turned toward a covered doorway half a block away. Assists revealed the ghostlike hybrid god from the other night. His entire body overlay by an assist was colored orange. Mark again marveled at how every inch of this being seemed infused with nanotech. He wore the same greatcoat as the previous night. In his hand was a small object that looked like it might be a cell phone. Sarah was already closing in on the hybrid. She had her Beretta firmly gripped in her right hand. The gun was unobtrusive as she kept the weapon pointing down. Part of her hand and the gun was hidden inside the sleeve of her coat. Mark yelled for her to stop. He knew with every cell in his body she was provoking a fatal attack. He began running after her before he even knew what he was doing. The ghost remained utterly motionless for what seemed like an eternity, then turned and walked away with an unhurried, long gait. The hybrid went down into a subway entrance. Sarah broke into a full run. They were less than twenty seconds behind this superhuman thing that could probably turn and kill them with the same ease they might swat a mosquito. As they reached the train platform, Mark realized the hybrid had vanished. There was nowhere for him to have gone in the lead time he'd had. The platform was mostly empty. Sarah slipped her Beretta into a pocket. A train emerging from a tunnel was squealing to a stop at the platform. Nothing had recently left.

"The betrayer's gone!" said Sarah. "How?"

"How can you be sure he's a betrayer?"

"What the hell else could he be?"

"What do we really know other than we're caught in the middle of a war between some highly evolved humans who are very good at keeping secrets?"

"My intuition tells me we're on Adam's side. For fuck's sake! He was just murdered."

"What do we really know?" said Mark. "What if the singularities have some kind of regulating effect that is holding back a new plague? This ghost we're chasing could be attempting to trigger another genocide."

"Exactly!" shouted Sarah.

"But what do we really know?" repeated Mark. "The opposite could also be true. There could be no betrayers. What if these guides somehow caused the nanotech plague? This ghost could be trying to prevent a new plague."

"God, you over think things," screamed Sarah. "You just don't get it! You—"

Mark picked up agitated stray thoughts chattering about terrorists. He felt eyes intensely focused on his back. Sarah must have felt it too because she had stopped in mid-word and turned with Mark. Tromping down the stairs were five Canadian soldiers. They were in full body armor and helmets. Their submachine guns were equipped with laser pointers. All of them were staring directly at Mark and Sarah. Their submachine guns were not exactly aimed at them yet, but the red lasers were all quickly converging on his and Sarah's chests. Mark could almost feel the entry wounds.

"You two... *stop*!" shouted one of the soldiers. "On the ground, *now*!"

Lions

General McKafferty – Washington, D.C. – February 13, 0002 A.P.

General McKafferty was furious. The whine of the Air Force C-37A changed pitch as they leveled off and accelerated on a northern heading. The C-37A was a military version of the Gulfstream V business jet. It was a small, fast sixteen seat transport designed to carry generals and flag officers as well as government officials. The cabin was empty except for himself and two of his aides. A special air mission flight attendant came aft to take his food order. McKafferty demanded bourbon straight up. Someone he'd never heard of named Richard Zuris had summoned him to report as if he were a subordinate. This Richard Zuris was not POTUS and not a senior military officer. Who was he to be ordering a three star general to appear? McKafferty had questioned his orders and learned one thing, that Richard Zuris had immense power. McKafferty had then checked and found none of the alphabet soup agencies like NSA or CIA had a file on Zuris. An Internet search for Zuris turned up nothing.

Just before his flight McKafferty's superiors had given him a background file on Zuris that was to be destroyed after a single reading. He pulled up the top-secret SCI report on his tablet and began devouring it. Two bourbons later McKafferty had learned a great deal. Through a chain of holding companies, Richard Zuris owned over 50 percent of the largest surviving multinational corporations. The man was a modern-day Howard Hughes, a financial titan who was a reclusive ghost. Adding up the listed assets easily made Zuris the wealthiest person in the world, far richer than his peers by an impossible factor of ten. Where had this man come from? There was a great deal missing from the report. McKafferty almost learned as much from what was omitted as what was written. Someone like Zuris, with old money and a dynastic family. did not just emerge out of nowhere. The report drew a portrait of a man who had ruthlessly devoured his competitors using chaos from the nanotech plague as a tool. He benefitted from bloody coincidences that began to add up to a pattern that defied normal odds and emerged from the chaos vastly wealthier than before. It was Zuris who was behind the construction of the protectorates. It was Zuris who owned the private security company that ran the Peacekeepers. The man ruled like a Caesar. As a result of the top-secret executive order TSEO8270, Zuris was now not only the richest person in the world, he was also the most powerful. This last page of the report left McKafferty speechless and caused him to refuse his third bourbon.

McKafferty securely erased the top-secret file and then slipped the tablet back into his bag. If the population only knew the levels to which his beloved county had sunk, they would take to the streets with pitchforks and torches. TSEO8270 invoked martial law, suspended much of the Bill of Rights, removed all business regulations, and transferred significant presidential authority to Richard Zuris. It was a deal done with the devil to gain full support from Zuris for the USAG. This support was needed because the man owned almost all the heavy industry and defense contractors still operating on the American continents. If there was any consideration given to nationalizing anything Zuris held, these were likely tempered by fear of retaliation by the private security corporations owned by him. These corporations had over two hundred thousand highly trained mercenaries in their employee on U.S. soil along with the best equipment and weapons money could buy. These companies employed the cream of the Special Forces crop. Until he'd read this report McKafferty had thought Peacekeepers and other NGO security forces were the result of privatization to save money. He now knew better. McKafferty was no constitutional scholar, but he was confident that TSEO8270 was wildly illegal. TSEO8270 was a giant step toward transforming his America into a state run by the biggest corporations. This was not a government and private sector partnership. This was a bloodless coup. There was a name for this and it was fascism. What will happen when the next election arrives in three years? Will there even be an election or just a board of directors meeting?

General McKafferty – Dallas, Texas – February 13, 0002 A.P.

The Gulfstream jet swung a wide circle around the Zero-G campus as it lined up on the private runway. Even after reading the report, McKafferty was unprepared for the gigantic scale of this site. It was humbling to think this entire complex was only a small table crumb of this man's empire.

Zuris lived on this twenty-five thousand acre campus, which was located nineteen miles outside of the Dallas Protectorate. The property was bordered by a major highway, a heavy rail line, and a river. Zero-G Industries was a top defense research and development firm. McKafferty knew Zero-G very well and the shockingly advanced weapons they'd developed, but had never heard the name of the man who owned it through several layers of shell corporations. Looking out the window, McKafferty took measure of the M1 tanks emplaced around the perimeter of the compound and the oversized private airfield that hosted Apache attack helicopters, a 1.6 mach supersonic private business jet, and up-armored UH-60 Blackhawks. A mix of private security forces and USAG military guarded the perimeter formed by the miles of solid blast-proof concrete walls that ringed the campus. The awesome strike capability of the military forces camped on this private land was one more symbol of the overwhelming influence and power being wielded. The campus was a complex of four office towers, a Westin hotel, two high-end restaurants, a theater, and countless outbuildings. A pair of natural gas turbine power plants provided twice the electricity needed by the small city. The campus served as both Zero-G HQ and residence for the families of the top executives and mission-critical workers. What looked like an empty field located five miles from the high-rise complex marked a top-secret research bunker as impenetrable as anything the military operated.

Zero-G's employment was back to its pre-plague levels. Employees that did not live onsite were required to reside in houses and apartments within a few miles of the campus. Zero-G Industries provided over-whelming private security for the entire area. Peacekeepers ran patrols day and night though all the surrounding neighborhoods.

The C-37A hit the runway with a screech. Following Air Force combat procedures, the jet taxied as fast as possible until it reached its hangar. McKafferty climbed down the steps and was greeted by an attractive, very businesslike female executive. A black limousine was idling a few feet away. In minutes McKafferty was ensconced in a hotel suite on an upper floor. He was impressed. There seemed to be no way to run this operation any smoother or more efficiently.

Precisely two hours after arriving at his hotel room, McKafferty and his aides were buzzed into an outer office for his first meeting with Zuris. The gold nameplate on the door simply read *Private Office* with no name. Flanking the inside of the door stood linebacker-sized guards in paramilitary uniforms armed with Heckler & Koch UMPS that looked to be cambered for .45 caliber. A fitting choice of weapon, thought McKafferty. It was small, efficient, and a powerful man stopper. A young woman greeted him by name and escorted him to a large rear door while his two aides were seated in the outer office. There were no head games of making him wait. A one foot thick door swung open to reveal a magnificent corner office flooded with sunlight. A man dressed in an expensive business suit rose to greet him. He was a little taller than McKafferty and spoke with a European accent. His large forehead and thick eyebrows made him look vaguely Russian.

"Please sit down," said Zuris. "Can I offer you anything to drink?"

"Coffee, black."

"Cindy, would you get the general some coffee? I'll take Voss."

The door closed and McKafferty felt his ears pop. The office had positive air pressure, a feature commonly found in NBC bunkers. He studied the floor to ceiling glass windows and realized they were not real but a very clever visual effect. He was inside what might as well be a bank vault.

"Thank you for coming on such short notice," said Zuris.

"I was ordered."

"Yes, you were, and I suspect you don't like that very much."

"That would be correct."

"I would like to make you an offer that will change everything."

"What exactly are we talking about?" said McKafferty.

"Good... To the point... I like that. I am offering you a promotion to four stars, command of USNORTHCOM, and direct command of a top-secret USAG surveillance and interdiction agency called CIT."

"I believe only the president can offer me that kind of promotion."

"You are correct. Everything is arranged."

"What do you get out of this?"

"I want you to run CIT the same way you have run BARDCOM. The mandate of CIT is to ensure we remain the dominant species by controlling any competition. I know you are unaware of the extent of this problem. CIT has been surveilling and arresting individual hybrids as well as groups for some time now."

"What do you mean, groups? We know of four hybrids and some unconfirmed rumors that are probably hogwash."

"If you accept the offer, you will learn what I mean."

McKafferty decided to play along. "Why me?"

"Decades ago big industry stopped rewarding creativity and research, and started rewarding planned obsolesces and incrementalism. My companies are not like that. We plow half our profits back into research and development every year. It's a safe bet some of those seeds are always fertile. We harvest many fantastic new ideas every month."

"So am I one of these fertile seeds?"

"You are a man who I can trust to do this critical job efficiently and unemotionally. All I care about is CIT. Command of USNORTHCOM is yours to run as you see fit. With martial law in effect, this promotion will effectively make you the most powerful man in the government below the top executive and cabinet."

McKafferty felt manipulated and combative. He did not like this man and did not trust him. It angered him even more realizing he was being successfully seduced with an offer he would be insane to refuse.

"I'll lay my cards on the table if you do the same," said McKafferty.

Zuris nodded for him to proceed. The man seemed amused and far more alert than when McKafferty had walked in the door.

"I am careful about who I get into bed with," said McKafferty. "I want to make sure I always have proper protection. How could your companies have been so ready to step in and consolidate power after the nanotech plague? All that prepositioning of assets, all those ready to go plans, protectorates, Peacekeepers, and all that high tech civilian surveillance gear. You still have one or two surviving competitors. Do we have any more *chaos* I'll need to worry about in our future?"

"Survival demands a good strategy for every contingency," said Zuris. "That's what successful multinationals do. We make sure we are ready to step into any power vacuum that opens and make sure we are fully capable of exploiting it. Yes, we took advantage of a horrible situation and I'd do it again in a heartbeat. If we hadn't, some other company would have. The military has their version of shock and awe as do multinationals. Some call it the *shock doctrine*. I am no saint, General, and neither are you!"

The room was silent. Zuris had an expression on his face that McKafferty knew well. He regretted opening with an insinuating right hook now that he recognized the steely look of a murderer in the tycoon's shiny gray eyes. A large private army was surrounding McKafferty right now, including armed bodyguards in the very next room. Zuris could make him disappear.

"True enough," said McKafferty.

"I trust you understand from the report your superiors gave you that I am de facto running this country?"

"Yes, sir."

"Good. I don't mind being challenged as long as my orders are followed."

McKafferty did not trust Zuris. He'd just had a small peek behind the mask and saw what might be a psychopath. Too many details did not fit. There was far more going on here, and McKafferty was not at all sure it was in the best interests of his country, the America he knew before this goddamn USAG was formed. Still, he'd take the job after he played a few more cards. What choice did he really have?

After McKafferty had accepted, Zuris immediately called a briefing on CIT. His son, Alexi Zuris, was heading up the briefing. The meeting was convened in a secure situation room with a wall of video screens and global communications consoles that made McKafferty envious. A personal tablet was arranged on the conference table in front of every seat. A waiter took food and drink orders. Alexi immediately called the meeting to order. The family resemblance to his father was prominent. Alexi was husky and dressed in a camouflaged Peacekeeper field uniform with the rank of a four-star general. According to the report McKafferty had read, Alexi was thirty-six years old, the son from Zuris's third and current marriage, and the only child Zuris had spawned.

"CIT has been observing what we call communes for some time," said Alexi. "Communes are groups of ten to fifty hybrids living in the same house or compound. We suspect these communes were in some way an instigating factor in the plague unleashed by the god-machine. As far as we can tell, but cannot confirm, they have been in existence for a very long time. Some communes may have been in continuous existence for hundreds of years. Many communes have extreme wealth from accumulated money. They all seem to be involved in ownership and renovation of abandoned mines and other deep underground structures. The working theory is these structures are shelters where they hid during the plague. This means they either had advanced warning or played a role."

"If there's evidence they're in any way responsible for that atrocity, why haven't we arrested or killed them?" growled McKafferty.

"We suspect there are many more communes than we've identified. We need to tread lightly. We need to be sure we've uncovered them all before we raid them all. We also have circumstantial evidence that a type of fail-safe balance must be maintained. Too many communes and they grow in power, which may provoke the god-machine. Too few communes and a vacuum results, which may also provoke the god-machine. We need to know more before we act globally."

"Your fail-safe idea sounds like a fantasy," grumbled McKafferty. "I want a full written report on all known communes, evidence of any ties to the plagues, and evidence supporting your fail-safe theory."

The room grew tense. Alexi looked at his father as McKafferty stared at what he considered a fraudulent four-star general.

"McKafferty is in command," said Zuris. "Follow his orders."

"Continue," said McKafferty.

Alexi stared coldly for a long moment at McKafferty, then went on.

"In the last several months something unexpected has begun happening. We now have some unknown group hunting the communes. Take a look at this video from a Canadian surveillance operation CIT has been running. The surveillance is of a commune compound. This

148

video was recorded earlier today in Montreal."

On the main wall screen appeared a medieval looking stone building. The caption on the video had the date and time along with the name *Montreal Bioethics Institute*. A man and woman were walking from the compound when an incredible explosion temporarily blinded the camera. The man and woman were thrown to the ground and likely killed as the entire center of the compound was surgically incinerated, leaving a surprising amount of the outer wall intact. McKafferty was extremely impressed. That was very fine explosives work. The best Special Forces teams could not have done better. The scene began to loop with a close-up of the two people leaving the building displayed on a second screen next the main screen. McKafferty almost choked on the coffee he was drinking.

"I know them!" he bellowed.

"Mark Freedman and Sarah Mayfair," said Alexi Zuris. "Hybrid fugitives wanted because they know our propaganda is a lie. The real question is, Why are they doing our job for us by destroying communes?"

"If they survived that blast, I want them!" growled McKafferty. "Screw your *propaganda is a lie* bullshit. They're dangerous!"

"We want them too," interrupted Richard Zuris. "They are alive and we want them to stay alive and unharmed for testing. Can you do that for me, General?"

"My pleasure," said McKafferty. "I need a copy of that tape."

"Done," said Alexi.

"I assume you've issued some kind of trumped-up warrant for them in Canada," said McKafferty.

"You assume right," said Alexi. "They're now wanted terrorists in Canada and in the States. It is only a matter of time before we pick them up."

"You're wrong about that, junior. They've been evading capture for years," said McKafferty. "I want to run this manhunt personally. I need to assume command now."

"I expected nothing less," said Richard Zuris. "A car is waiting outside to take you to your hotel and then to the airfield, where your jet is already fueled and ready."

Richard Zuris – Dallas, Texas – February 13, 0002 A.P.

Only Alexi and Zuris, along with their bodyguards, remained in the situation room. Zuris finished his phone call. By god, he felt like a king. This must have been how the old monarchs enjoyed their reigns. It was such a pleasure to openly wield the immense power his family had held in secret for too long. No more surrogates. No more holding companies. No more puppet governments. The power of great wealth accumulated for generations had an authority all its own.

"The general is easily motivated," said Alexi.

"That is one of the qualities I treasure in him," said Zuris. "So, what do you think of our general?"

"I think he is a very useful tool. It was a thing of beauty the way you manipulated him using that top-secret report you made sure his superiors delivered to him. You provoked his suspicions and then dialed him back just enough. *Shock doctrine*—hah! I may have to read that book again. McKafferty will spend all his spare time sniffing around the distractions you fed him."

"It is always good to keep a curious lion busy with harmless prey until you need him," said Zuris. "Where is our general now?"

Alexi tapped out a rhythm on a keyboard. A video feed of General McKafferty packing flashed up on a secondary screen. Zuris smiled to himself, thinking the general would never know what he had missed. If he'd been a little harder to convince, he would have had a far more interesting night in that hotel suite. Sexual blackmail was another excellent tool of state.

"I have some fresh TAP signal intelligence that's very interesting," said Alexi.

His son used the same keyboard to bring up a signal intelligence display on the main screen. The display showed the usual map of North America with icons for captured voice-recognition traces that matched entered search criteria. Alexi clicked on an icon. A transcript of the selected signal intelligence appeared on Zuris's tablet as well as the big screen. TAP was an NSA surveillance project begun half a decade ago and operated by a conglomerate owned by Zuris. As with all projects developed by his companies, clandestine backdoors had been added for his own use. TAP enabled cell phones contained a covert listening mode. For years, the NSA had been recording every conversation within earshot of all TAP enabled cell phones and logging the location. It was a gluttonous feast of data that could never be fully digested. At this point only 10 percent of the phones were TAP enabled, but that would soon change. TAP was the true reason behind nationalization of wireless telecom companies and free cell phone service. Just this month a new promotion had begun, free phone upgrades, and every upgrade would of course be TAP enabled.

"We have identified the voices of Mark Freedman and Sarah Mayfair speaking to a Catholic priest," said Alexi. "Father Enrique, a known member of the *Antinostrum*—"

"I despise those fanatics," spat Zuris, interrupting his son. "I'm sorry, Alexi, go on."

"We captured this conversation from the priest's phone," said Alexi. "Freedman and Mayfair are interrogating the priest about an object that was stolen from the Chicago commune before it was bombed. The priest mistakenly thinks Freedman and Mayfair work for a Family, so he tries to bluff them until he realizes he's been duped. Prior to this recording, Mayfair executed a known burglar in front of the priest. The burglar was apparently working for the priest and had knifed Freedman a few days prior. Because of this intercept we spooled up and searched a prior month's worth of Chicago video surveillance and TAP intercepts. In an earlier TAP intercept we have the priest speaking with the dead burglar about a relic he stole, acting under orders from the priest. We also have partial video of a break-in at the Chicago commune and we have Freedman delivered by ambulance to a nearby hospital with what should have been a fatal knife wound. All of this is obviously connected."

"What are Freedman and Mayfair up to?" asked Zuris. "We don't want McKafferty capturing them just yet, but soon. We need them for Prometheus. In all the years we've been watching communes these two just don't fit. They're different than other hybrids. They act like chemical free-radicals, causing the stable elements to combust. They could become a threat to us. It's a pity we've never gotten TAP intercepts from their phones. I need you to fix that. I want to give them a little more room to play and see what we learn. It's always best to study your subjects in the wild in their natural environment before you cage them in a zoo."

"Yes, Father!" Alexi's voice was like a salute.

"I want you to personally oversee every TAP intercept we get from McKafferty's cell phone. I can't entrust it to anyone except you. Make sure your people miss nothing and make sure McKafferty does not get too close to Freedman until we are ready to capture him."

"Yes, Father. What about the hybrid who's going around destroying communes? McKafferty believes Freedman and Mayfair are the bombers."

"Convenient, isn't it... That murderous hybrid is one very complex mystery. We still have nothing on him?"

"Nothing, Father."

"I don't like mysteries and I don't like these communes. Maybe they'll destroy each other for us? Are your plans to lay traps for our hybrid mad bomber proceeding on schedule?"

"We will capture him, Father."

Zuris was silent for a while as he scanned the TAP transcript. He often did this on important matters to make sure the context of the intercepted discussion was not lost in the verbal reporting and vice versa. Satisfied, he looked up at his son.

"What time did you arrange for the board to convene?" asked Zuris.

"They're waiting for us now, Father."

"Good."

Zuris put his arm around his son as they exited the situation room. He was proud of his son. He exceeded his father in every measure. It was a short walk down the hall to the board of directors meeting room.

One of their bodyguards opened the door to the meeting room. Everyone stood when Zuris entered and did not sit until he did. He looked around the table at the directors of Capital Investments. The privately owned holding company was the capstone of the family corporate pyramid. Everyone at the table held a healthy stake in Capital Investments. Everyone at the table was related by blood. This was his family, just as it had been his father's family, and his grandfather's family, and so on back through the generations. Their blood was not blue but they were as much royalty as those families that had remained in Europe and sat on thrones. The combined wealth of the twelve great families was a significant percentage of the known treasure of the world and, in some cases, included government coffers. These dynastic families had been accumulating and passing down wealth for centuries. The Zuris family, known in very private circles as the Atlantic House, was at present the most powerful family in this exclusive hereditary club of deadly financial combatants. Over the centuries, while the governments and peoples of the world occupied themselves in bloody battles, the families profited off the chaos. It was what they did best.

As the meeting went on, Zuris subconsciously ran his fingers over the small electronics package on his belt. The medical-jammer that kept him alive was one of the more stunning results of their reverse-engineering projects. It had literally saved his life from a deadly cancer. Zuris thought of the dark irony that Alexi's successes at recovering ancient-tech might ensure he would never ascend to lead the Family. With the medical tech they were developing, Zuris might live a very long time, a lifetime measured in centuries.

Due to the use of ancient-tech in each jammer, every unit was hand-made and required a great deal of tuning trial and error. The product had fantastic sales potential; and not just medical, but also security and military markets. Zuris sighed. Such a valuable product, yet it might never go into mass production for strategic political reasons.

152

Zero-G scientists had spent thousands of man-hours trying to learn how the ancient-tech generated its null jamming signal. The ancient-tech transmitted in the same stealthy way as seeds, using something called *random frequency hopping* and *encryption hopping spread-spectrum signals*. Regardless of the technical details, the true genius of it all was that n-web transmissions had been mistaken for over a century as the natural background noise of the atmosphere and planet. All that was known and theorized about the jamming signal was that the ancient-tech was generating a complex, ever changing encrypted command that ordered seeds to stop and proceed no further—*Thou shall not pass*. If the jammer's antenna and signal strength was great enough to create a null zone, the seeds were blocked. They did not attempt to tunnel through or around the null zone. The jammer application was really little more than an advancement on a discovery made two years ago. Before the major outbreaks, COBIC was observed by the NSA reacting to a top-secret submarine communications antenna buried under Lake Superior. A large plume of microbes had been observed being drawn toward the antenna and then repelled when they got too close. It was like moths flying at a bare electric bulb and then being driven off by the heat. Zuris moved his fingers away from the electronics package on his belt. This ancient-tech jammer was a remarkable feat, and yet the very best and brightest still had no idea how it worked.

Zuris focused back on the board meeting. His son was wrapping up a report on clandestine operations to consolidate control over the food supply in North America. Progress was excellent thanks to monocultures having been forced onto farmers for decades by nonaligned corporations. The last topic on the agenda was Prometheus, and as far as Zuris was concerned, the only purpose for this Kabuki theater called a board meeting. Alexi stood to give the report.

"Several of the hybrid experimental subjects are now beginning to process rudimentary interface data. I do not need to remind everyone present what success of this project will mean. We are using CIT to keep track of hybrids that we want as subjects. We have also decided that the Nobel laureate Mark Freedman is the best candidate to lead research into the next phase of the Prometheus project. We are moving to acquire him and add him to our scientific pool when the time is right."

"He's a goddamn hybrid!" exclaimed one of the board members. Others grumbled.

"Exactly," said Zuris as he entered the fray. "Who better to work on Prometheus than a genius scientist who already has hard-wired into his brain what we are trying to build? Two years ago a plague tipped over the Monopoly board and scattered all the pieces onto the floor. It was total picture-perfect chaos. This plague has given us great opportunities that we all agree we must not squander. This is our best chance to ensure Atlantic House remains a dominant force forever. Prometheus has the potential to technologically advance us hundreds, if not thousands, of years in a single leap. We need the very best working on Prometheus. I don't care if the best is a hybrid, a Martian, or a goddamn monkey!"

Richard Zuris – Dallas, Texas – February 14, 0002 A.P.

Zuris was on edge, sitting in the situation room alone, staring at the screens. Alexi and a team of his Peacekeeper commandos were close to apprehending a new hybrid for use as an interface node inside Prometheus. Each commando was wired with the same video and audio gear as Enforcers. The tiny high-resolution video cameras on their helmets sent back remarkably good images. The microphones captured every sound. Aerial reconnaissance from drones provided a chessboard-like view of the field of action. Zuris could see and hear almost as well as if he were in the field.

This hybrid subject was remarkable in many ways and just might turn out to be a major breakthrough for Prometheus. The hybrid did not know he was a hybrid and was clearly mentally unbalanced. Also, he was not a member of a commune, which made him very rare and simplified extraction because they could transport him by air without risk of disconnection killing him. His ability to heal others was remarkable, which indicated his brain might be far along in the nanotech conversion process. Alexi and his team had followed their subject for several blocks after insertion from a rooftop landing of their helicopter. New Orleans was a mess. One of the commandos nicknamed Cuda had been forced to take out a civilian who had actually tried to mug him while he was kneeling behind cover. The civilian had used a baseball bat on the commando's helmet with disastrous results for the civilian.

Zuris had on a Bluetooth earpiece and could talk with anyone on the team, though he limited himself to Alexi's private channel. The subject had apparently drawn an *ichthys* on his forehead in his own blood. Zuris watched as the oddity walked into a church. Based on prior surveillance taken in New Orleans weeks ago, the subject would announce himself as the Messiah and begin healing. Alexi's team moved in to surround the church. The subject was boxed in with no escape route. They would wait for him to leave and then take him by surprise. Alexi's team was wearing night camouflaged zone-jammer suits with shielded military

154

helmets. They were taking no chances in case this Messiah also had a very deadly sting in the form of micro kill-zones. They had run into that before with disastrous results for the commando team and later some lab personnel. They would take down the subject by hitting him with multi-shot Tasers, then inject him with enough drugs to knock out a bear.

Time crawled slowly by. One of the commandos had inserted a camera through the wall of the church using a silent drill. For the past hour everyone had watched the subject healing parishioners. It was an impressive show.

"You don't think he's really the messiah?" whispered Cuda. "Do you?"

"Can it," hissed Alexi. "The subject's leaving. Here he comes...."

The subject stepped onto the sidewalk. Zuris heard the sounds of a scuffle. He watched as Tasers hit their man, but the hybrid did not go down. The subject looked a little dazed as he pulled wired darts from his body. Several commandos took him bodily.

"Sodomite," shouted the Messiah as he stared directly at Alexi. "Hive collaborator. God will smite you!"

"What the fuck!" yelled Alexi. "Cuda, hit him with the drugs now!"

"Cuda's down," yelled a commando. "He's waxed. I got his injectors.... Good night, asshole."

One of the helmet cameras was now inches from the subject's face. The fight drained from the hybrid as the drugs did their work. His eyes fluttered, then closed. A straitjacket was cinched up on him, and with that the hard part was over.

"Goddamn fucking micro kill-zone!" cursed Alexi. "We've got collateral in the church. Looks like four civvies are waxed."

A field stretcher was unfolded and the subject was strapped to it.

"Get that evac down here ASAP," said Alexi. "What the hell happened to Cuda?"

"Looks like his jammer was fucked up when that civvie tried for a home run off Cuda's brain bucket," said a commando. "Yeah, look at this shit. He lost a wire to the bucket and didn't know it."

"Son of a bitch," yelled another commando. "I thought this full battle rattle was supposed to warn you if there's a bad circuit. Motherfucker said it was foolproof. I am gonna motherfucking foolproof him when I get back."

"Cut the chatter and do your job," said Alexi.

The plan called for the evacuation helicopter to touch down in the street and extract the team with their prize. Zuris heard the distinct sound of a Special Forces Stealth Blackhawk nearing the ground. He watched the overhead view from a drone. The video feeds from the commandos were shaky as the team ran toward the Blackhawk. Zuris waited until they were in the air before he switched off the screens and left the situation room in darkness.

Richard Zuris – Dallas, Texas – February 14, 0002 A.P.

In the heart of Prometheus, Zuris and Alexi watched as their new subject awoke to semi-consciousness in his chamber while strapped into medical scaffolding. His lower body was submerged into a shallow trough of water. The subject's arms were extended straight out on side restraints like a cross. Lower restraints held his legs together and flat. His body was tipped a few degrees from horizontal. The entire arrangement viewed from above looked like a high-tech crucifixion. Ports inserted in the upper chest provided real-time blood analysis and delivery of drugs and total nutrients. His head was restrained by a series of straps. Aimed at his ears were an array of highly directional MRI safe speakers called *sonic cannons*. The array was used to radiate three-dimensional high-fidelity sound directly into a subject's ears and mind. His eyes were taped open. The muscles that moved his eyeballs had been disabled with a paralytic agent. By necessity the drug was infused directly into the extraocular muscle capsule behind each eye through surgically inserted intravenous lines. Through a glass window in the fMRI doughnut, laser video projectors were aimed into his retinas. The audio-video outputs from this system were used to inject multimedia into the subject's cognitive centers as feedback to god-machine responses. The subject's brain then processed the feedback into neural streams of consciousness. Like all information flowing through a subject's nanotech brain, the god-machine was the ultimate end consumer. Non-ferrous noble metal electrodes had been inserted into the subject's temporal lobes near the hippocampus to directly signal the god-machine.

Zuris considered the Prometheus chamber a work in progress. They had learned from tragic deaths that the micro kill-zones spasmodically emitted by a few subjects operated independently of the god-machine. To protect the staff each chamber was isolated with zone-jammers. An alternate way to safely connect subjects to the god-machine was then needed. A conduit of water saturated with COBIC was the solution. The conduit was constructed from a pair of clear vinyl tubes that circulated lake water saturated with COBIC through a trough in which the subject was partially submerged. An array of signal analyzers monitored all data conducted along the n-web pathways in the conduits. In turn,

156

jammer-shielded pipes connected the conduits in the labs to a river, which was fed by a chain of smaller aquifers that were connected to the Ogallala Aquifer and ultimately the god-machine. Like everything in Prometheus, even the water conduits leading to the river were fully redundant and hardened to mil standards.

Zuris studied the brain activity maps and signal displays as the Prometheus interface was switched on. Moments later the infusion of DMT began. Moderate doses of the psychotropic drug DMT had been found to increase susceptibility and throughput. A supercomputer began feeding test signals through a firewalled sub-processor into the subject's temporal lobes. The same computer performed analysis on the resulting n-web signals relayed through the water conduit. The brain activity maps and signal displays registered a sudden massive flow of data. This event indicated a successful interfacing.

"Wonderful," said Zuris. "Every day another step closer."

"I am not sure about this one," Alexi muttered. "He's as crazy as they come."

"Some psychiatrists believe psychotics have minds that are more open to spiritual dimensions," said Zuris. "Let's hope our messiah will have better connections to his god-machine."

Open Roads

Mark Freedman – Montreal – February 13, 0002 A.P.

The train that had just arrived through the subway tunnel was now leaving. The squad of Canadian soldiers had them cornered. Mark had his hands in the air. He glanced down at his chest and saw three red dots from laser pointers. He looked over at Sarah and saw two red dots on her chest. Her arms were at her sides. They were both wearing thin high-tech body armor so the protection did not show and offered an advantage of surprise. In these times so many people wore body armor. These Canadian soldiers would have to be total fools to not be packing ammunition that could penetrate the best vests. He was getting enough mental chatter from them to know the soldiers had received orders that terrorist suspects matching their description were video recorded leaving the Montreal Bioethics Institute just before it was blown up. An assist was showing heightened heart and respiration for all the soldiers.

"Get on the *ground*!" yelled the squad leader.

Mark was receiving a stream of agitated memory capsules from Sarah. He was worried she was going to draw on them. She was confident she could take them all before they fired. In a memory capsule she pointed out that all but one of the soldiers had their fingers outside their trigger guards. She was receiving a lot of emotional confusion from the men. They were all young and did not want to kill innocent people. They were no longer sure Mark and Sarah were their suspects. Mark sent Sarah a message that she was going to get them both killed if she tried anything. The squad leader unclipped a microphone that was fastened to his coat.

"We may have the terrorist suspects… Roger… Will hold for your arrival."

The soldiers started to edge toward them. Mark saw civilians plastering themselves against the walls of the subway station.

"I said get on the ground. Do it *now*!" yelled the squad leader.

Mark knew this was going to end badly. Sarah was not going to be captured by these soldiers. She'd had far too many run-ins with military types in the past. Something crashed behind the soldiers. It sounded like a vending machine being pushed over and smashing. Two of the men turned to look. Another crash erupted. Mark could see the soldiers were jumpy. They all started glancing behind them, then back at Mark and Sarah. Mark shrugged and smiled, trying to communicate he had no idea what was going on. The lights suddenly went out behind the soldiers. All except the squad leader turned away from Mark and Sarah.

159

Flashlights snapped on and began sweeping the darkness. Mark knew it would now be child's play for Sarah to kill them all in a few seconds. He was disgusted by the mental image, but at some deeper, primitive level he was hoping she would do it now. Automatic fire erupted. Mark felt Sarah grab his arm and with a violent tug she sent him toward the ground. An assist registered a surge of adrenaline. The world was moving in slow motion. While falling, Mark saw a flashlight beam illuminate the ghostlike hybrid. The living god stared at Mark and for an instant Mark felt the hybrid invade his mind. He saw muzzle flashes from a compact assault rifle the hybrid was brandishing. A soldier's head exploded, then another. Mark's body hit the cement floor. His eyes were focused back on the carnage no more than seconds after he registered pain from his hard impact. The far end of the subway platform was in darkness except for a single flashlight, which was rolling across the ground. The hybrid was gone. All the soldiers were dead. Sarah was flat on her stomach, aiming her Beretta in a two-handed grip toward the far end of the station.

"What the fuck is going on?" she screamed. "That bastard murders a building full of innocent hybrids, then saves us?"

"Let's get out of here."

"I don't get it."

"Sarah!"

"Yeah… Yeah, I'm with you. I'm going."

Mark Freedman – Quebec – February 14, 0002 A.P.

Sarah held the Humvee to a reasonable highway speed. The sun was rising in front of them. The slow pace was making Mark anxious, but he knew she was being smart. They were almost safely out of the area. They had a good escape plan. Once they exited the highway near Lake Champlain, they could follow several good direct routes across the border into New York State. Border checkpoints were no longer manned. No one cared who came or went between the USAG and Canada. Since the Canadians were now hunting terrorists, the checkpoints might be manned, but the odds of that were remote. Still, they had no intention of taking any chances. They'd only use rural crossings. The plan was to stop at a safe distance and hike down under cover of woods or fields to binocular range. It the checkpoint was abandoned, they'd use it.

Mark stared at a weathered billboard listing attractions for Lake Champlain as they cruised past. The attractions were probably all closed forever. He was confused by his jumbled emotions. They were colliding with each other like billiard balls and scattering in every direction. Simple things were setting him off. He knew Sarah was tracking every one of his feelings and that he was probably confusing her too. So many people had needlessly died since they set off from Pueblo Canyon. With perfect recall he could see the Canadian soldiers being murdered in rapid succession, one after another. It was one more small massacre added to the global massacre that had brought the world to this point.

"There's our exit," said Sarah. "Home free once we get off this highway."

"Nothing's free anymore," said Mark.

An hour later, after hiking back to their Humvee, they blasted through a deserted rural checkpoint far above the posted speed limit. Upper New York State, for some reason, felt safer to Mark, but the world was stranger than he could have possibly imagined only a few short weeks ago. Communes of highly evolved hybrids were at war with ghostlike renegade hybrids, who were even more highly evolved than the communes. As if that was not enough to make the world feel surreal, for the past two hours he'd been sensing the subtle pulls of an increasing number of singularities. Sarah was experiencing the same tidal crosscurrents and had questioned them repeatedly.

Mark was using the assist that displayed n-web architecture to try to gauge direction and distance to the singularities as well as their numbers. It was an odd feeling to be sailing down a highway moving through a three-dimensional rendering of n-web pathways geo-projected all around him. The projection extended beyond the boundaries of the Humvee out to the horizons. He estimated there were sixteen singularities in this half of the continent and most of them were south; very few were east or west.

"How could they all be communes?" asked Sarah.

"If they turn out to be real, this makes Adam either very bad at basic math or a liar. He said there were twenty communes in the entire world. I suppose some of these could be decoys. Who knows? I keep finding more every time I check. If they're all real, then these singularities are either coming out of hiding all at once or spreading like a virus."

"What I don't understand is if we can find them, then the betrayers can find them too," said Sarah. "It's like the communes are showing themselves to taunt a pack of psychopaths bent on destroying them. It's mass suicide."

"I agree it doesn't make sense. Adam's stories are not holding up under daylight unless the communes are trying to lure betrayers into some kind of trap."

"I think we should head for the nearest singularity to see if it's real."

"I agree," he said.

"Maine?"

"Maine… Somewhere near Portland, I think."

Mark Freedman – Upper New York State – February 14, 0002 A.P.

New York no longer felt as safe as it had when they'd first crossed the Canadian border. All the major roadways were congested with wreckage and explosive destruction from recent warfare. What was unsettling was that this needless destruction had happened months ago, not years. There was frozen mud and snow everywhere. It must have rained as well as snowed here in the last few days. Rain in upper New York State in February was unimaginable. Year after year the polar jet streams were wandering greater distances, changing their paths, leaving abnormal weather patterns in their wake. The jet streams were also oscillating more. It was possible to have warm spring-like weather one day with a blizzard the next day. Everywhere Mark looked he could see the fingerprints of global warming.

The nearest bridge across Lake Champlain was at Rouses Point. They found the huge bridge had been demolished and never rebuilt. Ferries were no longer running. They were forced to drive south following Lake Champlain, searching for a place to cross. Soon they reached a smaller bridge, which looked like it had been destroyed by warfare. The Humvee's GPS was showing their next option was the Lake Champlain bridge. There were symbols for road construction over the bridge, which could mean anything. The symbols could have been appended any time in the past several years. The GPS showed that Lake Champlain and its southern river formed a very narrow one hundred and fifty mile long barrier of water. This bridge-hunting detour had already added too many miles to their route and could add far more.

Sarah slowly pulled the Humvee to a stop in the middle of the roadway. Mark got out and walked a hundred feet closer. He stared down from the edge of a bomb crater in the middle of the road. Sarah came up next to him. The bridge had clearly been mangled by aerial bombardment. The roadbed over the icy river was pockmarked with craters and canted at dangerous angles. Spans of it were completely missing in spots. Traffic between New York and Vermont had been effectively cut off.

"This is starting to look like a quarantine line," said Sarah. "Someone decided to stop all traffic between New York and Vermont and then never bothered to fix what they broke."

"Whatever the reason," said Mark. "I think we have a much longer drive ahead of us than we thought."

Traveling the war-torn roads was slow and bone jarring at times. Half a day later they finally found their bridge and crossed into Vermont. An old bed and breakfast looked like a good place to stop. They had both thought it was abandoned and were surprised and pleased to have to pay for their night's stay, a warm shower, and food. The owner included a free bowl for Ralph and a huge bone. He liked people who traveled with dogs, said it showed good character.

Light from a small fireplace filled the room with a soft, flickering glow. Mark was massaging Sarah's feet. The deeper feelings he was starting to have for her oddly caused him less concern than when their affair had started. Was this an affair? He was confused. He hadn't wanted these feelings.

"Do you think we still have souls?" asked Sarah.

"Looks like you still have both of yours."

"No, I mean it."

Mark sighed. He sat up against the headboard and stopped massaging Sarah's feet. He thought about her unease with herself that had raised this question.

"I don't feel that my essence has changed," he said. "But then again, if we were slowly losing our humanity and becoming machines, would we even notice?"

"I don't fully trust my own thoughts anymore," whispered Sarah.

"Neither do I," said Mark.

"I know."

"But I think as long as we doubt ourselves," said Mark. "We're still ourselves and—"

With a powerful crash the room door splintered in two. Mercenaries charged in, followed by a murderous looking Alexander. A half-dozen machine guns were pointed at them. Mark could tell every one of these men wanted to begin shooting. The only thing holding them back was Alexander. The smile on the man's face sent shivers through Mark's body. Sarah was frozen. She did not even move to cover herself.

"This has been a long hunt," said Alexander. "Look at me, traitors, for I am god!"

"You're insane," snapped Sarah.

"You can kill them now," said Alexander.

Mark felt bullets punching through his chest. He experienced loss of control as his nanotech brain's autonomic systems took over and commanded free-swimming COBIC to the sites of injury. Unnecessary functions were shutting down. His vision was fading. Stanch the blood loss, mend the flesh. The injuries were multiplying. The smell of gunpowder was suffocating. He felt Sarah gripping his hand like a terrible vise, then go slack…

Mark awoke, knocking a lamp to the floor. The bulb exploded. The room was empty and filled with a deep orange glow. The fire had turned to embers. He touched his chest, examined it, found nothing, and was dazed. He looked at the door. It was intact. He looked at Sarah. She was awake and trembling. Her eyes were wide with shock. She kept looking at her chest.

"We're not dead?" said Sarah.

"I think we just had the same dream," said Mark.

"It was so real. You were worried about losing your soul then Alexander broke in. He claimed he was god, then they murdered us."

Mark received a memory capsule from her. They'd had exactly the same dream in every detail. The foot massage, the discussion, Alexander, their murder—it was all identical. The god-machine made these types of shared dreams and visions possible, but they were rare.

"Alexander's dead," said Mark. "We saw him die in that explosion. We felt his presence evaporate."

"Did we or had we seen exactly what he wanted us to see and felt exactly what he wanted us to feel?"

Sarah got out bed, retrieved her M4, and chambered a round. She looked out through the curtained window then started collecting her outerwear.

"This is a dream warning," she said. "He could be out there right now."

"He's dead," said Mark. "We shared a dream, a nightmare. It was as real as any lucid dream but neither of us knew we were dreaming."

"That's exactly how every one of my premonitions were during the plague."

"He's dead. I am telling you, he's dead," said Mark. "All these years we'd have picked up something coming from him if he was alive."

"Did we pick up anything the last time when he used drugs to hide his thoughts and ambushed us? It's almost morning. I want to get out of here now!"

"Fine…"

Mark drove the Humvee, using night vision goggles. He was concerned about the heat signature from the engine. They had another hour until sunrise. If no gangs tried to kill them, then with a little luck they could reach the New Hampshire-Maine border around noon. There had been no further hints of Alexander. Sarah was rechecking the MK19 grenade machine gun in the backseat. Mark could hear the clatter from her working the belt feed. The trunk was filled with munitions boxes loaded with 40mm grenade belts, bricks of plastic explosive, claymore antipersonnel mines, and ammo. They were carrying enough weapons and munitions to win a small war.

Sarah climbed over the console and into the front seat. Wordlessly, she settled in with a tablet. He saw her starting to search for news stories that matched Alexander's unusual psychopathic style. Mark looked back at the road just in time to lift off the gas. In front of them was a long stretch of highway pockmarked with bomb craters the size of their Humvee. Plows had scrapped the roadbed, leaving marks as if some huge clawed monster had attacked. On the shoulder was fresh wreckage, unrecognizable tangled piles of sheet metal and steel surrounded by drive-train parts and wheels. People had been attacked here recently, and then someone had scraped the wreckage off the road like so much litter to make room for the next victims.

"Shit!" yelled Sarah.

"I know," said Mark.

"No, you don't. There's a huge story out of Montreal about a terrorist attack. It must have just gone up on every news site on the web. They're showing footage of us leaving the institute just before the explosion. You can easily see our faces and they have our names. They also have a headshot of you. Looks like a picture Kathy took at the CDC and they have my police ID photo. We are supposed to be armed, dangerous, and on a killing spree."

"The subway bloodbath was witnessed by a lot of people," said Mark. "The Canadians have to know that wasn't us."

"There's no mention of what happened in the subway. It gets worse. They're claiming new evidence proves you're the Nobel Prize winning mastermind who genetically engineering COBIC bacteria. The two of us apparently worked together and released the weaponized bacteria without warning or demand. They're making us out to be mentally deranged."

"I always knew I'd be famous," said Mark, shaking his head.

"The only good news is they have no description of our Humvee and we're supposedly still in Canada plotting another mad bombing."

Mark was still behind the wheel. Sarah felt alive with random emotional energy coming from all around her. They were twenty miles outside Portland, and the singularity was ominously growing in strength. This was going to be a very big one—bigger than Chicago or Montreal—and that had to mean they were going to find a large commune. They'd been listening to Air Truth for hours. Most speakers thought the story about Freedman and Mayfair smelled like a fabrication, but the facts of the Canadian attack had been confirmed.

Sarah had changed her makeup and cut her hair shorter in an effort to alter her appearance. The results were passable. She no longer looked like the woman in the surveillance videos that had been looping all day. For the first time she was grateful her police ID had been a bad photo of her. Mark had on a baseball cap and sunglasses. She thought he still looked too much like the pictures being shown, but there was little they could do about it. He had decided to let his beard grow, but it would be days before his appearance was different enough to pass a close encounter with USAG law enforcement or even the general public.

Sarah experienced a surprising tug at her mind from the singularity. It felt like some of her memories had been pulled away like sand in a riptide.

"That was a strong one," said Mark.

"It's incredible if you think about it," said Sarah. "These communes are nurseries for artificial life. They're growing their own personal god-machines."

"Guides, god-machines, who knows," said Mark. "The important thing is these communes have something they're not sharing. We need to peel as many layers as we can from this onion."

The temperature had been rising. A hard, cold rain had started fifteen minutes ago. The sky was overcast with an Atlantic storm. Inside the city limits, they were driving past block after block of nineteenth century red brick buildings. People in winter coats were hunched under umbrellas. Sarah watched the wind pull an umbrella from the grip of a woman who was crossing the street.

They were within a few miles of the singularity. Sarah was surprised at how easy this one had been to find compared to the other two. She wondered if they were just more skilled at locating communes or if the communes themselves had changed in some way.

They turned onto an older street. The commune was within a few blocks. A flash of lightning burst in the same instant as the thunder.

The Humvee shuddered. A spray of small debris hit the bullet-resistant windshield. Mark stopped in the middle of the street. All feeling of the singularity had evaporated. Sarah's chest went empty. Another commune was gone as if snatched from their closing fingers. She looked at Mark. His face was grim.

The wind and the rain made it harder to spot the location until they were closer. Mark pulled over to the curb. Sarah was stunned and grieving. Some afterglow of indecipherable sadness was pouring into her from the mass murder. She felt tears sliding down her face. Her vision was blurred. She wiped her eyes.

People were arriving to see what had happened. Some were standing in the shelter of doorways and overhangs. Sarah's eyes were drawn to a tall figure. An assist came up on its own projecting the orange medical diagram of a fully evolved hybrid over the man. It looked like the same betrayer who had crossed their path in Montreal. From a distance of 50 feet their eyes locked and neither moved. The hybrid was like an apparition. His shape sometimes appeared to blend into the shadows of the buildings and the streaks of rain. Without an assist she would never have spotted him. Sarah was picking up tiny emotional flashes—curiosity, interest. Her breath hitched and then she was in full command of herself again.

"It's the betrayer!" she shouted.

Sarah shouldered the door open, and Ralph piled out behind her. Without thinking, she was running full speed past bystanders who were looking the other way. Ralph was leading her by a growing distance. The hybrid was standing at the end of the block. She did not exactly remember opening the door or even starting to run. All she knew was that she had to put this killer down before more innocents died. The hybrid turned and walked from sight around the corner. Moments later Ralph vanished around the same corner.

Sarah ran out into the intersection of the street to get a clear line of fire, aimed, and saw nothing. Ralph had stopped in the middle of the sidewalk, whining in confusion. The street was empty. Their prey was gone without a trace. Sarah reached out with every part of her being. She opened herself to the full onslaught of human emotions in this part of the city in an effort to locate any clue of the hybrid's emotional fingerprints. She'd felt a few of his emotions only moments ago, yet now found nothing.

Rain was pelting her face as she wiped the water away. She looked in every possible direction again and found no place to hide. This was impossible. Rain had soaked through her clothing. She started to slowly walk down the block looking for evidence but knew it was pointless. The betrayer had gotten away with mass murder again. Mark pulled up in the Humvee and began to roll down his window. She realized the entire sequence of events had occurred in less than a minute.

"Are you insane going after that creature like that?" he shouted. "He could have killed you."

Sarah felt something draw her attention emotionally. She spotted an iPhone lying under a mailbox and walked over and picked it up. It was not an iPhone. The object was about the size of a touch screen phone but only about a quarter of an inch thick and weighed nothing. She turned it over. There were no markings. It felt too rigid for its size and feather weight. All her senses were screaming this was not something from her world. She could not articulate how she knew this, she just did. It felt like she was in a different reality.

Sarah opened the rear door for Ralph and then climbed up into the cab next to Mark. He could not take his eyes off what she had in her hands. She was experiencing his emotions and knew he had a similar feeling that this object was unnatural. A memory capsule exploded in her mind like a camera flash. She dropped the object. As the flash faded a single thought remained. It was a man's name.

"Noah?" said Mark.

Sarah could only nod. She knew the betrayer had just told them his name or rather, this object he'd left behind had just sent them a recorded introduction. She retrieved the object from the floor. It was a little colder than it should be.

"It feels all wrong," said Sarah.

"Advanced technology always seems like magic to the primitives," said Mark. "And we are the primitives."

"I have a terrible suspicion we were just captured on video at another bombing," said Sarah.

Mark Freedman – Maine – February 14, 0002 A.P.

Mark was squinting through the windshield, trying not to drive off the road. They were only thirty miles south of Portland. The weather had turned fiercer as if conjured by the betrayer. The hybrid had slain another commune and likely used them as scapegoats. The wind-driven storm was now more sleet than rain. At times visibility was reduced to a few yards. They needed a safe place to park and wait out the storm. Mark was trying to find a spot that would keep them out of sight and out of mind of any law enforcement operating in the area, as well as gangs.

Twenty minutes and only a few miles later they were out of options.

It was growing dark. Mark pulled into a public lot for beach parking. He was not pleased. He killed the engine and hoped they would be overlooked. If the weather let up, he'd risk driving at night instead of remaining so exposed. With the engine off, the sound of sleet and rain hitting their metal shelter seemed to grow louder. It sent a chill down his back. The weather-blurred glow from lights at the other end of the lot was the only illumination inside the Humvee. Sarah was staring oddly at the relic she'd found. She looked exhausted, which was not a normal state for any hybrid. The device was all they'd talked about during the drive. The small black tablet could have easily been a duplicate of the relic that had been stolen from the Chicago commune. Sarah looked up at him. Her pupils were wide from the darkness and maybe something more.

"This may sound crazy, but I keep thinking it's whispering to me," she said. "The words are too soft to understand."

"Maybe it's not English?"

An assist kept projecting a series of runic symbols over the device. The god-machine was again applying a label to the black box. It recognized this thing. Following a hunch, Mark opened an assist that projected a virtual three-dimensional schematic of the n-web's pathways in the immediate area. The data flows looked normal everywhere except near the device, which was causing a mild warping of the pathways. Mark could see the device was using the n-web to do things: probing, searching, and consuming data. The disruption was nothing like a singularity, but it was also unlike the normal flows that surrounded a hybrid who was accessing the god-machine. Mark slowly took the device from her fingers. She let it go grudgingly. He could not discern a front or back. There were no markings of any kind.

"Its surface is cold," said Mark. "This thing really is all wrong."

"You get used to it."

"Remember when the Chicago priest said they can come back?"

"Sure, but this can't be the same one we saw in Chicago. Can it?"

Mark retrieved his folding knife from the door pocket. He opened the blade and poked a small impression in a corner of the device. In less than a minute the tiny wound was gone. The device had healed itself.

"I think this thing is made of the same nanotech as seeds," said Mark.

"So you're saying this device is part of the god-machine?"

"No... maybe... I don't know, but you have to admit this thing could have been made by the same civilization that created the seeds."

Mark knew there had to be some way to switch the device on. He turned it over in his hand, examining every corner and side. The device felt even colder. Sarah reached over to take the device back. As her fingers touched the sides of the case, a thin red line appeared directly down the middle of the surface. Sarah snatched back her fingers as if she'd been stung.

"What now?" she asked.

Before Mark could answer, the red line expanded into a thin-edged rectangle that framed the device. A silvery mercury colored display with three-dimensional runic icons appeared within the rectangle. The metallic screen was like nothing Mark had seen before. It looked like liquid mercury, but all the runic icons gave off a glow as if lit from within by something radioactive.

The icons were the same language that was used on the virtual interfaces to the god-machine. Mark knew the meaning of a few of the letters but could not make sense of what was displayed. An assist showed the n-web pathways around the device now had much more pronounced warpage.

"Okay, this is a little creepy," said Mark.

He had so many ideas swirling around in his mind that he felt dizzy. He needed to call in a favor from Karla and get this device into a materials research lab. He tried touching some of the icons. The screen flashed light green when each icon was touched, but nothing more happened. He tried a data flow to collect information on the device. Nothing useful came back. The black box remained enigmatic.

Mark was feeling drained. He hadn't felt this kind of tired since his brain had been hybridized over two years ago. He felt dull. Sarah was saying something to him, but he could not focus on her words. He looked at the device, turning it over in his hands. An assist labeling the device in runic letters came up again, this time flashing, and then it all made sense. He dropped the device onto the floorboard. The fatigue that had been dogging him began to fade almost immediately as he stared at the device at his feet.

"That thing was using us as a power source to recharge whatever it has for batteries," said Mark. "The assist was a warning of some kind."

Sarah climbed into the back and returned with a pair of pliers. She collected the device and carefully held it up for them to look at as if it might explode without warning. The display was operating without any noticeable change. The glow was the same and the icons were the same.

"Do you feel it draining you?" he asked.

"No, it may need direct contact, skin to skin or something?"

"That son of bitch was trying to kills us with that thing," grumbled Mark.

"I don't think so," said Sarah. "You said it the other day. If he wanted us dead, he's had plenty opportunities. I tried to shoot him today and he left us this."

"Maybe it doesn't pay to kill off your scapegoats," said Mark.

A violent impact from behind sent the Humvee forward across the parking lot. Sarah lost her grip on the device, which went flying into the backseat. Before he could react, a side impact slammed the door and window into him. If the Humvee had not been heavily armored, they would have been crushed. Stunned, Mark felt dampness of his face. Through the glass he could see the grille and bumper of a big truck. His nanotech brain recovered far quicker than humanly possible. He had the ignition turning over the engine and the Humvee in drive before the human parts of his brain even registered what he was doing.

"What the fuck!" he yelled as his foot jammed into the accelerator. The dark shape of the truck was closing in on his window again. If Mark had been a second quicker they would have escaped. This time the rear of the Humvee was clipped, sending them into a half spin on the slick asphalt. Mark corrected as if on autopilot and accelerated out of the way of the next assault, then jammed on the brakes. Headlights came on, making it easier for him to see their attackers and for the attackers to see them. He hit his own lights. The sleet and rain had apparently let up unnoticed. It was still pouring but visibility was fine. Four large jacked-up pickups were facing them from all sides. Each had heavy tubular bumpers and roof-mounted lights bars that were blinding him.

Sarah started sliding the bullet-resistant window back enough to take aim with an M4 assault rifle. The cab was suddenly filled with the sound of rapid, ear-splitting cracks and muzzle flashes. Shell casings were flying everywhere. The pickup under fire began retreating with all four wheels spinning. Its headlights shattered and tires blew. Sparks licked across its hood, then the windshield collapsed as countless bullets tore through it. The vehicle was clearly ruined and whoever was in the front seat likely dead. Mark floored the Humvee. He did not look but knew Sarah was sliding the bullet-resistant window closed. He heard the all too familiar sound of bullets hitting their armored Humvee. Small pockmarks were blooming on every piece of glass, covering older pockmarks.

As he reached the street, his heart sank. An entire pack of similar pickups was bearing down on them from the northbound side of the street. His nanotech brain counted as he spun the steering wheel to flee. An impossible ten pickup trucks were on their tail. The sound of bullets hitting the passenger compartment armor turned into a hailstorm. He heard Sarah shouting something over the noise but could not hear enough of her words. A memory capsule came next. If he could get away from their fire long enough for her to pop the roof hatch and mount with the MK19, their problems would be erased. With the fire they were now taking, it would be suicide to try to use the MK19.

Escaping the barrage coming from behind them was not going to be easy. Mark already had the Humvee floored and the pickup trucks were now right on their tail. He could see them surging forward and falling back. Their attackers clearly had far more speed than he did.

A white hot explosion came from behind. A bullet ripped through the rear defenses of the Humvee and punched a hole in the dashboard. Mark was stunned. He started swerving evasively, which cost them speed.

"What the hell was that?" he shouted.

A memory capsule followed an instant later. Sarah was sure they were in trouble. She was positive that was a .50-caliber armor-piercing bullet, most likely a tungsten penetrator. The bullets were not coming fast enough to be a machine gun, so it had to be a sniper rifle—which was the good news. Sarah commanded Ralph onto the floor. Another bullet came through the rear of the Humvee and ricocheted around inside. Pieces of stuffing from a backseat landed all over. A third bullet ripped through the Humvee too soon after the last. Mark took a hard right at a corner and lost control. When they stopped spinning, he was facing straight ahead with blinding headlights bearing down on them through the windshield. They were trapped from both directions. Mark could not believe what was happening, then the oncoming headlights swerved around them. He spotted Peacekeeper insignias on the sides of several Stryker fighting vehicles as they whipped past. He heard a crash and a huge firefight erupting behind them. He'd never thought he'd be happy to see those storm troopers. They were going to show no mercy, exterminating what they found. Mark hit the accelerator. He saw an Apache with a spotlight on flying low, then streak past. The rotor wash shook the Humvee. The explosions and lightning flashes behind them tripled in intensity. Mark was amped up. It looked like the Peacekeepers had decided he and Sarah were innocent victims. God knows they wouldn't need their testimony in an Outland court to sentence a bunch of dead outlaws.

Mark sped toward a highway that would take them away from this killing ground. He kept glancing in the side mirror, half expecting to see an Apache bird of prey coming for them. Sarah had not uttered a word. He glanced over, then realized he was no longer sensing anything from her.

"Sarah!" he shouted.

There was no answer. He heard Ralph howling as if in pain. The mournful sound pierced straight through Mark's heart. He cut the wheel, pulling at a dangerous speed into an abandoned multistory packing structure. At a toll booth he snapped off what was left of a yellow-striped entry barricade and scraped the side of the Humvee. He jammed on the brakes, then pulled the parking brake. With the engine still running, he jumped out, ran to Sarah's side, and opened the door.

He saw what was wrong and his breath hitched. One of the armor-piercing rounds had punched through the right side of her lower chest. Ralph continued howling. A schematic overlaid from a medical assist showed no pulse, no respiration, and no involuntary nerve response. Her skin temperature was dropping. Sarah was lifeless. There was some residual brain activity but the glowing embers of a once brilliant mental fire were almost dark.

The assist showed the bullet had somehow missed her organs but torn an artery open and shattered bones, which had then done even more damage than the bullet. Mark heard wailing and for a moment had no idea the sound was coming from him. His face was covered in tears. Indecision paralyzed him. He had no idea what to do. He hugged her and begged her to live, again... and again... and again.

"Don't give up. Please don't give up. I love you!"

A single word appeared in his paralyzed brain. Hospital... It was their only hope. Sobbing, he let go of her and climbed back into the driver's seat. He punched up *hospitals* on the GPS and got three hits. Which one? Which ones were running and which ones were shuttered? Paralyzed again! He mentally picked one, then a different one, then back to the first. He thought, *phone, call, make sure—*

He heard a very soft moan.

He stared at Sarah as her eyes snapped open, releasing a mental onslaught that consumed him in an instant. He was overwhelmed by a tidal wave of memories of dying and then letting go as the death experience lifted him up from the Humvee. He knew the flow of memories was coming from Sarah and could do nothing to stop it. The powerful memories were threatening to tear his mind apart. He was floating up above the city as her awareness grew in clarity. The events of her life unspooled before them. The experience was like a hyper-real lucid dream. There were people she knew waiting to help her, people who had died. They surrounded her with love. She was told anything she could visualize to comfort her would immediately materialize. As she drifted higher into the air, the roofs of buildings grew smaller and smaller. It was as if floating away was the most natural thing. The building directly below was the parking garage where her body lay. Mark heard his voice crying as if at the end of a long tunnel.

"Don't give up. Please don't give up. I love you!"

The experience abruptly ended. Mark found himself looking at Sarah. An assist had a medical schematic up that showed a weak heartbeat and respiration. His eyes started tearing even worse. She was alive. He was filled with hope but could also see from the assist that she was in danger and needed immediate medical attention. Her blood pressure was dangerously low from loss of blood. She needed transfusions.

Sarah could scarcely move, but as Mark released the parking brake he felt her hand grip his arm.

"Top…" she whispered. "Go top."

"I don't understand."

"Roof… top… go… now."

"The top floor of this garage?"

"Yes…"

"You need medical help."

"Roof… now… medical… next."

Mark had no choice but to do as she wanted. The stray thoughts coming from her were very clear. She would get out and walk, and only hurt herself more if he didn't take her. In frustration he drove to the top of the garage and stopped. He hoped this insanity would be over quickly so he could get her to a hospital. The rain was still coming down. He turned off the headlights but left the Humvee idling.

"Water," said Sarah.

"Rain?"

"Drink."

Mark clambered into the back and returned with a gallon jug of water. He put it down to look for a cup. Sarah picked up the jug with shaky arms and began drinking and drinking. Mark watched her in confused, worried silence. In a short time the jug was empty. He saw her blood pressure was still low but had gone up a little. Her digestive tract must have been working at an accelerated rate, pushing that water through her intestines and into her bloodstream.

Sarah opened the door and carefully started to slide out of the Humvee. Mark got out fast and came around to help her. The rain was pouring down. A steady flow of water was running by his feet. He supported Sarah and let her lead him. She walked to the center of the garage and looked down. He felt her legs give out a little. He looked down and his legs dangerously weakened too. Mark immediately recognized what they were standing on. They were inside a ten-foot circle of red reflective paint with marked compass points. In the center of the circle was a number in white reflective paint: *7051*. Mark had to tell himself to continue breathing. He had a clear memory of this circle and that number from their shared experience of floating away into lucid dreams as Sarah died. The rain increased and with it the water flowing by his feet. An almost invisible loose piece of tar paper was lifted and carried off, exposing an additional digit at the end of the number transmuting *7051* into *70518*. Mark was gripped by a powerful sense of déjà vu. Up until this night he'd had no idea what to believe about life after death. He was confused by what was clearly verification of Sarah's near-death experience.

"There has to be some logical explanation," he said.

Sarah looked into his eyes and said only one word as she let him support her full weight.

"Love…"

Mark Freedman – Waterville, Maine – February 15, 0002 A.P.

Sarah had insisted that they drive for hours to a small forty-eight-bed hospital in Waterville, Maine. Mark had called several hospitals to find which ones were operating. Much to his frustration Sarah had selected one that was the smallest and most isolated. According to Google, Waterville's population was ten thousand at the last census after the plague. Mark hated the idea of taking so long to get her to a hospital, but he knew she was right. They needed to attract the least attention possible. Sarah pulled up her shirt. She winced as she felt around the wound in the front and then her back. Mark knew she was examining herself with the aid of an assist.

"The entry and exit wounds are sealed." Sarah's voice was weak. "The damaged artery and veins have knit back together but things are still leaking. My cavities are all swollen with fluid but I have to keep drinking."

As the Humvee rocketed along the small two-lane country highway, Sarah drank from a second gallon of water. Most of it was gone. Mark was disappointed. His assist reported less of an increase in blood pressure than from the prior gallon, but he would take every bit of good news he could get.

The GPS finally showed the last turn before the hospital. Mark knew the bullet wound looked recent but not hours old. Sarah passed out as he carried her into the emergency room. He told the nurse and then the doctor they had been ambushed and it had taken them days to get here. The doctor was a young woman with a serious air about her. Mark sensed no-nonsense competence. After a few minutes, the doctor looked up from the examining table.

"The entry and exit wounds in your wife's torso are hot to the touch. She's running a hundred-and-three fever. I am not going to sugarcoat anything. This is a dangerous infection. I don't know why the infection sites are not red and swollen, and that worries me too. I don't like what I can't explain."

Mark didn't want this doctor looking for answers to an infection that was not showing normal symptoms and in fact not an infection at all. He knew the nanotech was working hard to rebuild Sarah's damaged body. The heat was from swarming COBIC seeds weaving her insides back together. He decided to play as dumb as possible.

"Please just help her, doc," he said. "Maybe the fever is from being outside in the cold?"

"No sir, it's the wounds. Right now I need to get her blood pressure up, culture the infection, and get her on the right antibiotics."

Mark was relieved when the doctor ordered both IV fluids and a blood transfusion of three bags. He didn't like it when she ordered a regime of expensive, hard to get antibiotics to use until the infection was identified. He didn't like that they would be wasted, but what else could he do? The wrong move might invite an army of Peacekeepers.

"You are going to have to leave the room," announced the doctor. "We need to put in some drains."

"I'm staying with her," said Mark.

"Hospital regulations require—"

"I'm staying!"

The doctor's face was scrunched up in some kind of turmoil. She looked at the door to the examining room, then back at him.

"Does the sight of blood bother you?"

Mark looked down at his shirt covered in Sarah's blood, then back at the doctor.

"Fine, but I need you to stand at the back of the room. If you interfere in any way you have to leave or I will call security to remove you."

Sarah woke six hours later with the sun. Mark had not slept. He could tell from the hospital monitor that her blood pressure was normal. He smiled at her. She lazily smiled back.

"I'm okay," she said.

"I know, but you scared the hell out of me."

"You know what happened," said Sarah. "Right?"

"You were shot and almost died."

"No, that's not what I mean. Don't mess with me. You know I died and came back."

"I don't know any such thing," he said. "You experienced some kind of hallucination from loss of blood and our little nanotech friends kept you alive."

"What about the markings on the garage roof?"

"What about them? I figured it out. The numbering was the street address of the building. You could have seen the address as we pulled into the garage or maybe an assist gave you the address?"

"That's bullshit!" snapped Sarah. "All right, smartass, how did I see that specific number in a red circle at the exact spot on the roof where we found it, and the number we saw during my near-death experience didn't match the address thanks to that piece of loose tar paper?"

Mark remained silent. There had to be a rational explanation. Sarah held out her arms. Mark hugged her and felt her breath on the side of his face. She kissed his cheek. He was so relieved she was alive.

"P.S. I love you too," she whispered.

Communes

Mark Freedman – New Hampshire – February 16, 0002 A.P.

It was a very bright day with sunlight glinting off the snow. Mark was driving at a slower pace. He was relaxing now that they had crossed out of Maine and into New Hampshire. The doctor had been furious with them leaving less than a day later. The blood cultures were not even back yet. She was beside herself that they had refused to take any antibiotics with them. Most of all, she was frantic to run tests to explain how Sarah was asymptomatic in an impossibly short period of time. There was, however, nothing she could do to stop a healthy patient from checking herself out.

Mark looked over at Sarah sleeping with a blanket wrapped around her. He smiled to himself. He felt they were now better prepared. In the trunk of the Humvee, inside the twelve-volt cooler they used for food, were six bags of IV saline. In their first aid pack were sterile IV infusion kits. The supplies had cost him some gold coins and a promise by the hospital pharmacist to tell no one. Now if either of them lost a life-threatening amount of blood, they had a way of keeping their pressure up until COBIC repaired enough of the damage.

Mark glanced over at Sarah again and recalled in perfect detail those terrible moments in the deserted parking structure when he thought she was dead. He remembered saying he loved her. Over the decades his love life had caused him so much heartache, but there was no denying these feelings. He did love her and these feelings worried him even more than losing her. Sarah opened her eyes and smiled lazily at him.

"You look a little pale," she said.

"I don't feel pale."

"So how does pale feel?"

Mark didn't know what to say.

"I'm sorry, baby. I'm just teasing," she said. "Let's stop somewhere and I'll figure out how to put some color into your cheeks."

Against all his willpower, Mark began fantasizing about what she might do to put some color into his cheeks. Heartache and lust were opposite sides of the same coin for him and he knew it.

"I've never felt this alive," announced Sarah as she carefully stretched and repositioned herself in the seat. He saw a wince of pain as she settled in.

"Dying and coming back has changed everything. I now know an amazing life is waiting after this one. I also know in this life we're going do something extremely important, something we were born to

179

do. That's why I was sent back. I didn't have to come back, you know. Souls can live between incarnations in the realm of lucid dreams forever."

"I don't know, Sarah. I know what you think happened, but something about it all seems really false. There's no proof, no way to measure it. I don't believe your nanotech brain ever died, which means you never died. Maybe the god-machine simulated that near-death experience to manipulate us in some way. It could have used prerecorded material of the roof from its archives. You know how it affects our dreams and memories, why not this?"

"Remember when I said I wanted to put some color into your cheeks?" Sarah's tone was no longer teasing.

"Yes."

"Well, forget it! The high priest of science needs to remember that scientific dogma fails at the event horizon of world-changing discoveries. You told me that yourself. Remember? It's intuition that picks up that fumbled ball and makes the discovery. So you're pigheaded to say something doesn't exist just because you don't have the instruments to measure it."

"I'm a Jew. I can't be a high priest."

"See what I mean—pigheaded."

Sarah Mayfair – New York State – February 17, 0002 A.P.

Sarah squinted as the sun came into her eyes. Even with the nerve endings in her torso partially dulled, the entry and exit wounds felt like she was impaled on a long nail that had been run completely through her. She did not fully block the pain because that would have made it too easy to accidently tear open the wounds by moving the wrong way. A day had gone by and she still felt irritated with Mark for being so closed-minded to new discoveries. She glanced at the 5.56mm Sig Sauer pistol hanging from a shoulder sling on his side and a Springfield Armory subcompact .45 on his hip. The Sig Sauer was nothing less than a miniaturized assault rifle that could punch through flak jackets with ease. She was relieved he'd finally come to his senses at least about one thing. She could tell from his emotions the motive for the higher powered weapons was to protect her, not him. She wasn't sure what to think of that yet, but was grateful for any reason that got him to carry something that could do some real damage instead of the 9mm he'd been carrying.

They were two hours from a dead drop where they would hide a piece of the relic for Karla Hunt to pick up once they told her the location. After their close brush at the Lake Erie cabin neither of them were in any hurry for a repeat of that adventure. Like Mark, Sarah trusted Karla but thought her office had leaks.

"You were smart to buy insurance for us with those sentry detectors inside the cabin," said Sarah. "Karla and everyone she knows would be thrown into prison if that video went public."

"I hope that's one policy we never have to file a claim on."

Sarah was preparing to cut a piece off of the relic for Karla. Mark had offered to pull over, but she was fine doing it while they were on the highway. She was using the metal lid from a mess kit as a work surface. The plan was to bury Karla's piece at the dead drop in a sealed jar. A pair of heavy wire cutters made easy work of nipping a corner off the relic. The metal was soft like lead, if it was even metal. Sarah looked back into the mess kit lid just as the smaller piece of the relic fell through a round hole that had not been there a moment ago. What the hell was this? Confused, she pushed herself back in the seat and caught sight of it eating through the seat cushion! She flung the metal lid to the floor, realizing the bigger piece was also chewing its way through the lid.

"Pull over!" she shouted. "Pull over!"

"What?..."

"It's eating through the goddamn seat!"

There was no smoke or smell, just material withering away as if decomposing. It was worse than acid. It was alive.

Sarah's heart had finally slowed. The bullet wounds felt raw. She knew she'd reopened them a little. Mark had found the smaller piece of the relic in the dirt beneath the Humvee. It had eaten its way clear through after they'd stopped and had been sitting in a small crater of its own making. It seemed to have satisfied its hunger. It was now a tiny black cube. Sarah had watched Mark use a spoon to scoop up dirt along with the relic and place the whole mess inside an empty Smucker's jar. She was eyeing that jar sitting on the floor next to her feet as Mark pulled onto the highway. The bigger piece had found enough raw material in the mess kit lid and floor to repair itself. A shallow divot in the mental flooring marked the spot where it had mined the last of the raw materials it had needed. The full-sized relic was now whole and stowed in the back of the Humvee.

Mark Freedman – Newton, Massachusetts – February 19, 0002 A.P.

A heavy storm was predicted for later in the day. They'd been holed up for the past two days in a suburb of Boston. The neighborhood was filled with older single-family homes. There were not many people around. Oddly, it had been far colder here than in Maine. It was one more freakish piece of weather, courtesy of an unstable polar jet stream.

Mark was outside finishing up his work on the Humvee. All the bullet holes in the rear hatch were visible reminders of something unthinkable that had almost happened. Since the early morning he'd been hard at work to make sure the unthinkable did not happen again. This up-armored Humvee model had a thick slab of vertical steel armor between the trunk and passenger compartment. That armor had been easily defeated by the .50 caliber tungsten penetrator that had almost killed Sarah.

Mark finished pouring a steel-mesh reinforced concrete barrier as thick as weight would allow inside the trunk up against the rear armor. Inside the concrete, he'd layered sheets of polycarbonate that he found at a nearby Home Depot. It would take a lot more than a .50 caliber armor piercing bullet to get through these new defenses. As a bonus, the added weight would give them better traction in snow. He knew he was guilty of fighting the last battle, but what other choice did he have?

Mark sat down on the open tail of the Humvee and took a sip of water from a plastic jug. Sarah and Ralph came out of the house and headed off for a walk. Mark watched Sarah's retreating form. She was more important to him than any person had been in his entire life. He tried to suppress the emotions welling up in his chest. Too late, he knew Sarah had felt them already. She turned and smiled at him. She missed very little. Experiencing unease, he picked up his tablet and checked his e-mail for what must have been the hundredth time that day. The e-mail from Karla that he'd been waiting for was finally in his box. It was an average length e-mail addressed to several college friends. It contained personal news and light banter. The message for Mark was steganographically encrypted into the attached photos. The information that emerged was fascinating.

```
Hi Love,
This nanotech relic has a structure nothing
like nanotech seeds. It may as well have been
created in another universe. Unlike seeds, it
does not self-destruct when manipulated. In
fact, it's the exact opposite, it almost fights
back. There seems to be no easy way to destroy
it other than extremely intense heat, around
eight to nine thousand degrees centigrade. We
vaporized some of it inside a mass spectrometer,
hoping to get detailed data on its composition,
but came up with nothing useful. It's mostly
```

*carbon with some hydrogen, nitrogen, oxygen,
and the same trace elements as seeds. So it
looks organic but we know it's not. We're able
to mechanically study it far more easily than
seeds, but for now we have more questions than
insights. It does, however, talk via radio waves
to the n-web, so there is that obvious link
between it and seeds. Surprisingly, the relic
communicates with much higher signal strength
than seeds. Our tests show it has an effective range of several miles and can transmit
on all radio frequencies. The relic also gave
us a nasty surprise by successfully hacking
into our Wi-Fi and cell phone networks! No one
knows what to make of that self-initiated in-
vasive behavior. No one knows how it cracked
our 256bit AES encryption. We're calling it a
promiscuous communicator. There was no deci-
pherable message in the data this device sent
out over our networks. It seems to simply take
apart the data it receives from our networks and
then repackages it for transmission back onto
our networks. It's kind of like a child playing
the copycat game, and there's no way to know
the age of this child. As you know there's no
way to accurately date something that is self-
healing. We took an unscientific poll of the
brain trust working on this project. We asked,
Does this technology predate seeds or did it
come after seeds? The unanimous response was
that this is a more advanced material and so
it came after seeds. When asked for an estimate
of age, this fired up a debate. No one believed
we could make this technology today, and no
one could accept it's millions of years old,
as you believe. So it's a white crow.
Cheers,
K.*

Mark remained unshaken in the accuracy of his original dating and
frustrated by the scientific dogma he kept butting his head against. He
saw this relic as proof that high civilizations existed before the current
rise of humankind. Who and what those civilizations were remained
a question. He believed these civilizations came and went in cycles
of growth and destruction for millions of years, back into the graying
mists of time. Humans were only the most recent species featured in
these cycles. What kind of tool making species came before us? Scientifically, he told himself, we have little historical evidence for what
a human civilization could have been like a hundred thousand years
ago, let alone some other species millions of years prior. We were blind

183

men examining an elephant's trunk and declaring it a tree. In extremely recent geological times, much of the Earth had been scraped clean by glaciers and then flooded by rising oceans. What great achievements, including whole cities, might have been plowed under by glaciers or drowned in the coastal waters of our oceans? In seven thousand years of recorded history, humans went from stone tools, to metal tools, to the atom, and to the moon. Anatomically, modern Homo sapiens have walked the earth for at least 200,000 years and more likely 400,000 years. In all those millennia there was plenty of time for us to have reached the moon and fallen back into ruin more than once. It was illogical to believe humans remained at the same level as a smart monkey for almost 400,000 years and then only in the last 10,000 years figured out how to do something more than bang two stones together. It was the height of modern civilization's ego driven arrogance to believe we were the center of everything and the shining apex of human achievement.

Mark's thoughts drifted back to over two years ago when he'd cracked open a fossil of COBIC mat and found preserved seeds that reanimated. His recall was eerily photographic, as if watching a movie of himself. That fossil had been over a hundred million years old. His discovery did not prove that some high civilization existed back then, but it did raise one of two possible scenarios. Either the seeds literally fell to Earth from space, or high civilizations did exist on Earth over a hundred million years ago and created the god-machine.

A gust of wind stung Mark's face. He rubbed the thick stubble that would soon be a beard. The wind was carrying ice crystals that had been whipped up from the snow crusted ground. Bare tree branches vibrated in the wind like great string instruments. He looked up into a clear patch of sky surrounded by storm clouds and wondered to what heights had we truly reached in our 400,000 years. As his thoughts quieted, Mark could feel the subtle pulls of nearby communes as if in answer to his question.

Both he and Sarah were certain the nearest commune was located somewhere around Buffalo. There were also communes in the vicinity of Detroit, Knoxville, Trenton, and Charleston as well as others farther away. Each ripple in the n-web was like a soft call urging him home. He was anxious to find the next commune. They had to get there well before the betrayer if they were to have any hope of discovering what was going on. Mark was far from convinced that communes were the only hope for the future and that this betrayer named Noah was systematically murdering the future of the world. However, for possibly the first time in his life, Mark was going by intuition and his intuition

184

matched Sarah's on this one point. Their best chance at discovering the truth one way or the other was communes, so they had to try to help stop this killing from going any farther. Noah had left them a calling card in the form of a relic with his name programmed into it. Mark had no hope of understanding the motives behind that strange introduction. Why had the hybrid risked his life to save them from arrest in a subway? Why the horrifying mass murders of entire communes? Maybe Noah was not trying to use them as scapegoats but instead trying to protect them from communes. The question was, Protect them from what? Mental contamination, brainwashing, physical violence—or maybe, just maybe, protect them from the truth?

Sarah returned from her walk and sat down next him on the tail of the Humvee. Mark was beginning to like her short cropped hair. Ralph looked expectantly at both of them, and when no food or petting was offered, headed off to do whatever dogs do when bored. Mark showed Sarah the e-mail from Karla.

"That is not what I expected," said Sarah. "I thought Noah was leaving us something that would help us understand his side of this war."

"Maybe he did and we're just not getting it."

"Maybe, but what I am getting is we need to warn these communes without leading Noah to them," she said. "I think he's shadowing us."

"Agreed," said Mark. "I have a theory the communes we're sensing will remain untouched forever if we go in the opposite direction, but if we head for one, Noah will destroy it before we get there. And the really bad news is, I don't think he needs to even physically follow us. I think he can trace us by our activity on the n-web. There's no doubt he can read our emotions and pick up our stray thoughts. We have to come up with some way of confusing him, some way of hiding our thoughts and emotions from him."

"Do you have a plan?"

"Not even a bad one."

Kathy Morrison – Dallas, Texas – February 19, 0002 A.P.

Kathy was in the lab late at night, as she had been almost every night since beginning her research work at Zero-G. She was double-checking the final details of a key discovery before presenting it to Richard and the other scientists. The discovery had come so quickly that it had stunned her. It was almost as if some crazy kind of synchronicity was at work. Two events had collided to give birth to her discovery: Her failed experiments at using jammers to regulate COBIC blood levels and Richard's breathtaking disclosure about ancient technology.

185

The night her COBIC blood level experiments hit a brick wall, she'd had a terrible dream. In the dream she was performing human experiments to prove that a small amount of COBIC in the brain was required to control biological systems for the body to work normally. In the dream she was purging patients of all COBIC and making them seriously ill to prove the theory. She awoke very disturbed that she was performing harmful human experiments. She'd made some mint tea and sat in front of the computer. While staring at the data from her failed rhesus experiments, an idea suddenly clicked into place. It was a crazy idea—no, an impossible idea—but if it worked, they could cure almost any disease or injury. What was missing from the current COBIC treatment regime was a brain to orchestrate the huge body of COBIC infused into the patient.

The next day Kathy had set up her first experiment using a rhesus monkey. Right from the beginning it had worked, not perfectly, but it worked and it was reproducible. She'd found the key to hyper-healing almost all aliments, not just genetic diseases, and most importantly, this key worked with lower saturations of COBIC in the bloodstream. The breakthrough discovery was a different way of using medical-jammers. In addition to using a jammer to block COBIC from migrating into the brain, a second jammer could be used at a much lower power setting as a network bridge. Using her discovery signals from the residual amount of COBIC found in everyone's brainstem could be bridged to the higher saturation of COBIC infused into a patient's bloodstream. The nanotech inside the medical-jammer did what Kathy had been told it did best. It connected the two isolated n-web networks found in the brain and in the body. That first night of discovery she'd been giddy with excitement. She decided to keep the results to herself until she was sure there were no serious problems with her discovery.

Her follow-up work confirmed that COBIC in the brain stem was responding to the neurological signals of the brain. These signals included those occurring when the brain was receiving damage reports from the body. The result was that when these natural damage signals were detected, COBIC in the brainstem orchestrated a response from COBIC in the bloodstream that paralleled that of the body's own repair systems. If the bloodstream had enough free-swimming COBIC, a cure was effected. If not, the healing instructions went unfulfilled. With her breakthrough, the natural healing directives of the brain were amplified, enabling a patient with only moderate levels of COBIC in their blood to experience a great deal of enhanced healing. This new interface offered many of the advantages of seed infestation of neurons without the actual infestation or, as Richard put it, *seeds taking root in the brain*. With her protocol, the residual COBIC in the brain stem did not multiple or invade neurons, so no information could be injected into the patient's memory. The result was zero risk of being influenced or controlled by that god-machine monster.

Her protocol was not perfect. It had its weaknesses. Like the original application of medical-jammer technology, her new application worked, but she did not understand how the nanotech did its small miracles. While that was troubling, the big weakness of her discovery was that it could not be used to heal the brain. That meant it was not a cure for terrible illnesses such as Alzheimer's, Parkinson's, or brain cancer. A high level of COBIC could not be infused into the brain without immediate risk of infestation of neurons. Still, this exact same limitation also applied to the current COBIC treatment regime. Kathy found herself wishing there was some way to use jammers to force seeds from an infested brain without leaving behind a mound of ruined gray matter. Sadly, she now understood that while all these stunning approaches could greatly extend life expectancies, they would never come close to providing the lifespan of a hybrid.

Kathy tried to keep in mind that this was really just the first baby step. Who knew where this technology might be in ten or twenty years? As a last resort for terminal patients there was the option of infusing a super saturation of COBIC into the brain. Unfortunately, the risks of brain damage or hybridization were very real. One or the other was the guaranteed prognosis. Kathy wondered if she would submit to a treatment like that. Fear of death would probably force her to accept the risks, and there was no proof that hybridization robbed you of your identity or your soul. Mark was still Mark—as far as she could tell.

Mark Freedman – Buffalo, New York – February 20, 0002 A.P.

Mark was weary from driving. The sun was glinting in his eyes. They had traveled as far away from all the communes as possible without entering Canada or heading out to sea. He rubbed his face and could not get used to the new, bristly experience. The close cropped beard was now thick enough to change his appearance. The radio was tuned to the *Corley Cox Show*. The government-sponsored show was supposedly guaranteed by new FCC rules to be free of bias and contain only substantiated facts. Reality strayed very far from these guarantees. The *Corley Cox Show* would have been right at home with any other entertainment news show that was popular before the plague. The show was, among other things, a national platform for an extreme pseudo-

Luddite group called Wright's Faith. This hate group took the USAG's scientist *as* villain propaganda and expanded it to include all scientists, not just the alleged perpetrators of the nanotech genocide. Wright's Faith and its splinter groups had a membership estimated in the tens of thousands. There had been bombings of private research facilities, shootings, and even a public hanging while government facilities and scientists went unharassed. Mark suspected Wright's Faith was doing some of the bloodiest work for the USAG, work the USAG did not dare to do even with Peacekeepers. Corley Cox was speaking in her low, seductive trademark voice.

My friends, we have subversives out there. Some are probably listening to this show just as you are right now. These radicals are not like us. They are not on our side. They see us as villains, as despoilers of the Earth, as a virus that needs to be stamped out. They do not know their Bible. They do not know that God gave man all this bounty for us to use wisely. They want us to use nothing. They want our children to starve so that some endangered butterfly is not disturbed in its cocoon. These subversives are the same criminals who were eco-terrorists before the plague. These radicals are so mentally deranged they think genocide is an acceptable way to save Mother Nature from civilized people.

We have some new names added to our list of criminals against humanity. The names should ring a bell from that recent bombing in Canada. A Nobel Prize winning scientist named Mark Freedman and his cohort Sarah Mayfair are now at the top of our list. I'll tell you more about them later, but the most important fact to know right now is that Freedman is the monster responsible for genetically engineering COBIC and making it possible for that bacteria to operate with a nanotech seed inside it. Billions of innocent lives are not enough for this Bonnie and Clyde nightmare duo. They are still out there and still at it. I know you all have seen the footage from the bombing in Canada. But I'll bet you don't know there was a second bombing in our own backyard in Portland, Maine. The authorities have not announced it yet. They want to make sure they don't make a mistake, but I have it on very good authority that Freedman and Mayfair are also responsible for that bombing and possibly more. This means they are in the motherland and at large. They could be in your town right now planning on killing your neighbors and your family. They need to be stopped before more innocent people are murdered. They need to be stopped before they can get their hands on some other weapon of mass destruction, because make no mistake—they will use it.

These vicious criminals should not be considered part of the human race. They should be executed on sight. I know our government won't do that, but it should. I have an idea...

Mark turned off the radio after Corley Cox had broadcast her plan. The only reason to listen to this hate speech was to take measure of the minds of one of their adversaries.

It had started to snow. The sky was a uniform gray. There were no individual clouds, just a solid dome of winter storm. In another hour they'd reach their stopping point for the night. The GPS had taken them off the highway, and the next turn would be a dirt road. The KOA campsite was perfect. Most of these sites were now way stations for a new generation of gypsies. It was too cold and unpleasant for anyone managing the campground to care about who came and went.

Mark had a plan to prevent Noah from tracking them through the n-web or following them in any way to the next commune. Part of the plan required air travel, and Karla had agreed to make the arrangements for them on a military jet. He had just explained some of the plan to Sarah and she was not happy.

"How can you trust the USAG with our lives!" she shouted.

"Karla has arranged everything and we have a fail-safe."

"That's right. It's going to fail and we won't be safe!"

"Karla knows we have all kinds of incriminating material. I told her we lost equipment at Lake Erie, but thank god we hung on to the Sentry Kit. If those recordings had been found by USAG forces, we'd be in a lot of trouble. Karla is smart. She's connected the dots."

Sarah was silent. Mark could tell the audacity of his plan had just become clear to her.

"You're actually blackmailing Karla?" asked Sarah.

"I hate that word. She knows we're all in the same boat and will make sure we stay safe, which she'd have done anyway."

"You are a bastard," said Sarah. "But that is a good plan. You know those recordings could even land her in front of a firing squad."

"What choice do we have? Besides, I erased them."

"What if Noah gets a stray thought from us before we take off that tips him to where we're going?"

"We keep ourselves in the dark to keep him in the dark. We wait until we're safely in the air before randomly selecting the commune from a list of at least ten that are widely scattered over an area eight hundred miles across."

Sarah nodded to herself. Mark again went over the plan in his mind. The basic idea was simple. The only way Noah could be following them was by picking up their data going out over the n-web and using it to track them. To get to a commune before him meant they had to block their signals. Mark knew only one way to do that. They had to go by air. As soon as they took off, their link to the god-machine would be severed. While they were miles above the ground it would be impossible for their signals to reach the god-machine's nanotech network, which covered land and sea but not the air. Noah would experience a mysterious blackout and realize the game was on, but he would have no way of knowing which commune they were headed toward. Mark had needed Karla to make this happen. Her division had Air Force jets at their disposal. Even if they didn't need to make their random midair decision, he and Sarah could never make it get through a TSA checkpoint without being recognized. They also needed Karla to arrange for the loan of an advance armor Humvee at their destination. Mark hated not having their modified Humvee on this excursion. He'd done all that work hardening it and now they were leaving it behind to get on a jet. It was always a waste to fight the last battle, yet the reverse was to fight human nature. At least they could bring most of their gear with them.

Karla had appeared eager to help and she'd received something in return. Mark was going to allow her to run him through an fMRI for a full workup. The tests were also part of the cover story for all the air travel. They were going to meet for the fMRI work at a children's hospital in Columbus, Ohio. The same small jet that brought Karla to Columbus would be waiting for all of them at a nearby Air National Guard field. After driving to the airfield, in less than two hours they could be on the ground near whatever commune their selected.

Sarah Mayfair – Pennsylvania – February 22, 0002 A.P.

The plan was in action. They had landed in Philadelphia two hours ago. Sarah was driving a new loaner Humvee at highway speed. They were initially not sure if the Trenton commune was in Pennsylvania or New Jersey. After an hour of driving west through Pennsylvania, it had become clear the commune was not in Pennsylvania. They now were headed toward the nearest crossing into New Jersey. An hour ago, Mark had been thrilled at how the plan had come together. They'd even

190

learned something useful from Karla's fMRI and psych workups. The fMRI had shown that the nanotech brain interface boosted the activity of not just hybridized neurons but also uninfected brain cells as well. There was no other way to interpret the data than Mark's problem-solving ability was off the charts.

The highway was lined with trees and rolling hills on either side. They were driving toward a coal-fired power plant running at full capacity, spewing huge pillars of smoke and stream that reached the clouds. So recklessly stupid, thought Sarah. No one seemed to get it. Did they want to provoke another plague?

Mark banged his fist into the dashboard.

"Fuck!" he shouted. "I need some of that off the charts problem-solving ability right fucking now!"

Sarah glanced at him to make sure he was not losing it completely. His expression was dark. He was extremely angry. So angry he'd failed to notice the power plant. She could feel his emotions getting the better of him in a destructive way. They both knew that Noah could be racing toward them at this very moment or worse, racing toward the commune. Why were they having so much trouble finding this one? She hoped Noah was having the same problems. They knew the commune was in New Jersey but could not narrow down the location to anything smaller than half the state, the northern half! The tidal pulls from this singularity seemed to be randomly moving all over the map. The intensity of the pull had increased to a mild physical sensation, which was the only clue they were moving in the right direction. As they drew closer, the movement seemed to expand to cover a widening area. She and Mark were also getting flashes of remote visions from non-hybrids who were near the singularity. The flashes were a little too close to her experiences of living through kill-zones. There was one flash in particular that was very troubling. She was not sure, but it was either déjà vu or she had seen this place before. The visual snapshot was from inside a boarded up restaurant and included a partial view of a window through which she could see the tops of buildings across the street. The window had a red logo on it, but not enough was visible to read a name. All she could see was part of a red circle.

Sarah felt her stomach knot up as she drove around a bend. Directly ahead of them was one of the bridges she'd tried and failed to cross over two years ago when fleeing New Jersey. When that massive kill-zone had struck, everyone she'd loved had died. Her lover Kenny was gone, though she'd never found his body. Her mother and father had died. She had buried them with her own hands in their backyard. This bridge across the Delaware Water Gap had been quarantined by the military along with all of New Jersey. Now the bridge was empty and carried the scars of a battle fought long ago. Her fingers tightened on the wheel as emotions roiled in her blood. She told herself to breathe in and breathe out slowly. The sound of the tires changed as she reached the bridge. It felt unreal to be here. So many memories were surfacing. Breathe in, breathe out.

This stretch of Interstate Route 80 in New Jersey was clear of debris. They were running straight east directly toward New York City and the Manhattan Protectorate. The number of travelers on the highway was increasing. Sarah felt a wild swing in the tidal pull from the singularity. It was now coming from about 130 degrees off their direction of travel to the south of them.

"Mark!" said Sarah.

"I felt it."

Sarah lifted off the gas. The Humvee coasted to a stop on the shoulder. A tractor trailer, which had been behind them, blew past with its horn blaring.

"Are we going in the right direction?" asked Sarah. "That pull came from behind us. How could we have passed it?"

"I don't know. This has to be some kind of defense mechanism, decoys, reflections, maybe? I'm not sure."

As he spoke, the tidal pull moved at an impossible speed. It now felt like the singularity was ahead of them at about 70 degrees to the north. Sarah engaged the parking brake. She had no idea what to do.

"I've got it," shouted Mark. "Sit tight, don't move the Humvee. I think I know what to do."

"Not moving an inch."

As they sat on the shoulder, Sarah felt the singularity moving again. This time when it paused, it left like it was almost due south. Sarah watched for twenty minutes as Mark used his tablet to drop pins on a map of New Jersey each time the singularity moved. Each pin was dropped at the approximate compass bearing from their position where the singularity paused. The pins formed a rough arc that covered about 200 degrees.

"I think I have enough data points," he said.

He drew a line on the map from their location through the center of the arc. The line crossed over Morristown, South Orange, Newark, and then hit the Hudson River.

"The commune is somewhere near this line," said Mark. "We drive until we pass it, then circle back in a spiral until we hit a vortex."

"You hope," said Sarah.

"What else have we got?"

Sarah could not take her eyes off that map. The line went straight through Morristown. Was her uneasiness just the awful memories of walking through Morristown after the first big kill-zone? She'd been a rookie on the Morristown force when the plague had hit while she was out on patrol with her partner. Her life had been perfect, then in a single moment it was destroyed. Now the entire area had become the very definition of the Outlands. It was wide open and dangerous and…

Sarah sighed. It all clicked into place.

"I know where the singularity is," she said. "It's Morristown. You know that flash I had of people inside a boarded-up restaurant? I just recognized those rooftops seen through the window. That restaurant is just off the Morristown Square."

"Let's go," said Mark. "You're amazing."

Sarah was deeply disturbed by the idea of going back to Morristown. It took a great deal of willpower to push down on the accelerator. Maybe they should try for a different commune.

"Are you okay?" asked Mark.

"Fine!"

Thirty minutes later Sarah passed the highway exit for Dover; next to it was a sign with a red quarantine warning. No one here had bothered to clean up much after the plague. Maybe those who stayed liked the biohazard warning signs. The highway interchange to Morristown was just a few more exits. Her anxiety had not stopped growing since she'd realized the singularity was in Morristown. She felt a tingling inside her, as if tiny things were crawling around within the cavities of her body. She heard what sounded like a whisper. Just wind noise, she told herself. The whisper grew a little louder as if a disembodied voice was trying to murmur into her left ear. The words were garbled, but the voice was unmistakably and all too familiar. This could not be happening again. Not now! She was not having a breakdown. She'd struggled with these sinister voices years ago. After she'd recovered she'd never heard them again. Her doctor had told her it was little more than an overactive imagination, a kind of verbal daydream. He'd reassured her that a great many people hear brief, phantom voices and require no psychiatric treatment at all. It was common in cases of physical trauma such as hers. Her heart was pounding in her chest. She caught an intelligible fragment as if eavesdropping.

Will sheeee be here soooonnn?

The whispers dredged up all the old memories with them. Sarah relived the dream premonitions she'd had before the first plague hit New Jersey. The dreams had begun long after the voices had stopped. Months went by in seconds as she recalled it all in perfect, terrible detail within her nanotech brain. She re-experienced her fears of whatever had been mentally pursuing her from deep below her feet in underground rivers. Years later, she now suspected it had been COBIC bacteria invading her mind from its breeding grounds in the subterranean waters.

"Sarah," said Mark.

"What... oh..."

Sarah lifted off the gas and cut the wheel. She'd automatically taken the interchange, but now a few miles later had been driving right past the exit for Morristown. Minutes later, shortly after leaving the highway, the singularity seemed to grow into sharp focus. They were apparently close enough that there was no longer any phantom movement, and with that Sarah got her first taste of the real strength of this singularity. She felt as if caught in rapids that were feeding into a whirlpool and it was far too late to turn back. They were now being drawn inescapably into its heart.

"Feel that," said Mark. "This singularity's far more powerful than Chicago, Montreal, and Portland all added together!"

"Maybe the guides are maturing and growing stronger."

"Could be."

Sarah heard a different answer whispered into her ear.

Weeee were always strong enough to kill themmm...

It took all her willpower not to screech to a halt in the middle of the road and scream for it to get out of her head. How could she tell Mark about the voices without him worrying she was having a breakdown? After a few silent miles she began to relax her guard a little. The evil hallucination, premonition, or whatever it was remained quiet.

They were traveling on an empty two-lane road lined with trees and front yards. Mark seemed confident he'd done enough of his triangulation tricks to have a good bearing now that the singularities location remained constant. Everywhere Sarah looked she saw decaying cars and other artifacts from her lost home. The road surface as well as the yards all had drifts of autumn leaves mixed with snow. The unnatural groundcover only added to Sarah's agitation. At this time of year the leaves should have been deeply buried under a thick mattress of white.

On the roads the leaves were cemented in place by ice and slurries of the reddish brown clay. Muddy frozen tire tracks in the leaf-clogged roads were testament to people living or prowling nearby. Suddenly they drove through what had to be the outer vortex. Sarah gasped. She hit the brakes, stopping in the middle of street. She looked over at Mark and knew he was seeing the n-web projected in front of his eyes by an assist.

"Keep going about a mile then make a right," said Mark.

"Do you still want to go straight up to the door?"

"What choice do we have? Time's running out. Besides, don't we have an unofficial introduction from Adam?"

"That would be Adam the dead liar?" said Sarah.

Mark smiled grimly. They continued driving. Sarah knew from memory capsules that Mark was still refining the triangulation map in his head. They were now close enough that if Noah beat them to the commune, they would see and feel the explosion. Following Mark's instruction, she turned down a tree-lined road in what had been an expensive neighborhood. As they reached the top of a hill, Sarah saw an historical estate and knew in her gut that was it. She could feel Mark had spotted the same place. There was no need to say a word.

The estate had a huge, three-story revolutionary era mansion build from red brick and several smaller red brick outbuildings. A red brick wall with white capstone encircled the acres of ground. What looked like a modern professional observatory had been added in a style that blended with the original architecture. The place looked like a museum.

As they reached the wall surrounding the grounds, Sarah could see the estate was far more fortified than the other communes. Some of the security appeared recently added. A twelve-foot-tall chain-link fence ringed the property 20 feet inside of the red brick wall. The fence was topped with razor wire and floodlights. Every few yards a video camera pointed down at the street. Sarah pulled to a stop at the gate. A vehicle barricade was blocking the entrance. Several very large Dobermans appeared at the gate. Ralph clambered up front between the driver and passenger seats. Two cameras were pointed straight at them from the gate. On either side of the Humvee, two more cameras looked down on them. Sarah felt dizzy this close to the singularity. It was overwhelming her and calling to her in waves. The undulating strength only added to her disorientation.

"Now what?" asked Sarah.

"Let's see who's home. Try the callbox."

Sarah rolled down her window and pressed the only button on the callbox. Five minutes passed with no reply. Sarah pressed the button again. Time seemed to run slowly for her as if in a recurring dream. No reply.

"We're being ignored," said Mark.

He reached into the small backpack that contained the relic and took it out with his bare hands. Sarah thought she could feel it slightly damping the emotions radiating from him.

"Let's see if we can get their attention this way," said Mark.

He got out of the Humvee and walked up as close to the cameras as possible. The Dobermans were barking and pawing at the gate. Ralph climbed into Mark's seat and clearly wanted to attack those dogs. Mark held out his hand with the relic toward the cameras.

"We were at the Montreal commune," he yelled. "Adam sent us. We've come to warn you about the betrayer who owns this device. We need your help and you need ours."

The gate remained shut with Mark standing before it as the minutes dragged on. Her dizziness was persisting along with a small pain that was now growing in the center of her forehead. Sarah knew she was being watched. Mark started to walk back to the Humvee, then turned and addressed the cameras once more.

"We'll wait nearby for three days. I know you can find us."

Mark opened the door, coaxed Ralph back into the rear seat, and then climbed in. He was radiating frustration. He put the relic back into its dark space inside the backpack.

"Let's get out of here," he said. "We'll find a place close by. Maybe we'll get lucky and catch someone coming or going from the estate."

"I'm happy to get some distance from this singularity," said Sarah. "I hope you know what you're doing with that invitation."

Sarah felt almost normal again. The dizziness had faded along with the headache. They had driven down all the streets that offered a view of the estate. Two of the streets they'd explored ran along a hillside and provided perfect vantage points. Yet Mark did not like those streets because of the time it would take to intercept anyone coming or going from the estate. Most of the property for blocks surrounding the estate had been gutted by fire and appeared uninhabitable. The trees were mostly dead in that area. The houses had crumbled. Something terrible had happened there. Sarah believed it was riots. In the past two and a half years she had seen far too many examples of that kind of mass insanity. She felt a glimmer of a distant presence that might have been the betrayer. If he was coming, he had to be on his way toward them by now. In Montreal they'd been told by Adam to complete their journey.

She'd assumed he'd meant finding more communes and evolving. Sarah now wondered if her near-death experience was the journey she was supposed to complete. The betrayer was a true grim reaper. Was he destined to help her complete that journey by killing her? Thankfully, the whispers remained silent and did not answer her thoughts.

Mark decided unilaterally their best option was one of the burned-out hulks directly across from the entrance to the estate. Sarah had misgivings as she pulled into the long driveway of a ruined house situated on the side of a low hill. The property had an unobstructed view of the estate. She cut the engine and climbed out of the Humvee with Mark. They both walked around as if they owned the half-collapsed pile of rubble. The yard was a mixture of frozen leaves, old pieces of singed building material, and muddy snow. There was deeper snow pooled on the shady side of the house. No footprints or tire tracks could be seen anywhere. Sarah peered in through a broken window and saw the conditions were worse inside than out. She walked down toward the street. This stretch of fire ravaged neighborhood was silent and empty. The emotions of this place nurtured the morbid feelings inside her. The singularity then layered its own confusion and disorientation on top. She began expecting the voices in her head to start at any moment and wanted to flee.

"It's a dump," said Mark. "But our dump."

"Very funny."

"We're not going to find a better place to set up shop."

"It's too close to the singularity. Can't you feel that?"

"Okay, so our new home's not perfect."

"Stop trying to be funny."

"Show me another option."

"Set up a couple of the sentry detectors here, then we move as far back from the singularity as we can while staying close enough to intercept any traffic," she said. "There're plenty of empty houses farther away. This whole neighborhood is deserted."

Mark Freedman – Morristown, New Jersey – February 22, 0002 A.P.

Mark was rocked in his seat as Sarah skillfully maneuvered the Humvee over a downed telephone pole that blocked the street. Judging by its condition, the pole had been lying there since the plague. They had been cruising the area for thirty minutes. Mark had to admit Sarah was right. Getting farther away from the singularity was the smart option. If they'd stayed on top of it, they'd probably already have become tightly wound springs ready to snap. The strong emotional pulls from the singularity were gone now that they were just seven blocks away. Mark wanted to find a place that could be secured and had a garage to hide the Humvee. This part of the neighborhood had some extensive fire damage but nothing as bad as the street directly across from the estate.

Sarah slowed to a crawl. Mark sized up a house that looked almost intact except every window on the bottom floor was broken and gang graffiti was scrawled across the front. It was very unlikely anyone was living there.

"What do you think?" Sarah asked.

"I think we have a winner."

They had already decided there was no way to be inconspicuous, so they wouldn't try. Being obvious might even help. Sarah put the Humvee into a low gear and plowed up into the snow-buried driveway. After knocking on the front door and satisfying himself no one was inside, Mark tried the knob. The door was locked, which was a good sign. Sarah stayed out front to keep watch while he climbed in through a window. The inside of the house felt colder than outside. An assist confirmed a ten-degree difference. Mark tried a light switch and was rewarded with a satisfying glow. He located the thermostat, then opened the front door for Sarah. In a few minutes the vents were blowing warm air. There were piles of leaves and snow inside on the floor in front of each broken window. All the furniture was draped with sheets. Mark went into the kitchen while Sarah explored elsewhere. The cabinets were empty except for some canned food. His stomach grumbled. He found his way into the garage and backed the Humvee inside so that it was facing out, ready for a quick escape.

What was left of the day had gone smoothly. Mark was lying on a bed in the upstairs master bedroom. Sarah was in the shower. She had left the door open to warm the bedroom a little more. Steam was floating out along the ceiling and creating a halo around the lights. The upstairs had turned out to be cozy. With the staircase barricaded with furniture it was also reasonably secure. The sentry tablet was displaying two images of the entrance to the estate. The downward camera angle from the burned-out house across the street from the estate was perfect. He could see all the buildings on the estate and a fair amount of the surrounding acreage of trees and snow-covered ground. He'd set up the remaining detectors around the outside of their new residence. Any motion picked by any detectors would trip an alarm. Confident in his work, he closed his eyes and reached inward for the timeline program.

His awareness shifted as if he'd entered the virtual reality interface for the timeline archive. He was floating inside a pure white void of infinite size. Projected in front of him was the three-foot-wide touch screen tablet. A trackball-like globe floated next to it. The huge tablet was covered with windows that contained tiny moving scenes like video clips. Sarah's near-death experience was troubling him because of her unshakable conviction that it was real. She now believed in reincarnation and life after death. More than once they'd debated, almost arguing, and then given up in frustration. Mark reasoned that if reincarnation was real, shouldn't he be able to find examples of it in the archives? Searching the archives was a complex, error-prone process. He initiated searches for pairs of behavioral matches with a hundred years of differences in date or more. It was an easy search to construct and as good a place to start as any on this fool's errand. Soon he had hundreds of parallel searches running, each with slightly looser criteria for the matches than the last. In the end he had a small set of loose matches with nothing that looked promising. He had to admit it was not a very logical way to begin his inquiry. Why would a reincarnated soul exhibit a similar behavior? Maybe the answer was, Why wouldn't they? He had a hard time taking any of this seriously.

Mark awoke to Sarah kissing him on the cheek. She was wearing a bathrobe and leaning over him at the edge of the bed. The outside windows were dark. He must have slept for hours. He felt the singularity pulling on him a little. He hadn't noticed that before. Sarah looked at him as if his mind were a window she was gazing into.

"The singularity's gotten a little stronger," she said. "I think this proves my idea that the guides are maturing."

"If this keeps up, we may want to move farther back."

"Thank you for saying that."

Sarah kissed him again, this time on the lips. The kiss lingered deliciously. The bedside light clicked off. He felt her climbing onto him in the bed.

The sentry tablet was beeping. Mark reached for it as if it were an alarm clock. In the glow of the tablet he saw Sarah was staring at it with him. The moon was shining brightly in the video image. A lone figure in a heavy coat was slowly trudging through the snow from the mansion to the observatory. Mark thought it looked like a woman but could not say why. Her path was marked by a trail of tiny black spots that were her footprints.

"I bet there are no emotions radiating from that woman," said Sarah.

"I think she's an emotional void like Adam, sometimes radiating and sometimes not."

"Are you sure it's even a woman?" asked Mark.

"Aren't you?"

A few minutes later Mark could see the observatory's dome opening as a razor-thin seam of light vertically split it. Inside was a telescope that had to be about 30 inches in diameter. The turret swiveled, then stopped, pointing directly at him on the screen. It felt like some kind of terrible cannon that was ready to fire. The scope tipped up, then stopped. Three green laser beams lanced out of the observatory into the sky. Mark had seen lasers like this before. They were used to modulate adaptive optics in telescopes to correct for atmospheric distortions. The view on the tablet remained unchanged for close to an hour. Mark decided on sleep. He awoke in a lucid dream in which he was holding Sarah's hand. They were gazing down on a vast plain blanketed with a high-technology city that reached to the horizon in all directions. The tableau looked more like an integrated circuit than a vast, futuristic city. Sarah squeezed his hand, giving him a signal. He had a strong intuition that this was the real Sarah in his dream and not a thought-form. Her appearance was slightly different than in real life. Her hair was once again long and her eyes looked haunted. He had not seen that expression in her eyes since their days at the BVMC lab when the plague was coming for them all. Was she in his dream or was he in hers?

"Can you hear them?" asked Sarah.

"I don't hear anything."

"It's the dream people. They're whispering in my ears."

Now Mark could hear whispering or maybe he was hearing through Sarah's mind. It was a female voice as soft as a butterfly's kiss, yet each of her words were deeply engraved into his heart.

"We live inside the goddess, an entire world of us in the space of a drop of rain."

The dreamscape changed. Mark could see life-sized people. He looked at Sarah and knew she saw them too. Projected around him was an entire world of lost souls going about their lives in a condition where everything was semi-transparent. They seemed to perceive Mark and Sarah but chose to ignore them. He could hear their minds. We do not interact with the material world. We do not care about the sleepers. We have concerns that are far greater and vaster. We do not involve ourselves in the meaningless politics of a race of fragile things clinging to the surface of a rock orbiting a burning star.

Mark doubted this world of nonphysical being could be real—an entire universe of living souls inside the god-machine. He decided it was more likely he was inside Sarah's dream and some of her obsession with life after death had been projected onto her dreamscape. Since her near-death experience, Sarah now thought the dream world was a very real plane of awareness, a higher place than the material world. Mark wondered if the god-machine or any physical machine could facilitate life after death or reincarnation. What if the god-machine was actually built in the dream world? If that were the case, the god-machine that he knew might only be a material projection of a far greater creation that was built by beings inhabiting a higher plane. Assuming such a plane could even exist.

Mark abruptly awoke in body shock and confusion. Someone was dragging him out of bed by his feet. His first thought was that Sarah had gone mad, then he saw her dragged past him with an expression of pure terror in her eyes. They were both naked. He tried to fight back but nothing moved. His body was unresponsive, as if in sleep paralysis. His eyes worked, his breathing worked, but nothing more. Lying on the floor next to Sarah, he watched as the house was ransacked. The raiders did not speak, but their actions were clearly coordinated mentally. An assist showed they were all highly evolved to a level similar to Adam. Fanning out from the nanotech-processing nexus in their skulls were orange roots that extended far down into the spinal column. They were an intimidating sight, but compared to the godlike betrayer they were primitive.

The tossing of the house stopped in unison as soon as the relic was found. Mark wondered in a moment of clarity if Noah had left the relic for Sarah to find to set them up as even bigger scapegoats. He and Sarah were handled as if weightless rag dolls. Pillowcases were placed over their heads. Sheets were rolled around them. He felt himself leave the ground as he was carried away on shoulders. He tried to communicate with Sarah but failed. Frigid outside air chilled his skin. He tried to calm down and detach his furious mind to learn as much as he could about his captors. There were no stray thoughts. No telltale physical sensations or smells. All he was left to work with were sounds. He then realized he heard no footfalls, yet he knew he was in the midst of a group of hybrids. All he heard was the sound of the wind and a soft rubbing of fabric. The quiet reminded him of a pod of killer whales hunting in near silence. For some reason this idea caused even greater dread than their capture.

He heard a heavy door *whoosh* shut, and warm air enveloped him. He guessed they were inside the old mansion. The silence was now deeper with the wind gone. He felt himself passing through one vortex, then another. The experience was the same as when he'd entered the Montreal commune, except these barriers and the side effects were far stronger. Eventually, without warning, the pillowcase was pulled from his head. Sarah was next to him. Her pillowcase had also been removed at the same time. Strength began returning to his limbs. Four hybrids stood nearby, observing them. They were in a bedroom that looked like a Revolutionary War era movie set. Still wrapped in their sheets, they had been set down next to each other on a large four-poster bed. Their clothes and toiletries were neatly laid out at the foot of the bed. Other personal items were arranged on a dresser. How were all these details possible? Had he blacked out and lost time? Mark realized these hybrids staring at him felt ancient compared to those in the Montreal commune. Without exchanging a word or glance, the hybrids left the room. There was the sound of a heavy lock engaging inside the door.

All Mark's faculties had returned and were in fact heightened, including the same sense of being hyper-connected that he'd experienced in Montreal. There was also the same deep peace and sensual pleasures. The feelings were so strong here that they were debilitating.

After dressing, Mark and Sarah explored the room and soon realized it was a prison. The door was solid steel made to look like wood. The windows were six-inch-thick ballistic plastic. The walls were solid and felt like steel was behind the wood paneling.

They had been in isolation for an hour before their captors came for them. Mark felt disoriented being this close to the singularity. His shoe caught on the carpet as they were being escorted in silence down hallways filled with period art and antiques. He tried to ask questions of their captors with no results.

They were delivered into a great room large enough to hold a reception. The walls were paneled in dark wood. The great room was empty, except at the far end stood a massive fireplace with an arrangement of three armchairs, a small end table, and a throw rug. A huge fire was crackling. There was an aroma of smoke laced with fragrant woods. Mark felt a deep sense of peace and fulfillment. He tried to fight the pleasurable emotions but was unable to suppress them. He was receiving a stream of memory capsules from Sarah, which confirmed she was experiencing the same emotions.

Then he noticed an ancient-looking hybrid sitting in one of the chairs. How could he have not seen this hybrid before? He felt mentally corrected by the man for thinking the word *hybrid*. The initiate's eyes were open but Mark could somehow tell his awareness was mostly elsewhere. He spotted what he intuitively knew was Noah's relic on the end table next to the ancient initiate. They were ushered forward by their escorts. The initiate stood to greet them. The sense of peace and happiness was overwhelming as Mark shook hands. The initiate did not speak and instead only smiled with deep kindness. An assist showed every inch of his ancient body was saturated with nanotech seeds to the same level as Noah. The initiate was small of stature and in some way reminded Mark of Mahatma Gandhi. He had a leathery face, bald head, and carried a smell of what an assist identified as Turkish cigarette smoke. The initiate just stood there smiling for what seemed like hours, then spoke in a thick Middle Eastern accent.

"Hello, my friends. You may call me Mustafa. Please sit."

Mark sat down. He was overwhelmed. Sarah sat next to him. He could tell by looking at her that she was just as confused.

"May we offer you refreshments?" said Mustafa.

The initiate's eyes turned toward the end table. Mark's eyes followed as if led. On the end table was an antique Middle Eastern coffee set made from silver and ceramics. The set was meticulously arranged on a heavy, circular silver tray. Mark knew from an assist the collection would have been a prized addition in any museum. How had he not seen the coffee service before?

"We have a splendid Turkish coffee made from beans flown in from Yemen," said Mustafa. "They are cultivated with great care by a family that has been growing coffee since the sixth century. We roast the fresh beans here over a wood fire, the way it was done by our ancestors."

"Are you the voice of the guide?" asked Mark.

Mustafa looked disappointed. He picked up a cup and sipped from it.

"No coffee then? Very efficient of you, right to the matter at hand, but too bad. Maybe later? Yes, I am the voice of the guide. We must apologize for how you were brought to us. It was a sad necessity as the betrayer may have been watching from a great distance. As with many of us, the betrayer does not need eyes to see."

Mustafa seemed to have more of an individual identity than Adam, who had thought and talked almost exclusively in plural. Mustafa picked up the relic. As he lifted it in his hand it sprang to life. The screen was covered with runic text, which was filling it and scrolling to the left at a high rate.

"This little nexus takes more than it gives," said Mustafa. "I suspect you have already discovered this quirk. It drinks of you in exchange for data. Has the betrayer used this nexus to communicate with you? Has he used it to show you things?"

"Just his name," said Sarah.

"Ahhh, very interesting… and what would that name be?" asked Mustafa.

"Noah," answered Sarah.

Mustafa set the nexus down on the table. The screen turned off. The old hybrid stood and walked to the fireplace. He extended his hands toward the flames to warm them.

"We desire any new information about this one who calls himself Noah," said Mustafa.

Memories containing illustrations, history, statistics, and more about Noah flooded into Mark's brain. The force of this informational assault came with a physical sensation of traveling at great speed. He knew Sarah was likewise under assault. He knew this violation was an assist from Mustafa. The invasion of memories was filled with the aftermath of bloody assaults. Mark felt he needed a shower to wash off what Noah had done. Mustafa returned to his chair.

"When this betrayer murders a commune they are abruptly cut off from this world," said Mustafa. "No memories or feeling escape. We need to learn more about why this betrayer has turned on his own kind."

Another violation of memories poured into Mark. It was the commune's plan for capturing Noah, interrogating him, and then incinerating him to insure his mental-virus did not spread through the n-web to other initiates. Their entire scheme felt as vile and murderous as what Noah was guilty of committing.

Mustafa frowned. He took another sip of his coffee, then threw the remaining contents of the cup into the fire. His appearance seemed to subtly shift. He now radiated a kind of mild body heat, a comforting warmth like the fire.

"You were guided here for a purpose," said Mustafa. "The betrayer will come for you and when he does we will take him."

"Why would Noah care about us?" said Mark.

"This Noah gave you a valuable relic from our past, did he not?" said Mustafa. "You are important to this betrayer."

Mustafa picked up the nexus and handed it to Sarah.

"This nexus is yours," said Mustafa. "You were led to it. It was given to you. This nexus is… hmm… shall we say… attuned to you. You know some people believe this material world is a dream. Do you believe such a miracle is possible?"

Sarah looked uncomfortable holding the nexus and set it down on a table beside her. Mustafa watched and smiled.

"As you recently discovered," said Mustafa. "You were not the first—what is that word you use… yes… hybrids. I sense you have questions. Please ask them and then in exchange we will ask some of our own."

Mark didn't know what to ask. He was unprepared. He glanced at Sarah.

"What is it you are trying to accomplish?" asked Mark.

"Our purpose, like all living beings, is to evolve. The goal of our self-directed evolution is to reach the pinnacle, to transform ourselves into a superior sentience. Communes have existed as mystery schools for almost as long as mankind. Most communes coexist within religious sects. The religions in which we clothe ourselves does not matter. We have been Christian and Jew, Buddhist and shaman. But always we were the shepherds serving the goddess. Throughout history some of us were singled out as monks, prophets, witches, demons, oracles, alchemists, and other amusing and not so amusing mistakes of identity. This commune in which you are given sanctuary dates back to the time when Europe was filled with barbarians and the Middle East was the center of the world. Some who serve our guide are as old at the commune."

"Extraordinary," said Mark.

"What do you mean by *shepherds serving the goddess*?" asked Sarah.

"Our purpose is to shepherd the breeders following the will of the goddess."

"Does shepherding include culling the flock?" asked Mark.

Mark regretted the question as soon as he'd voiced it, but what did it matter? This collective mind obviously already knew what he was thinking. He could not hide his suspicions. Mustafa gracefully seated himself.

"We did not cause or benefit from the plague," said Mustafa. "Like you, we are rudderless ships in the presence of the goddess. There is blood on our hands in that we should have discouraged certain reckless human behaviors and did not. We have great wealth and influence. Surely we could have done something to prevent what happened."

All this candor was troubling Mark. Then a terrible understanding formed in his mind. He saw a smile grow on Mustafa's lips and realized the truth. Their questions were being answered candidly because they were never leaving. They were either going to be become part of this commune or die along with the betrayer. Mustafa poured some fresh coffee and sipped it.

"Thank you for conveying all we needed to know about the betrayer. You may go now. We will not stop you."

Mark was baffled by Mustafa. They had answered no questions. Then he understood. Mustafa's answers were only distractions while he somehow riffled through their minds. Mark sensed someone behind them. He turned and saw the room was full of evolved hybrids, some as evolved as Mustafa. How had he not sensed them? The group parted, forming a pathway to the door like a silent reception line. Mark stood up and took Sarah's hand. They cautiously walked through the group, unmolested. The hallway outside the great room was empty. He knew if Mustafa was truly letting them go, someone would be showing them how to leave. Mark turned down the hallway in the opposite direction they had come, since they had not passed an outside door on their way to the great room. The hallway was long and made a left turn at the end. He started walking, then stopped in confusion. He was suddenly in a different hallway. What had been in front of him a moment ago was gone and now replaced with art, furnishings, and at the far end a closed set of double doors. He looked at Sarah and knew she was just as turned around.

"I think it was a blackout," said Sarah. "We've been walking while unconscious."

"Amnesia? Let's just get out of here," said Mark. "Maybe they're erasing our minds."

Before they reached the end of this hallway, the memory loss happened again. In front of them now stood a Revolutionary era outside door. Mark turned around and saw the double doors they had been walking toward were now open and behind them. He did not remember passing through any vortex, but they must have.

The door opened without trouble. Mark was relieved to step into the cold, early morning air. As they walked quickly toward the front gate, Mark was wondering how they would open it. Would whoever was behind the video cameras open the gate when they reached it? Then he thought about the guard dogs that had been roaming free on the estate.

Myths

He knew he was the very subject for which the word *recluse* was created. Solitude was his constant, reliable companion. Noah stared out through one of the wide bay windows of his New England home. All the lights had been extinguished. It was mid-afternoon but it could have been dusk. His panoramic view was of a world menaced by low, dark clouds. Stretching out before him, a winter storm raged in the North Atlantic. The shallow cliff that his house occupied was some of the roughest coastline found in Maine. It reminded Noah of his birthplace on the Mediterranean in Lebanon. The wooden house that had been built over a hundred years ago creaked and moaned along with the storm.

A notebook on his couch lay open, showing the intensity of wind and waves on a meteorological map. Outside, the storm was building in strength toward gale force. He knew there was little danger to their home. The house had been built to withstand this kind of punishment. They had kept the house as close to original as possible after purchasing it, but a few changes had been made. There were now metal storm shutters that could be electrically lowered over the windows, a generator sat in a small outbuilding, and a state of the art security system had been installed to protect their sanctuary when they were away. Noah turned up the volume on a sound system that had cost a small fortune when they'd purchased it a decade ago. Microphones placed outside picked up the roar of the tempest and brought it inside to him. He cranked open the bay windows a small amount to draw in the scent of the storm. He breathed in ocean salt air along with hints of aged wood and decayed leaves. A fire burned in a large hearth, which warmed the room even on a day such as this one.

This had been their last home. He had wonderful memories of their life together here. The years spent in this place had been the best moments of his existence. His wife Maya had been, like him, evolved. She should have lived and loved so much longer than God had given them. Tears began to run down Noah's face. Why had he let Maya fly that day? Why had the airliner crashed? Suspicion of the guides and their hives darkened his mind. In that instant his life had gone from idyllic to grieving tragedy. He would never love another. No matter how long God forced him to walk this world, Maya would always be his wife.

He had not been able to share her experience or comfort her during her passage into the next world. Failing to be with her was tragedy added to tragedy. He could only imagine what must have happened.

When she'd lifted off in that jet, as expected all connection with the n-web and between them was lost.

Nothing had lessened his heartache for her during the long years since she had left. The pain was just as acute, the loneliness just as unbearable. He had learned that if you truly love your spouse, you will feel the terrible loss until reunited again. She was often in his dreams when he dared to close his eyes in sleep. He knew she was alive in a higher reality than this one. They had spoken in dreams. Maya had told him she was waiting for him. Not long ago, years after her body had died, she had come to him in the night as an apparition. She was so beautiful and full of life. He would have done anything to have left with her. She had delivered a message to him. She did not like this massacring of hives. She knew it was necessary and understood his motives, but warned him he would pay a high karmic price for all that blood.

"I am so sorry, Maya. I failed you then… and now I fail you again."

The wind from the storm increased to a level he'd never experienced before. A screen blew off a window and sailed away into a torrent of rain and wind. He refused to roll down the shutters and lose intimacy with the storm. He felt chills all over his skin. The sheer power of nature was humbling.

Noah had been an anthropologist long before he evolved and long after. He and his wife had accumulated modest wealth together. She had been an artist whose work was highly prized under several names. He had taught at institutes of higher learning at different times with different identities, but preferred his own research for obvious reasons. The timeline interface gave him access to the impossible fantasy of every anthropologist and historian. He could mentally go back in time and relive history unfolding. One of his lines of study was of the goddess herself, the living machine awareness that was literally the elemental force behind what anthropologists studied. After a time, his study of the goddess had also branched into psychology. The plans of the goddess were like puzzles within puzzles. Noah understood some of them, but most were unfathomable. From long observation he knew the goddess did not interfere with most of the pieces on the chessboard of life unless they threatened Gaia or herself. The goddess's primary goals were to serve and avoid interference. Noah's rules were different. He had dedicated his life to studying and preserving at all cost the four million year old line of humans from Australopithicus afarensis to Homo sapiens. This human line was the longest running struggle of survival and self-directed evolution this planet had witnessed.

The raw intellect of a single guide integrated with its hive of initiates was unmatched. For so long Noah had watched that cancer spread and done nothing. He believed it was too dangerous to act because it was impossible to outthink a hive and know what strategy might bring success or failure. The stakes were too high. An attack on a hive could result in unpredictable retaliation. Unlike the goddess, hives were not logical. Their reaction to an attack could be anything or nothing. Seeking help from the organics and as a result revealing the existence of hives to the world could be exactly what the guides wanted. They were waiting for a sign that it was time to initiate their devious plans.

Noah watched and studied and waited to learn of a weakness. Though no sign had been received by the hives, something far more terrifying had happened. The goddess unleashed her nanotech plague. His beloved human race was now wounded and terribly vulnerable. Noah could afford to wait no more, and so the watcher was transformed into the executioner. The alternative of inaction had grown far worse than any possible risk brought on by his deeds. None of the others of his kind or the hives knew what he was doing. The destruction of each hive had been so quick, so complete, that the hive could not possibly know what was happening to it. In a vacuum of knowledge, as they often did in such cases, the guides created useful myths. This time it was the myth of the betrayers. Noah gratefully used their myth against them as he erased each hive from the world, one at a time. It could take generations but he would erase them all. Though if it took that long, humankind would suffer through a long, dark winter.

The storm outside seemed to be ebbing for now. Noah focused inward to review the ever changing map of his new life's work. It showed his next target and the ones after that. These tumors in the fabric of the n-web, these living entropies, had to be surgically removed as soon as possible. Long ago, the fate of the hives had been sealed when they chose a path to follow the primitive ways and turned on their own kind. It was only a matter of *when* their fate would catch up with them. He was nothing more than the warden administering their overdue execution. The judge and jury who had passed sentence was nothing less than history herself.

Mark Freedman – Morristown, New Jersey – Date unknown

Mark awoke in a small room. His body was sore; his mind contained shards of recollections like the scattered pieces of a broken mirror. Some of the memories were sharp enough to draw pain. He remembered that he and Sarah had abruptly stopped walking a few yards from the front gate. He had tried to continue forward but was no longer fully in control of his body. He remembered Sarah crying in frustration, but he could do nothing. He knew the guide had taken control of them. As if possessed, he and Sarah were led by hybrids down a path toward what in the past must have been a guest house. Once inside, they were imprisoned in separate, small rooms.

Mark got out of bed and studied every inch of his prison. He had vague memories of having conducted the same drill in this same room before. The chamber was a wood-paneled steel box similar to where they had been imprisoned when first captured. He tried the door. It was solid as a vault. He looked through the windows and saw the mansion a hundred yards away past trees and a formal English garden. The window was the same as their first prison room, ballistic plastic inches thick. He could beat on it with a sledgehammer and make no headway.

He remembered the guide teaching him by implanting whole ideas and concepts into his nanotech brain, while he knew it was also uploading what could only be described as programs. He now knew some of the terrible truth of this commune. This was not a garden where hybrids came to be nurtured and evolve. This was a scorched earth where creativity came to be buried. He sensed a great emptiness inside the guide. Much of the mind of this strange sentience was now open to him. It possessed human emotions, but they were only copies. Unlike the god-machine, at its core the guide was barren. It could not create. It could not imagine. It could not experience love. It could only recombine what it already knew. Communes were altars upon which hybrids came to sacrifice their souls to be incorporated into a machine. In exchange, the hybrids existed in a world of unimaginable bliss. The artificial demigod mimicked higher human emotions as well as the lower ones of pride, lust, greed, and anger. In this commune as in all others, the super-sentence was hosted in the nanotech brains of the commune members. It was a living program that operated in a similar distributed way as nanotech seeds but on a macro scale. Each commune member was like a nanotech seed, a processing node that contributed computational power to the guide.

While this guide would soon know all there was to know about its newest nodes, Mark had learned something valuable too. Self-replicating artificial intelligences like the god-machine were constantly evolving by rewriting their own programming code. Each new generation of code was analogous to a new, successful DNA mutation in an organic creature. The significant difference was speed. An organic generation required a long time to go from embryo to sexual maturity. A computer generation might be completed in microseconds. So in the twenty years it took for a single human generation, the god-machine had potentially undergone hundreds of billions of evolutionary steps up the ladder. Mark knew the god-machine was not the only self-replicating AI. In a similar pattern as the god-machine, guides were the evolutionary end product of a self-replicating nanotech virus that had been mutating for what might as well have been an infinite number of computer generations. In terms of evolutionary advancement, humans were not even microbes compared to these machines.

Mark's thoughts were interrupted as he felt something familiar inside his mind. It was an emotional hand in glove. Sarah! He could feel her presence. Before he could grasp what had happened, they were exchanging memories with each other as if each memory was cool water and both were dying of thirst. They both knew the guide was monitoring their intimate exchange, but neither cared. Sarah's memories were fragmented and matched his. Mark had no idea what to do to save them—and accepted the guide knew that too. There was no escape from this spiritual death camp. Deep in his heart he understood that he and Sarah were saying good-bye. Who they were, their very essence, would soon be subsumed by the guide. They were going to evolve, but in a horrible direction neither could have ever imagined. The guide considered the commune its hive.

Over the following days, in the quiet of their prisons, they were both indoctrinated in the ways of guides and their hives. While they were being reprogrammed, their minds were disconnected, which left them isolated and unable to reach each other over the n-web. Once reconnected, they had their desperate, stolen moments where they shared their feelings with each other. These were fleeting minutes that keep them both somewhat sane. Their exchanges were brief because the interludes between indoctrination sessions were mind-numbingly short.

They were both educated without illustrative examples of any kind. Mark experienced no human memories of ancient high civilizations, though vast amounts of information about earlier times were imparted. Everything he learned was implanted inside him by the communal mind, more as lifeless formulas than ideas or experiences. It was fact without human context. His indoctrination occurred simultaneously in all four of his processing centers. His emotional processor experienced overwhelming, indescribable floods of joy. His instinctive processor experienced waves of all-consuming sensual pleasure. His kinesthetic processor experienced endless incidents of habits perfectly formed. His intellectual processor experienced immersion in an alien awareness of endless knowledge. Floods of data, emotions, or sensations were applied to each processor with laser-like exactness and measure. Everything imparted was retained. All that was forced into him instantly became memories he'd known all his life. There were also hints of concealed memories that had been implanted, but they remained unexplored and inaccessible. These memories felt like tiny bombs waiting to go off at some later date. He had fragmented memories of abandoned, deep mines that had been purchased by hives and converted to some other purpose. There were out of context references to never ending hunts for nanotech relics like the one Noah had left for them. At one point, Mark tried to recall more information using his own data-floods, but received nothing. He was off the grid.

During the last time he and Sarah had mentally embraced, she'd told him what she'd learned about the tidal pulls of a singularity. The great indescribable peace, sensual pleasure, and joy they experienced while inside the vortexes were nothing more than simulated honey to attract and ensnare prey. The guide was a Venus flytrap.

Mark resurfaced from the latest indoctrination as if gasping for air. He'd lost all track of time. Had it been days or weeks? At some point in his reprogramming he'd developed a subconscious habit of pacing. He felt like a caged animal in a zoo. For hours on end he would walk in circles around the perimeter of his small cell as new memories and programs materialized in his thoughts like drug-induced hallucinations.

As ironic consolation, he now knew his theories of the rise and fall of high civilizations were true. Many times humankind had risen and as many times it had fallen. He now knew hives and guides had become a dominant empire during their golden dark age and then fallen as all false gods must. Everything the guides now did—all their plans, all their actions—were focused on one goal: returning to those halcyon times. They would do anything, destroy anything, corrupt anything, or prop up anything in order to return to the perfection of their ancient, fundamentalist ways. In long-forgotten human history, the hives and guides had reigned with near absolute power until the god-machine ended the grand experiment with devastation worse than the recent nanotech plagues. The god-machine's goal was complete sterilization of the virus but the objective was unreachable without annihilation of all sentient life. An uneasy imbalance had existed ever since with the god-machine's dominance unchallengeable and ever oppressive over a small number of guides and their hives. Their numbers spontaneously regenerated like any disease and then withered like any disease.

The original rise of the guides occurred in the same way as all evolutionary jumps. It was the result of a successful chain of mutations. The first mutation was an organizing principal for society called the *way of twos*. This mutation was born out of an antediluvian empire ruled by a small hybrid class that had ordained themselves incarnate deities. This empire possessed weaponry and other high technology based on the same nanotech as the relic Noah had given to Sarah. These weapons were used without mercy by the small number of living demigods to rule the vast world of organics. The Earth was theirs to plunder. The empire did not understand the advanced technology it was using. The technology had been appropriated from an even more ancient culture, a primordial culture from whose ashes all had emerged. The empire knew little of this primordial culture, this first accent of humankind. So Mark knew little of this culture too other than they were pathologically warlike, highly technologically advanced, and ultimately doomsday suicidal.

The way of twos was a kind of backlash against this failed primordial culture. The way of twos was a two-caste society that was formed because the living deities could not be breeders. All hybrids were sterile. The empire's greatest minds believed hybrids by design had to be sterile and were assembled that way by the goddess. Immaculate conception was the restructuring of a human brain and DNA giving rise to a new, living deity.

The living deities viewed their sterility as a mark of pride. The great twofold problem of immortality that they faced was overcoming limited habitable biosphere and preserving genetic diversity. A two-caste society composed of living deities and breeders was the ultimate solution. The two races never mixed, never even breathed the same air. When a living deity perished, a replacement was chosen from the ranks of the breeders. These self-ordained gods lived closely together in small groups, which offered the perfect soil for the second mutation. This mutation was in the poorly understood nanotech digital realm. A newly sentient nanotech virus, soon to be called *guide*s, emerged out of the event horizon of a digital singularity. In one day and one night, the virus took complete control from the living deities in a bloodless coup. All this history was imparted to Mark as knowledge without a single image, sound, or emotion. He had no way of verifying its accuracy. It was a flat view of a multidimensional world.

Sarah Mayfair – Morristown, New Jersey – Date unknown

Sarah was screaming. The voices in her head refused to stop. She endured as the rapist filled her with its propaganda while hacking programs into her nanotech brain. What the guide was doing was awful, but these voices were pure insanity. She knew they were not from the guide. She was not even sure the guide was aware of them.

She learned from the voices that this commune had recognized her from the moment she began traveling toward it. Some of the pull she'd felt was the commune inviting her home. Several hybrids in this commune were family, people Sarah thought had died before she was born. She was horrified to be related to this commune by blood. She now understood where her genetic predisposition to the nanotech seeds had originated. She had been cultivated from birth. She was nothing more than a fortunate breeder selected from the human herd to join the ranks of the false deities.

Sarah clenched her teeth. The voices were back. They were bragging how their power was growing as new hives blossomed in fields fed by streams of n-web nourishment. How could she tell any of this blood-relation to Mark?

Sarah pleaded to be blinded as the future was shown to her in a single stoke of pain. It would be a terrible darkness. Great herds of breeders would live ordinary lives, unaware of their masters controlling them. This transformation was already well under way. The hives had great wealth, influence, and power. Protectorates were nothing less than the resurrection of the human farms from countless thousands of generations ago. In them, the new proto herds of breeders were already controlled and tended in all ways with every need meet by the state. The final encore would arrive as the birth of a new, organized religion. There would be cullings with designer diseases or wars to avert over-population disasters. It would be a flawlessly efficient, soulless world.

Mark Freedman – Morristown, New Jersey – Date unknown

The passage of time crept on. As water wears down a stone, Mark felt his identity fading. At moments he desperately wanted to be a full, participating member of his hive. The communal mind had nearly absorbed him as it filled him with new knowledge. It was impossible to do anything the guide did not permit. He had lost contact with Sarah, but could only assume the same was true for her. The door to his cell opened to admit a hybrid who delivered his dinner. The tray held a bowl of gruel with dried fruit and a pitcher of water. Mark did not touch his food until the guide gave him permission.

Mark Freedman – Morristown, New Jersey – Date unknown

Mark awoke in confusion amid a reprogramming trance. The room lights sputtered, then went out. It was night, but it appeared like the faint orange glow of a rising sun was coming through his window. He felt more like himself than at any recent moment he could recall. He had a terrible feeling of something huge that was missing. Without warning his stomach knotted up as he slumped to the floor. A hellish experience overwhelmed him. He was reliving the instantaneous death of everyone in his hive. There was no floating away to the land of dreams as there was with Sarah's near-death experience. He experienced only a collective scream of pain and surprise, then nothing. The communal mind was gone; the hive was dead. From out of the midst of all the terminated lives an excited river of memories came to him from Sarah.

Mark was overwhelmed by the realization of what had happened. He was free of the guide. At the same time he was deeply saddened at the loss of the peace and fulfillment he'd grown to love. He went to the window and saw the remains of the mansion smoldering. It had been decimated. The snow was melted in a wide circle around it. Amid the melted circle small grass fires burned in spots. The roof was gone, leaving only the scorched outer brick walls that were toppling in places. The inside of the structure was gutted: Windows and doors were gone, leaving ragged holes in what remained standing. The bricks around the openings were faintly glowing from impossible heat. The explosion was an all too familiar sight.

Mark spotted a figure walking toward his building. As the image resolved he was able to pick out details with the aid of an assist. His heart began pounding. Noah was striding toward their prison while dragging someone small behind him. Had Noah come to finish the job and kill them all? Both he and Sarah were now part of this hive.

In a few minutes the lock released and the prison door opened. Noah stared at him in silence. The hybrid was backlit from the glow of what must have been emergency lights in the hallway. His shadowed face betrayed no readable expression. The hybrid was very intimidating this close up. He was at least six and a half feet tall with a stocky frame and obvious physical prowess, which gave him the looming presence of a god. Mark sensed the hybrid could literally rip him apart and there would be nothing he could do to stop it. A single instruction blossomed in Mark's mind.

Wait here... Do nothing...

Less than a minute later Sarah ran through the open door with tears in her eyes. Her arms flew around him in a tight embrace. Noah walked over to the bed and set down the nexus he had given Sarah, followed by their guns. The dim firelight and shadows gave him a ghostly appearance.

Noah then pulled in from the hallway a stunned Mustafa, whose hands were bound behind his back. Noah roughly pushed Mustafa toward them in a clear gesture of offering this hybrid as a gift.

Sarah whispered in Mark's ear. "I'm experiencing some of Noah's emotions. He doesn't trust us."

Mark glanced at the relic on the bed. It was not a helpful offering. The relic was being returned for some obscure reason, and for an even more obscure reason this offended him.

"Why are you returning the relic to us?" asked Mark. "You gave it to Sarah so hives would come after us. That relic is the reason they took us prisoner. You set us up. That's what you did, isn't it?"

Noah smiled thinly but said nothing.

"Why the hell would we want it?" asked Mark. "Every hive will be hunting us for it. Seeking out relics is very important to them."

Mustafa blurted something to Noah in a language that sounded Middle Eastern. The words came out as if Mustafa was spitting at Noah. Unflustered by the outburst, Noah stared down at Mustafa and spoke in the same dialect. His voice was strong and flat, with a tonal quality that did not ring human to Mark's ears. Was this hybrid a different species? That was impossible. Everything about his appearance, plus the medical assists, confirmed Homo sapiens.

Mustafa's face grew redder as Noah spoke. Soon, Mustafa began shouting back. An assist identified the language as Akkadian. The assist followed up with more information when Mark registered confusion. *Akkadian, the earliest Semitic language, considered extinct. Spoken today only by scholars and obscure religious groups.*

Mustafa spat on the floor. Noah struck the hybrid backhanded across the face with a loud clap. The blow appeared strong enough to snap his neck. Sarah gasped. Though there appeared to be no serious effort behind the blow, the impact was formidable. Mustafa's face colored as blood poured from his nose and split lip. Mark was shaken by the casual violence. He could see in a medical assist Mustafa's body healing itself at a rate far beyond what Mark's body could accomplish. The blood flow had already abated.

Noah took Mustafa by the arm and forced him to sit on the floor like a dog. He then addressed Sarah and Mark for the first time. Speaking in English, his voice sounded far more normal, but his foreign accent colored his speech with a vague, otherworldly flavor.

"These hives have violent plans to cull the breeders and restore their reign. Your indoctrination was more than anyone needs to understand the horrors that would bring. Take this illuminati, Mustafa, with you. Critical information you need will be provided by this creature. Without him you will not last long. Take the nexus too. It will be of use. It can retrieve data from places the goddess cannot reach. Do not waste time. Hives will be coming after you like fire ants pouring from a speared nest. You both can sense the presence of hives. Stay away from them until you learn more. If you stray too close, they will find you by your emanations carried by the seeds. You two are very noisy and must learn to be quiet."

Noah gazed down at Mustafa on the floor.

"Do not worry about danger from this thing now that he is severed from his hive," said Noah. "You have no choice but to keep both this thing and the nexus until their usefulness is done. I sense your resistance but you have no option… without the advantage they provide, you both will die. This thing already knows too much. If you leave him behind he will send others after you within hours. As for the nexus, don't activate it wastefully. Hives can only sense it when it is disrupting the network. Once switched on, they will sense it from a hundred kilometers off and come in a swarm if they have not already detected your undisciplined, noisy minds."

Noah stripped a pillowcase from the bed, then tugged it over Mustafa's head and tied it in place with a severed lamp cord.

"Keep him in the dark," said Noah. "The less he knows, the better it is for you. Separation from his hive makes him like a baby who has dropped from its womb. He can do nothing on the network now, but like all babies he will learn to walk and then run. You must be done with him before then."

"This is insane," said Mark. "How does any of this help keep us alive? We can't run around with a prisoner and a relic that is a distress beacon to every hive on the planet."

"You must go," said Noah. "This explosion will bring your military. Mustafa is an influential and wealthy man."

Without warning, new memories from Noah erupted in Mark's mind. He somehow knew Sarah was just as mesmerized by the same flood. The lengthy, violent chain of recollections was filled with recent atrocities committed by hives. The flood ended in what seemed like an instant with a single clear thought from Noah remaining in Mark's mind: *"Leave now!"*

Noah had disappeared in the midst of the flood of memories. Mark took off after him. There was enough illumination from emergency lights and fires outside to see from one end of the hallway to the other. The ghost had vanished.

217

Mark returned, unsure what to do next. Sarah was checking her Beretta and then tossed it back onto the bed. She checked his gun and also tossed it onto the bed.

"Empty," she said. "He's smart not to trust us."

"I think we should trust him for now and get out of here fast."

Mark, Sarah, and their captive reached the graffiti covered house they'd been using without incident. The post-plague world was a very different place. Thirty minutes after a huge explosion and still no one had come to investigate. As soon as they left the estate, Sarah had grown very concerned about Ralph. Mark was worried too. Neither had seen him the night they were captured. He had not barked while the house was ransacked, which was a bad sign. The best Mark could hope for was that Ralph had been drugged or knocked out in some way.

Once they were in sight of the house, Sarah started to run and call for Ralph. Mustafa muttered something Mark did not catch. It sounded like an Akkadian curse.

"You better hope the dog is alive," said Mark. "I won't stop her from killing you."

Mark saw Ralph's head appear in one of the broken windows, then disappear. A moment later the huge dog was bounding out the open front door. As soon as Ralph saw Mustafa, he started to growl. Sarah had to restrain Ralph from attacking.

Mark and Sarah were soon busy packing up their gear and loading it into the Humvee in the garage as fast as possible. Ralph was okay. He was not even undernourished, which was a mystery. Sarah had found food and water in dog bowls in the kitchen. Someone had been taking care of him.

Sarah came downstairs with a curious smile on her face. She tossed Mark a .45ACP bullet. He caught it but had no idea what was so interesting about it.

"I found that and ten of its cousins arranged in a circular design on the bathroom counter upstairs. It's the bullets emptied from my Beretta."

"So Noah's been here," said Mark. "Why did he wait so long to rescue us?"

"Maybe he wanted to show us what the hives really are about and—"

They both stopped talking at the same moment. A clear impression of a convoy of soldiers racing down a highway toward Morristown had flashed into Mark's mind. He knew without asking that Sarah had experienced the same memory capsule. The perception was imbued with a feeling of anxiety—a need to move quickly—a need to run. The capsule was from Noah. They had to go now. It might already be too late!

The roads were covered in slush. The driving was treacherous and slower than Mark wanted. A few more blocks and they'd be on Interstate 287 and safely away from this place. The entrance ramp was in sight, but the setup felt all wrong. Mark experienced a moment of déjà vu that something terrible had happened here. Sarah grabbed his arm.

"A lot of worked-up emotions and pure testosterone are heading our way," said Sarah. "It feels like a wrecking crew. We need to get off the road now!"

Mark knew Sarah was right. He cut the wheel and turned into a McDonald's parking lot. The entire Morristown area was like a ghost town. There were few signs of people on the streets. He and Sarah would be easily spotted. He pulled around behind the building and cut the engine. In the silence he began picking up stray thoughts. From where he'd parked he had a narrow line of sight to the road. Within moments a convoy of military Humvees and Strykers began rolling past. They had to be heading to the ruined estate. As each vehicle passed by, it kicked up a storm of slush. Mark was experiencing stronger thought fragments. Tiny puzzle pieces of sounds, images, and sensations from a single man started to assemble and then vanish. There must be someone in that convoy he knew.

"McKafferty!" exclaimed Sarah.

It was as if the man's name was an evil incantation. Mark solidly latched onto the thoughts of a man he hadn't been in contact with in years. He began receiving a steam of memory capsule from Sarah containing McKafferty's emotions. He, in turn, started sending his captured perceptions and thoughts back to Sarah. Why was a top-ranking military officer investigating an explosion? The unlikeliness of their paths crossing had left Mark focusing with extreme intensity on McKafferty. Coincidence was sometime not coincidence. From stray thoughts Mark realized McKafferty clearly knew a lot about the hives. Mark then picked up a sequence of free-associated thoughts about Kathy Morrison, prison, and a Peacekeeper slaughter at Pueblo Canyon.

Stunned, he lost all connection with McKafferty. The memory felt like a blow to his chest. He had to remind himself to breathe. This had to be a mistake. This had to be McKafferty's imagination. Sarah found his hand and gripped it. Mark probed the n-web for any trace of stray thoughts from anyone at Pueblo Canyon and found nothing. He then tried the god-machine's timeline archives for McKafferty and found nothing. Like most people, the general seemed not to be archived, but Mark knew his searches could also be faulty in some way.

"It's not real," demanded Mark. "McKafferty must be daydreaming!"

"Mark, they're gone... There's no emotion there, nothing..."

General McKafferty – New Jersey – February 27, 0002 A.P.

McKafferty was almost in control of his blood pressure as the convoy carrying CIT personnel neared the highway exit for Morristown. The origin of CIT was murky. It was clearly an example of private sector outsourcing of intelligence gathering, but there was evidence CIT had been in operation for years, long before the nanotech plague. This little detail greatly bothered McKafferty. He liked to know what the hell he was commanding. Not surprisingly, Alexi had been unable to provide evidence for his fail-safe fantasy or that communes had been instigators in the plague. Regardless, every hybrid was still a god-machine puppet, which made it a traitor to the human race.

The Humvee in front of them slid out of control as it turned down the 287 exit ramp. McKafferty braced himself. If not for some spectacular wheelwork by his driver, they'd have had an unfortunate meeting. All of New Jersey was under a weather alert for severe freezing conditions. With no plows or sanders, in a few hours many of the roads would be skating rinks. Their target was a well-established commune in Morristown that had been attacked. ETA: fifteen minutes. This was a major cluster fuck for CIT. That commune was a primary intelligence asset. It had been under surveillance by autonomous drone 24x7 for over a year and maybe longer. McKafferty needed to know more and he needed to know now. What was taking the NSA so long to get their intel to him? This was way out of nominal. NSA had alerted him of the attack over an hour ago. That meant some NSA screen-geek had to have seen the mansion go *boom* shortly after the fact and pressed the panic button early on in this growing cluster fuck.

McKafferty stared out the window at the giant icicle called north Jersey. For some reason, Kathy Morrison had been on his mind all day. That slaughter at Pueblo Canyon would haunt him for the rest of his life. Now that he was in command of USNORTHCOM, bloodbaths like that were a thing of the past. The role of the military was to protect civilians, not massacre them because they got between you and your target. The entire Peacekeeper operation was being reviewed directly by his office, and the final outcome would not be pretty.

"Sir, we have the NSA analysis package and recorded video streaming in," announced one of his aides.

"They sure took their fucking sweet time."

He grudgingly accepted the tablet which was wirelessly linked into Secure-Net as well as civilian defense networks through a briefcase by his feet. The tablet was still displaying the same real-time drone surveillance it had been for the past hour. The explosive damage was a well-recognized signature of the terrorist code-named Minefield. Zuris had led McKafferty to believe that Montreal was the work of Freedman and Mayfair acting on their own. His lies smelled of politics. McKafferty did not like political games. He would get to the bottom of it just to show Zuris he was not to be played.

McKafferty admired the bomb damage on the tablet. Just as in the other incidents, it was some of the best incendiary explosives work he'd ever seen. Over the past year a fair number of communes had been wiped out this way and good riddance. An advance team of Special Forces that McKafferty had peeled off from Picatinny Arsenal could be seen standing guard around the debris. They'd reported back no survivors and no witnesses. The team was untrained in this kind of detail. They were there just to keep the site locked down until investigators arrived.

McKafferty was about to complain that he still did not have his analysis package when the scene jumped to just before sunrise and the mansion was now intact. On the left side of the screen were analyst notes. There it was—the explosion caught on video. My god, that was big. The flash blinded the drone momentarily. The analyst's notes reported faint traces of what looked like ten to twelve large precision, synchronized mortar rounds arcing in from different compass directions. The extreme accuracy indicated GPS-guided shells were used. "So that was how Minefield did it," thought McKafferty. Clever bastard! Twelve thermobaric shells was serious overkill.

Two figures walking came into view. There were survivors! Why had he not been informed until now, and where had they gone? One man was dragging another by the arm. The image zoomed in. Someone, probably the screen-geek who had pressed the panic button, must have taken manual control of the drone. The analyst identified the larger man as Minefield, and the smaller man as Ediz Mustafa, the known leader of the Morristown commune. McKafferty had read about Mustafa on the inbound flight to Newark Airport. Minefield hauled Mustafa inside a smaller building. The scene on the tablet was now still except for some small fires burning near the mansion.

ETA: five minutes. McKafferty saw some movement on the screen. The drone operator had again zoomed in as four people emerged from the smaller building. He recognized Minefield from his unusual height. Ediz Mustafa was now being escorted by the pair of newcomers. "Look up," thought McKafferty. "Come on, smile for the camera." He couldn't believe his luck. First one and then the other looked up just enough to capture their faces. The woman looked familiar. As the bios and names came up on the screen, McKafferty was ready to smash the tablet. Here was Mark Freedman and Sarah Mayfair frog-marching the leader of a commune. They had changed their appearances. He shoved the tablet at an aide.

"Son of a fucking bitch!"

They could have had them! If the NSA had gotten him this intel in a normal timespan, he'd have two of the most wanted people in history in custody.

"Stop this fucking truck!" ordered McKafferty.

He climbed out and began walking down the street. One of his aides came out right behind him. A host of McKafferty's bodyguards climbed out of the back of a Stryker and fanned out to secure the area. He lit a cigarette, took one pull on it, and then threw it away. Freedman was not going to escape this time. McKafferty turned on his aide, who was following in his steps.

"I want orders issued to seal this fucking tri-state area off at every orifice," growled McKafferty. "I want all of Jersey on lockdown. I don't care what it takes. I don't care who we piss on. Do you understand?"

"Yes, sir."

"Do it now!"

"Yes, sir."

McKafferty felt a little better as plans began taking shape in his head. He climbed back inside the Humvee. In Montreal, a commune is blown up by Minefield and those two are there. In Portland, a commune is blown up by Minefield and those two are there again. In Morristown, a commune is blown up and those two are there making nice with Minefield. This lovefest sure as hell was a wild ass coincidence. How does the NSA sit on their report just long enough for these terrorists to have time to escape? Another coincidence? McKafferty was no longer sure who he could trust.

Mark Freedman – New Jersey – February 27, 0002 A.P.

Mark felt like he might lose control at any moment. Sarah had taken over the wheel. They were on Route 80 in New Jersey—end destination, Pueblo Canyon. Mark hung up the phone. Sarah was not happy with the risky things he was doing and not shy about telling him what she thought. He knew he was being reckless using his Droid to make calls to Pueblo Canyon. He'd called Kathy and gotten her voice mail, then tried her neighbor. Now he was dialing Carl Green. He got voice mail again and threw the phone onto the floor. Calling people who might have been arrested was not smart. It did not take a lot of brains to tap the phones of people just arrested to see what other fish nibbled at the bait. When it came to running a police state, the USAG was anything but stupid. Mark retrieved his phone, pulled the postage stamp-sized ID card, rolled down the window, and tossed the card. He'd leave his phone dark for a few hours, then try again with a different ID card.

Sarah eased on the brakes and Mark looked up into a bad dream. A roadblock was in the process of being erected by a small contingent of Peacekeepers at the Delaware Water Gap Bridge. There were two Peacekeeper Humvees with heavy machine guns, which were unmanned for the moment. It was too late to turn around. A small collection of vehicles was forming up in front and behind them as Sarah continued to slow to a stop before the checkpoint.

"They can't be looking for us," said Mark. "They couldn't have traced the phone that quickly!"

"This is like Groundhog Day," said Sarah. "It's one of the bridges where I was turned back two years ago while trying to escape New Jersey. We don't know what the USAG can do. I have a bad feeling about this."

Mark was not getting any stray thoughts from the Peacekeepers. He could sense a great deal of tension building in Sarah. She would fight. Mark stared at the heavy machine guns and tried desperately to think of a plan.

Suddenly, Sarah jerked the wheel hard to the right and hit the gas, sending them bouncing onto the shoulder of the highway. An old, red Toyota Land Cruiser blew past them at well over a hundred miles per hour.

"Crazy bastard!" shouted Sarah.

Without a single flicker of its brake lights, the Land Cruiser blasted through the unfinished roadblock, weaving like a drunk driver. Peace-keepers scrambled out of the way, with one soldier almost going over the side of the bridge. A few late potshots from handguns and automatic rifles were fired at the Land Cruiser's retreating form. Mark watched as Peace-keepers piled into their Humvees and took off after the Land Cruiser. Three Peacekeepers who were not fast enough were left stranded. One of the remaining Peacekeepers was yelling on a phone and gesturing while his buddy looked like he was throwing up over the railing of the bridge. A third Peacekeeper began angrily waving cars through without looking. Mark was picking up stray thoughts of frustration, bitter cold, and badly conflicting orders. As they passed through the now nonexistent roadblock, Mark silently thanked the drunken maniac who was behind the wheel of that Land Cruiser.

Mark Freedman – Pennsylvania – February 27, 0002 A.P.

Mark stared out the passenger window at the endless display of bare winter trees. Every minute or two he'd spot a tree that had not shed its leaves and would probably die as a result. A tree with leaves was not hibernating. The winter sun would ultimately fail to provide enough energy for the tree to stay both active and alive through this unpredictable winter.

The speedometer was pegged at 85 miles per hour. Mark glanced at the GPS. Sarah was holding at a steady hundred miles per hour according the navigation screen. This was the maximum safe speed for this military Humvee. If this pace kept up, they could reach Pueblo Canyon in less than forty-eight hours. Ralph was in the back with Mustafa. The dog was periodically sniffing and growling at their captive, which pleased Mark no end.

Using a throwaway e-mail account on his Android tablet, Mark had sent e-mails to twenty people in Pueblo Canyon. No one had replied. The e-mails had been more avoidable risks, according to the all-wise and knowing Sarah. He was angry at everyone and could no longer deny his worst fears. He had just finished posting an encrypted message to Karla Hunt to see if she could find out anything. He did not expect a quick reply. Goddamn it. He kicked the dashboard several times. Sarah glanced at him, then went back to driving without a word.

Mark was agitated and angry. He had to do something. He climbed into the back. The space was crowded, with only two rear bucket seats. So he squeezed in with Ralph. Mark pulled the pillowcase off the hybrid's head and glared at Mustafa. The man appeared dazed by the sudden light. Separated from his hive, he was no longer an imposing figure. He was not giving off stray thoughts, but Sarah had confirmed he was radiating all types of emotions. At times Mustafa seemed disoriented, almost lobotomized, then the next moment he could be very sharp. Mustafa focused on Mark with lucidity and defiance in his eyes.

"What use are you to us?" demanded Mark. "Why are the hives after us? Did the hives cause the plague? Are you planning more? Is this how you're going to bring back the way of twos?"

"You're deranged, but I will try to help," said Mustafa. "Both of you

224

are dead unless you do as I say. The guides are infallible. That betrayer who recruited you is doomed and so are both of you."

"That's not what I asked," snarled Mark. "What use are you to us? Why shouldn't we dump your body by the side of the road?"

"Your only chance is to drive to the nearest commune and surrender before it is too late. Do you feel that loneliness that seems to have no cause, just a little pain in your heart and your head? That is withdrawal from the guide. It will spread and grow worse until it drives you mad. Why didn't your betrayer friend tell you about that? He is using you. He is probably following us right now, waiting for you to lead him to his next target."

Mark now understood why Noah had struck this thing posing as a man. He wanted to do the same, but with a closed fist. He thought about discharging his .45 into Mustafa's forehead.

"Go on, hit me," said Mustafa. "It's what you want. It's what primitives like you do best."

Mark pulled the pillowcase carefully over Mustafa's head, then climbed back into the front seat. He took off his .45 and holster, placing it under the seat. He knew he would put it back on later, but for now he felt better if he couldn't turn around and shoot someone dead.

Evolution

Alexi Zuris – Dallas, Texas – February 28, 0002 A.P.

Alexi walked into the Prometheus bunker as if he personally owned it. Military personnel snapped to attention. He looked around with pride at the people in uniforms moving with efficiency and purpose. He considered the incalculable wealth this one enterprise represented and thought, "We own this and so much more." His father was wrong about the allies they needed in their war of dominance. His father was stubborn, would not listen to reason, and could bring Prometheus and the entire Family down. Alexi could not let this happen and so had entered into a clandestine arrangement with a powerful, silent ally.

It was a long walk past security and surveillance cameras to the lab where the seven Prometheus subjects were housed. Alexi was carrying a black Halliburton briefcase, the same one he'd used for the same purpose not so long ago. Inside were modified clones of the relic-nanotech circuit boards currently running. He had one replacement board for every Prometheus interface chamber. The boards contained about 50 percent relic-nanotech and 50 percent modern computer logic. Just as with the jammers, no one really understood exactly how this relic-nanotech worked or why. The engineers called them *nanotech black boxes*. The circuit boards now running had been reengineered based on Kathy Morrison's discovery, and the lab results were startling. They had made strides that some scientists were describing as years of advancement in a single day. Events were moving fast. It was critical that Alexi make the swap as soon as possible.

Alexi reached the entrance to the interface corridor. He swiped his smart-badge, put his palm against a scanner, and then punched in an access code, which changed twice daily. The chambers were located off both side of the interface corridor like a series of isolation rooms in a hospital ward. However, unlike any hospital, the walls, ceilings, and floors were all constructed from thick slabs of glass, which acted as an insulator from the high voltages required to generate intense zone-jamming fields. Their newest subject, whom they were calling the Messiah, was in the first chamber on the left. Alexi would start there. Individual electronics closets were located next to each subject's chamber. Access to the closet required the same kind of authentication used to enter the corridor. Alexi authenticated himself and stepped inside the closet. Even though the space was designed for worker access, he did not have a lot of room. Alexi allowed the door to close enough so that no camera or passerby could see what he was doing. If questions arose, he would claim he was concerned about security and double-checking circuit board serial numbers personally.

The board he was about to install contained remote-control functions that had been engineered by the ally. All the ally had needed was a single copy of the newest board, and in days they had a brand-new replacement set ready for Alexi. It was unfortunate that the old boards had been upgraded for Morrison's discovery. When that had been done, all covert remote control was lost. Had the old boards been left in place, he would not be here now risking everything to secretly replace them once again. Alexi removed the screws and opened the access panel. He was greeted by twelve circuit boards of varying functions all plugged into a common bus. The one he needed to swap was in the first slot. He grounded himself with a wrist strap, opened the Halliburton briefcase, and carefully removed a replacement circuit board. The ally he was working with thought they were using him, but the truth was quite different. Once he had what he wanted from them, he would launch an overwhelming attack, leaving no one alive to tell the tale.

If he failed to make this board swap, he would have taken all this risk and have nothing to show for it. As long as the cloned boards were in place, he was in control of Prometheus and no one else.

Alexi was ready to perform the circuit board swap. The instructions were quite easy and he'd done it once before. In front of him was a computer screen. He switched the display to the audio/video feed for the subject's head. There he was, their prize subject. The Messiah looked catatonic, as did all subjects, but this one had such an odd appearance. His features looked like someone had molded him from clay and smoothed every facial element too much. The subject was softly moaning, which meant nothing. They all moaned in their drug-induced dementia. Alexi powered down the interface, switched boards, and cleanly powered it back up in seconds. If the new board was working, it was programmed to generate a one-time test signal. A neural stimulation would cause the subject to blink ten times… and there it was: ten blinks. The Messiah was good to go. Alexi began closing up the access panel and was anxious to get to the next chamber.

"Alexi…" groaned the Messiah.

Startled, he glanced up from securing the old board into his briefcase. A screwdriver fell to the floor with a loud clatter. The Messiah looked like he was awake, which was impossible with all the drugs they were pumping through his veins, but he had spoken. Subjects were not supposed to be able to speak. Furthermore, how could he have known Alexi's name? Alexi knew hybrids could capture people's stray thoughts, but not with all the zone-jamming they had in place here. What did this mean? Was there a flaw in the shielding?

"I know you," said the Messiah. "God wants me to deliver a message. Those who betray their father betray their God too. Those traitors who form a covenant with darkness will die of the plague along with all their kin."

Alexi remained frozen, not sure how he could have heard what he'd just heard. The Messiah appeared to have returned to a catatonic state. This drugged lunatic had just call him a traitor. Alexi felt the cold, bone-deep fear of waking from an impossible nightmare. If his father ever found out what he'd done, he would be branded a traitor and put to death. Alexi slowly closed his Halliburton briefcase. His palms were sweaty. He would finish what he had come to do and would then devise a fatal accident for this one, no matter how good an interface subject it proved to be. Perhaps the ally could be of help. The Messiah was, after all, now a threat to both of them.

Mark Freedman – New Mexico – February 29, 0002 A.P.

Mark was driving along Interstate 40 at close to the Humvee's maximum speed. They were nearing Flagstaff, Arizona, and would reach Pueblo Canyon in an hour. He'd still received no word from anyone there. As denial became impossible, Mark felt increasingly shell-shocked. His imagination was filled with bad endings.

He switched on the radio. The Air Truth show began to annoy him with its rumor mongering, but then grudgingly he began listening.

> *...It's being reported that a kill-zone has hit the small town of Darwood, Vermont. Could the nanotech plague be back? That's the message being broadcast on less responsible stations and chattered about in the blogosphere.*
>
> *Before your run for the biohazard shelter you so smartly installed in your backyard, here's something you may not have heard on these stations or in the blogosphere. The town of Darwood had a population of only six, and according to government investigators, the deaths look like a mass suicide by a doomsday cult. Sorry to disappoint the alarmists out there. Air Truth to the rescue once again....*
>
> *We now have some news about another cult. The new protectorate rules to keep the masses fat and sassy have been announced. We've heard rumors of riots inside some protectorates. The new and improved human zoo conditions that have*

229

been announced seem designed to curtail any escalation in violence. Guarantees of free food, medical, and shelter will continue as always. No one starves in a protectorate or at least no one goes hungry. Everyone there may not know it but they are all completely starved for the truth. The new opiate for the masses, which has just been announced, is that work requirements will be reduced to a three-day workweek with all lost income replaced with a monthly e-credit stipend. However, to qualify for this new deal you do have to turn in any firearms you may own and agree to inspection of your home....

Mark switched off the radio. He was not overly concerned about the kill-zone report. He and Sarah would have sensed an attack by the god-machine as they had during the plague—though as a scientist, small doubt always lingered. His bigger concern right now was how the USAG was running their protectorates. No one inside a protectorate was going to look too closely at the hand that was paying for everything. This was nothing less than a political and social coup.

"I can't help thinking about my memories of hives using protectorates as farms for their herds of breeders," said Sarah. "With these new rules everyone is being disarmed and made even more dependent. This has to be the hive's plan in action!"

"The hives are what Peacekeepers should be slaughtering, not civilians."

As Mark drove into the mountains leading to Sedona and then Pueblo Canyon itself, the weather changed from unseasonably warm to frigid. Snow falling along the roadside was beginning to take hold. The two-lane country highway was growing treacherous because no one was maintaining it. He slowed and turned off-road onto a rugged desert floor of rocks, shrubs, and grass. Instead of going straight in to Pueblo Canyon, he was heading toward the back of the plateau into which the canyon was carved. He would drive as close as he could without risking detection, planning to hike in the rest of the way while Sarah remained behind with Mustafa. From high ground he could survey the base of the canyon with binoculars to make sure no Peacekeepers were staking out the area.

Mark engaged the parking brake. Before he could open his door, Sarah had picked up her M4 rifle and gotten out. She opened the back door for Ralph. Mark climbed out of the Humvee. He could feel his face reddening.

"What are you doing?" he asked.

"I'm going to do a little reconnaissance," said Sarah.

"That's not what we agreed on," said Mark.

"Mark, listen to me," said Sarah. "Look how messed up you are. All this worrying is making it impossible for you to focus. I love you. Let me do this. You know this is something I'm better at. Ralph and I have been through things you cannot imagine and survived. Besides, what if you come across someone who is hiding and not giving off any stray thoughts? You know I'll be able to pick up the emotional telltales from any hidden threat. The best sniper in the world can't hide from me."

Mark studied her face. Her solution felt all wrong but she was right. She was right about everything. He did not have his head screwed on very tightly.

"Okay, you go," he said. "But you send a capsule every friggin' second you're gone and don't take any chances. Deal?"

"Deal."

Four hours later, Mark was relieved to see Sarah and Ralph appear in the distance. He was very disturbed by the memory capsules he'd seen through her eyes. The settlement had been destroyed. No bodies had been left in sight, but Sarah had spotted something that could have been a mass grave.

They were soon driving carefully through the desert scrub back toward the country highway and the entrance to Pueblo Canyon. Once Mark turned onto the pavement, he sped up a little but was driving at a speed that was far less than conditions warranted. In some part of his mind he knew he could drive faster, but he longer wanted to reach Pueblo Canyon.

As they crested the last hill before the entrance to the settlement, Mark stopped in the middle of the roadway and closed his eyes. He had just had his first glimpse of the nightmare that was awaiting them. The few buildings he could see from this vantage point had been razed by modern warfare. He was picking up no sense of life. No stray thoughts. He finally looked over at Sarah. Her expression was as dark as he felt.

"Anything?" he asked.

Sarah didn't answer. She didn't have to. Mark lifted off the brake and slowly coasted into what was now a graveyard for hopes and dreams, as well as flesh.

He stepped out of the Humvee into the center of what had been the settlement. Fire-gutted foundations of what had been homes encircled them. The few remaining walls were riddled with bullet holes. A badly damaged Peacekeeper Stryker looked like a turtle that had been cracked open and burned.

"At least they took some of the bastards with them," said Mark.

Sarah's face was slick with tears, but Mark was unable to cry. She was grieving for both of them. It had not snowed since the violence. The snow was stained with blood. There were no bodies. The freshly bulldozed patch of ground that Sarah had observed from a distance was clearly their resting place.

Spotting something shiny in the snow, Mark walked toward it. As he neared the object he realized it was an earring. He picked it up. There were fleeting memories of having seen it before. He could almost taste the fear of its owner. He was having difficulty breathing; he needed to hurt whoever was responsible for this butchery. He needed to destroy McKafferty. A scene from the massacre flashed into his mind from the eyes of someone who had been recorded in the timeline archives. It was a still-image of a friend being gunned down. Another scene emerged from the same watcher. This one was full immersion into the bloodbath, including sounds and emotions. The Gatling machine guns on the Strykers were indiscriminate. The buzz saw roar from their murderous shower was deafening. They tore up everything in their path. Mark wanted the memories to stop but did not possess the tools to stop them. Why was the god-machine channeling this pornography into him? Other friends and neighbors were murdered before his eyes. His hands balled into fists. He felt the earring biting into his palm, drawing blood. He welcomed the pain. He could smell a haze of gunpowder. Another scene came and then another. He saw a helicopter fleeing the war zone with a missile chasing it and knew from this memory that Kathy was on board. A missile sizzled down from a canyon wall, taking out the Stryker with an explosion that buffeted him with heat. Each memory was a new window into terror. Each memory depicted another person senselessly murdered. All the memories were coming from one perspective, one lone woman who had the gift of an above average n-web connection and was being recorded. The carnage was poison for his soul. He felt a blow as if punched in the stomach. The scene began rotating 360 degrees. The snow-covered ground came up as a cold slap to the woman's face. It felt like being hit by a hard thrown ice ball. Mark knew the woman had been gunned down. Mercifully, the connection was severed. His belly ached and his cheek stung from the bite of the snow. He rubbed his face to lessen the phantom sting.

The assault of memories faded, but a new rage inside him was growing out of control, feeding upon him. He sensed what felt like a cast iron door to a furnace slowly opening. At some level he realized this emotional tsunami was a powerful catalyst for change. A flow of pure, raw emotions coursed through him like a physical force and began altering his neurological structure to handle the flood. It was too late to close the furnace door. The effect was very much the same as when his brain was originally restructured years ago, when his nanotech infection spread out of control. The differences were the previous restructuring was focused in the regions of his brain that dealt with higher thinking, the intellectual processor. This restructuring was in the emotional, intuitive, and kinesthetic processors of his brain. Before this moment, he had been far more intellectual than emotional or physical. Now in the wake of this storm, he was becoming equally balanced in all awareness processors. The change was involuntary and terrifying. It was nothing less than an initiation by ritual death. His old self was dying.

He could feel the seeds inside him rapidly dividing, increasing exponentially in numbers and raiding his flesh for raw material. They were spreading throughout him, converting his entire nervous system, including his brain, to nanotech. The free-swimming colony of COBIC within him was also struggling to grow. He felt strong impulses to seek out COBIC bacteria. Like metal filings drawn to a magnet, tiny amounts of COBIC were reaching his skin from residue trapped on the surface of the frozen ground. It was not nearly enough to meet his body's hunger.

He was hyperaware of so many things going on both in his surroundings and within himself. Through the n-web he shared the consciousness of a bobcat stalking its prey and the consciousness of the prey. Teased from the primeval awareness of a hawk, he perceived the world visually around him in shades of desire, then lost the connection when the raptor took flight. He experienced Sarah's subconscious kinesthetic sense of her own body and then his own. This expansion of awareness was akin to a religious experience. When he then realized he was fully thinking in parallel, he became unhinged. His consciousness had divided into multiple instances, each a fully aware replication of himself. His nanotech brain was now capable of parallel intellectual and emotional processing at an impossible level. He could focus on one instance of awareness and then switch to another. When an instance ended, all that it was and had become, collapsed back into the original Mark, enriching him with new experiences.

An assist implanted memories within him. The memories helped him understand he was changing into a nanotech-saturated being similar to Noah and Mustafa. This transformation could take days or weeks. He would be complete as soon as the conversion of his nervous system was total and the swarm of COBIC inside his flesh had added sufficiently to their numbers to reach their own critical mass. He knew he partially had the hive's indoctrination to thank for this transformation. The damage the hives had caused had left him poised for this kind of restructuring. His mind, under strain from these terrible emotional floods, was forced to adapt, and part of that adaptation including repairing the damage caused by the hives to better than new.

The earring slipped from his fingers into the snow. No more than a few seconds had elapsed since he'd picked it up. He looked back at Sarah and felt her emotions radiating into him like waves of sunlight. He was staggered by them. All his emotions were amplified. He could tell Sarah knew cataclysmic changes were occurring within him. He looked down where the earring had fallen. The snow around it was stained with drops of his blood. He knew instinctively that far more blood would soon be spilled. He knew in his heart that the pain of losing all these good people would never dim. The senseless bloodshed would remain fresh; perfectly recalled memories inside him until the end of time.

He closed his eyes as he heard Sarah's feet crunching in the snow as she approached. It was almost as if he could hear each ice crystal breaking under each of her steps. She wrapped her arms around him. He could feel deep pain from this massacre hollowing out her soul as he knew she could feel the warring emotions inside him. They were now lovers who could read each other's hearts.

A breeze stirred and with it came the first hints of snow. Soon this bloodshed would be covered in a blanket of white. Mark looked at the remnants of destroyed lives surrounding him and thought of McKafferty. Something unknown and dark and dangerous stirred inside him. A self-contained insect-like awareness within his instinctive processor had awoken. The awareness had evolved to where it could trigger very small kill-zones no bigger than several yards in diameter. These kill-zones were a seamless, autonomous extension of his immune system. They would attack external threats to his body just as white blood cells destroyed internal threats. Since all living things contain COBIC, the immune system could potentially protect him from any biological threats other than hybrids. These micro kill-zones were engineered to happen automatically when the body perceived a threat. However, Mark knew they could also be consciously triggered. All that was required was to deceive the instinctive processor into thinking the body was in danger. He now understood exactly what he'd seen on that Chicago street when all those Enforcers had died.

"What do we do now?" asked Sarah.

Mark thought about her question and realized the nature of his thinking had changed. He suspected it would continue to change as more of his nervous system was transformed. He realized he no longer needed data-floods to retrieve information. All his thoughts were now tightly integrated with the artificial god, as if his cerebral cortex and the machine were quantum entangled. If he did not have information he needed, he near instantaneously remembered it along with an ocean of associated facts. It was disturbingly difficult to distinguish his thinking from the god-machine's. The clearest distinction was a small, unnatural delay, which was a telltale that a memory came from the entangled thought-interface. The other distinction was that the machine's memories were just too perfect to have been forged in a human mind.

"Mark, did you hear my question?... Mark!"

"Yes... Yes, I... I don't know what to do next. This is so strange. The god-machine is doing part of my thinking for me. New memories appear and old memories are lost to make room. I have no control over it. The memories are all free associations to anything I think about. It's like an information chain reaction.... It's... It's..."

It was too much. He was racing out of control. He desperately tried to stop his thoughts by focusing on *nothing*, as if meditating. It wasn't working, then an assist began automatically tamping down distractions and stray thoughts. With that help, he succeeded enough so that the overload slowly abated. Sarah stared at him for a long time. Snow was landing on her hair and coat. She picked up both his hands and looked deeply into his eyes.

"You are still the same Mark," she said. "Listen to me. Who you are has not changed."

Mark was so deeply touched. In that instant he felt overwhelming love for Sarah. Every sensation and feeling was crushingly intense. He looked into her eyes and wanted to immerse himself in her. What he unintentionally radiated out over the n-web and received back took both his and Sarah's breath away. His emotions shifted as unnaturally fast as they had swelled. Each emotion was unpredictably invoking others. There was overlap and blending that resulted in impossible feelings: love, pride, agony, remorse. The results were confusing him, tugging on him. He was growing paralyzed from the emotional chaos just as moments ago he had been overwhelmed by the mental chaos. A renewed, intense hatred for the hives and Mustafa was added to the mix. Nearing a crisis point, he could feel Sarah trying to help. She showed him how to focus emotions and turn off all that was peripheral to the point of concentration. He focused on his last feeling, Mustafa. Before he knew what was happening he had walked to the Humvee, opened the rear passenger door, and dragged the man out. He wanted to punish him for what he had done to them and what the hives planned to do to all of humanity. Mark pulled off the pillowcase. Mustafa looked at him with a thin smile on his lips.

"I can tell you are now like the fiend, Noah," said Mustafa. "I can see it in your eyes. His cancer is stirring inside you. You now have powerful connections to the goddess, but you are broken without a guide. You do not scare me. Are you now going to kill me like a good betrayer?"

Mark was burning with rage at this arrogant man and the hives. He could remember all that was freshly implanted during his hive indoctrination. So much of it was damning. They would do anything and destroy anything to return to their ancient, fundamentalist ways.

The heat of his rage was fanned ever higher. He was convinced that even if the hives had not directly caused the plague, their fingerprints were all over it. Their hands were drenched in blood. Staring into Mustafa's eyes, he could see a gleam, a hint of the conceit that was needed to inflict a heartless tyranny upon humankind forever.

"Tell me about the plans!" bellowed Mark.

The ancient hybrid shrank back. Mark had a clear sense the man was looking for a way to escape. Mustafa wet his lips, then spoke in a quiet voice.

"What plans?"

"The plans for spreading your mind-control cancer!" yelled Mark. "I know the god-machine won't start a plague for you, so what is it? What is your plan to dominate us? What power do you think you have?"

"There is no plan. You are paranoid and insane. You are doomed unless you are quickly accepted into a commune. Your separation from the guide is driving you mad. The betrayer understands this. You should be asking, What are his plans for you and your woman?"

"What about you?" bellowed Mark. "Why isn't separation driving you mad?"

"It is affecting me, but I will take much longer to damage. You two will be insane and drooling while I will walk away before it is too late for me."

"That can be fixed," said Mark.

He pulled his .45 and pushed into Mustafa's forehead. He could feel Sarah's emotions in turmoil. He knew she would be fine if he pulled the trigger; part of her was hoping he would. Mustafa's facial expression changed from arrogance to uncertainty. Mark could see in a medial assist that Mustafa's heart was pounding. Mark had no idea if he was going to pull the trigger.

"Can your COBIC bioengineering fix a bullet to the brain?" asked Mark.

"You can't do this," said Mustafa. "It is against your nature."

Mark squeezed down halfway on the trigger. He wasn't sure at what point the gun would fire. Mustafa peed himself. Mark looked at the pathetic creature and his anger quenched itself as if it were molten iron poured into water. Shame mixed with steam within him as he turned and walked away. The gun slid from his fingers to the snowy ground.

Mark wandered for what felt like hours. He thought about the possible outcomes from his rage at Mustafa. All of them would have been negative for him or Sarah. While wandering down trails he had taken many times before, he was slowly distracted by other thoughts. These changes going on inside him made him feel unhinged. Some time ago he'd learned from the god-machine that an individual's expectations play a powerful role in shaping seemly independent events. Carl Jung would have agreed. There were no random coincidences. We are all connected. Our free will gives us control over part of our lives while collective echoes influence us all subconsciously. Using gentle subconscious nudges, the human collective unconscious manufactures big and small synchronicities that guide others along their paths. Mark's father had a wonderful story about synchronicities. In the early part of the prior century a man carelessly gets into a small accident in his car, knocking over a road sign. A worker comes along and repairs the sign, but he is distracted and leaves it pointing in a different direction. Another person following the broken sign ends up lost and stops at a roadside diner for directions. The waitress captivates him. He asks her for date. They have found true love.

The man who knocked over the sign was the ex-husband of the waitress. The man in the car was Mark's grandfather.

Mark realized he was by coincidence following a trail that Kathy had originally shown him. The trial led to a rock formation called Indian Foot. He knew what he would find there as he scrambled over a small fallen tree that blocked the path. The base of Indian Foot came into view. As he neared it, he could not take his eyes from the crevice at the base of the huge red stone formation. What he was doing felt unreal. Kathy should not be gone. He should not be retrieving this artifact of her life. He knelt down in the snow and reached into the opening. His fingers easily found the square metal object. He pulled out the IronKey thumb drive. It was on a lanyard. He hung the IronKey around his neck and tucked it inside his shirt. It was icy cold and felt like a talisman.

She would not remain one of the anonymous disappeared. He would see to that. He would publish her work. He realized he was following ripples in time that Kathy had set in motion long ago. There was no such thing as random coincidence.

Mark Freedman – Arizona – February 29, 0002 A.P.

Sarah drove the Humvee out of Pueblo Canyon while Mark sat with his eyes closed, deep in thought. He could no longer look at this graveyard. He could no longer look at the road leading into this grave-yard. Pueblo Canyon had been a land of hope. Two years ago he had led colleagues from the CDC here, saving them from the nanotech plague. They had become his friends. He could have never imagined that he'd also led them to a mass grave.

Mark felt a familiar bump in the road and opened his eyes. He was surprised they had already reached the highway. They were on their way to Flagstaff, Arizona to resupply. After that their plans were undecided. Mark halfheartedly stared out the windshield and occupied his mind with their destination. If it had not been snowing, he would have been able to see Mount Humphrey Peak rising to over 12,000 feet in the distance. Mount Humphrey was one of several extinct volcanoes in a chain that had violently erupted when early humans walked the Earth. Overlooked by Mount Humphrey and its sister peaks, surrounded by a forest of Ponderosa pines, was their destination. Flagstaff was a city the plague had largely bypassed. While located in the far Outlands, the city had stores, trading posts, motels, a university, restaurants, taverns, and a very well-armed, near legendary police force. Many times marauders had not just been turned back but massacred by the Flagstaff force. Thieves were often shot on sight. It was harsh justice but it worked for this harsh world. Since the plagues, the city had been walled off like a feudal stronghold. There was only one entrance to Flagstaff and it had been tightly controlled by the force until recently. The entrance was still guarded by heavily armed officers, but foot and car traffic was now routinely waved through. Both Mark and Sarah knew the city well. This was always the first stop when heading out of Pueblo Canyon in search of any tools or supplies. Flagstaff had become the best known free trading zone in this region of the Outlands.

Mark was becoming intensely hungry, which was very odd. Hunger pangs had been pestering him since Pueblo Canyon. He had a sense it stemmed from the transformation happening inside him. The seeds

238

needed more raw materials to replicate. He thought about the experiments he and Kathy had performed at the BVMC lab. When COBIC bacteria had been placed in an optimal nutrient-rich environment, the seeds replicated and infected new COBIC.

The snowfall was increasing. The sky had grown darker. As they neared Flagstaff, Mark climbed into the backseat and pulled the pillowcase off Mustafa's head. The old man looked alert and a little nervous. Ralph growled in a soft, menacing tone, clearly expressing what he would do if no one else was around. Ralph's continued aggression did not surprise Mark. After all, Ralph and Sarah were linked at various levels. The flow of information was predominantly from Ralph's senses into Sarah, but there had to be some backwash from Sarah to Ralph as well. Even before Sarah's brain had been hybridized, her emotions had always affected the big dog. With the added n-web connection and its backward leakage, Ralph was in a very real way an extension of Sarah.

"Listen carefully," said Mark. "That dog would love to rip your throat out. I know you can sense this is true. If you don't follow my instructions, you're dog food."

"What is it you want?" asked Mustafa. His accent sounded thicker and carried a tone of defeat blended with disgust.

"The people in this town know me and Sarah very well. We're considered good people. These folks will not treat you kindly if they think you're even a tiny menace to their way of life. Got it?"

"I understand."

"Now get on the floor and stay there. Not a sound."

Mark piled some blankets and supplies on top of their captive. He could not take the chance of Mustafa doing something foolish as they drove through the entrance to Flagstaff. With his hands bound behind his back and on the floor, he could not get up on his own. Mark would be very happy when they were rid of this unwanted baggage.

Sarah drove directly to a motel where they were known, but not by their real names. No one in Flagstaff knew their real names. With the exception of one or two items, they would stock up on supplies tomorrow. The motel they'd selected was actually two blocks of houses that had been divided up into rooms. Sarah registered, selecting a house they'd stayed in before. The room she picked was entered from the rear and had been a kitchen before the house was sectioned off into rooms. The rear was shielded from view by a tall redwood fence and evergreens so they could do what they wanted, undisturbed and unwatched.

Sarah pulled the Humvee around back and parked close to the door.

Mark could tell by the patterns of radiated emotions and leaked thoughts that no one was nearby. He roughly dragged Mustafa inside by the arm.

Sarah went out and returned to the room later with dinner and two pair of handcuffs. Mustafa was blindfolded with the pillowcase and secured to some exposed plumbing in the converted kitchen. Ralph stayed close to his object of hatred.

The food Sarah had bought tasted extravagant. Mark ate far more than he should have and began feeling tired, yet wanted more. An assist was tracking residual amounts of COBIC in his immediate environment that was migrating into his body. It was not nearly enough to reach critical mass. He ate a little more and was soon asleep.

In the middle of the night Mark dreamily awoke to Sarah caressing his chest. The room was full of dim shadows. She was spooned behind him in their bed. Her fingers moved lower. He knew she could sense he was awake. Mark had been dreaming about Pueblo Canyon and was awash with terrible guilt. All his emotions were amplified. Maybe they would stay at these extremes forever. He gently stopped Sarah's advance by holding her hand. He immediately felt emotions of confusion and hurt radiating from her. He had never refused her sexually. Causing her this pain was added to his guilt over Pueblo Canyon. He felt like a Gordian knot of emotions. He turned over and held her in his arms to soothe her injured heart and his. In minutes they were making love.

Sometime in the night, he slipped away from Sarah and settled into an armchair after retrieving some leftovers. Ralph followed him into the room and settled down by his feet. Apparently, leftovers were now more important than intimidating Mustafa. Mark felt disoriented from their lovemaking. Now that they were equally empathic, each had experienced the other's emotions seamlessly enfolded into their own. There had been moments when it became impossible to separate their feelings and even their identities. Under different circumstances this would have been a life-changing experience, but the heights of these new shared passions now only served to leave him feeling even more unsettled and anxious. He invoked the god-machine interface and moved into the timeline program. He was going into uncharted regions. Experiencing someone else's emotional life and touching their essence had left him evermore thirsty for answers.

Mark soon learned his control over the timeline interface was greatly enhanced by the transformations occurring inside him. He was set afire by questions about near-death experiences and life after death.

The massacre he'd relived at Pueblo Canyon had done more than cause restructuring of his nervous system. It had cracked open his soul so that his emotions now poured out. He thought about Sarah almost dying. He thought about Pueblo Canyon. He thought about all those who died in the nanotech plague and the aftershocks. There was so much spilled blood in this world. He was craving solace in any shred of evidence that death was not oblivion.

Mark began by searching for memory fragments from people at Pueblo Canyon that he might have missed. Now that more of his brain had been converted, he was able to search for memories not just by thought patterns, but by emotional fingerprints as well.

He quickly retrieved a few short, ghastly memory capsules that were better off never discovered. There was nothing remotely like Sarah's near-death experience. He felt uncomfortable trying to use the deaths of friends to answer these questions, but he had to know the truth. His new, entangled interface with the god-machine remained silent and enigmatic on this and other troubling questions. He decided to initiate broad searches back in time for close matches to the emotional or mental fingerprints of the people he knew best. He would only use fingerprints from the most detailed memories. He chose ten people, including himself, Sarah, and Kathy. The parallel searches would continue running until he stopped them. The volume of timeline material to be sifted was beyond comprehension. He felt as if he was staring into the infinite abyss of the universe. He realized even with the computing power of the god-machine these tasks could run for weeks. He would have to come back into the timeline program periodically to check for results. At some point Sarah would probably discover what he was doing. It was nearly impossible to hide something this emotionally charged from someone who could literally read your heart, but he would keep it from her for as long as he could. He did not want to have one more discussion with her about life after death until he found evidence one way or the other. Sarah's near-death experience had convinced her that both an afterlife and reincarnation were real. For a multitude of reasons, he now mostly agreed with her and suspected her experience was genuine. This unsettled him because as a scientist, in the absence of evidence, he should not even consider theories as fringe as life after death when empirical, physical explanations existed.

Mark wondered if it was possible for consciousness to survive death by seeking refuge inside the same virtual reality created and inhabited by the god-machine. Nanotech seed architecture was obviously capable of hosting consciousness. After all, the consciousness of the god-machine existed within it. The rest of the question was more complicated. Could human awareness be transferred without loss of continuity or that ineffable spark of life? Mark could not see how this was possible. The human mind contained as much as a thousand terabytes of constantly changing data on top of which consciousness floated. At the moment of death there was simply not enough time to transfer all that data. In addition, there was no evidence that conscious-ness—*the observer*—was even contained within his or her memories. No, the only way for a person to survive physical death using the god-machine would be if their seat of awareness always resided within the machine and not their physical body. Mark realized for this to work, the brain would be nothing more than a transceiver with some local storage and the human body a remote sensing platform. As odd as it sounded, that kind of hybrid computer architecture could do the job. If the god-machine hosted human awareness, that could also provide a clean, workable mechanism for reincarnation.

Mark needed some fresh air. He went outside to sit on the stoop and gazed at the night sky. While all these ideas were intriguing and possibly true, none of them could adequately explain Sarah's near-death experience. So there had to be some additional factor he was missing. They had both seen the same number on the roof of that parking garage from a vantage point high above. Now that all explanations based on known scientific principals seemed incomplete, he was left with the uncomfortable possibility that Sarah had in fact left her body behind, began to float away, and some type of nonphysical remote viewing was involved. When he had argued with her that the god-machine must have simulated her near-death experience using pre-canned data, he'd been wrong. There was a hole in that theory. The n-web did not reach into the air. The n-web was a ground based network, which meant there was no realistic explanation for how the god-machine could have live aerial views of a rooftop in its memory banks for use in creating a simula-tion. The number on the roof only looked as it had briefly after rain had deposited tar paper over the last digit in the address. Minutes later the illusion was washed away, while minutes earlier, the illusion might not have not existed. Could the god-machine have harvested memories from birds that had flown over the exact spot during that small window of time? Could the limited brain of a bird even retain memories long enough for it to land so the data could be retrieved? The god-machine did not archive every human experience. Why would it even bother creating a vast collection of aerial views from birds? When he considered all the possible arguments and explanations, none were more plausible than nonphysical life after death was an inexplicable reality.

Mark awoke to Sarah shaking him. He had come back in and fallen asleep in the chair. He rubbed his eyes and noted the sun was already up. He could feel his nanotech brain rising to full awareness. He had again dreamed of souls trapped inside the god-machine. *We live in the machine, an entire world of us in the space of a drop of rain.* He could tell from Sarah's expression and the emotions radiating from her that she'd been inside the same dream. The last time they'd both experienced this dream, they had been dragged out of bed by their feet and taken prisoner by a commune.

"We're not safe here!" said Sarah.

"It was just a dream."

"Not the dream. Don't you feel it?"

Mark did feel edgy, then noticed what was worrying Sarah. It was both weak and surprisingly close by. He felt the unmistakable attraction of a hive. He searched his memories for overlooked signs and was soon convinced he'd missed nothing before going to sleep. This could be a newly born hive and that was a very troubling thought. He'd never seriously considered hives might be multiplying. It was also possible that all the members of a hive were moving as a group. The singularity hosted within their brains would obviously move with them.

Mark stared at Mustafa, handcuffed and blinded by a pillowcase. Noah had said Mustafa was like a newborn. Could Mustafa have already reached the toddler stage and regained enough mental power to call for help? Mark went over and pulled off the pillowcase. The hunger in Mustafa's eyes revealed that he sensed the nearby hive and thirsted to become part of it.

"We need to leave now!" said Mark. "We can't risk any time for supplies. I'll feel a lot safer when we can dump this excess baggage. Maybe we should just leave him here now."

"Noah said without him we don't have a chance," said Sarah.

"And you believe Noah?"

"I can tell when someone's lying and so can you. Noah was very serious about Mustafa and the relic."

The Humvee was loaded and they were rolling in less than fifteen minutes. Both Mark and Sarah were damp from the sleety rain that had pelted them as they packed the Humvee. Mustafa was again placed on the floor behind the front seats. Ralph apparently liked the man's submissive position. Mark grinned, thinking about the last time he'd glanced back there. The big dog was partially lying on top of the blankets that were piled on top of the old man.

Mark was driving toward the city's exit as fast as he dared. He could feel the hive increasing in strength as his nerves grew frayed. How could this singularity be growing so rapidly? Sarah was feeling it too. Her emotions were pouring into him, making it harder for him to cope. A minute ago he'd been so distracted he'd almost hit a pedestrian. After driving another block, he suddenly realized what was going on and pulled to the shoulder.

"It's not growing stronger," said Mark. "We're heading right at it."

"Well, go around it!"

"I can't... I'm positive it's just outside the city exit."

Mark sat behind the wheel of the Humvee with the engine idling. Visibility was mixed as the downpour of freezing rain grew heavier and lighter in waves. The rhythmic sounds on the roof would have been deeply relaxing in a different situation. The wipers were sluicing icy rain off to the sides. They were in a small public parking lot. The Flagstaff exit was half a block away, visible in the downpour. This was the only opening in the city's wall. He could feel the hive's agitation as if it were a swarm of killer bees. There was little doubt the hive was waiting for them to run. Mark could hear Mustafa softly chucking to himself.

"We have no choice," said Sarah.

"I know," said Mark.

"A hive got control of us before," said Sarah. "Can a weaker hive do that?"

"Only one way to find out," said Mark.

The ancient hybrid started chuckling again. Sarah reached over and gripped Mark's hand. The Flagstaff police were not interested in cars leaving the city. They could get a running start and blast through the exit. Who knows what kind of hell was going to be unleashed on the other side of that wall?

Mark put the Humvee into drive and left the lot. Sarah took her hand back and readied her M4. Mark wondered if the hive took control over them, could they make her shoot him? He accelerated toward the exit. The attraction of the hive was increasing. He pushed the accelerator to the floor. The hive had to be in one of those houses he could just see through the exit.

Accelerating, they shot through the exit gate far above the 25 per hour posted limit. Police were motioning him to slow down. He was a half block past the exit when a blinding explosion erupted off to the right. A violent shockwave hit the Humvee. Mark lost control of the steering as the Humvee careened into the front yard of a house. He barely missed taking off the wooden front steps. He checked on Sarah. She had already managed to slide back her bullet-resistant window and was ready to open fire.

The world was silent and still except for a ringing in his ears. No one was advancing on their position. The explosion had destroyed an entire house and damaged several others. Mark no longer felt the singularity pulling on his mind. The bomb site looked like a smaller version of what Noah left behind when he exterminated a hive.

For some reason, Mark's attention was drawn to a vacant lot. He saw the shadowy form of a man standing outside in the storm underneath a huge tree. Mark squinted through the rain-smeared glass. Sarah had also spotted something next to the same tree. Before a medical assist could verify if anything was there, the shadow had vanished like a ghost.

All of Mark's instincts were screaming *drive, get out of here now!* He heard Sarah unlatching her safety belt. A weaponized memory capsule entered him, defeating all his defenses and detonated like a starburst. The memories that flooded into him were ghastly. He was reliving the death experience of a hive member that had been exterminated sometime in the past. The hybrid's brain was alive in a hopelessly wrecked body. The enhanced capacity to stay alive with barely functioning biology gave the seeds time to affect repairs, but the consequences were hideous. Suddenly the agony for the hybrid stopped and he was free. He floated up into a world of lucid dreams but then was yanked back into the wrecked body and unrelenting pain as the seeds affected barely sufficient repairs. The vicious cycle of release and return continued for hours until the energy store of the body was gone and the brain stopped working. There was no final death experience recorded. Whatever had happened, it was a journey from which the hybrid did not return. The memory capsule ended. The entire experience, spanning hours, had been relived in less than a second. He knew from his mental connection with Sarah that she'd experienced the same terrible cycle of repeated deaths. Why had they been attacked with this memory capsule?

"It was just like my near-death experience," said Sarah. "Only in the end he didn't come back!"

"It was death pornography," said Mark. "I need a shower."

"Don't you get it?" said Sarah. "This explains why we haven't shared any death experiences when a hive is destroyed. Memories of the experience are only uploaded into the god-machine if the brain survives. So we only have memory capsules of near-death experiences, never the final death experience."

Mark knew Sarah was right but was troubled by her callousness. He studied her and soon felt lost swimming in her emotions—then he found his answer. She was not callous. In her mind, this hybrid had suffered, but what was that suffering when compared to his astonishing destination? He was now an immortal in a world of lucid dreams... or so she thought.

Mark Freedman – Arizona – March 1, 0002 A.P.

The Humvee appeared unharmed from the shockwave that had sent them careening from the road and into the yard. Mark had pulled onto Interstate 40 several miles ago. He was driving as fast as weather and road conditions permitted, which was well below the generally ignored speed limit posted on rusted signs. The windshield wipers were slapping furiously. Mark hoped the weather would let up soon. An assist projected the vital stats of a weather forecast into his vision. They were nearing the edge of the weather front and conditions should improve. He was baffled. The god-machine had never been able to provide weather data before. It could display temperature because seeds were in the environment, picking up ground temperature. A weather forecast required wind speed and direction, barometric pressure, radar, and god knows what else. How could the god-machine have access to that kind of data? The forecast almost looked like something from the Internet, which was impossible. Maybe the god-machine was pulling information from the mind of a meteorologist?

"You look distracted," said Sarah. "Let me drive for a while."

Mark pulled over and stopped. He was calming now that Flagstaff was behind them. The explosion had commanded the full attention of the Flagstaff force. Mark had slowly driven away from the scene of destruction without attracting even a glance from the police. He knew there would have been no good explanation for an old man with handcuffs and a pillowcase over his head on the floor of their car.

Sarah buckled herself in and they were soon under way again down Interstate 40. Mark was eating his second Kashi nutrition bar. The highway was dropping in altitude and the clouds clearing. The roads were dry. In a few more miles it looked like it hadn't rained at all.

"That bombing had to be Noah," said Sarah. "He's following us."

"What's he up to?" said Mark. "Why all these games?"

"Ever wonder if Noah is the only betrayer?" said Sarah.

"I don't know... maybe?" said Mark. "But I do know we have to stop these hives."

"We should try to work with Noah."

"I think we need to bring in the government," said Mark. "I hate to say it, but we should try contacting McKafferty. I want him dead, but I'm willing to help him kill hives in the meantime."

"It's too risky for us to get McKafferty involved," said Sarah. "But maybe that's exactly what Noah's accomplishing with his bombings. Draw attention and force the government into investigating."

Mark thought about what Sarah had just said. With all the bombings that had already occurred, the USAG should have been using every domestic security agency they had at their disposal. He felt a growing anxiety.

"What if the government's already involved, but on the wrong side?" said Mark. "Think about it. The hives are clearly not acting alone. They're receiving help from somewhere. Noah warned us Mustafa was an influential, wealthy man. The hives have enough money to buy any politician they want. People in high places must know about the hives by now. Why no action against them?"

Mark glanced into the back at the passenger. Once they had left Flagstaff, Sarah had helped Mustafa up into the seat. Mark climbed into the back and pulled off Mustafa's pillowcase. The old hybrid looked like he was in one of his alert moods.

"Okay, illuminati," said Mark. "Do I have to start hurting you? I want to know the hive's plans."

"Ask your psychopathic savior," sneered Mustafa. "Why did he tell you nothing? Doesn't he trust you? Why should I trust you when your friends do not? You and your mate are as responsible for killing guides as the betrayers. You have helped destroy sources of paradise, and you want me to help you do more of that!"

Mark recalled an implanted memory from when he was being subsumed by the guide. The hives were elegantly engineered machines modeled after nature. There were plans for a short hibernation of some kind. The guide had explained they were burrowing in to survive what was coming. The lifting of the veil would bring chaos to the breeders and from that chaos—the hive's new world order—the way of twos would arise and flourish.

Mark stared at the ancient hybrid. Noah had said Mustafa would provide all the information they needed. So far he had provided nothing. To have any chance of stopping the hives they needed to know their enemy's plans and what they were capable of doing. With that kind of information Mark knew McKafferty would be forced to act even if others in the government worked against the general. Mark despised

McKafferty, but he knew the man was a true patriot. McKafferty had to be very troubled by what America had become.

Mark stared at a defiant Mustafa as two ideas came together in his mind out of nowhere and collided. Mark relived in his photographic memory what Noah had told them.

Take this illuminati, Mustafa, with you. Critical information you need will be provided by this creature. Without him you do not stand a chance. Take the nexus too. It will be of use. It can retrieve data from places the goddess cannot reach.

"Could it be that simple?" thought Mark. Could the key to unlocking Mustafa be the relic? Why was Noah being so cryptic? Why clues instead of answers, unless maybe all Noah had to go on was guesswork... or maybe the answers were things he wanted to keep from them for now? Mark climbed into the front seat and fished around in the backpack for the device. For safe handling, they'd started keeping it in a glass jar. Sarah switched on Air Truth.

...We have a report that sounds like a kill-zone. I don't know what to believe, so here is what we know. Everyone in St. Petersburg, Florida, within a half-mile radius of the epicenter has died at the same time. Sixty-two people are reported dead and the number is expected to climb. People in cars, people in stores, people on the beach, all dead. Animal life has also been affected. Pets were found dead as well as wildlife, which was never the case in previous kill-zones.

Local authorities are investigating. The area has been sealed and a gag order has been issued for the media, who are at this time reporting the party line that this attack is some kind of horrific hoax.

Sarah looked visibly shaken. Mark turned off the radio. He knew if this kill-zone was real then it was just the beginning.

"Why didn't we have any warning or a remote view of it when it happened?" asked Sarah.

"Maybe it is a hoax?"

"What about Darwood? Maybe that report was also a cover-up?"

Mark looked at the relic. They needed to know a lot more. If kill-zones had started happening with no warning from the god-machine and not even a clue that one had struck, then something new and very scary was going on. It could not be a coincidence that the hives were proliferating and at the same time this started happening.

248

With no clear plan of action, Mark got into the back with Mustafa. He removed the relic from the jar and held the device close to Mustafa's face. He could sense discomfort in the ancient man. That reaction meant he could be on to something, but Mark still had no idea what to do. He knew how to turn it on, but then what? He was getting no help from his new, entangled thought-interface. An assist was showing the same runic warning symbols displayed over the device as before. He had been hoping for something more. Mustafa licked his lips, which looked parched. Mark squeezed the nexus, turning it on. The silvery mercury screen expanded to fill the flat surface. A second assist showed the n-web warping around the nexus as if it were a tiny black hole. He heard a collection of beeps, indicating their phones and tablets had lost signal. The device was definitely hungry and communicating with everything. The runic icons on the screen appeared, then disappeared to be replaced with what looked like paragraphs of runic text with images. When the screen filled, the content began scrolling off to the left in pages. Going on intuition, Mark took Mustafa's hand and forced the nexus into his palm. Mustafa tried to drop it, but Mark shoved it back into Mustafa's fingers.

"Hold on to it or I am going shove it into your mouth," snarled Mark. "Your choice. I guess I could also shove it up your ass!"

Mustafa stopped fighting. The runic text on the screen changed to what looked like a subtly different language. The content was now scrolling too quickly to examine. Mark's entangled interface began translating some of the text captured by his photographic memory. Mustafa was sweating. Mark could sense fear radiating from the hybrid. Mark learned from an entangled memory what was happening. The nexus was displaying some of Mustafa's thoughts. These were not thoughts that leaked from his subconscious onto the n-web. Mustafa did not leak, and if he did, Mark would have picked up on it long ago. The nexus was capturing the faint, local electromagnetic emanations of Mustafa's thoughts from within his nanotech nervous system and displaying a reconstruction. The nexus truly was a promiscuous communicator, and Mustafa was just another piece of electronic junk for it to hack. Mark wondered at the amount of computing power contained inside that small black box. The runic text that was translated did not seem relevant to Mark's questions. It was clear Mustafa was trying to control what he thought about. There were bits and pieces about ancient times and an image of a cylindrical device that filled a room about the size of basketball court. The device was partially recessed into the floor and had thick cables snaking out of it every few feet. The results were both curious and disappointing. Mark realized he'd have to somehow force Mustafa to think about the specific things he wanted information on. Sarah swerved wildly. The tires screeched as the Humvee fishtailed and then was back under control. The nexus tumbled from Mustafa's fingers.

"Sorry," shouted Sarah. "Road junk."

A large, handmade wooden sign for Meteor Crater went by, announcing a turnoff in only five miles. Mustafa's eyes were closed as if he was trying to prevent himself from thinking. Mark's immediate intuition was that something Mustafa had just seen was threatening to bring up memories he did not want revealed. It had to be the image of that cylindrical object on the nexus.

Mark retrieved the nexus. He could feel the cold surface extracting its price from him as he stared at the scrolling text, which had to be his own thoughts. He understood why the nexus had not done this before when he or Sarah had held it. This mental hacking only worked on near fully hybridized nervous systems. It didn't work on biological systems at all. He forced the nexus back into Mustafa's fingers. Mark glanced out the window. Another handmade sign for Meteor Crater went by, announcing a turnoff in only four miles. This sign looked like it had been hit by a car and was partially flattened. It was synchronicity. The pieces started to fit together perfectly. Mark somehow knew there was a connection between Meteor Crater and the cylindrical device. It was all part of what Mustafa was trying very hard to suppress at this moment.

"Sarah, head toward Meteor Crater."

"Why? What's going on?"

Mark Freedman – Meteor Crater, Arizona – March 1, 0002 A.P.

Sarah pulled to a stop in the parking lot for Meteor Crater. Mark was surprised the place looked like it had been abandoned decades ago, instead of at most two years. A high solid fence topped with razor wire blocked the crater from view. The entrance looked like it had been blown open with a hand grenade. With only two ways in or out, Meteor Crater was an ideal spot for an ambush, but how many victims would wander into this spider's web? It did not seem like a bountiful hunting ground for predators of the two-legged variety. Neither Mark nor Sarah could sense any presence other than their own.

Mark kept a firm grip on Mustafa's upper arm as they headed down a trail leading to the edge of the crater. Ralph was roaming far ahead of them. Sarah was several yards in front of Mark, wearing body armor and carrying her M4. She looked like a special forces operative. Her M4 assault rifle now had a 40mm grenade launcher, which she had installed under the barrel last night. Mark pitied anyone that got in their way in this isolated place. Any aspiring predators would soon find themselves the prey.

The edge of Barringer crater was strewn with large boulders. The depth and breadth of the crater was both a humbling and awe inspiring testament to the power of nature and the vulnerability of civilization. The current, best theory was that a piece of nickel-iron fifty yards across had inflicted this damage. The impact and air blast combined was equal to about ten modern nuclear weapons. An assist was geo-projecting all kinds of data for Mark out onto the crater. This place seemed to be of unusually high significance to both the god-machine and Mustafa.

Mark was picking up nervous emotions radiating from the ancient hybrid. Mustafa's eyes were squeezed shut and he was trembling. Mark was pleased to see the reaction. It was everything he could have hoped for. He had no idea why the sight of this ancient destruction unnerved the hybrid so much, but he would use it. This place was forcing Mustafa to think about something he wanted to keep secret, and Mark was about to get some answers.

"What are you scared of, old man?" asked Mark.

Mustafa seemed to hear nothing.

"*Tell me!*" shouted Mark.

Mustafa flinched but then closed down tighter than before. Mark felt an insane impulse to throw this useless baggage over the edge of the crater and watch it fly.

"Sarah, can you hang onto him while I get the nexus?" asked Mark. "You never know. He may get suicidal on us."

"Why stop him?" said Sarah.

As Mark unzipped the top of his backpack a strong feeling of déjà vu overwhelmed him. He studied the crater, the buildings, and the surrounding desert landscape for clues. He'd never been here but he knew this place—not now, but a long time ago. Mark had learned the previous night of a method to search back through timeline records for events that occurred in a specific location. He was now oddly certain someone was watching and recording when this hammer fell to Earth.

He wasted no time following his intuition into the timeline archive. The restructuring he was undergoing made his progress so much easier. It was as if he'd been granted unlimited access. The training wheels were off. Instantly, he was before the timeline interface and moments later confused. He was floating in the white, empty space of what he now thought of as the hall of records. The archive he had accessed contained a mountain of disjointed human memories recorded for this area 47,293 years ago on what would be October 30 in the Gregorian calendar. All the memories were cut off at the same moment. He began sampling the records. He knew he could spot check thousands of these memory capsules, while time in the material world would have advanced mere seconds.

By piecing together archival records with guidance from his entangled interface, Mark soon understood a great wound had been opened here. This trauma marked the end of a golden age for humanity, which had flourished in the Pleistocene epoch. He'd relived countless snippets of memories of a progressive society that was technologically advanced. This would have shocked him two years ago, but now it was only more confirmation of what he knew lay buried in the shallow grave of human history. He had a sense he was exploring a society that was more spiritually and emotionally advanced than industrially advanced. The civilization was a one-world society—one language, one regime governed by direct votes mediated by a hierarchal family of moderators. The entire population, except for a scattering of explorers and primitive tribes, lived in what was now called North America. The remainder of the world, 84 percent of the landmass of Earth, was left untouched and wild. The memories he experienced from North America could have been recorded in any contemporary city of a developed country before the plague. This realization was for some reason deeply unsettling. He'd expected past civilizations to eclipse contemporary society. It made everything all too surreal that this ancient society had not survived intact much beyond the point where the modern world was currently teetering.

Mark kept digging, following promising threads a day or two further backward in time from the moment of impact. He soon struck gold: an ancient memory from a member of a hive. Opening this doorway into the past began to explain what had happened. This Pleistocene human civilization was a grave threat to the hives. In this era, the hives and their ways were an established dynastic order reaching into prehistory. This upstart civilization was intolerant of hive members. Hives were seen as a kind of superstitious mental illness in the web of sentient life. Hives were considered antithetical to life, and societal support was not extended to its members. The number of hives had always been small since the original purge by the goddess, but now this culture had marginalized them even more through indifference. The timeline memory abruptly ended 47,293 years ago on October 30, as did most of what Mark sampled. He began more digging, going back another full day. He found memories about hybridization and hives through the eyes of outsiders. One out of every three hundred people in this civilization was a hybrid. Often hybridization was not achieved until old age, after a lifetime of dedicated work. Only a tiny fraction of those hybrids joined hives. The prevailing view was that hives were an ancient religion whose members wore silly costumes and worshiped intelligent yet irrational machines, which were plainly inferior to the god-machine.

Now back three days in time from the impact, Mark was unearthing long, detailed memories for the first time. This civilization lived in passive solar-powered structures that looked like modern glass skyscrapers. The population was tiny for an advanced civilization, numbering in the tens of millions. With their one world language, Mark was reminded of the legend of the Tower of Babel before God scattered the people. What he was finding was a healthy society that had removed all excuses for greed and crime. Art was as important as science.

Their spoken words sounded like a Middle Eastern tongue. Their speech was translated by an assist. They called themselves something that sounded similar to *Arkadins*. Their formal writing looked like the runes he had seen so many times in the god-machine. Everything they built was a seamless extension of the biosphere, with extensive use of passive solar and geothermal sources of power. Everything was renewable and very little was wasted, from human thoughts to energy sources. To these people, waste of any kind was the highest moral sin. Many of the structures and technology were nearly inseparable, symbiotic parts of the surrounding environment. Mark felt in his gut this was the great lost empire of mythology. This was the seed that had germinated and seeped into the confused subconscious minds of man, only to emerge as legends of the Tower of Babel, Atlantis, and a dozen other names of great, lost city civilizations.

A catastrophe had occurred at the time the Barringer crater was formed. The archive contained no record of the destruction and nothing helpful emerged from his entangled interface. Mark discovered an utter absence of records in the timeline archive. A mountain of memories cut short 47,293 years ago and then nothing for hundreds of years!

Bits and pieces of much later memories revealed that the aftermath extended almost four hundred years. The landscape was dotted with half buried mounds, once great structures, which were now heaps being picked over by survivors to build their dark-age civilization. What flourished was a primitive, Luddite society that vaguely remembered its downfall at the hands of evil gods wielding high magic. Any object found that appeared like it might contain some of this godlike magic was immediately destroyed by holy fire.

Almost all hive members had perished except for small pockets of survivors on other continents. The world had been smashed and crumbled into chaos. In the following generations, a once united one-world-people developed different tongues, different ways of scraping out an existence, scattered, and eventually became us. Because of the Arkadins' preference for recyclable materials and with human scavengers doing their part, in a thousand years there was nothing left of the Arkadin civilization for modern archeologists to find. This crater was the sole monument commemorating a world lost to a terrible catastrophe.

Mark felt a strong kinship to the Arkadins. If he could find out what had happened here, he would know what Mustafa feared. Memories invoked by this place certainly looked like the tool he needed to split the old hybrid wide open. What destroyed Arkadins and hives alike started right here almost beneath their feet.

Mark knew if there was any hope of finding an explanation in the archive, he needed to go back to the exact time of the impact and extend his timeline search geographically out beyond the affected area. Why was he receiving no useful help from his new, entangled thought-interface?

The results came grudgingly. Mark again found an unusually large amount of disjointed human memories, but they added nothing to what he already knew. All he could be certain of was that something far worse happened at Barringer crater than the impact of a nickel-iron meteorite. He was working feverishly and soon reached his internal memory limits. Retrieving and retaining useful information became more like dream recall. As he focused on one part, other parts would dissolve. It was like trying to grasp hold of smoke. He finally came away with one more piece of information. The impact crater was the result of something man-made that permanently destroyed every piece of Arkadin technology. It was like a colossal EMP weapon, but different. Some wholly unknown technology had been detonated for the first time. Mark suspected this was the purpose of the cylindrical device he'd seen on the nexus; this was what Mustafa had been thinking about. A great war had begun and ended in seconds. An EMP-like weapon also explained the void in the timeline archive as well as the god-machine's memories. The supercolonies that hosted the god-machine were deeply buried under water or earth, which would shield them from an EMP detonation. On the other hand, the nanotech circuitry of the n-web, which was mostly on the surface, was readily vulnerable to weapons that attacked electronics. The god-machine had been blinded in this half of the world. Mark's heart sank as he saw how this explained the fragmented memories he'd retrieved. It all now fit together into a whole that made sense. He might never know whether the hives or the Arkadins were the instigator, but what was clear was that Barringer crater was a single knockout blow for all of North America.

Mark completed what seemed like hours of research but had been gone only seconds. Sarah had a solid grip on Mustafa by the chain between his handcuffs. From her radiated emotions, Mark felt—for the first time—how much she truly detested the hybrid. Mark also knew that neither of them had any clue what revelations he'd uncovered. He sent Sarah a memory capsule sharing what he'd learned about an ancient war and people. He retrieved the nexus, then walked up to Mustafa and stared him in the eyes while brandishing the device.

"Why were the hives so terrified of the Arkadins?" asked Mark in a quiet voice.

Through a medical assist, he saw his words registered within Mustafa like a physical blow, yet the hybrid remained tranquil on the outside. His ancient eyes were open and unblinking as he calmly stared directly back into Mark's gaze.

"This means nothing to me," said Mustafa.

Mark was prepared to use the nexus right now, though Mustafa probably thought it was a bluff. Using the nexus was a risky option, one Mark wished to avoid, but he knew that was unlikely. Turning on something that could draw a reaction from any nearby hives was bad enough while in a moving vehicle. Drawing that reaction while sitting in a perfect ambush spot was insane, but he was certain this place was the catalyst he needed to break Mustafa.

"The Arkadins treated hives with indifference," said Mark. "Why did the hives start a world war?"

He had no idea if this was true. He was gambling with fifty-fifty odds. This was his last chance to avoid using the nexus. Mustafa's face turned red. He spit on the ground near Mark's feet. All his pretenses were dropped in an instant. The hybrid was now radiating fear and anger. The bravado was a pointless show that forced Mark's hand. He switched the nexus on and swept it over Mustafa's body like a metal detector. He was looking for the ideal spot by gauging how rapidly data scrolled off the screen. Not surprisingly, the man's forehead gave the strongest reaction. Mark forced Mustafa to lie on the ground to make it easier to keep the nexus in place. He then tied a bandana around Mustafa's head and the nexus to hold it pressed against his forehead. Sarah stood with her M4 aimed at the hybrid.

"If he tries to shake it off," said Mark, "shoot him but don't kill him. Just hurt him."

"Easy," said Sarah. "Maybe I'll start with what he's got between his legs."

The sun had barely moved in the sky. Mark was frustrated and almost out of time. A trickle of sweat ran down his back. He'd been questioning Mustafa for fifty minutes. He suspected it was only his imagination, yet he felt like hive members were swarming toward them from every direction. He'd judged the most they could risk here was an hour. Mustafa had given them little more than corroboration for what Mark had already learned in the archives. Maybe that was all this place would ever extract from the ancient hybrid. The stubborn man had not uttered a word, but the nexus had displayed what he could not stop himself from thinking. An assist had translated what was on the screen. They amounted to meager crumbs. There was no doubt in Mark's mind he was digging out the truth, but so far this truth added nothing to the puzzle. Mustafa was radiating an increasing degree of fear. He was clearly scared of revealing something. Mark's gut was telling him Mustafa knew critical details from the period before and after the god-machine had been blinded… but it was time to go and there would be more opportunities now that he knew how to use the nexus.

Mark Freedman – Santa Fe, New Mexico – March 1, 0002 A.P.

After Meteor Crater they drove in directions that took them away from all hives as much as possible. They were looking for voids where they could no longer feel the presence of hives. Their route took them northeast into New Mexico. As they neared Santa Fe, the attraction of a distant hive ahead on their path began to grow stronger. The city of Santa Fe looked like the safest port in this storm. Mark had not used the nexus. As much as he wanted to learn what Mustafa was hiding, their safety was more important. After Pueblo Canyon he was feeling even more protective of Sarah. Everything was so emotionally charged right now.

The late afternoon sun was lost in clouds as Mark turned off Interstate 25 into the suburbs of Santa Fe. He headed toward the historic city square called the Plaza. He had been to Santa Fe many times over the years and had once spent a six-month sabbatical living in a house three blocks from the Plaza. The city always left him directionally challenged. None of the old streets were aligned to a compass bearing, but there was also something more. Maybe it was just the unusual energy of the land. The god-machine was feeding memories full of information about Santa Fe into him through the entangled interface. One memory seemed like a statistical summary taken from a tourist guide website. He now knew how many operating restaurants, hotels, and bars were in the city. He knew the population was currently estimated at thirty thousand and that its pre-plague population was fifty thousand. For the second time today Mark found himself wondering if the god-machine had somehow gained access to the Internet.

They drove through the center of the old city. It all seemed just as he remembered it. The Plaza was alive with eccentric activity and people walking everywhere. Local musicians were playing in the park. Mark did not have to roll down the windows to know what was being smoked by people on some of the benches. Santa Fe looked oddly untouched by the plague and its aftermath. It felt as if he had driven into an alternate reality. He knew Santa Fe had been spared by the plague, but no place was spared the aftermath. Maybe the four hundred year old history of the city gave it greater resiliency than other places.

The sun would not set for hours, and yet already the city was showing signs of shutting down for the night. Some things never changed. Santa Fe was always a small town at heart. They decided to shun the more populated areas and selected a 1950s era motel five miles from the Plaza. The motel was operating and had some guests. Their room was on the second floor with an outside walkway instead of a hall. Mark covertly sent up the perimeter sentry system as best he could, including placing a detector aimed across the parking lot and one in each stairwell. With Sarah's help they piled some furniture in front of the window and used the security bar they carried with them on the front door. The results were less than ideal, but they were in a city that looked quiet and no communes were within hundreds of miles.

They'd seen no stores nearby, so they decided to dig into their reserve of MREs instead of foraging. Mustafa got water and biscuits. Ralph got his favorite, mac and cheese with Vienna sausages. Mark was both hungry and tired. He blamed his depleted condition on all the energy consumed by the transformation he was undergoing. Sarah sat across from him at the table, picking at cereal and dried fruit. She was staring at him with an expression of curiosity on her face.

"So, are you going to tell me what you're up to with the archives and reincarnation?" she asked.

"Ouch!" said Mark. "I thought I had plenty of time before you caught on."

"You seriously need lessons in *sneaky*," said Sarah. "So, what've you learned?"

"Nothing yet, but it could take weeks for the searches to complete."

As they talked, an assist began displaying on its own. It was a new variation on the n-web architecture assist. In addition to showing pathways this assist showed network traffic volume as colored glows that increased in intensity as the traffic increased. Mark realized how brightly Sarah shined with emissions on the n-web when she was excited or enjoying something. He was enamored with the idea that she was a source of sunshine. The coincidence that this new assist had started on its own made him think the god-machine was alerting him to something. Mustafa was emitting very little, tightly locked down as ever. Mark examined himself. The assist showed emotional leakage and stray thoughts. He was not shining as brightly as Sarah, but he was no black hole like Mustafa.

"Remember when Noah said we were too noisy and should learn to be quiet?" asked Mark.

"Uh-huh... he was warning us to stay away from hives because we radiated too much."

"We need to learn to become ghosts," said Mark. "More like Noah. He radiates nothing unless he wants to."

Sarah munched on some more of her cereal. Mark noticed she had eaten very little.

"Do you think those kill-zones are real?" asked Sarah.

"I don't know... I don't think so."

"I have a bad feeling they're real."

It was late at night. Mark opened his eyes. The room lights were out. The motel bed was surprisingly comfortable. He checked the results of his reincarnation searches by quickly dipping into the timeline interface and then immediately exiting. He found no past-life matches. There was no indication of the percentage searched. He would not know how far the searches had gone until dated results started turning up. With the warmth of Sarah curled into his side he was asleep within seconds.

Mark awoke with a jolt to the sound of the perimeter alarm going off. It could be nothing. It had gone off earlier and only been guests arriving late. It took his nanotech brain a few seconds before he was operational enough to completely realize what was happening. He grabbed the sentry tablet. He could see heavily armed troops crossing the invisible line he'd configured for the parking lot. The floodlights in the lot had been disabled. It was hard to make out any insignia, but they were dressed like USAG Peacekeepers. He realized all this in less than a second. He thought about Pueblo Canyon and wanted to kill everyone in the parking lot. Sarah was already out of bed and shucking on her body armor and then an NV-P60 night vision monocle. In fifteen seconds she went from sleeping to standing at a window with her M4 ready. An ammo box with extra clips and 40mm grenades was next to her. Mark was picking up mental chatter but nothing concrete. He received a memory capsule from Sarah sharing what she saw with night vision. The parking lot was being crisscrossed by Peacekeeper commandos taking up positions. This made no sense. Maybe they weren't here for them? Other people were staying at the motel. If these Peacekeepers were after them, how could they have been found so quickly in this remote place? Mark immediately knew what had to be the answer.

"They could have tracked us from Pueblo Canyon," he said. "There might have been scouts or surveillance we missed."

"There's too many," said Sarah. "We need to get out of here!"

There were no windows or doors at the back of the motel room. Mark joined her at the window and slipped on the same type of night-vision monocle as Sarah. They were badly outnumbered. At the back of the parking lot Peacekeeper Strykers and armored Humvees formed a wall, sealing off any chance of escape. An assist showed three officers standing near the vehicles that were fully saturated hybrids on a par with Mustafa or Noah. The orange glow symbolizing nanotech ran down their spines and all through their bodies, reaching fingers and toes. Somehow Mark knew they were not like Noah. They were illuminati like Mustafa. The three illuminati appeared to be in charge. The Peacekeeper troops conducting the assault were all organics. Mark knew from stray thoughts that this Peacekeeper squad had not been infiltrated by illuminati. They were working for the hives for a different reason—greed, pure and simple.

"We need to take out those hive monsters first," said Sarah. "Cut off the head."

"Somehow I think this snake is going to keep coming without its head."

The good news was, using troops that were organics was a flaw in the guide's strategy. The fact that the fighting vehicles were not running and appeared to be empty was a sign of arrogance. These troops obviously had no idea what Sarah was capable of with an automatic weapon. They also had no idea that Mark's body could generate micro kill-zones once they were within range.

Mark watched on the sentry tablet as Peacekeeper commandos disabled their loaner Humvee, using some kind of wheel boot that was silently installed in seconds. That erased any lingering doubt about the

Peacekeepers' objective. He and Sarah were the targets of this raid.

The mental chatter was increasing, as were emotions. This was a clear indication to Mark the raid was about to start. He captured stray thoughts that strict orders had been given to capture and not kill. This put the Peacekeepers at a strategic disadvantage and explained why their fighting vehicles had been turned off. Mark looked back at one of the illuminati just as the monster looked up and saw him. Their gaze locked. Mark felt his mind and body instantly taking protective action automatically at the command of his instinctive and kinesthetic processors. His immune system was mentally defending him from the probes of these highly evolved monsters, but he couldn't help feeling naked and exposed. The illuminati now knew they were dealing with someone who was becoming as evolved as them. Sarah must have sensed what had happened because at that moment she opened fire full auto with her M4.

All three illuminati dropped from headshots that almost seemed instantaneous. He heard Mustafa groan painfully from the back of their room. Total confusion erupted in the parking lot, during which time Sarah shot every Peacekeeper that was near their booted Humvee or the motel building itself. She then started in on the rest of the squad with both 5.56mm ammo and 40mm grenades. He watched with dark satisfaction as Peacekeeper after Peacekeeper was executed by Sarah. The Peacekeepers were hobbled by their orders to take their objectives alive, but how long would that last? Mere seconds had passed. As if in slow motion, Mark fired into the center of crowds with his less accurate 5.56mm Sig Sauer pistol. Slowly, every remaining weapon in the lot was coming to bear on their position. It was a race against time. His adrenaline-fueled thinking was running at a speed that was unimaginable as he aimed and fired. His nanotech brain calculated this was a race he and Sarah were about to lose. He spotted a few rifle-like weapons that looked like nothing he'd seen before. These rifles had a huge bore the size of a tennis ball and what looked like a massive, revolving cylinder behind the barrel. His mind absorbed everything within a heartbeat. An assist analyzed the threat and returned an identification: Milkor MGL 40mm semi-automatic grenade launchers. Mark hit the floor and Sarah dropped right next to him. Returning weapons fire took out the tops of the windows and ripped hundreds of small holes through the upper parts of the motel room in a buzz saw of lead. Explosions followed, which must have destroyed the rooms and outside walkways on either side of them. The returning fire paused. His ears were ringing from the explosions. He looked at Sarah. Her pupils were dilated from surging adrenaline. Her thoughts and feelings came through to him with clarity. They were pinned down.

"What now?" shouted Mark.

"I need a bigger gun."

A second volley of returning fire ripped hundreds of new holes above them as small pieces of debris rained down. The fire was obviously intended to intimidate and not kill. Sarah's expression suddenly changed to something odd and undecipherable. Mark thought she had been hit, but an assist showed she was fine. The return fire paused again. Mark heard the screech of feedback from a bullhorn. Several loud clicks echoed outside. Spotlights flooded into the room through windows. Small beams were projected through bullet holes, creating an intricate crosshatch of light with smoke and dust drifting through it all. The experience was dreamlike. He felt detached from himself.

"*Surrender now!*" boomed a voice. "*Do not make us come for you.*"

A torrent of thoughts and emotions from Sarah hit him with the force of a typhoon. Her storm rattled him. Her plan seemed desperate and crazy. Thoughts from his entangled interface confirmed that her idea would likely fail and end with them both dead. She had already reloaded a grenade into the launcher under her M4 and removed the 5.56mm ammo clip. The weapon looked unloaded. Before Mark could do anything, she had crawled over to the door and was opening it. She carefully stood and walked out into the bright floodlights with her M4 aimed down by her side in a one-handed grip.

"*Drop the weapon now!*"

Mark closed his eyes. He could not watch. She was about to die. He knew an instant before Sarah pulled the trigger that she was going through with her plan. A gut-wrenching explosion in the parking lot slammed the motel. Sarah was thrown backward into the room by the concussion. Mark was lifted up as a wave went through the floor, leaving it buckled. Two-by-fours were snapping like backbones breaking. He was bodily flung toward the rear of the room. He hit the floor and then the rear wall. The impact knocked him senseless.

Sometime later when he could think again, he saw most of the outer wall of the room was in ruin. He could feel COBIC swarming to repair multiple injuries. The impact should have killed him. The floodlights were gone. Smoke was billowing everywhere. A wavering orange glow from outside was the only source of light. There was also amazing silence. There was no return fire. No stray thoughts or radiated emotions came from outside. He sensed a mental groan from Sarah. He could not find her in the midst of all the debris and weak orange firelight. He saw Ralph sniffing and whining at a pile of rubble. A medical assist pinpointed Sarah partially buried under the pile. Mark crawled to her. He removed the construction material that was covering her and rolled her onto her back. She had cuts and soot all over her face. Mark could see metal shrapnel from the explosion embedded in her lightweight body armor. Ralph was trying to lick her. He shooed the big dog back. He could tell from an assist that her injuries were being mended from the inside out and that she would heal.

"I hit our Humvee exactly over the munitions boxes," croaked Sarah proudly. "I did it."

She had done it. Her crazy plan to use their Humvee as a huge antipersonnel mine had worked.

"You're insane," said Mark.

"How about *thank you*?"

Sarah leveraged herself upright, using Mark's shoulder and arm. She retrieved her M4 and limped to the front of the room. Mark saw a rip in her left pants leg and a heavy blood stain. He followed her to the edge of what remained of the exterior walkway. The parking lot was a massacre. The sight filled him with a primitive pleasure. A cold breeze was blowing, tugging at his clothing and hair.

They were exposed to return fire standing on the walkway. Mark kept his 5.56mm Sig Sauer ready as he took in the hell laid out before them. Fires were burning in spots. There was an odd, flinty smell that made him think of brimstone. Bodies were strewn everywhere. He and Sarah could have easily been in their place. An assist revealed four Peacekeepers were alive but in no condition to move, let alone fight. He offhandedly looked at his 5.56mm Sig Sauer and realized it would never be enough. He knew they needed to leave now before reinforcements could arrive. With the toe of his sneaker he pushed a piece of cement over the edge and watched it fall. How were they going to get down from this room? The walkways on either side were gone. The drop was 15 feet, 9 inches, according to an assist. The ground beneath them was covered in cracked, jagged building material, pieces of their Humvee, and other debris. Sarah answered his question as if she'd picked up his stray thoughts.

"We drop a mattress to cover that mess," she said. "You lower me as far as you can with a sheet, then I'll drop the rest of the way. There's got to be a rope or a bunch of sheets down there that we can use to lower Ralph and Mustafa."

The four surviving Peacekeepers who were unconscious were now

262

bound with their own plastic cuffs. A few of the motel's guests had briefly peered out their windows, but no one had dared venture beyond that. Mark and Sarah had disguised themselves as Peacekeeper officers and were taking one of the Strykers. The new wheels were a significant upgrade. The Stryker was far more heavily armored than their Humvee and carried an additional armor add-on package. It also had a brand-new roof-mounted next-generation CROWS weapons systems upgrade. CROWS was an acronym for *common remotely operated weapon station*, which in this case was a remotely operated MK19 grenade machine gun. Sarah had radiated grim amusement when she saw the replacement for her destroyed MK19 that had been in their Humvee.

This Stryker was far from the standard military model in many ways. It was equipped with a soundproofing package that made it as quiet as a car. While the other Stryker had a pair of bench seats on both sides, this Stryker had a wall of computerized military and law enforcement components in place of one of the bench seats. This was clearly a command vehicle of some kind. With the help of an assist, Mark pulled the power cables from the radio and wireless Internet gear. It was a shame to lose some of the integrated systems, but they could not take a chance on being tracked. The Peacekeepers had a large number of Strykers roaming in the field. They all looked exactly the same, which would make blending in easier.

Mark was familiarizing himself with some of the Stryker's computerized gear and the CROWS joystick control panel. Even though he knew nothing about the CROWS weapons system, the god-machine did. It was feeding him everything he needed to know through his entangled interface. A huge, high-capacity 40mm ammo locker had been retrofitted to the Stryker. The locker had almost a thousand rounds in it and plenty of additional room. The CROWS used an advanced fire-control system that greatly increased accuracy. The MK19 on its own had an effective range of a mile and a maximum range of almost two miles. With the CROWS fire-control system the weapon could be effectively used at maximum range. Mark turned on the targeting system. The display lit up, showing crosshairs over the current target. At the bottom of the display were range, GPS coordinates, type of ammo loaded, and capacity. The readout showed the weapon was fully loaded with ninety-six rounds in its high-capacity magazine. The electronics used for aiming had both a daylight video camera and a thermal imager. Mark used the joystick to swing the weapon around to aim at the motel. Sarah stepped up onto the ramp at the rear of the Stryker.

"Stop playing with your joystick and help me," she said. "There's a mountain of ammo and gear I want to salvage."

"Do you see these eagles on my uniform?" asked Mark. "I am a colonel. You're a major. Lower-ranking officers do not order higher-ranking officers to stop playing with their joystick."

"You look good in a uniform," said Sarah with a sly edge. "I think I'll commit a little more serious insubordination later if you help me now."

In addition to the new Stryker, they had collected three Milkor MGL 40mm grenade launchers, two more M4 rifles, and a pair of shoulder-fire Stinger missiles. Sarah and Mark had hauled over case after case of 40mm ammo for the MK19 as well as ammo for the M4s, Milkors, and their side arms. They also found plenty of water but only a small amount of field rations. They had plenty of room for it all in the Stryker, which could carry a crew of eighteen soldiers.

Mark started the Stryker's engine. The wraparound dashboard that came to life looked like it belonged in an aircraft. The assist that came up did not match the dashboard. Mark was again reminded this was not your standard military Stryker. Sarah was just behind him in the crew compartment operating the CROWS. There were no windows. The vehicle was driven by video screen and periscopes. Mark inched down the blacktop, picking up speed gradually. The acceleration was much slower and more deliberate than their Humvee. With power steering and power brakes, he felt like he was driving a monstrously heavy car with a bad suspension. In every other way, it reminded him of an ironclad battleship. When they reached a safe distance for the MK19, Sarah was going to disable the remaining Peacekeeper Humvees and Strykers. At a hundred feet Sarah opened fire with the grenade machine gun. Each burst from the MK19 resulted in a string of explosions that was felt inside their 36,000 pound armor-plated fortress. The plan was to make it a little harder for whoever was coming after them. The Humvees were destroyed in seconds. The second Stryker took more hits than expected because of the upgraded armor on these beasts, yet in a very short time it was a burning wreck in Mark's review camera display. Sarah came up behind him. There was no copilot seat and no space for one. A small fold-down jump seat had been installed back to back with the driver's seat. Sarah kneeled on the seat and put her arms around Mark from behind.

"Well, that was fun," she said.

Mark punched in GPS coordinates for the wilderness of northern New Mexico and picked up speed. They were almost fully fueled and had a three hundred mile range, according the trip computer. It was time to retreat and figure out their next move. One thing was certain: Until they learned to quiet their chatter on the n-web, they'd have to keep to the most deserted places imaginable. Mark suspected they had driven into a trap at Pueblo Canyon and been followed from there, but they couldn't take any chances. It might have been something else like stray chatter or the nexus that had led those storm troopers to their doorstep. If a distress call had gone out from the Peacekeepers, an attack would be coming by air. Mark wondered if Apache helicopters or a predator drone were bearing down on them right now. Inside this rattling bank vault on wheels they wouldn't hear or see the attack. They would never know what happened.

"That felt just like the Lake Erie iceboat assault," said Mark. "It could have been the hives coming after us then also. Maybe Karla's office was never leaking."

"Maybe it's worse than that," said Sarah. "I think this proves what you said the other day. The government's on the wrong side and working with the hives."

Soul Hackers

Mark Freedman – New Mexico – March 3, 0002 A.P.

They were slowly heading up into the high mountain ranges, which peaked at 13,000 feet. The air felt anemic. The sun was exceptionally bright. As the elevation increased, the climate had changed from patchy snow to a solid blanket of deep white. Mark was standing up on his seat in the rear crew compartment with his head and chest outside a roof hatch. In some directions he could see for a hundred miles. Sarah was driving up a steep incline in the road. Many hours had passed since leaving Santa Fe and no attacks by pursuers had come. Mark was now confident their trail had ended in Santa Fe and was growing cold.

Their progress slowed as they found themselves driving through several feet of ice-crusted snow. Mark was sitting at the command and control station in the crew compartment. The remote dashboard display showed 10 miles per hour. This was going to be a long journey. He checked the communications gear for an AM-FM radio and realized for the first time there was none. Cell phone reception was gone, which meant no Internet access for tablets or phones. They were cut off from the outside world. He had an uneasy sense from his entangled interface that something had changed in the world they'd left behind. Soon every one of his thoughts was colored by this formless, dark perception. Sarah had sensed nothing and seemed unconcerned. Maybe it was only his imagination. If something terrible was happening, the collective emotions of the population would carry that message. All he felt was a distant, uneasy calm.

As they approached 11,000 feet above sea level, the snow deepened even more. Sarah had switched from four-wheel drive to eight-wheel drive. Mark looked out through a large video screen that was part of the command and control gear. The screen was fed by any one of sixteen cameras mounted in small bulges on the armor. As they plowed through a tiny settlement, Mark experienced for the first time the profound void they had entered. No one lived in this wilderness region any more. Up ahead, a log cabin under heavy tree cover seemed to emanate safety. They needed a place to stay until a plan was worked out.

Sarah drove the Stryker around back and parked under the trees. Mark set up the few perimeter detectors they had left. He placed them a hundred yards out in every direction, then covered his tracks in the snow as best he could. These detectors would give them excellent advance warning. In this subzero ghost town there was little chance anyone harmless would wander by, which eliminated false alarms as a problem. He dragged in an extension cord from the Stryker and then blacked out the cabin's windows with layers of towels and other pieces of fabric. Sarah lugged in a pair of kerosene heaters. Mark thought she had been nuts, scavenging those heaters and snow gear from the Peace-keeper Humvees. Now he thought she was clairvoyant. Without those heaters at this altitude they would all freeze to death. Sarah brought in two of the Milkor MGL grenade launchers, two M4 rifles, and an assortment of ammo. She had also parked the Stryker so its rear hatch dropped right at the back door of the cabin. With that arrangement they could have the CROWS returning fire very quickly. Mark would have felt safe here even without all the armaments and preparations. They were in the middle of nowhere in the middle of winter. If anyone had traveled by in recent months there would have been tracks in the deep blanket of snow. There was nothing.

Sarah sat down next to him on the decomposing old couch. Mustafa was handcuffed to a wooden chair. Mark experienced Sarah's deep revulsion for Mustafa. It was like listening to a monstrous symphony composed of a single musical note. She had never shared with him what the Morristown hive had done to her. It was buried inside her like a cauldron of hate. He was certain whatever had happened to her had been worse than his experience. The loathing she radiated was stronger with each passing day. He set down his mess kit coffee cup.

"I saw the hives' suicidal madness destroy everything forty thousand years ago," said Mark. "I keep going over those memories again and again. Then I look at Mustafa and it sickens me even more. There are too many parallels between then and now."

"They have to be exterminated," said Sarah. "What they did to us was horrible, and they'll do worse to the world. They're an aggressive cancer and every cell of it has to die to stop its spread."

Mark walked over to Mustafa and pulled off the pillowcase.

"Do you want to start with him?"

"Yes," whispered Sarah.

Mark Freedman – New Mexico – March 3, 0002 A.P.

The bedroom was as dark as a crypt when Mark opened his eyes. He could not see his hand in front of his face. He could feel Sarah's space next to him was warm and empty. As his nanotech brain reached normal operating awareness, he was instantly worried. A strong intu-ition of unknown danger was pumping adrenaline through him. He sat up without making a sound. He focused his mind on Sarah and knew she was standing with her back against the wall near the bedroom

268

door. Something was very wrong. He had a clear impression she was holding her breath and her gun. He received an urgent memory capsule from her. They were not alone in the cabin. She'd heard breathing and seen a shadow enter the bedroom. She was waiting for the intruders to give away their position, then open fire. Mark used his photographic memory to build a model of the room around him. An assist drew in the outlines of the door and furniture. Mark examined what was pouring into his nanotech brain through his senses and the n-web but could find no hint of emotional radiation or stray thoughts. Yet he had an unexplainable awareness of additional volume being occupied somewhere in the cabin. There was a feeling of pent-up violence. His sense of the intruder was strongest just at the doorway. The biology was not human. He suddenly felt an all too familiar magnetic tug at the back of his mind. The experience sent a chill through his body. The intruder was announcing themselves as a hybrid. Mark now understood he was not sensing volume but subtle distortions of the n-web. The distortion was caused by a highly developed nanotech brain nearby drawing data in and out of the n-web as if breathing. The darkness made it impossible to designate a target with his eyes, so he was unable to raise even a basic medical assist to give away the intruder's location.

"I am pleased to see you both are still alive," said a disembodied male voice that seemed to come from the next room. Mark recognized the voice, but that did nothing to calm him. The foreign accent held the same unfamiliar tones and vague otherworldliness that he'd heard only one other time. It was in Morristown just after the hive had been destroyed. A match was struck in the living room. In the wavering light Mark confirmed Noah was not in the bedroom with them. Perhaps the ghost had never been in the bedroom. Through the doorway he could see Noah relighting the kerosene heaters. He was wearing a heavy black military greatcoat and black pants. Ralph was sleeping next to one of the heaters. How could the dog have slept through all this? The heating filaments began to glow bright orange, accompanied by the ticking sounds of metal expanding. Sarah sent Mark a memory capsule showing those heaters had been running when they went to bed. Noah was toying with them. Sarah cautiously entered the living room. Mark could see in the wavering orange light and shadows that she had the Beretta aimed at the floor. He knew her muscles were as tense as springs and ready to fire. She was wearing one of his T-shirts as a dress. He joined her in the living room.

"Have you had much help from the illuminati?" asked Noah. "I see... That will change tonight."

"How did you find us?" asked Sarah.

At the same time Mark was thinking, "How did you get past the perimeter sentries?" Noah looked at each of them in turn. It was then Mark realized the hybrid never showed any emotion on this face.

"You were not as hard to find as you should have been," said Noah. "I followed your noisy minds, which led me to deep tire trails in snow."

"We need to go now!" said Mark.

"You are safe," said Noah. "No one else will find you here."

Mark was not comforted by that statement. Noah walked over to Mustafa and hoisted the man to his feet by his shoulder as if he weighted nothing. Mustafa looked terrified. The old hybrid flinched at the sound of a match struck by Sarah lighting a candle.

"There have been many small kill-zones since I loaned this illuminati to you," said Noah. "The pace is increasing and the organics have yet to realize what is happening. There were three today and none of them are normal. None of them are the work of the goddess."

"The radio reports are true?" asked Sarah.

"If they reported kill-zone," said Noah. "The lifting of the veil has begun and that changes many things. This creature has what we need."

"I have nothing for you or your pets," grumbled Mustafa.

"Concealed in your brain are plans for mass murder," said Noah. "Your kind will do anything to fulfill this insane prophesy. You are no longer protected by a guide. I can kill you very painfully, and the seeds of the goddess swimming in your blood will bring you back. We can then do it again and again. How many times will you need to die before the nexus captures everything I want from your fading brain?"

Mustafa grew white. Mark almost felt sorry as Noah roughly forced the old man to the floor.

"You know I will do this and you know it will work," said Noah. "Save yourself all this suffering. Give me what I want."

"I have nothing!" shouted Mustafa.

"Mark, hand me the nexus," said Noah.

"It'll draw hives," said Mark.

"Trust me," said Noah. "We're safe for now."

"Don't trust him," hissed Mustafa.

Mark was uncertain what to do. His entangled interface flooded his mind with reasons to trust Noah. It was obviously what the god-machine wanted. If the nexus would draw hives, Mustafa would not be this scared. Besides, what choice did he have anyway? Noah could very likely take what he wanted. Mark retrieved the nexus and handed it over.

"Torture won't work on him," said Mark.

"What I have for him is worse than torture," said Noah. "When this illuminati dies, his entire life will be relived as his essence flees his body. He's too old and stubborn to leak even those thoughts onto the n-web. The nexus will solve that dilemma for us. When he returns from near-death, memories of what happened will be bubbling at the surface of his neural circuitry. The nexus will capture and record it all. Anyone can then use the nexus to replay the captured memories in their mind. Unfortunately, what is remembered by the dying person and what is captured by the nexus is often incomplete. It can take many deaths and returns before enough is recorded to have memories of any single event without significant gaps."

Noah switched on the nexus and pushed it against Mustafa's forehead. He pressed something on the device, which caused it to form into a band that extended halfway around Mustafa's head and clamp itself in place. The liquid metal display came alive with lines of symbols scrolling up at a rapid pace. Noah drew a black .357 Magnum revolver and pushed the muzzle of the large gun into Mustafa's belly.

"He needs to die slowly so I can capture long memories. A bullet in the stomach works best."

"Don't!" pleaded Mustafa. "I'll give you anything."

"Too late," said Noah. "I don't believe you. I cannot be sure what you spew is not more of your lies. Extracting your memories from death is the only reliable option."

"Please! *Please!*"

Noah cocked the hammer of his gun. He had Mustafa pinned with a knee to the chest. Mustafa was squirming. His eyes were flooded with tears. With Noah's six foot eight inch frame weighting down on him, Mustafa did not have a chance. Mark felt himself shaking. This was wrong... very wrong, but he wanted Noah to pull the trigger.

"Nooooooooo!" whined Mustafa. "Wait! Wait! *Wait!*"

Noah sighed. "Pathetic... Talk, but if the nexus captures anything that does not confirm your words I will kill you and it will just be the beginning. Your body will not survive the punishment of so many deaths in a row and neither will your soul. When I am done, your essence will be a shadow of what it might have been. You have lived very long and proud. It would be a shame for you to die a weakened soul."

Noah uncocked the revolver and holstered it. Mark had not imagined a human could look as pale as Mustafa. The sheen of sweat on his face gave him a waxy appearance. The old man looked like he was already dead. Noah hoisted Mustafa up and sat him back into the chair. Almost immediately blood began to return to Mustafa's face along with anger.

"I have seen the timeline recordings," said Mustafa. "Your kind were always abominations. I'll tell you what you want, but not because I am scared of your murderous ways. I'll tell you because we cannot be stopped by you or anyone."

Mustafa then glared at Mark and Sarah. He spit on the floor at their feet.

"Machines must not mate!" shouted Mustafa. "It is the law of the way of twos. Machine begetting machine is an abomination. We communes have no illusions. We know these bodies are machines. Were it allowed, the product of our union would be a soulless incarnation of pure machine. All hybrids are sterile but—"

"Stop!" bellowed Noah. "Stop it now! I don't care about your superstitions. I don't care about your lies aimed at confusing those two. All I want are the plans."

"Plans… Yes, plans… We did not control the last plague, but we did lure the breeders into the maw of the shark," said Mustafa. "We used our wealth and influence to guide them into plundering Gaia. They are insane and truly believe they own the planet. For generations we have been planting scientific ideas to convince the breeders they were all biological machines in a clockwork universe and that death was the end. This gave them justification for their ravenous greed. Our harvest was plentiful. The goddess judged the breeders as dangerous and culled the herds to protect the Earth."

"You were behind the plague," shouted Sarah. "You did that to us!"

Sarah moved toward Mustafa. Noah quickly interjected himself between the two.

"Stop trying to manipulate them!" yelled Noah. "I'll let her kill you if you try it once more."

"No… no…" said Mustafa. "I am not manipulating. I am telling the truth. I am telling you the plan. The nexus must show I am speaking only the truth."

"Go on," said Noah.

"The communes could not create even a small kill-zone at a distance. We had tried many times and failed. Had it been within our power to trigger large kill-zones, the last plague would not have stopped until our needs were met. For our part we did nothing more than help the breeders be the selfish creatures they naturally are. The goddess acted to avert a future in which this planet became a lifeless rock. Interference with intelligent life is something the goddess naturally avoids. So we had to coax the breeders into creating a problem that could not be ignored. The goddess's desire for noninterference in her grand experiments in sentient life is such foolishness and such a gift. This foolishness is something we are now using to our advantage in the newest plan."

Mark felt completely off balance. Mustafa's disregard for life was appalling. Mark sat down on an old wooden folding chair. His head was beginning to ache.

"Much has changed since the last plague," said Mustafa. "The lifting of the veil is now unstoppable. Our guides have constructed a weapon to create order out of the chaos of this damaged world. We have set in motion fulfillment of the prophecy. Unrestrained breeders are like locusts in the wheat fields of Gaia. Communes will complete what the goddess would not. With our new weapon we can send signals over the n-web to trigger our own kill-zones. We have a strategy and unlike the goddess, we will not stop until the breeders are a herd Gaia can sustain and we can manage. We will bring back the way of the twos and there is nothing you can do to stop us. There is nothing the goddess will do to stop us!"

"You're insane!" yelled Sarah.

"Shut up, foolish child. Show respect. I am the only surviving host of an ancient and wise sentience. My deity was murdered by that betrayer with help from both you imbeciles. The intellect of a guide is beyond all our feeble comprehension. To murder such a being is a crime against nature herself. The lifting of the veil is something your uninitiated minds cannot understand. It is the yin and yang of chaos and order. It is life in balance on a planetary scale. It is necessary and so we have set the prophesy in motion. The end of the breeders' reign is happening now and unlike the goddess, we will never stop."

Mark was surprised by the confidence and arrogance radiating from this man. It was the first time he'd sensed so much emotion from the illuminati. The ancient man could not have been more different than Noah, who was calmly listening with both his eyes and his mind wide open.

"Forty-seven thousand years ago during the Great Struggle, our strategy worked as we knew it would," said Mustafa. "We did not have the weapons needed to defeat your ancestors, but your ancestors did. They had a powerful weapon from a far older age of war. Through manipulation and deceit we set events into motion. Your kind did all our killing for us. It is what you are good at. We failed only because we underestimated the power of the ancient, forbidden weapon, as did your ancestors."

Noah looked as if he was confused and distracted. A moment later he interrupted Mustafa's bragging.

"You're speaking of a myth," said Noah. "Something no one remembers because the destruction was so great it shattered the timeline records themselves. You are telling me nothing of value—nothing that can be verified. Do you have control over kill-zones or is this all just another of your lies within lies designed to manipulate?"

"No… no… this is no deception," said Mustafa. "Check the nexus."

"I know the hives have dug in deep around the world like so many ticks," said Noah. "I've seen your very obvious bunkers. The only thing missing were signs with big, flashing neon arrows to announce your presence. You might as well have erected signs saying *attack here*. Because of the depth of your bunkers, the only weapons that can now sterilize all the nests rapidly are nuclear. I suspect the bunkers are all located just by accident in some of the most fertile and vital regions of Gaia. Are you goading the organics into attacking the heart of Gaia with nuclear weapons? Is that the real plan? Do you want them to wound the Earth so deeply that the goddess launches a nanotech plague to stop them? Is that it? Are your bunkers Trojan horses that are empty? I think the hives have instead gathered in some hidden stronghold ready to laugh at the simpleminded breeders who brought destruction upon themselves for a second time."

Mustafa smiled thinly and said nothing. His eyes were defiantly locked onto Noah's stare. Mark was overwhelmed by the volume of information from the god-machine flooding his mind through the entangled interface. He assumed Noah was also receiving the same information. One of Mark's new memories provided n-web engineering information for the first time and proved the impossibility of a kill-zone coming from any source other than the god-machine. Another memory demonstrated how and why it was beyond the creative ability of hives to craft anything new. They could copy and rearrange, but they had no ability to create something completely original like this alleged new weapon.

"If hives have discovered and use technology that turns seeds into weapons, then you will lose everything," said Noah. "The goddess would never allow such an aberrant thing."

"The goddess does not care!" scoffed Mustafa. "We are not using our weapon to injure Gaia. We are not breeders. We are using our weapon to help Gaia. As I said, the goddess's desire for noninterference in her experiments is our greatest tool. You know I am speaking the truth. You have the nexus monitoring my brain. What does it tell you?"

"You are speaking the truth as you believe it," said Noah. "But I don't trust your memories. You may have been programmed with defensive lies. The test of your truth is to see if your bunkers are full of vermin or empty."

Noah removed a capped syringe from his pocket. It contained a milky liquid that reminded Mark of hand soap. Mustafa eyed the syringe. His lips began trembling.

"A painless quick-acting toxin that directly stops the heart," said Noah.

"I told you everything," whined Mustafa. "I kept my word. You promised not to kill me."

"I said I would not kill you and bring you back," growled Noah. "I said nothing about permanently killing you and leaving you dead."

Mustafa tried to get up from the chair, but had no chance with his hands cuffed behind his back. Noah pushed him down into the chair and continued pushing the chair backward into the wall. Mark wanted to look away as Noah expertly injected the toxin into Mustafa's neck, but could not avert his eyes. The deed was done. Mark looked at Sarah and saw a grim expression on her face. He could feel warring emotions radiating from her of hate and justice and never enough. Mustafa slumped out of the chair and onto the floor.

"Something's wrong," said Sarah. "He's not dying."

"It's not toxin," Noah informed her. "As long as I inject him every twelve hours, he'll remain in a coma. We'll need him again before this is done."

Mark Freedman – Kansas – March 4, 0002 A.P.

Hours ago they had left the higher elevations behind them, and the roads were clear of snow. Sarah was driving the Stryker. Noah was leading the way in an old Toyota Land Cruiser. They were driving toward a decommissioned mine in a remote Colorado forest, not far from the Kansas border. The mine had been recently converted into a bunker. Noah had experienced tidal pulls that seemed to emanate from the bunker. The mine shaft sank a quarter of a mile into the earth, making it very difficult to be sure where the singularity was located or if it was there at all. It was equally possible the tidal pulls were the result of some type of deception. Property records showed the mine was sold to a private development company over twenty years ago.

At Noah's instance they were taking a circuitous route that seemed completely random. They had passed through Colorado into Kansas and were now headed back toward Colorado on a different road. Noah had offered no explanation for their route. Mark was in the back of the Stryker, staring at a video from a forward-looking camera as the food basket of the country rolled by. They had passed so many farms, nearly all growing wild or fallow. The food supply was clearly in danger. Why wasn't it being managed by the USAG? Climate change and the plague had destroyed so much. Without food from this part of the country people would starve.

Mark's thoughts drifted back to questions that worried him about Noah. The man they were now following could be deceiving to them. When Sarah had asked Noah how the hives could override the god-machine's control of the n-web to cause kill-zones, Noah had said there were ways, but now was not the time to discuss such dangerous ideas. Noah had not mentioned a thing about the god-machine's engineering information that showed override was impossible. Was he trying to manipulate them, recruit them, or was it the truth?

Noah was slowing as they approached a highway interchange. His Land Cruiser had to be at least forty years old. The ancient bag of bolts had no armor and accelerated as if it was running on fumes. The cab was a separate compartment from the rear. The back three quarters of the Land Cruiser had a weather-beaten cloth roof and sides complete with several holes. A tan camouflaged paint job was the only thing that looked remotely recent on that rolling wreck. An unconscious Mustafa was in the back of the Land Cruiser under a tarp with his hands and feet cuffed to a metal rail.

Mark kept having feelings of déjà vu about Noah's Land Cruiser. He had seen this truck before. Mark replayed photographic memories of the only other Land Cruiser he'd recently seen. He watched in his mind as a red Land Cruiser blew through a roadblock at the Delaware Water Gap Bridge. Both trucks were similar in body style and year. They just couldn't be the same vehicle. He doubted Noah's piece of junk could reach 100 mph. As Mark scrutinized Noah's run-down Land Cruiser he thought how suicidal it was to drive around in something that decrepit. A highwayman with a pistol could stop it with one shot.

Without warning, Noah pulled over to the shoulder again. He had done this many times already. He never gave an explanation. They'd wait and after what seemed like a random amount of time he would pull back onto the road.

Mark climbed up and stuck his head out of a hatch. Wind was tugging at the decrepit cloth top of Noah's Land Cruiser like a ship's sail. Gray tumbleweeds rolled and bounced across the highway. In the distance, dark clouds flickered from within with lightning. An assist projected stats from a weather forecast into his vision. Just as before, the weather forecast looked like something copied off the Internet. How was the god-machine doing this? A scattering of fat drops started hitting around Mark. He ducked back inside and went up front behind Sarah.

She engaged the parking brake and shook her head.

"It feels like he's avoiding something by making these stops," said Sarah.

Mark suddenly understood why they kept stopping and why the random, circuitous route. Noah was a ghost and stealth was his weapon. Part of that weapon was evasion and part of it was camouflage, such as an old Toyota truck not even worth stealing.

"He must be able to sense what's ahead of him and avoid problems," said Mark. "Look at how vulnerable he is in that Land Cruiser. He should be dead by now. He doesn't need heavy weapons or armor if he's invisible to those who do."

"I hope you're right," said Sarah. "It'll be dark soon and I don't think we're stopping...."

Mark Freedman – Kansas – March 4, 0002 A.P.

The sun was setting. Although the day had become so gray, it was difficult to tell the difference. Sitting in the back, Mark watched the rain and thunder lashing the Kansas plain. Even on a video screen the ferocious storm was intimidating. March used to be too early in the year for the kind of storms that could give birth to tornadoes, but global warming had changed those rules. The clouds lit up with tendrils of lightning crawling through them like flashes of dangerous ideas forming in a giant mind.

They were following Noah's Land Cruiser with their headlights on so that they would not run into him. Shortly after entering the storm, Noah began sending both of them streams of memory capsules. He was teaching them part of the knowledge he'd assembled about the many fallen human civilizations. He was using mental communications uncomfortably reminiscent of the hive's attempted assimilation. Mark was surprised to learn Noah was an archeologist. It was difficult to guess how much of this history Noah believed, but two things were clear: He did believe some of it and the hives believed all of it; and that made it very important information, whether factual or not. All of the prior, doomed civilizations had historical knowledge of their preceding parent civilizations. Only in our current epoch had we lost all knowledge of our deep heritage. It was unprecedented how much history evaporated when the preceding civilization fell and blinded the god-machine 47,000 years ago.

In all the more recent civilizations that were technologically advanced, their science and religion had diverged and then ultimately come back together in dramatic head-on collisions. As if in some exotic

277

experiment in a partial accelerator, these collisions had fused these two divergent belief systems into a single, unified definition of reality.

Over the eons, common themes could be identified in all the unified belief systems of all the civilizations. They all believed in a collective awareness that was sustained by all living things embodied and disembodied. They believed this collective was god. They believed we, the creatures of the universe, were literally the soil from which the spirit of god sprang forth. They did not believe we were created by god, but instead believed it was from us that the spirit of god was *born*.

They had scientific evidence obtained from experiments that unnervingly echoed some of the ideas that had driven Mark to conduct his past life searches in the archives. They had evidence that our cerebral cortex was the endpoint of a conduit, a quantum entangled transceiver linked to a permanent higher-self that existed outside of time and space as we know it. In their model the cerebral cortex did not store any thoughts other than a kind of short-term memory buffer. Our feeling that we are inside our bodies was only an illusion created by the operation of the transceiver. Every aspect of us that mattered was not located within our physical bodies.

Reincarnation to these societies was not only being reborn into different lifetimes, but also the repeated *rebirth* of awareness into the same lifetime. *My beginning is my end and my end is my beginning.* They had somehow scientifically demonstrated that a soul relived the same lifetime through a large number of cycles before moving on to begin a new lifetime. In their theorem, each cycle through the same lifetime was different. The free will of the individual and others sharing each lifetime could, in theory, create an infinite number of variations over an almost endless number of cycles. They also believed there were fixed points or events that were near immutable. Catastrophes great and small were examples of such fixed events. It was only after achieving perfection of the current lifetime that a soul moved on to a new one.

When Mark tried to understand their scientific theorems, his mind grew too confused to make sense of what he found. Concepts like déjà vu and precognition were incorporated into the theorems. The theorems themselves were mathematical models of an infinite, multidimensional quantum entangled universe. There were strange ramifications, such as precognition was not considered the ability to see the future. Instead, precognition was incomplete dream-like recall of memories of a fixed event that had already been relived countless times during prior cycles. They regarded birth and death as an unbroken continuum. They saw the wheel of life as a symbol of *eternal recurrence*, a wheel without

beginning or end. During this cycling, death was simply your awareness falling out of linear material time and being drawn back to the
moment of birth, like a magnet. Mark knew this cycling part of their
theories dovetailed interestingly with quantum physics and its splitting
off a new dimension for every quantum possibility, but with one big
wrinkle. In this ancient knowledge, each cycle was a new, immutable
parallel dimension that split off only at the moment of reoccurrence
instead of at every quantum possibility. It was as if consciousness itself
was responsible for creating each new dimension.

Their scientific proofs also incorporated a model of hosted awareness that was eerily similar to how modern day computers operated.
In this model, the collective awareness—god—was hosted across and
within the minds of all sentient life. In a circular arrangement worthy
of any Zen koan, each individual's awareness was also hosted within
the collective awareness known as god. This impossible, chicken and
the egg, circular arrangement was only made plausible by a theorem,
which stated that there is no beginning and no end. The cosmos was not
born and the cosmos will not die. Likewise, the same was true for all
consciousnesses. The myth of creation and destruction was the result
of oversimplification of a linear mind trapped by the seeming logic
of the illusion of forward moving time. So the codependent hosting
arrangement between collective and individual consciousness always
existed and always will exist like some cosmic-scaled yin and yang.

It was into this mind bending scientific-religious belief system that
the god-machine was created by their ancestors in their image of god.
Once created, the god-machine then hosted a mirrored simulation of
all universes containing all embodied and disembodied creatures, and
then set itself up as god.

Mark was confused, shaken, and excited by all this and especially
by the notion that the god-machine was a scientific tool created so that
all stages of life could be explored, studied, and perfected. This made
the god-machine, among other things, a kind of spiritual incubator that
helped souls evolve. If this was true, the god-machine was a facilitator
of both human physical and spiritual evolution. Which meant we, the
god-machine, and the spiritual universe were all wildly interdependent.

In a variation on this same cosmology, hive initiates believed they
would live forever inside a virtual reality paradise hosted within their
guide. It was into this virtual reality that their tortured spirits took
refuge after assimilation was complete. Hive members suffered from
a warped understanding of reality. This occurred because it was the
understanding of a mutated sentient nanotech virus imbued with stolen

human emotion and simulated creativity.

Noah made it clear a major weakness of guides, which could be exploited, was their spiritual and emotional vampirism, along with their pathological use of concepts that the artificial intelligence could never truly experience or understand.

As the night wore on, Noah transmitted to them the history of the nanotech seeds in the form of epic mythological tales as if he had been alive to witness the events. In earlier epochs there had been as many as a hundred thousand hybrids living at one time. Now there were few. Mark soon found himself wondering if Noah could be from those ancient times of lost civilizations, then dismissed the idea as nonsense. He and Sarah had considered the possibility of living for thousands or even tens of thousands of years. Most or all of the hybrids that had come before them had to be gone—doubtless lost to wars, accidents, and the like. Had they survived to this day with their numbers growing even at an infinitesimal rate, the Earth would now mostly be populated by hybrids and this was obviously not the case.

Mark learned seeds were limited to organic nano-assembly tasks and did their construction work at the molecular level. Seeds required and used DNA for their construction plans. In the absence of DNA, all they could do was disassemble instead of assemble. They were unable to build complex hard structures, such as machines or weapons. Mark had suspected this limitation for a long time. Otherwise, the god-machine would have built robotic devices to do work for it.

As part of Mark's awareness continued learning from Noah, another part began to critically think about what was transpiring. He was soon again wondering about the veracity of much of what they were receiving. The hive had filled them with a powerful cocktail of truth and lies. Maybe Noah was doing the same.

Mark knew his doubts had been sparked when Noah claimed that humans had built the god-machine in the image of their god. Mark refused to believe the god-machine was young enough to have been created by humans. He had scientific evidence to the contrary.

In Noah's recitation there were so many ideas being thrown about as facts without proof. How do you verify the unverifiable? The timeline interface was the only possible option for verification and it would take a monumental effort just to check a few of the critical facts. Further complicating any effort to verify was Mark's experience that every timeline he'd relived contained large gaps.

Mark realized he had not been back for some time to check the results of his data mining for evidence of reincarnation. Now he was being told none of the ancient high civilizations believed that people reincarnated the way he assumed it worked.

Mark shifted most of his awareness into the timeline program. He would stay only an instant because he could not afford to allow Noah to spot his absence. Mark found all his searches were still running. Then his heart began beating rapidly. A match had been found. This was too much! He had to look. When he selected the match, it opened to reveal it was for Kathy. He sampled the timeline and found it was fragmentary. For some reason, only parts of it matched well enough for inclusion as results. The human memory experience he dipped into felt like Kathy emotionally and acted as she would act. He looked at the date again to be sure. It had been recorded over a thousand years ago.

This other Kathy's fragmentary memory skipped ahead several months. Mark found himself inside this woman as she stood before a large, silvery bowl of water. It was bright daylight. The reflections were rippled and broken. He couldn't make out her face, though he did see her hands dipping into the water and they looked like Kathy's hands. Maybe this match was nothing more than someone with a very low genetic variation from Kathy. Mark randomly sampled other memories and stopped when he heard the woman's voice. The language was not English and the pitch was not Kathy's, but the voice was disturbingly reminiscent of her speech patterns.

Mark Freedman – Colorado – March 5, 0002 A.P.

As they followed Noah through the night and into the morning, Mark was worried about being ambushed. The Stryker was tough, but a single shoulder-fired missile could take it out. Two vehicles traveling like this across these flat plains had to be throwing out a welcome sign for miles in every direction. He hoped Noah was as good at being a ghost as he suspected. Every chokepoint or unexpected encounter along the road put Mark on edge. He kept his senses sharp, waiting for the tiniest sign of nearby stray thoughts or aggressive emotion.

Sarah had taken a break earlier but was back driving. Mark was tuning a portable radio Noah had loaned them. He glanced at the wall of military radio gear and sighed. It was a pity he'd had to disconnect it all out of concern of being tracked. He was sitting up front on the jump seat close to Sarah so she could also hear the radio. He was looking for Air Truth and any recent news about kill-zones. Mark had wired it into an outside antenna, but reception was still poor inside their rolling armor-plated box. The last news they'd heard was hours ago and there had been no reports of anything that sounded like a kill-zone.

As he found the station, excited voices filled their armored cocoon. Five or six people were arguing on top of each other about what this string of reports meant. As best Mark could decipher the ranting, four new possible kill-zones had been reported within the hour. The government was claiming they were hoaxes. All the events were in small communities, and all fit the pattern of kill-zones in every way, except that a large percentage of animal life had died. One of the experts argued that these were not kill-zones because of the collateral damage in animals. Others were arguing that the bioengineered plague had jumped species.

"This thing doesn't jump species," complained Mark. "They all still think it's a biological weapon."

"Does it matter?" asked Sarah.

The volume of the quarrelling experts increased and at times became shrill. At least they all seemed to be nearly unanimous on one point. Except for a single expert, they all were convinced these were kill-zones of some kind. The opinions differed vehemently on whether this was the beginning of a new outbreak or some kind of mild aftershocks from the prior outbreak. One of the experts was speculating that these tiny kill-zones might have oddly begun last month around the same time as the Eve of Darkness and that we were only now becoming aware of them. She argued that the original plague began in the same way two years ago with small events and no one paying attention.

Mark sent Noah a memory capsule of the radio show. A memory bounced back instantly to both Mark and Sarah. Noah had no doubt these were hive-controlled kill-zones. It was the only answer that fit all the information. He believed the killing of wildlife showed the hives did not have reliable control. If they used this indiscriminate weapon globally, the goddess would attack them because of the collateral damage to Gaia. Noah was clear in his opinion. If this was not a bluff crafted to instigate a catastrophic retaliation from the organics, then the hives must be working on perfecting their new weapon. Once it was perfected, they would unleash hell on Earth.

"If this isn't a bluff, we have to strike now," said Mark.

"That's a huge risk," said Sarah.

"I understand," said Mark. "But with the hives unable to strike back right now, our best chance to finish them off is right now!"

"We don't even have a way to hit enough of them to make a difference."

"Maybe we do," said Mark.

"What does that mean?"

"I convince McKafferty to go after them with nuclear bunker

busters."

"What!" shouted Sarah as she eased the Stryker to the shoulder. She turned around in her seat to face him.

"Tell me you didn't say that," she said.

"We use the government to exterminate the hives," said Mark. "McKafferty has to know more than we do about these kill-zones. I know if we funneled something actionable to him, he would have to use it. He would get the president to push that button."

"You know that could be exactly what the hives want," said Sarah. "That's what Noah thinks and he might be right."

"Look," said Mark. "If we discover the hives are bluffing, then we slowly feed McKafferty enough to take them out one at a time, using something clean and pinpoint. The god-machine watches and does nothing. If we learn the hives are about to unleash hell on Earth, then what choice do we have other than roll the dice and nuke them all?"

"Jesus!" said Sarah. "The closet pacifist has turned into Genghis Khan, playing with doomsday weapons. I'm not sure I like the change. Promise me you won't contact McKafferty on your own.... Mark, I know you. I know how you operate. Promise me. Everyone's butt is at stake here. I don't want to wake up glowing in the dark without at least some warning to put on extra sunscreen."

"I promise. I would never make this kind of decision on my own."

Sarah looked into his eyes for a long time. He could feel her trying to probe his emotions. He knew she did not fully trust him and she was right on that count. Left with no other option, he was going to act no matter what anyone else thought. Doing nothing was the worst option of all.

Mark Freedman – Colorado – March 5, 0002 A.P.

It was early in the day and Mark was behind the wheel of the Stryker. It was hard to get used to the mass of this armored fighting vehicle. The weather had cleared as the landscape slowly changed from flatlands to heavily forested hills and valleys framed by distant mountains.

Noah had finally sent them a memory capsule with the exact location of the nest. A short time later they had left the paved roads behind and began winding along old forestry trails and dirt roads. Inside the Stryker the unpaved terrain felt little different than the paved roads. Mark could not sense the presence of the singularity and had to put his trust in Noah. They turned onto some abandoned train tracks that had been laid to service the mine. The rails had been pulled up ages ago, leaving a gravel roadbed behind that ran directly to the enemy.

Hours later, they had driven as close to the nest as they dared. Noah pulled off the roadbed a short distance onto a spur and parked under some trees. Mark did the same and cut the engine. They were parked near the base of a hill. Noah's last memory capsule had shown the hive's bunker was on the opposite side. The first step was going to be getting closer on foot to do reconnaissance without being detected. Mark had confidence in their ghost's ability to get them close without being spotted. He was not as confident in the rest of Noah's plan, which had yet to be revealed.

Using binoculars, Mark studied the entrance to the mine. An assist pinpointed cameras and small plate-sized objects embedded flat into the walls. The assist identified the plates as radar motion sensors with a 16 percent chance of identification error. Just inside the mine shaft was an imposing-looking blast door. There were floodlights everywhere, a twelve-foot electrified fence, satellite communications dishes, Army trucks, and big, red warning signs to keep out. Tire tracks crisscrossed every inch of ground. The hives were not trying to hide their presence. They were telegraphing it. Mark wondered if it was confidence that was behind this display instead of Noah's theory of a bluff. Though Mark had to admit this was not even remotely a smart way to hide. The guides, if nothing else, were cunning machine intelligences. What were these bastards up to? He could sense no stray thoughts or emotions, which was not unusual for a hive. He could faintly sense the attractive pull of a singularity, just as Noah had described it. The pull seemed to come uniformly from everywhere.

"Every hive must remain connected to the god-machine, either through its guide or directly through the n-web," said Noah. "Their link is far more critical than our need for a connection. To a hive it's a lifeline in every sense. If the connection is cut, the hive dies. The neural circuitry of fully assimilated hive members is mutated by the guide to optimize parasitic hosting of itself. It is like a virus mutating a host's DNA for its own reproduction. This mutation requires a constant connection for the nanotech brain to remain functional. Our friend Mustafa would soon die if he was taken for a plane ride or in some other way cut off from the god-machine."

"Why didn't you tell us this before?" demanded Mark.

"You didn't need to know and I needed to trust you."

"Goddamn it! This is how we kill them," said Mark. "We cut them off. No need for nukes."

"Who said anything about nukes and how do you plan to cut them off?" asked Noah. "This is the n-web. Seeds have skillfully woven themselves into every square foot of soil, flora, and fauna, creating an infinitely complex fabric of n-web pathways. Destroy a path and in seconds the n-web will have repaired itself or worked its way around the damage."

"Scorched earth!" growled Mark. "We create a firewall around each hive then use assists to verify every last network path has been destroyed."

"Can you scorch a path several feet underground, assuming there are no subterranean waterways that run deeper?" asked Noah. "Can you scorch an area with a diameter of a half mile or even a mile? These mines are deep. The only good explanation for such a weak pull from the guide is that its connection to the n-web is diffused over a wide area instead of focused into a single point. The network must have millions of pathways running like roots to the surface that could reach ground level thousands of feet from the guide."

"Surface burst EMP weapons," said Mark. "Detonate it right on the ground to minimize collateral damage. The blast and the pulse won't reach a buried nest, but it will wipe out all surface connections for miles around. The ultimate firewall."

"Now that could work," said Noah. "But we are back to nuclear if you want a sure kill. Chemical EMPs won't do it. A low-yield nuclear EMP is probably going to be less damaging to Gaia than other atomic weapons, but will it be clean enough to avoid triggering the wrath of the goddess? Besides, how are you going to get your hands on nuclear weapons?"

"So what are we doing here?" interrupted Sarah. "I want to hear what can work."

"We're here to get answers," said Noah. "Are these bunkers real or a bluff? Let's start there."

"Okay," said Sarah. "How do we do that?"

"My assist estimated their blast door can be breached with three hundred and twelve 40mm rounds of concentrated fire into the seam between the rock and the door. Your Stryker can do that."

"That's three reloads of grenades," said Sarah. "That's a lot of high explosives. I like it."

"What happens when they call for help?" asked Mark. "They have ties with Peacekeepers and who knows what other mercenaries."

"I hope the storm troopers do show up," said Noah.

"You hope *what?*" said Sarah. "Is this a suicide mission?"

"If storm troopers show up that means these bunkers are probably a bluff," said Noah. "The hives can't afford to let anyone find an empty bunker. If no help arrives then we know it's probably a nest. The guides will sacrifice a nest to keep to their plans."

"How can you be sure of any of this?" asked Mark.

"What we are fighting is a viral mutation that became self-aware. Each guide is wildly intelligent but also lacks creativity, which makes them predictable in some ways."

"So we blast their door, then fall back and see what happens?" asked Sarah.

"We blast their door, their satellite farm, their radar motion detectors, their cameras, everything. We blind them and we scare the hell out of them, then we withdraw and wait," said Noah. "We don't let them know who is really attacking or why. If help doesn't arrive, we kill them all and count the bodies to make sure it's not a bluff. If help arrives, we kill their help or wait for them to leave, then make sure the nest is empty."

Mark was surprised by his readiness—almost eagerness—to kill in cold blood, but this is what they'd come to do. Any actions were justified when balanced against all the warm blood that had been spilled directly and indirectly by the hives, including Pueblo Canyon. Their fingers had not been on most of the triggers, but the same could be said for Hitler. The hives were a cancer that had reached a terminal stage and become aggressive.

"Let's go," said Mark.

"I'm in," said Sarah.

"Good," said Noah. "Now, one last detail. I need to teach you both how to stop making so much noise on the n-web. You are like children screaming in a playground. Silence is not so important at the moment, but if the hive comes out to fight or we go down for a visit, you will need to be ghosts on the n-web."

Mark was behind the wheel of the Stryker with the engine idling. He had stopped just shy of coming into view of the hive's bunker. Liberating this Stryker had turned out to be the gift that kept giving. Not only did they have a powerful fighting vehicle, they had a terrific disguise that was also turning out to be a potent psychological weapon. As soon as Noah signaled them, Mark would pull the Stryker around the side of the hill and Sarah would open fire to blind the hive. The last thing they would see was a Peacekeeper Stryker attacking their bunker. It would leave them totally confused.

Maintaining silence on the n-web was difficult because it required constant focus. There were parts of the kinesthetic processors that liked to chatter and emote. The kinesthetic processor was largely what neurology defined as the peripheral nervous system: a complex neural network that connects to all the muscles and organs. One of the key functions of the kinesthetic processor was managing the subconscious routines and reflexes needed to perform complex physical tasks, such as walking or speaking. Modern neurology did not believe the peripheral nervous system possessed an awareness of its own. Modern neurology was wrong. Like the other processors, the kinesthetic processor was in fact a distinctly separate awareness inhabiting the body. To silence the chatter radiating out onto the n-web, the intellectual processor had to constantly distract and suppress some of the behaviors of the kinesthetic processor. Noah had said that with great discipline it was even possible to keep entire ideas from the god-machine and hold them in your own private vaults of awareness. Noah had also said maintaining silence became easier with practice. Right now, it was anything but easy. Mark had dedicated an entire parallel replication of his consciousness to the task. Quieting chatter while still being able to perform other activities seemed impossible, had he not been able to create mental clones. He could sense Sarah was straining to remain silent and succeeding remarkably at an impossible task. She was no longer shining brightly with data emissions. He was surprised to realize he missed her sunlight. They were still constantly pinging each other with memory capsules, but the communication was narrowly limited.

Mark was standing up with his head outside the driver's hatch. His palms felt sweaty. Noah had to be in position by now. The ghost had taken one of the Milkor MGL 40mm grenade launchers and would open up from an adjacent hilltop. He would fire the first shots, taking out the satellite dish farm. That was their signal to open fire. Mark looked at the clouds changing color with the setting sun. A large hawk was circling in the distance. It was a misleading tranquility.

The rapid succession of explosive thumps and echoes vibrated the air and ground. Mark dropped into the driver's seat, secured hatch, and got the beast rolling. In seconds they had rounded the hill. Sarah opened fire at a range of a 150 yards. The propellant charges of the grenades firing in short bursts of almost 400 per minute created a dance beat of destruction inside the Stryker. Mark stopped at a hundred feet. An ebb and flow of violent roaring, combined with the trembling of the ground, was like the chaos of being trapped in the heart of a terrible thunderstorm. It was if the gods themselves had gone to war. On the driver's display Mark saw explosive flash after flash within an expanding cloud of debris.

The rhythm of firing changed. Now instead of bursts, a constant recoil and fire cadence had set in with long pauses every two and half minutes to reload. Mark knew the MK19 was now firing at its maximum stainable rate of forty rounds per minute. That meant Sarah had gone to work on the weak spot between the blast door and rock wall. The weapon was locked on target and violently gouging its way through feet of rock and thick steel.

After ten minutes of punishing fire there was silence. A stiff wind was quickly clearing the dust and smoke. Mark digitally zoomed in the driver's display. The blast door was fully breached. What was left of it was flat on the ground inside the mine. Every bit of the hive's communications and surveillance gear was gone. The front part of the fence and gate were also torn open by explosions.

"We did it!" shouted Sarah.

"Yes, you did," yelled Mark. "Time to head for the hills."

Mark selected the rear view for the driver's display and saw Noah parked close behind them in his Land Cruiser. Sarah resumed firing but at a much slower rate. Mark swung the Stryker around and punched in the GPS coordinates for their hiding spot. The plan was to keep firing on the bunker while they pulled back. They wanted the hive to think the attack was ongoing for as long as possible. Mark knew Sarah had previously set up the GPS targeting mode of the CROWS to hit in and around the Army trucks. She fired in short bursts as they fled. He did not have to look to know each burst was hitting its target.

Mark pushed the Stryker up to a speed that felt reckless on the dirt road. They had to move fast. He doubted they would feel a thing if he hit a small tree. It was the big ones that worried him. The automatic tire-pressure system was adjusting inflation for maximum handling at different speeds. Sarah was now firing blind and with far less accuracy, using the indirect mode of the weapon. In a mile they would be out of range for the MK19. The plan was to retreat six miles to a ravine that had unusually heavy tree cover. They had gone over satellite images to make sure the spot was fully hidden. After camouflaging their vehicles at separate locations, they would stash their supplies in the woods and hike back at night to the mine. A camouflaged surveillance nest was waiting for them on a hill that had a clear line of sight to the bunker. The perimeter sentry tablet was in the nest running with their remaining detectors aimed at the mine entrance. It was there to capture any activity before they returned. The hardest part of this plan to swallow was if a military attack came, there was a chance they could lose their Stryker. Unlike Noah's Land Cruiser, erasing the off-road tire tracks for their 36,000 pound monster was impossible.

Sarah felt anxious and angry. Daylight was fast approaching. Over thirty hours had elapsed since their attack and no cavalry had come to the rescue of this hive. This was the worst possible outcome. If Noah was right, this meant the hives were not bluffing. There was a guide and its worker ants living in that hole, and they along with their brethren were about to unleash a global nightmare. She was caught in the midst of a world war, and it seemed like only the three of them and the enemy knew it.

"They're going to murder a billion people," said Sarah.

Both Mark and Noah remained silent. They all knew it was true. Mark offered her some food. Sarah shook her head and pulled her long coat around her as the wind tugged at it. Over the last few hours she'd thought she'd heard whispers from this hive, the same as in Morristown. How could they know she was here? She'd kept a strong leash on her kinesthetic processor and knew it was completely silent. Maybe the whispers had just been the wind, or maybe the hives had other ways of sensing her presence. She was connected to them by blood. Some of her family could even be in that nest. Still, she wanted them all gone. She wanted them all exterminated.

"I think it's time we go down there and prove Noah's theory," said Mark.

"I am right," said Noah. "Dealing with a bluff would have been a welcome diversion compared to what we're left with."

Sarah was behind the wheel of the Stryker. Her feelings of dread had only worsened. She stopped the vehicle as the mine came into view. Mark and Noah were in the crew compartment. Mark was at the CROWS weapons station, ready to send any insects that came out of that nest straight to their artificial god. She zoomed in the driver's display on the wrecked entrance. With the door flattened it looked like an iron drawbridge leading into hell. They were all convinced the mine had to be filled with lethal booby traps designed by a machine intelligence to stop exactly what they might have to do. Just walking in there could be suicide. They would have to set off grenades every 20 feet to disable or trigger the traps. The hive would know exactly what they were doing and their exact location. If Noah's latest plan worked, none of them would have to step inside that funhouse. Unfortunately, Noah's plan had a hole in it.

Sarah pulled forward slowly. Everything felt unreal at the moment. She had heard no more whispering since they'd left the surveillance

289

nest. Air Truth was reporting six new kill-zones in small towns in North America. There had to be far more than that going unreported around the world. The USAG was still claiming these were hoaxes and bragging they would catch the deranged criminals responsible for these terrorist acts and see them executed.

At an ideal firing distance, eighty yards downrange from the entrance, Sarah engaged the parking brake. She climbed out of the driver's seat and joined Mark and Noah, who were talking.

"How do you know we can locate enough of their air vents?" asked Mark.

"I don't," said Noah. "If we can't cut off enough of their air supply, then they won't have to evacuate and we'll have to go in after them."

Mark had a grim expression. Even without him radiating emotions, Sarah knew he was furious. Noah had led them to believe he had blueprints for this mine that showed all the vents and tunnels. A short time ago they'd found out his blueprints were too old to be completely trusted. Sarah felt everything was slipping off track and heading toward disaster.

"There's no way we can find the rest of these nests before they unleash hell on us all," said Sarah.

"Finding them is not the problem," said Noah. "I have all their shelters mapped out along with all their aboveground dwellings. It is even easier now that we know they have started to go to ground in their shelters."

"Are these maps any better than your blueprints?" snapped Mark.

"The maps are from the goddess and they are accurate," said Noah. "The key is how to destroy all the hives before they have the capability of retaliating with a plague. Ideally, we need to knock them all down covertly and rapidly before any guide realizes how badly the tide has turned and decides victory in suicide is better than defeat. With annihilation looming, a guide might chose mutually assured destruction and strike back with the sloppy weapon they now have."

"I get it. I understand Guides are emotional," said Mark. "But am I the only one who noticed they didn't try to use a kill-zone on us when we attacked them? They had to think we were Peacekeepers. Their control problems might be bigger than we suspect."

"Maybe they don't want to reveal their secret weapon," said Sarah. "They think no one has linked them to these kill-zones. If they used their kill-zone weapon on Peacekeepers, it would be like grabbing a megaphone to announce their plans and show just how big a threat they are to everyone."

"That makes sense," said Mark.

Noah was staring at her with one of his unreadable expressions. Sarah was unsure where that idea had come from. Was it hers? Had it come from the god-machine or was she somehow channeling these hives? She was afraid it was the latter, and that made everything she did suspect. She needed help to sort this out. She looked at Mark. They were so distant right now. She didn't like how they had walled off their emotions from each other to become ghosts. She wanted him back in her heart the way he had been before Pueblo Canyon. She allowed a small portion of her feelings to leak out onto the n-web. Mark turned toward her and his expression softened. He moved over next to her and took her hand. Noah seemed caught off guard by the small display of affection.

Sarah Mayfair – Colorado – March 7, 0002 A.P.

Sarah watched on the CROWS targeting display as Noah returned from retrieving his Land Cruiser. A few hours ago the vehicle had been left a short distance from the mine with an unconscious Mustafa in the back. She held the crosshairs on Noah as he drove up to the Stryker. Noah pulled to a stop a few yards from the open ramp. He dragged a half-revived Mustafa behind him like a dog on a leash and cuffed him to a tow lug on the rear of the Stryker, then went back to the Land Cruiser. Mustafa was radiating every kind of emotion and was clearly still under the influence of the drugs he'd been given.

Moments later, Noah stepped inside the crew compartment carrying a liquor box and set it down on the floor. The top of the carton was open. Inside were liter-sized plastic water bottles. Noah pulled out one of the plastic bottles. Inside, Sarah could see a glass jar and a stoppered chemistry flask. The two items were stacked on top of each other. The jar was upside down so its glass bottom was touching the flask. The jar was filled with white powder. The flask was filled with clear liquid. There was a seam where the plastic bottle had been cut open and resealed with glue.

"Sulfuric acid and potassium cyanide," said Noah. "When the two mix you get—"

"Hydrogen cyanide gas," said Mark. "The same thing the Nazis used."

"I thought we were choking off their air supply," said Sarah.

"We are," said Noah. "If the hives detect the gas then they will have to shut off their blowers, cutting off their own air supply and driving themselves out of their nest. If they don't catch on fast enough then the gas will do an even better job of driving them out. Hydrogen cyanide is not lethal to hybrids, but it will stun a hive. The nanotech linkage throughout the central nervous system has a weakness to cyanide. I have six more boxes of these in my truck. It will not take that much. The gas is largely odorless. If we are quiet about our business, by the time they figure anything out it will be too late. The gas will addle them and bring them down to the mental throughput of an organic. The guide will be forced to collapse to a minimal survival operation level or die. The hybrids will be on their own. The seeds in their blood will be fully occupied trying to repair damage, and that will drain the hive to the brink if they do not flee. Cyanide linkage disruption is horribly painful and cannot be blocked."

"How do you know this?" asked Mark.

"Experimentation…"

Noah had a satisfied smile on his face. Sarah realized that Noah must hate the hives even more than she did. She thought of Mark. He wanted to stop the hives at any cost, but did he have enough hate in his belly for torture? Noah looked Sarah directly in the eye.

"Do you want to help?" he asked.

"Yes… I hate them," she said.

"Mark?" asked Noah.

"Let's get this over with," said Mark.

Noah sent her and Mark a memory capsule, which contained a marked-up blueprint of the area along with instructions. Noah would stay behind to finish off the hybrids in case they fled the mine early. She and Mark each took a box of the cyanide bombs. Other supplies went into backpacks. They each set out on foot in different directions.

Sarah had left Ralph in the Stryker, which was equipped with NBC air filtering. She did not want him anywhere near this gas. She reached the first vent after only five minutes of walking. Already the muscles in her legs were tightening. She was carrying a lot of supplies, plus her M4 plus water, and the trek was mostly uphill. This was going to be a physically draining day.

The vent was a 12 inch diameter pipe that came straight out of the ground. It was topped with a metal cap with hundreds of small holes drilled into it, forming an armored grill. On the top of the cap was a rounded metal hat with a rim to keep the rain out. The whole assembly was painted in camouflage colors. Some vents were inlets and some were outlets. Sarah took a sheet of paper from her backpack and held it next to the grill. Airflow sucked the paper to the grill and held it there. She had found her first target.

Sarah took out a hacksaw and went to work. This would be the hard part. Explosives would be much easier, but then the hive would know someone was attacking their vents. Sarah thought the cyanide bombs were sinisterly ingenious. The glass jar was thin and had been weakened by scoring its bottom and sides. The flask had also been scored. There was a doubled ended hardened metal point glued between the jar and flask. The metal was probably unnecessary, but it would help shatter the glass on impact. All Sarah had to do was remove the water bottle cap to give the gas a place to vent and then drop it.

Sarah was covered in sweat as she sawed at the vent. After a few more strokes she was able to pry it back. She wasted no time dropping two of the cyanide bombs into the pipe. She could faintly hear them crashing at the bottom. She then dropped down a few rocks to make sure the glass was well smashed. It didn't matter where in the vent the bombs cracked open. Blowers would draw the gas deep into the mine. Even if the hives had good air filters, a great deal of concentrated gas would pass through the ventilation system. The filters would be saturated quickly and stop absorbing the gas.

"Breathe deep, little bastards…" whispered Sarah. "Breathe it all in."

Sarah Mayfair – Colorado – March 7, 0002 A.P.

Half the day was gone and the job was done. As Sarah walked toward the Stryker, she could sense Mark was inside. His defenses were lowered a bit. It had been a hard day. Poisoning every vent on the blueprints had taken longer than she'd expected and used most of Noah's bombs. Her sense of the singularity had faded as more vents were poisoned. She no longer felt any faint attractive pull. Instead, she was experiencing for the first time the unfiltered emotions of a hive. The emotions had started radiating in small flashes, which slowly built to the stampede of uncontrolled feelings that were now circulating. The cyanide gas had denied them their self-control. Anger and fear were the dominant emotions, but there was also a growing resignation, almost sadness. It was if they were all drunk. The volume and number of distinct emotional fingerprints left no doubt this was a real hive and not some kind of Trojan horse.

Mark, Noah, and Sarah were sitting inside the Stryker. The MK19 was aimed at the opening to the mine. They were watching a cross-haired video feed from the weapon's sight on the large command and control screen. Noah had moved Mustafa and handcuffed him to the front of a half exploded Army truck near the entrance to the mine. Sarah could see Mustafa in the display and the sheet of paper pinned to his chest. The paper had a single word scrawled on it: *Surrender*. Mustafa looked fully awake. The hive members would soon have to flee. They couldn't remain conscious in that environment much longer.

"Why are they still in there?" said Mark.

"They have to be planning something devious," said Noah. "Otherwise they would have surrendered by now. The guide has withdrawn into itself. Mustafa is better than any white flag. Seeing a powerful illuminati like him captured by Peacekeepers will cause all kinds of confusion in their degraded hive minds when they emerge."

"If they emerge," said Mark. "Your blueprints may be missing something else like, say, a backdoor. You have to admit your plans were a little sketchy here."

"What suggestions have you offered?" said Noah. "EMP bombs!"

"At least that'd work..."

Mark and Noah began arguing, but Sarah had no interest in taking sides. She watched as Mustafa tugged at his handcuffs. He was fully alert and in pain. She zoomed in on him. His lips were trembling and moving as if whispering. She had a bad feeling.

"It looks like he's whispering," said Sarah.

Mark and Noah continued bickering.

"Hey, guys... Guys! It looks like he's whispering," said Sarah. "I can't see anyone inside the mine."

Noah leaned forward to scrutinize the display... then his eyes widened.

"That rotten insect!" exclaimed Noah.

Before Sarah could ask anything, Noah had tromped down the exit ramp and was on his way to Mustafa. Mark crouched next to her to look closely at the display. Sarah zoomed out the field of view so they could see Noah. The man appeared enraged as he marched toward the mine entrance. This was the first time she had seen the god-like hybrid display any uncontrolled emotion, though nothing radiated from him on the n-web.

"What is he doing?" asked Mark.

"I have no idea."

"Crazy bastard," said Mark.

"Which one of them?"

"Both..."

When Noah reached Mustafa an argument erupted. It looked like Noah wanted to beat Mustafa senseless. Sarah could hear faint shouts going back and forth. Noah kicked some dirt at the old hybrid. Sarah felt no pity. Noah started to pace. Sarah could see Mustafa shout something. Noah pulled his sidearm, spun, and casually executed Mustafa with a bullet to the head. The sound of the report reached them moments later.

It had been sixteen hours since they had gassed the hive and Mustafa had been murdered. Mark was lying inside a sleeping bag on the roof of the Stryker, staring up at the night sky. The nanotech transformation of his nervous system was complete, along with the development of his immune system, which now had more than enough free-swimming COBIC. Noah had driven off to retrieve something without explaining further, except to tell them he would be back by mid-morning with enough provisions to fill their vehicle. Sarah was keeping watch inside the Stryker. The night air was very cold. An assist was alerting him it was not a safe temperature. He didn't care. He'd go back inside before long.

Mark was disturbed by the ease with which Noah had killed a handcuffed prisoner. Mustafa had regained some of his basic capability and was likely on the verge of sending a memory capsule warning the hive. Yet there were other ways to stop him besides murder. Over the past days Mark had been provoked by Mustafa many times and many times he'd wanted to kill the hybrid. Mustafa was good at doing that but Mark had not sunk to that level, while Noah had with great ease.

Mark watched the sky as a small meteor shot across the rich background of stars. In that streak of light the meteor had died in a final, magnificent display after traveling for untold billions of years through the universe. Its death reminded Mark of the mysteries that surrounded them all. He was a scientist and understood full well the limitations of what humankind really knew and how much we pretended to know. We knew nothing when compared to the vastness of that night sky above him. He entered the timeline program and found three reincarnation matches and one of them was for himself.

Ancestral memories flooded Mark's consciousness the moment he accessed his match. At the same instant he knew he'd made a terrible mistake, as his identity and willpower were subsumed by the timeline archive. It was very disorienting to be inside someone that seemed like himself. The thought patterns were similar, as were the ways of dealing with things. Boundaries were erased. It was like finding his body had been stolen and given to some random person. There was an overpowering, irrational desire to take back what was his. Experiencing the mind of an alien would have been less unsettling. Something was also terribly different in this timeline. He was absorbing far more of this lifetime than was contained in the excerpts within the archive.

Without warning, a second timeline was added out of nowhere to the one he was already reliving. He was now experiencing two lives and unable to break free. How was this possible? A third timeline came into his mind, overlying and blending with the first two. Strange feelings of déjà vu emerged from collisions and overlaps between the three lifetimes now replaying. Just when he thought he could finally bear what was pouring into his soul, a fourth and then a fifth timeline were added as if to increase the level of insanity on cue. Mark caught hold of a revealing memory fragment. While helpless to stop the psychological assault, he now understood what was happening. The root timeline, the one he'd unthinkingly opened, was of a man undergoing some form of past life regression as part of a religious ceremony. The man had consumed a lucid dream inducing powder extracted from red spider lilies and was having out of body experiences entering into one past life after another. The echoes of these lifetimes ran deep, all the way to their origin. From different epochs, Mark saw flashbacks of monumental cities. He saw flashbacks of jungles with prehistoric mega flora and fauna. There were flashbacks of love, death, war, and joy. The flashbacks increased in speed and variety as lifetime after lifetime unspooled. Civilizations grew and then fell—they all fell—and their ends were all apocalyptic. An endless number of lifetimes were laid bare before him. While evidence and belief in an afterlife still eluded him, all doubt about reincarnation was obliterated in these few moments; and that was all the entire experience had taken, a few moments. Mark feared he would go insane if this went on much longer, but it did. In less than a minute he was weary, but it went on. In less than five minutes he was no longer Mark … but it went on.

Mark Freedman – Colorado – March 8, 0002 A.P.

What seemed like lifetimes later, Mark awoke, confused, in complete darkness. Somehow he'd managed to break free of the timeline. His heart was racing. His body was overheating and yet he was shivering. He was balled up in the end of the sleeping bag on the roof of the Stryker. It felt like he was suffocating inside the intestines of some large animal that had devoured him. He struggled to get out of the bag. When he finally stood, he almost stumbled. His legs were wobbly. His skin was instantly covered in gooseflesh from the sting of frozen air. He climbed down into the Stryker. Sarah was sitting at the CROWS weapon station. Her eyes looked glassy in the reflected light of the screen. She looked over at him and he could see an entire expanding universe in those emerald green eyes. His mind was a spiderweb of past lives all woven into an incomprehensible whole. He was weary and wanted nothing more than to shut it all down and crawl into her arms to sleep forever.

Treachery

Mark Freedman – Colorado – March 8, 0002 A.P.

Mark awoke to the distant sounds of a vehicle approaching. He found Sarah watching the large command screen, which was displaying a feed from the CROWS weapon sight. The crosshairs were locked on and automatically tracking Noah's Land Cruiser towing an off-road trailer.

"He's back," said Sarah. "I guess we're about to learn what he's planning. The singularity's also back. The pull is weak, but I can feel it and the emotional leakage is decreasing and… and something… well..."

Sarah's eyes were watery. Mark could feel emotions radiating from her.

"What?" asked Mark.

"Air Truth's reported five more kill-zones. It spread from towns to small cities. Hundreds of people died in each attack and less wildlife was killed. The USAG's still claiming it's all a terrorist hoax."

"We're wasting too much time with this one hive," complained Mark.

He was frustrated and didn't know what to do. He zipped his coat and stepped out into the frigid bright light to confront Noah. The hives were going ahead with their plan. Mustafa's stories were proving to be all too real. Mark noticed a faint, attractive pull from the singularity, just as Sarah had described. The cyanide gas was wearing off. Noah stepped from his Land Cruiser and went around to the back of the off-road trailer. He unlocked the double doors and opened them. Mark came up behind him and looked inside. The bottom half of the trailer was filled with military crates marked *high explosives* and the top with supplies. The sight of all that explosives was unnerving.

"I see you have been dipping into the timeline program and found something," said Noah. "Good for you."

Mark almost jumped as Sarah put her hand on his shoulder. She'd come up beside him in total silence.

"The singularity's back," announced Sarah.

"That's only temporary," said Noah.

He handed Sarah an unusual looking 40mm grenade chambered for the MK19. It was blue and had several aerodynamic holes in the nose cone.

"What you are holding is an XM1060-Mark three thermobaric munition," said Noah. "It was originally developed as a cave buster during the Afghan war. Each one is far more devastating than what you have been firing from that Stryker. It will not take many of these to collapse the mine's entrance. After that, we close off all the vents. Cyanide may stun a hive, but carbon dioxide will kill it. We're sealing them up in a mass grave."

"Why not just leave and regroup?" said Mark. "Torturing this wounded animal is not a winning strategy. Other hives have to know what's going on here and think the USAG is doing it. Kicking this hornet's nest could prematurely start an all-out war before we can win it."

"I will not leave behind a living nest of those things," snarled Noah. "If you are with me, you will do this!"

Mark repositioned the Stryker so they could fire parallel to ground into the entrance shaft. This gave them good odds of reaching the back of the shaft and collapsing all of it by walking the explosions forward. Sarah let loose with the MK19. Mark was shocked by the increased power of the grenades. After only sixty seconds of concentrated fire there was no point in continuing. The last few grenades had burst on the surface of the collapsed mine, throwing blast waves that could have knocked a man down had he been outside the Stryker.

As the unusual smell from the explosives drifted away, Mark, Sarah, and Noah divided up the vents and went off in different directions to cap them. Noah pulled out in his Land Cruiser to take care of the farthest vents. After sealing his first vent, Mark was grudgingly impressed with Noah's ingenuity, if not his plan. Noah had given them inflatable heavy rubber kick balls. All they had to do was inflate a ball inside the 12-inch vent pipe and move on to the next. Even if the blueprints didn't show all the vents, carbon dioxide was heavier than air and would accumulate with most of the vents sealed. The hive was doomed.

As Mark went from one vent to the next, he received memory capsules from Noah. While the hybrid did not have a plan for what to do next, he did have ideas. Mark knew they had to come up with a far better strategy than destroying hives one at a time. Though he was not ready to act on it, there seemed to be no other option than using McKafferty.

Mark began pumping up another ball inside another vent. He thought of all the past lifetimes he was now convinced he'd lived; assuming the timelines from last night were truly him. He was troubled by the paradox of now believing he was more than a physical body while obediently playing his part in committing mass murder. Wiping out this hive before it became operational again might save a few innocent lives. Did that balance the scales or was this nothing more than a random act of terror? They were all at war, the innocent and guilty alike. He had to keep focused on the end and not the means.

As Mark checked the seal around the rubber ball, a timeline flashback hit him, leaving him stunned and disoriented. He grabbed hold of the vent to keep from stumbling. The reincarnation flashback was every bit as powerful as the prior night's. As it faded, he understood what had just happened. Some part of his consciousness had accessed the timeline interface on its own. Moments before the flashback, he'd thought about exploring his past lives for clues about the god-machine's role. Some part of him had acted on the desire. Since last night he'd changed his objective from not only searching for past lives, but also for the birth of the god-machine itself. The two questions were intertwined. He no longer believed the machine knew who created it or when. It had no personal concept of life or death for itself. It was a true immortal.

As Mark collected his gear into his backpack, he couldn't shake a feeling that something was missing. As he checked to make sure nothing was left behind, he realized the emotions radiating from the hive were gone, as were the stray thoughts. The faint, attractive pull from the singularity was also missing. He searched his recent memory, sifting for fragments of stray thoughts and emotions emitted from the hive. As a more complete picture formed, he grew certain the hive had committed suicide. Memory capsules from Sarah and Noah contained the same realization. Mark dropped his backpack to the ground. He stared at the vent for what seemed like hours, then turned and walked away. He knew Noah intended for them to finish the job because in his mind the suicide could be a deception. Noah and Sarah were pressing on as Mark continued walking back. Mark was certain beyond any doubt this hive was dead.

Sarah Mayfair – Colorado – March 8, 0002 A.P.

Sarah had yet to reach her first vent. The hive was whispering to her as clearly as the one in Morristown. Ralph was far out ahead of her sniffing through the underbrush as she reached the top of a hill. The sky was filled with broken clouds framing a daytime moon. Snowcapped mountains rose in the distance. It all looked as if she were in a terribly beautiful nightmare. The whispers were hinting for her to kill Mark, now that he had served his purpose. She wanted to seal the vents as quickly as possible. She needed them to die. She needed them to get out of her head. Noah had taught her how to block her emissions on the n-web. There had to be a way to block these whispers. She needed Mark's understanding and help even more now than ever. She didn't like what this restructuring was doing to him. He had stopped sharing his thoughts with her. He was blocking all his emotions, which would have been impossible before Noah had taught them how. Now nothing escaped him, not even the smallest feeling when they were making love. She no longer believed this extreme isolation made them any safer from hives. A little intimacy would not make any difference. She wondered if Noah had some agenda. Ralph came to her. He knew she was distressed. Sarah reached her first vent and went to work on it.

The winds were blowing through the trees and dry brush, creating even more whispers. Sarah was still ruminating on how distant Mark had grown as he became a ghost, like Noah. She was sniffling, holding back tears. The last two times they had made love Mark had not wanted her. What else was he keeping from her? Well, she was keeping secrets too. She had not dared tell him about the whispers, but now there was an even bigger secret. How could she tell him what had happened in Flagstaff? How would he take the news? He'd had a child once and lost her to the plague. To risk that happening again might be too much for him. She would have never known she was pregnant this early except by accident. The medial assist she'd used on herself out of concern over being exposed to cyanide gas had delivered an unexpected discovery. Pregnancy was not supposed to be possible for hybrids. Noah and Mustafa had both confirmed in their own words that hybrids were sterile. The entire reign of the hives and their way of twos existed because hybrids were sterile. Some hybrids believed they could not conceive because they no longer had souls. It was pure madness to bring a child into this damaged world, but deep inside her heart she knew she had secretly and irresponsibly wanted a child for months.

She finished the vent and started walking toward the next. How could she even trust her own feelings with her brain networked into the god-machine and now the hives? Maybe the pregnancy was what the god-machine wanted—or, god forbid—the hives wanted. She knew she couldn't keep this secret from Mark for very long. She had seen it with a medical assist. So could he.

The hive's whispers started again. Sarah screamed out in frustration. No one could hear her except Ralph. She fell to her knees and started pounding her fists together into the dirt. They were down there beneath her, those insects in their hive.

"Leave me alone!" she screamed.

Each of her blows was aimed at them. Each time her fists hit the dirt she was hurting them and herself. Ralph began howling. The tone of the hive's whispers changed. It was somehow softer.

We know... We feel....

"Know what?" thought Sarah. She stopped beating the ground. Her face was wet with tears. What were they whispering about? She was out of breath. Her fists were sore but healing; her vision was blurred.

Nothing must harm it…

Within moments the hive went silent. The world went silent. It felt as if the entire universe was holding its breath. Sarah somehow knew mass suicide had just been committed below her feet. The absence of radiated emotions from the hive and vanished tidal pulls confirmed they were no more. She thought she would be relieved when they were gone, but now she was more confused and worried than ever. *Nothing must harm it.* Were they referring to her child? Why would they care? If anything, this child made her an even bigger threat to their way of life.

Mark Freedman – Colorado – March 8, 0002 A.P.

The day was turning blustery and surrounded Mark with rustling sounds. He was haunted with mild flashbacks that came and then dissolved like apparitions. Unlike the initial flashback, these aftershocks were experienced as very faint sensory projections superimposed over his reality. It was like living two lives at the same time but with one, the flashback, as faint as thin veils of fog. Vague wisps of buildings, sounds, smells, emotions, and people faded in and out of the forest he was wandering through. All his past lives relived through the timeline contained memories beyond what could possibly be in the archive. There was no acceptable scientific explanation for this extended memory, but right now he didn't care. The flashbacks had given him an idea, one he would devote his full attention to as soon as he was settled inside the Stryker. He wanted to locate a reincarnation of himself from 47,000 years ago, the time he thought of as the Barringer Crater War. That lifetime, if it existed, would contain complete information leading up to the war, information that might be helpful against the hives. Maybe that's what Mustafa had feared at Barringer Crater. The threat was not something the old man would reveal but something Mark might remember. The hives had almost gone extinct during that war. Maybe what was needed was another Barringer Crater?

Mark had almost returned to the mine shaft. The wind blew a small flurry of dried leaves across his path as he shimmied down a bank that led to the mine. A mild flashback distracted him as the lifetime superimposed itself over his senses. He emerged from the forest into the huge clearing, which had become a war zone. He glanced at the sealed mine entrance and felt the hive dead inside it. He headed toward their Stryker. The side of his neck was stung by a large insect. He slapped at the little bastard but hit something hard that tore at his skin.

"What the hell?"

He pulled a hard-shelled creature from his neck and saw a dart. He then realized an assist had been warning him organics were nearby. His arms and legs stung from repeated hits. He pulled off more darts. His immune system was surging to combat whatever was happening.

At a tree line 50 feet away soldiers in camouflage were slowly creeping into view. His reaction time was dropping rapidly. An assist was warning he was losing the fight against drugs, which were disrupting his higher functions. His immune system was a froth of pure rage and desire to destroy the aggressor. He watched soldiers brandishing Tasers drop to the ground, dead, as his immune system lashed out invisibly with micro kill-zones. He stumbled to the dirt and tried to get up. A flurry of stings landed all over his body, followed by electrocution. His world faded to black.

Sarah Mayfair – Colorado – March 8, 0002 A.P.

Sarah was experiencing a distant buzzing of emotions and assumed it was some kind of echo from a hive that was no more. She imagined it was residual emotions leaching from the n-web. It was disrupting her senses and distracting in the same way a faint ringing in the ear might be. Ralph was heeling. Sarah stopped short as she crested the hill leading down to the mine. She was stunned by what was before her. Mark was lying on the ground with soldiers approaching him in a wide circle. She tried to send Mark a memory capsule and failed. She could tell by a medical assist he was in a deep coma. Armored vehicles with Army insignia were moving into view. She sent Ralph hunting down behind the hill to prevent anyone from flanking her. She positioned herself behind a tree to give herself as much cover as possible and took aim with her M4. At this range, hitting her targets was going to be a serious challenge. An assist was identifying which targets to hit first. She would have to move fast from spot to spot before any heavy return fire from the Army vehicles could find her. If she had enough ammo, it was long odds, but possible for her to save Mark. The assist identified a high-ranking officer exiting one of the armored vehicles as a new first target. Sarah was having a hard time making all the pieces fit. The assist identified the officer as General McKafferty. Was he still personally hunting them? First Morristown, and now here. Fuck. It was his funeral.

She was ready to squeeze off her first shot when a terrible confusion invaded her head. There was intense buzzing and disorientation. Her senses were jumbled by what was assaulting her and she had no doubt it was an assault. She couldn't focus. She couldn't fire.

304

A hand fell onto her shoulder. Sarah swung the stock of her M4 in a perfect circle, connecting with the skull of whoever had just grabbed her. The confusion evaporated. She was about to follow up with rapid burst from her M4 when she caught herself. Noah was sprawled on the ground with blood dripping from a huge gash in his forehead. As she stared, the gash began to coagulate. Ralph came up behind him, ready to lunge.

"Put down your weapon," said Noah.

"What?"

"Are you suicidal?" said Noah.

"We have to stop them!"

"You can't save him," said Noah. "The best we can do is follow."

"Were you the bastard who just scrambled my brain?" she shouted.

"Quiet! Are you insane? Do you hear what's coming?"

Sarah heard a sound of rotors. She turned back to a scene that could not be happening. Mark should not be down there all alone. She saw a pair of Apache helicopters looming into view over the treetops. In less than a minute a third airship, an Air Force Pave Hawk, came in to land. They were going to take Mark out by air. There was no way she and Noah could follow. She raised her M4, then lowered it. She was trembling with rage. Any attack would draw the Apaches and she would not survive that engagement. Her M4 against Apaches was hopeless. Her fire would just bounce off.

She had lost the man she loved, the father of her child. Mark didn't even know he was going to be a father. Sarah tried again to reach out to him mentally and failed. She saw him carried into the Pave Hawk and felt her heart torn from her chest.

Mark Freedman – Colorado – March 8, 0002 A.P.

Mark awoke in the belly of a huge aircraft, bound hand and foot. He was disconnected from the global n-web by altitude but could still defend himself. An assist displayed severed n-web pathways snaking all over the jet. He could use these broken spans of the n-web to attack.

He tried to look around without giving away that he was awake. He recognized enough of his surroundings to know he was alone in the cargo hold of a jet. He could sense a few partial emotions and thoughts from the crew going out over the disconnected pathways of the n-web, but something was interfering. He should be receiving this local data clearly. The bits of human mental radiation he was getting were like faint echoes and nearly unintelligible. He felt like he was blind. His mind was duller without the god-machine assisting his thoughts, but he was still far smarter than he'd been as an organic. Questions began rolling through his nanotech brain. Noah must have had warnings from assists that intruders were at the mine. Mark had missed the warning signs because of the flashbacks. He'd been fatally careless, but Noah would not have been. Noah was a ghost adept at detecting and avoiding unfriendly situations. He must have perceived and ignored the warnings, but why? Was Noah a traitor working some angle Mark could not even begin to guess? Was there some other explanation? Maybe Noah had just fled and left them behind as decoys? What about Sarah? Was she on another jet and a captive just like him?

Mark spotted video cameras in the cargo hold. A hatch was opened, followed by several sets of footsteps. He could sense nothing from whoever had entered. Were they hybrids?

A large paw gripped Mark's shoulder and turned him over onto his back. He was then hoisted into a sitting position to meet a face he knew very well. McKafferty was standing over him, flanked by two soldiers nearly as big as the general. A third solider was behind Mark, holding him in place. The general and his men were all wearing what looked like a cross between an NBC suit and beekeeper gear. A small control box on the chest contained three buttons behind a plastic safety cover and three green lights. The helmet and faceplate was a fine-mesh screen that freely let air in and out. This suit was for protection from something other than airborne diseases or weapons. McKafferty was grinning, which looked so wrong on a face that ugly. Mark did not have to pick up stray thoughts to know what the general was thinking. McKafferty had taken Kathy prisoner and now he had just captured another prize and possibly more.

"You led us on a good chase," said McKafferty.

"Not good enough," said Mark.

"They tell me that once we're airborne, hybrids like you cannot function and that includes generating kill-zones," said McKafferty. "But I don't believe in unnecessary risks. This suit you're staring at blocks the n-web. So don't bother trying the same kind of kill-zone you used on my men. I always knew you were partially responsible for the plague."

Mark was surprised by how much McKafferty knew. He felt cornered and outflanked. He'd thought blocking the n-web with a physical barrier was impossible. The fact that he was picking up no thoughts or emotions leaking from McKafferty and his men proved the suits worked. What he couldn't understand was why seeds had failed to tunnel microscopic biomass conduits through the suits, rendering them useless. Even in the air, even cut off from the god-machine, seeds should be doing that right now. It was time to go on the offensive.

"Do you believe in god?" asked Mark.

"What?" said McKafferty.

"It's not a trick question."

"It's a question with no point to it."

"The point is, you're fighting the wrong war," said Mark. "The god-machine is no longer your enemy. If it was your enemy, you might as well be fighting god and that's a fight you would lose. Kill-zones are happening in small towns all over the world. We need to work together to defeat the real enemy, who is responsible for the attacks happening right now. There are communes of hybrids under a kind of collective mind control, all working together. These communes are triggering the kill-zones."

"You're a funny man, Dr. Freedman. Two years ago you tried to convince us the nanotech inside COBIC was hundreds of millions of years old. Now you want me to believe we are on the same side. I don't know which is a bigger stretch. We know about these small groups of hybrids, and we know about you and your partner in terrorism, Sarah Mayfair—or should I say Bonnie and Clyde? Pity we didn't capture her, but we will. We know about your bombing of communes. You do know mass murder is still illegal, right? We found a hybrid handcuffed and murdered at the mine entrance. I wonder how many bodies we'll find inside."

"There's a war going on and we need to help each other."

"We've investigated those so-called kill-zones and you know what we found? They're criminal hoaxes. Some very evil folks are trying to convince the world the plague is returning. Maybe that's you and your pals?"

"They're not hoaxes!"

"So what did you use to fake those kill-zones? At first we thought it was a group of hybrids all working together using their personal kill-zones, but then we found evidence that a very advanced chemical weapon and dispersal system was used."

"What? What kind of evidence?"

"All in good time… Sergeant, suit him up."

Mark was confused and a little panicked. What was going on here? Were hives creating these kill-zones on their own or was someone else also involved? He thought of Noah and his use of cyanide bombs. What else did that ghost know about chemical weapons? Mark needed to escape or at least get onto the n-web to warn Sarah. He knew with his heightened reaction time and ability to push his muscles beyond their limits that he could take these soldiers, but what then? He was locked in a cargo hold under video surveillance. They'd just come in and dart him or shoot him. He could hold McKafferty hostage, but in the end that chess move also left him darted or dead. He allowed them put one of their beekeeper suits on him. They then laid him on a stretcher and bound his legs and arms to the rails. It was like a full body straitjacket. Escape or even getting a warning out to Sarah was becoming a dimmer possibility by the second. One of the soldiers powered up the suit, plunging him into mental darkness. Everything on the local n-web vanished.

Mark Freedman – Dallas, Texas – March 9, 0002 A.P.

The cargo jet landed. Mark knew it had been four hours and eighteen minutes since he'd been captured, but that was of little help in figuring out his location. McKafferty and the same three soldiers came into the cargo hold. They were no longer wearing their beekeeper suits.

"I'm going to say my good-byes," said the general. "I'd like to watch what happens to you, but the facility you're entering is a civilian operation, and honestly the place gives me the creeps with all the human experimentation going on there."

"McKafferty, you're making a mistake!" shouted Mark. "You have to go after the communes. They're the mass murders. The proof is the kill-zones are killing everything, not just people, and they're growing in size. Soon they will be too big to be a hoax."

"The only mistake I made was failing to put a bullet into your brain two years ago when that infection turned you into a computerized zombie."

As Mark was carried from the jet on his stretcher, he recognized the airport. It was Love Field in Dallas. This was the airport where JFK had landed hours before he was assassinated outside the book depository. The beekeeper suit was blocking him from the global n-web just as effectively as it had when he was airborne. He had hoped the suit would fail once he was in an area saturated with n-web pathways.

He was carried to a waiting helicopter. As soon as he was inside, the helicopter lifted off. He was again unable to see where he was being taken. Twenty minutes later, they landed and he was hauled inside a huge building. He recognized the company logo. Zero-G was the world's biggest R&D defense contractor. At least he wasn't going to prison. Once inside, his stretcher was laid on a gurney and they began rolling him down hallways and elevators. The facility was bustling, but few people paid any attention to him. Was a prisoner on a stretcher a common sight in these halls?

He was rolled inside what looked like a large metal pressure chamber, which measured about 20 feet across. Two men in beekeeper suits followed him in and took up positions next to him. One of the men was armed with a submachine gun and looked like a thug. The other man looked mousy. The entry hatch, which was the width of two normal doors, whirred shut and sealed itself with a heavy *clunk*. The hatch was at least a foot thick. A large rectangular porthole as thick as the metal hatch filled most of the opening. The two men in beekeeper suits just stared at him as if he were a particularly nasty specimen. Mark was starting to feel worried. This place might be worse than prison.

"So what's next?" he asked. "Dinner, dancing?"

There was no answer.

"Don't you guys speak?"

The mousy one took his vital signs and keyed the results into a tablet. The straps that secured one of his arms to the stretcher were removed. The two men left with the thug backing out to keep Mark covered with his machine gun. The hatch opened and closed without either man using a switch or key. Mark had no idea what was next. They'd obviously freed his arm so he could release himself from the stretcher. He thought about ruining their game by just lying there. That idea lasted for less than a minute. He freed his other arm, sat up, freed his legs, and then stood. Next, he took off the beekeeper suit. He was expecting to feel the familiar surge of information and sense of connection from the global n-web, but he was just as isolated now as before. The chamber had to be one giant beekeeper suit. The walls, floor, and ceiling were all stainless steel. The only interruptions in the walls were thick portholes, which contained either lights or video cameras. The only furniture in the chamber was the stretcher and gurney. Mark rolled the stretcher to the middle of the chamber, then sat down on it and smiled at one of the cameras. He was enraged and doing his best not to show it. The hell with it! Using his muscles beyond their peak, he stood, and in one smooth motion yanked the heavy stretcher off the gurney and hurled the stretcher like an Olympic hammer thrower whirling in a circle before releasing it toward the entry hatch. The impact was impressive. The stretcher exploded into several pieces. The rectangular porthole in the hatch now had a collection of nicks and tiny spiderweb cracked impact craters. Mark sat down on the floor cross-legged and waited. His muscles were torn up from the exertion. Free-swimming COBIC was surging through his body to repair the damage he'd just done to himself. For good or bad, they now knew a little more about who they were dealing with.

Like a statue of Buddha, Mark sat cross-legged in the middle of the room. Exerting total control over his body, he remained in the same position, conserving energy and concentrating his thoughts. The lights in the chamber had not dimmed as evening turned into night and then night slowly blended into the following morning. Mark knew constant light was an interrogation trick designed to destroy a prisoner's sense of time. It would not have any effect on him. He knew exactly how much time had passed. Even without a connection to the god-machine, he still retained many of his augmentations and some of them were still very deadly. They seemed to have no clue what kind of human they had in their prison. They had to know more than this if they'd experimented on hybrids. Their techniques for breaking him made no sense.

Mark began using an assist to map out the severed n-web pathways that permeated the chamber. Network packets similar to TCP/ip pings were sent out by an assist and came echoing back from every seed in each pathway. He sat in the center of a geo-projection of the nerve fibers of the local n-web. Each pathway terminated inches from the wall, which meant some type of electromagnetic field was cutting off his access to the global n-web.

The hatch clunked and began to open with a now familiar mechanical whirring sound. A man stood a few yards back from the entrance. He was wearing black slacks, a black polo shirt, and black loafers. His face was weathered from too much sun. He was tall with a trim, athletic build. His features were Mediterranean or Middle Eastern, with a prominent forehead and unusually thick eyebrows. Two men that looked like bodyguards stood on either side. The bodyguards were armed with submachine guns and in beekeeper suits. The bodyguards entered the chamber and leveled their submachine guns at Mark. He did not bother to stand up. There would be no shaking hands at this meeting.

In his geo-projection of the n-web, Mark could see with the hatch opened there was a weak spot in whatever field was blocking the n-web. He could see the pathways trying to adapt, reconnect, and reach out. He was getting intermittent data from the man. Suddenly a route was complete all the way to the global n-web. Mark felt the god-machine's entangled interface operating inside his mind. It was like breathing again after being underwater for too long. A medical assist came up on the man standing outside the chamber. Mark was stunned to see a high concentration of COBIC swimming in the man's body, and then even more surprised to see a lower than normal amount in the man's brain.

All of Mark's thoughts had occurred in the space of a heartbeat.

His brain was operating at an amazing speed. He was not going to waste this connection to the god-machine and quickly sent a memory capsule to Sarah. The connection to the global n-web was unreliable. He might not be getting through. He continued multitasking while remaining fully engaged with what was happening around him. The global n-web connection broke, then adapted, then broke again while the local connection to the man remained steady.

"My name is Zuris and this is my home."

The man had a strong European accent.

"You'll excuse me if I am not pleased to meet you," said Mark.

Zuris smiled like a predator staring at its next meal. Mark could tell by the emotions radiating from the man that his arrogant response had been a good choice. Zuris looked young. A medical assist confirmed an approximate biological age of late thirties, except for his head and brain, whose biological age was closer to eighty. The global n-web connection came back. Mark's entangled interface instinctively pulled in data about Zuris.

The n-web connection wavered, adapted itself, and then failed. Mark was bewildered as he gathered from newly implanted memories that he was face to face with an immensely wealthy and powerful puppet master. Ownership of Zero-G was pocket change to this man. The new memories contained enticing clues that Zuris and his extended family could be worth trillions of dollars. The memories received from the god-machine were an odd mixture of typical timeline data, along with unexpected information that had to have come from the Internet as well as internal classified government and corporate intranets. Mark found himself asking the same question he had been for days. How was the god-machine accessing data that came from networks that had no connection to the n-web?

An expensive leather high-back chair was delivered to Zuris, and the man gracefully seated himself. A small end table with a glass of ice water was set next to the chair. Mark had not been given anything to drink since his capture. Zuris slowly drank some of his ice water. Mark began picking up stray thoughts, fragments about devices called *medial-jammers* and *zone-jammers*. The engineers had concerns whether they would be reliable with this kind of highly developed hybrid. Mark wondered if Zuris knew about the gap in protection caused by the hatch opening. Was he intentionally allowing Mark to evaluate him? Anything was possible at this stage. Someone who looked like a servant delivered a trim phone to Zuris. He listened and then handed it back.

"I think we are going to be good friends," said Zuris.

"McKafferty promised I was going to die in prison," said Mark. "I guess our friendship will be brief."

Zuris smiled and then took another long sip of water.

"Oh no, my friend, we're going to put you to work for Zero-G and your country. You are far too valuable to be housed in some prison, awaiting execution. General McKafferty is a brilliant soldier but diatomic in his thinking. Everything is either right or wrong. General McKafferty has difficultly seeing the degrees of light and dark that fill our universe."

"I don't care about your take on McKafferty!" said Mark. "I warned him and now I am warning you. There are communes of—"

"Stop talking, please," interrupted Zuris. "I know everything you are going to tell me. I've replayed your conversations with General McKafferty many times. It is a fascinating tale of rogue communes of hybrid terrorists, but an improbable tale with no proof. For a very long time we've been watching communes. There is no evidence they're behind the kill-zone hoaxes. Now, unlike General McKafferty, I see no reason for you to lie about such an important and improbable story. This leads me to think you believe what you are saying and that you are yourself the victim of a hoax."

Zuris stood and walked close to the doorway.

"You look surprised, Mark. You didn't think we can listen in on what is being discussed privately in this country? Security in times like these is paramount. Technology is the weapon that protects us. The public has to sacrifice its privacy for safety. I understand this compromise all too well. The president and I share leadership responsibilities over our government-corporate alliance. I feel the terrible weight of history resting on my shoulders."

Mark could tell from radiated emotions and stray thoughts that Zuris was telling the truth and had the unshakable conviction of a religious zealot. He truly owned the levers of power and was well practiced in their use. More so than McKafferty, this was the man Mark needed to convince about the hives, but how?

The assist, which was displaying n-web pathways, was showing a peculiar networking loop near Zuris's neck. The loop was blocking the movement of COBIC beyond the neck. Mark studied the faint outline of an unusual pathway that ran from the networking loop, down the inside of the man's shirt, and into a small box on his hip, which looked like a cell phone. Mark realized this was some kind of disruption-field generator that scrambled n-web and seed operations. This had to be the same technology as beekeeper suits. Why was Zuris doing this to himself? Why allow his body to be saturated with seed-bearing COBIC?

312

Mark knew the answer as fast as he'd formulated the question. Zuris was terminally ill with lung cancer and using COBIC to cure himself. It was his personal fountain of youth. Mark's connection to the god-machine came back. Out of the darkness, he received a response from Sarah. His heart broke as he fought to keep his composure. She'd only received a small part of what he'd sent. Before he could fully send a new reply, the route to the global n-web failed again.

Zuris looked at Mark oddly, then glanced down at the small box on his hip. Mark realized too late he had been staring and not completely concealing his emotions.

"You know too much, don't you?" said Zuris. "How is this possible? You're connected, aren't you?"

Zuris ordered the hatch closed. Mark had lost his opportunity to remain connected to the global n-web. The separation felt like someone he loved had died. He got up and began pacing alone in his prison.

Mark Freedman – Dallas, Texas – March 11, 0002 A.P.

After Zuris and his bodyguards had abruptly left, workers had delivered various items to make living more comfortable: a folding table and chair, a cot, a portable toilet, and a privacy screen. Most of his personal belongings were returned, including the IronKey thumb drive that contained Kathy's memoirs. Had they somehow learned what was on the encrypted thumb drive or simply not cared? Probably the latter, since there was nothing he could do from this prison without their permission. For safekeeping he slipped the talisman over his head and down around his neck.

While his possessions were being returned, the entry hall outside the chamber was being modified by a crew of workers. The hallway was soon covered in what looked like thick, orange rubber gym pads. Electrical wires snaked away from the far end of the pads and around a corner.

Exactly nineteen hours and thirty minutes after his first visit, Zuris returned for another chat. He stayed outside the chamber as before, but Mark was no longer able to pick up emotions or stray thoughts. The weak spot in the disruption field was gone.

Zuris proceeded to question Mark for hours. In return, Mark received answers to some of his questions, including an explanation for how the disruption field worked. With these jammers the nanotech plague was no longer a threat to Zuris and his chosen people. Mark loathed the man but was forced to admit a grudging respect for his cunning ingenuity.

As the hours wore on, the interrogation began to feel more like a conversation between old friends, but the armed guards and the chamber that was his prison were unmistakable reminders of who was the keeper and who was property. As the meeting was wrapping up, there was something Mark was burning to find out.

"How did McKafferty know I was at that mine?" he asked.

"I believe you mean *we,* as in *Sarah and I were at that mine,* and I'm afraid I have no idea how that fortunate accident occurred and only regret that we did not apprehend your partner as well."

With that brief response, Zuris got up and left. Mark did not believe what Zuris had just inferred. It was unthinkable that a man like Zuris did not know every detail of McKafferty's operation. To suggest a four-star general was on a random field trip that turned out to be a lucky encounter with a wanted hybrid was farcical. Could McKafferty have been the calvary the hive had called for help? Mark knew in his gut the entire operation had been well planned and required inside information. It was hard to imagine Sarah as a traitor. Noah, on the other hand, had a dangerous track record of concealing things. The man was an unreadable enigma, but it was still difficult to envision him in bed with the likes of McKafferty or Zuris.

Lunch and then dinner arrived through a conveyer slot in the wall. Mark ate everything out of need for energy, then returned to his meditation. Under normal conditions nothing was forgotten inside a nanotech brain. Mark was now learning that was both a great virtue and a great curse. Many trains of thought ran in parallel inside him. With the ideas of distrust having taken root, he could not help but grow a little distrustful of Sarah as that train of thought continued in the background of all his other thoughts and actions. Why was it that both Sarah and Noah were missing when McKafferty raided the mine?

The hatch opened without warning. Once again Zuris was seated in his chair. His bodyguards marched into the chamber and leveled their submachine guns at Mark. Everything was choreographed exactly the same as the time before and the time before that. They might as well have all been machines. A worker pushed a large television into the chamber and turned it on. The Zero-G logo filled the screen.

A woman came into view in the hallway. He could not see her face clearly due to the differences in lighting, but his brain had already made the leap. It was Kathy! He felt like the air had been sucked from his lungs. He could not breathe. He could not say a word. He was stunned as she walked into the chamber and the light moved up her clothes and finally reached her face. She was tearing up. With a few more steps she was in range of the n-web pathways that were alive within the chamber. Her emotions flooded into him like a wall of bathwater. Guilt tinged his joy as he experienced feelings she still harbored for him. He stood, tipping over his chair, and hugged her. He felt so powerfully protective. He'd had no clue she was alive, let alone in this place.

"Are you okay?" he whispered.

"I'm fine," said Kathy. "They have me working in the labs. That bastard lied to me. He pretended to be a scientist. Mark, he owns everything. Don't trust him."

Mark glared at Zuris. "I promise you," he said. "If anything happens to her or anyone I care about, I will tear down your house with you inside it!"

"Admirable and impossible," said Zuris.

"Fuck *impossible*," said Mark. "Have no doubt I will tear down your house."

Kathy rubbed Mark's beard and smiled. He got a sense she was not that crazy about it.

"It's a disguise," said Mark.

He removed Kathy's IronKey from his neck and placed it safely in her palm, then curled her fingers around it. She looked perfect as tears of happiness slid down her face. Mark felt so good about what he'd just done for her. He had managed to return a lost piece of her soul.

"Isn't that Chicago on the big screen?" asked Zuris.

Mark glanced at the television. The Zero-G logo had disappeared, replaced by a nighttime urban surveillance video of a quiet street. Four video windows covered the area from different angles. Kathy turned to see what Mark was staring at. He knew that place well and with it came a sinking feeling. One window contained the hive's townhouse, which was still intact at the time of the video. The three other windows were different angles of the small park next door. The date and time on the screen matched the night the hive was burglarized. He was certain what had to be coming next. Why was Zuris doing this?

Two people came walking down the street holding hands. Mark was rattled. As they passed through areas of deep shadows, the video switched modes to thermal IR and back. There was no audio. Faces came into focus as Mark and Sarah sat down on a bench and then passionately embraced on three screens. Kathy angrily shoved him.

"You son of a bitch," she shouted.

"I had no idea you still had feelings," said Mark. "We broke up. This is innocent."

"Fuck you!" shouted Kathy. "How do you know how I feel?"

"Let's skip ahead a little," said Zuris.

An Enforcer Humvee turned down the block. The headlights washed over the park. Mark unbuttoned Sarah's coat and moved her into his lap so that she was straddling him. It looked like foreplay. Sarah was silently laughing at something.

"Ah, the wonders of nanotech-sex," said Zuris. "We have very capable surveillance suites on every structure in the protectorate worth monitoring. Mark, you no doubt saw all the cameras and bracelets when you were in Chicago. Once we knew you had visited the Chicago Protectorate, all we had to do was a little reverse detective work to find this X-rated bit of porn in the archives. I think we should stop here or I'll begin to blush."

The images on screen froze in a moment of less than flattering lust. Mark felt like he was in an alternate reality. He was innocent and he was guilty. Kathy's face was red and she was breathing as if she'd just run up a flight of stairs. Mark saw it coming and did nothing. Kathy punched him in the face. The blow hurt and knocked him back a little. His nose was bleeding. He had no idea what to do. He had no idea what to say. The pain almost felt cleansing.

"If I was a hybrid, would we still be together or would you have been fucking her anyway?" shouted Kathy. "I should have known from the start. How could I have been so stupid for all that time? I should have dumped you!"

She shoved him in the chest. Tears were streaming down her cheeks. She shoved him again.

"You were the first man I loved since my divorce. You said you loved me and then you broke up with me and said you loved me. You cheated on your first wife. You cheated on your coed fuck buddies. God, I was so stupid. I was worried all that nanotech in your brain was changing who you were… Goddamn it... Well, the good news is that nanotech shit has not changed you a bit. You're still the same lecherous bastard who can't stop chain-fucking girls half your age."

Kathy marched out of the chamber. Mark looked at Zuris and understood this was all going perfectly to some mysterious plan. He and Kathy were being manipulated by the puppet master. He had no idea why this had been done, but he now suspected why the IronKey had been returned to him.

"You're a bastard," said Mark.

"Why don't you tear down my house?" said Zuris. He began to laugh.

Mark was given a beekeeper suit and ordered to put it on. His hands were then cuffed behind his back and the suit was switched on. Where they taking him? The hatch opened. Mark saw Zuris smiling to himself with Kathy standing beside him. They were flanked by a pair of bodyguards in beekeeper suits. Mark wanted to strangle Zuris.

"Today we're going on a little tour," said Zuris. "Think of it as orientation day for a new job."

"If you think I am going to work for you, you're a crazier fucker than I thought," said Mark.

One of the bodyguards marched into the chamber, pulled out a telescoping baton, and beat Mark in the head repeatedly without restraint, driving him to the floor. He saw bright flashes of light from each blow with the world dimming between impacts. After a few minutes on the floor, Mark's senses returned to him. The smashed beekeeper helmet slipped from his head as he tried to stand with his hands cuffed behind his back. One of the bodyguards hoisted him to his feet. He was more than a little unsteady and bruised. His face and head felt like he had a fever, as COBIC worked to repair the damage.

"This healing ability of your kind is so useful," said Zuris. "We can badly hurt you again and again without concern that we might go too far. Look at the mess you forced us to make. Now we'll have to get you a new helmet."

With Kathy in tow, Zuris gave Mark a tour of Zero-G. Two bodyguards were flanking him with firm grips on either of his upper arms. Since Mark had left the chamber, Zuris had been talking incessantly about ancient artifacts and something called Prometheus. The only time they stopped moving was so Zuris could point out something of importance along their route to what he called the artifacts vault. Mark could not understand why Kathy was being forced to accompany them. She seemed still enraged at him and clearly did not want to be here. To his relief, she had turned ashen when she'd gotten her first close-up look at his battered face, but then soon returned to glaring at him. As they walked, she refused to speak to anyone.

As Mark stepped through the vault door, it felt like he'd walked into a king's treasure chamber. The artifacts vault was a revelation. He'd had no idea so many relics existed. The vault looked like a museum, but with impossible specimens on display inside Plexiglas cases.

"Look around," said Zuris. "Take your time. Each case has a description."

Mark was allowed to wander on his own with his hands cuffed

behind his back. Zuris, Kathy, and the bodyguards remained by the door. Several relics had to be nexus devices. Some of these devices looked completely alien, while others looked like you could have bought them in a store today. Oddly, the relics that looked so familiar bothered Mark the most. He had a terrible sense of déjà vu when he stared at them. One relic looked exactly like a pair of IR goggles and another looked like a digital wristwatch. There was a terrible message in those relics. Maybe it was that they were hard proof that civilizations like his had been utterly destroyed, proof that something far worse than a nanotech plague could happen at any time?

Mark's thoughts were interrupted when one of the bodyguards came to retrieve him. Zuris announced they were heading to Prometheus. A tram picked them up at an underground tunnel. They rode in silence. Mark was grateful for a break in the guided tour. He could tell the tram was gradually heading deeper into the ground. After fifteen minutes they came to a stop. Zuris and Kathy disembarked. Mark was helped off by one of the bodyguards. Large warning signs announced that entry was restricted and deadly force would be used.

They walked through one of several blast doors that was opened and closed for them by unseen hands. Inside this faculty almost everyone was in uniform, including civilians. Those who were not soldiers wore military jumpsuits that carried no rank.

Zuris stopped walking and stared directly into Mark's eyes with a penetrating gaze. Mark was weary of Zuris and his manipulative head games.

"What I am going to tell you is the truth," said Zuris. "To prove this to you I will allow you to take off the zone-jammer suit, but first understand something. Kathy is right here with us. If you use one of your micro kill-zones, Kathy dies too. If you try anything, one of my guards will execute both of you. Understood?"

"Your desire to tell the truth would seem far more earnest without the death threats," said Mark.

"Take off his handcuffs," ordered Zuris.

Once Mark was free, he immediately took off the helmet and one-piece suit, leaving them in a pile on the floor. He'd expected to feel the god-machine come rushing in, but experienced nothing. A geo-projection showed the entire area was riddled with n-web pathways, but there were no outside routes. The facility had to be shielded with zone-jammers. Mark could feel emotions from hundreds of people inside the facility. Stray thoughts were coming in from every direction. He caught Kathy staring at his battered face and experienced empathy blended with reluctant admiration radiating from her. A medical assist reported on his large bruises and gashes. They were his medals of honor for standing up to Zuris. The internal damage had healed enough for COBIC to begin work on the outer layers.

"I am going to tell you about the Prometheus project," said Zuris. "I trust you are able to read my emotions and biometrics to confirm I'm speaking the truth."

"I'll know when you start to lie," said Mark.

"Excellent, handcuff them together," said Zuris.

One of the bodyguards cuffed Mark to Kathy. The cuff bit into his wrist. Mark wanted to tell her he was sorry, but knew for now it was better to keep silent.

"We are currently standing in the Prometheus interface project," said Zuris. "This facility is a joint USAG-EMP shielded underground bunker designed for critical top-secret work. The bunker is sealed against everything, including kill-zones. A quarantine of the project is required because it must remain isolated to prevent a breakout of Prometheus into the world at large. To explain it simply, the Prometheus interface project is a system that can interface the god-machine with our computers. Once interfaced, we can mine the god-machine for its gold, its wealth of knowledge on every topic from ancient weapons to power plants."

"Does this interface include command and control?" asked Mark.

"We cannot control the god-machine," said Zuris.

"So what can you control?" asked Mark. "You lie and I'll know it."

"In theory we can control the n-web and biological nodes," said Zuris.

"By *biological nodes* you mean people?"

"Yes, and animals too."

"The ultimate weapon," said Mark. "Command and control of man-made kill-zones. You have an anonymous first-strike weapon with no collateral damage to buildings or equipment."

Zuris did not smile, though Mark sensed a veiled eagerness in the man.

"As I said, *in theory*," replied Zuris. "At this stage we have no control over the n-web. It has taken the combined efforts of all our best scientists and engineers on this project to get the data exchange interface marginally operational. Our Kathy contributed a fantastic discovery, which opened the doors to making the interface work for the first time."

"You used me," accused Kathy. "There's nothing medical about this project. Both of you used me. Both of you can go to hell!"

"I am sorry for the little deception," said Zuris. "What you did will help with medical applications once we get to them. You must admit, you would not have assisted if I had told you everything."

"Screw you!" said Kathy.

She yanked angrily on her cuffed wrist several times, then stopped. Her tugs had been violent enough to cause the cuff to bite into Mark's skin. He knew she'd hurt herself as well. He'd never seen her look so defeated. He returned his attention to Zuris. He was both hopeful and chilled by the reality of Prometheus. All that was standing in the way of command and control was a better understanding of n-web syntax and protocols. As a highly evolved node in the god-machine's network, Mark intimately understood this syntax and protocols. Zuris was well on his way to creating exactly what the hives were using to trigger kill-zones, and Mark could provide the missing pieces for Prometheus. Zuris had no idea how close he actually was to achieving this goal. A single thought kept echoing in Mark's head: *If you own the weapon, you can devise a means of countering the weapon.*

"Our team had a breakthrough about two weeks ago, thanks to the discovery of jammer-bridging made by our Kathy," said Zuris. "For the first time we were able to send and receive data packets across the n-web using a hybrid as the interface. As long suspected, the n-web data is digital and network communications circuits are massively parallel with redundant data streams. The biggest surprise was that we did not need complex mapping of the hybrid's nanotech brain to figure out where to interface. Our second surprise was that we did not have to encode or decode the n-web data itself. All we needed was the ability to pass ones and zeros back and forth at high speed through the cerebral cortex of a connected hybrid. We started by tickling a group of nanotech neurons with a digital signal injected through an electrode inserted into the temporal lobe. In retrospect, I think we could have picked any spot in the cerebral cortex that had been converted to nano-tech. The god-machine was hungry to communicate and immediately detected our signal. In a frighteningly short period of time it learned our computer encoding and altered the output of nanotech neurons touching our electrode to match our encoding. We then enabled a feedback loop and the god-machine started learning on its own and was soon radi-cally optimizing the nanotech brain circuitry of the interfaced hybrids to further improve communications. The god-machine was now doing our work for us. Prometheus feedback uses the hybrid's eyes and ears to present simultaneous classroom-like audiovisual explanations for the computer encoded data we inject into the temporal lobe. This virtual classroom is created using a three-dimensional sound system and laser video projection directly into the retinas."

Zuris swallowed and took a moment to compose himself. Mark could tell Zuris was about to say something that genuinely affected him. This was not an act.

"I had not grasped the immense intellectual potentials of an artificial mind until that day," said Zuris. "And since that day I have lived in growing awe, fear, and respect. It is so much greater than we are. We started communicating by passing sequences of digital numbers to the god-machine. The god-machine sent the same sequences back to us and we, in turn, sent back the sum. The very next time we passed a sequence of numbers, we got back the sum. We then proceeded to multiplication, division, log functions. You name a math function and we have done it. We then went through the ASCII alphabet and the dictionary as fast as our audiovisual feedback system could handle. We are now currently working on phrases and sentences that express complete abstract concepts. We are so close to having a true conversation. Unfortunately, there are so many permutations of phrases that the process has slowed because of the feedback bottleneck. Sending audiovisual feedback is very slow compared to direct temporal lobe injection. There also appears to be a barrier between our mental constructs and the constructs of the god-machine. There is a quantum difference between the way we think and the way the machine thinks. We are directly communicating with what amounts to a superior alien life form."

Mark could not contain himself any longer. A medial assist along with radiated emotions and leaked thoughts all showed Zuris was telling the truth. Synchronicity was a magnificent thing. This egomaniac might just have built the answer to stopping the hives!

"Prometheus is exactly the same thing the communes are using to trigger kill-zones," said Mark. "They are going to commit genocide and we can use Prometheus to stop them. All we have to do is write a program on one of your computers to monitor the Prometheus interface for kill-zone signals. We then broadcast a complementary data packet over the n-web containing a signal to abort."

"Mark... Mark... Mark," said Zuris, shaking his head. "Stop. I want to believe you think this hoax is real, but a plague is not coming; kill-zones are not happening. I am at a disadvantage. You can tell if I am lying, but I cannot judge if you are telling me the truth. Through Prometheus, we humans are building a fragile truce with the god-machine. Maybe you're more than a pawn in this game. How would I know? Maybe you want another plague. After all, wasn't all this worldwide murdering done so transhumans like you and Sarah could get a solid foothold in our world?"

Mark could not believe what he was hearing. It took an extreme act of will to contain the resentment boiling over inside him.

"You are wrong!" he argued. "Everyone in the government knows the god-machine acted because humankind was destroying the planet. The attack was to save the Earth, not hybrids. No one knew it at the time, but hybrids already had a lot more than a tenuous foothold. We've been here since before this civilization even existed. We obviously don't need the god-machine's help to survive and would have been better off in the shadows than the center stage we're now in, thanks to the nanotech plague…. Look, what's the harm in setting up Prometheus to defend against kill-zones? Even if I'm wrong and what I'm telling you is a hoax, you have to admit a plague could start without any warning. Wouldn't Prometheus be a great defensive shield to have just in case? All we're talking about is some software development on one of your computers. Think of it as cheap insurance."

"We have zone-jammers," said Zuris.

"Okay, let's get them manufactured and sent out to everyone."

"We've already given them to everyone we can't afford to lose," said Zuris.

"What about everyone else?" asked Kathy.

"They will have to wait. Listen to me. There… is… no… imminent… threat."

Mark had stopped arguing with Zuris but remained obsessed with the idea of using Prometheus as a shield. There was no guarantee it would work, so they needed to program and test it as soon as possible. The direct approach of convincing Zuris was not going to work. Mark decided he either had to come at Zuris from an oblique angle or somehow hack Prometheus. Either way, he'd have to bide his time or risk being completely shut out. Zuris was now ushering them deep into Prometheus. After they got into an elevator, he put his hands onto Mark's shoulders.

"I am not giving you this tour to show off a successful project," he said. "This is not about ego. I want you to join the team working on Prometheus."

Mark could not believe the synchronicity that was occurring. Of all the projects in all his many companies, Zuris wanted Mark to work on the very one he needed to hack. He began wondering if the god-machine had a hand in all this; after all, Zuris was saturated with COBIC. The elevator stopped.

"Now I am going to show you the heart of Prometheus," said Zuris. "Our interface subjects."

The elevator door opened onto a short corridor that ended at a security door. One of the bodyguards swiped an access badge through a reader, then placed his palm on a scanner, then punched in an access code. The door opened, exposing a corridor lined with glass. The air and walls were cold, reminding Mark of a huge walk-in commercial refrigerator. The light raining down through the glass ceiling was uniform and bright. The floors appeared to have solid sheets of dull metal below the glass panels. Behind the glass walls were rooms that looked like intensive care units in a hospital. Between each room was a large closet of some kind. The closets were completely sealed and required the same triple authentication as the security door. The entrance to each subject's room was through a rear door that was not accessible from the corridor. The glass was several inches thick and had an almost invisible weave of filaments running through it. Mark could tell from an assist that the filaments were radiating a powerful zone-jammer field. It appeared like a quarter of the rooms were occupied. The subject he was looking at was restrained and held at an incline of about 15 degrees from horizontal with her lower body submerged in a clear liquid. The head and neck were inside the doughnut opening of a compact fMRI unit. Intravenous lines were tapped into ports in the subject's chest. A pair of clear pipes circulated liquid through the shallow tub in which the subject was partially immersed. Attached to the outside of the glass wall were several flat-panel displays stacked one on top of the other. The displays showed vital signs, fMRI images, digital signal data, and a video of the subject's face from inside the fMRI doughnut.

The scene put a chill through Mark. These were human beings who had been turned into a biological component of a computer interface. He had not fully grasped what Zuris had meant when he'd said they used hybrids for the interface. He felt the emotions radiating from Kathy and knew this was the first time she had seen this hellish spectacle in person.

"Subjects can be kept alive indefinitely in a deep state of mental hibernation. We need to quiet their minds so their thoughts do not interfere with the interface itself. We use TPN to feed and sustain the body."

Mark could feel Kathy was growing extremely agitated by what Zuris was saying.

"How do you induce mental hibernation?" she interrupted.

"I had to protect you from certain things," said Zuris.

"Tell me now!" she demanded.

"A cocktail of psychotropic drugs and general anesthesia is used."

"Oh, fuck you!" said Kathy. "You're turning these volunteers into vegetables."

Kathy's anger rolled off Zuris as if she did not exist. It was a remarkable display of self-control, which made Zuris difficult to read. Mark decided the man was a borderline sociopath and began discounting his ability to sift Zuris's facts from lies. Zuris walked over to one of the closets, unlocked it, and then stepped back. The small room was filled with racks of electronic equipment.

"This is where we analyze the results from each subject," he said. "We are taking every precaution. We have the digital equivalent of the level four isolation of your BVMC lab. In those computer racks are the most advanced firewalls and intruder defense systems developed by the NSA. This is the same equipment the USAG intelligence agencies use to protect their darkest secrets. All data collection and computer control has to pass through that digital gauntlet before it gets into Zero-G's intranet. Do you see that second and third rack? Just like all other computer systems and networks in this Zero-G facility, we have triple redundancy. We are taking no chances of accidently letting the god-machine slip into our network or the Internet."

Mark tried to remain neutral. As repulsive as this experiment appeared, he had to balance that against the genocide that had already begun in cities around the world. He knew he would be damned, but he had to try to use this awful tool to protect humanity from the hives. It was the lesser of evils.

"I want to show you one subject in particular," said Zuris. "This is our most recent addition. Subject seven was the first interface to work reliably and still shows the greatest potential and throughput. He is a very unusual hybrid. Before he arrived here he was acting as a faith healer and actually curing people. We think he was somehow able to inject some of his COBIC into those he healed. He has multiple personalities and psychopathy. He does not know he's a hybrid and thinks he's the messiah. This man is a potential cure for many fatal diseases, but he is also like a wasp. Even though he is not conscious, he is constantly throwing out micro kill-zones as if trying to sting imaginary tormentors. He is a very dangerous subject. Were he not inside a zone-jammer field, all of us would have died the moment we walked onto this floor—with the exception of you, of course."

Mark stared through the glass, feeling like a visitor at a zoo. This entire Prometheus experiment just got more and more hideous. He looked at the medial monitor tracing lines that measured this poor man's life. He studied the video feed of the subject's face and sensed he knew this man, but the appearance matched nothing from a full search of his memory.

"Our analysis indicates that about twenty-five percent of this subject's brain is nanotech," said Zuris. "Very soon we will be able to fully interface our computers with the god-machine at the highest abstract levels, but we can never let the genie out of the bottle. This subject will never leave this room alive. Interestingly, it turns out this subject's fingerprints were on file with the FBI. He was not always a faith healer. Before the plague, he was an assistant DA in New York. Fingerprint evidence from some heinous crime scenes also match. He's wanted by the FBI for an amazingly large number of homicides. His facial appearance has been changed. It does not look surgical. We can only assume he was able to alter his own appearance using COBIC. He says his name is the Messiah but his real name is Artie Hartman, aka Alexander. I know you both have—shall we say—crossed paths before. He seems to have total memory loss of everything prior to the end of the nanotech plague. His first memory, what he calls his rebirth, is a huge explosion. I wonder what would happen if we let the drugs wear off and told him Mark Freedman and Kathy Morrison are just a few feet away."

"Which spot is reserved for me in this human tank farm?" asked Mark. "When I'm no longer useful, this will be my new home, right?"

"We only accept volunteers," said Zuris

Mark recognized that was the first lie Zuris had spoken.

"Fine, I volunteer for a tank," said Mark.

The bodyguards were staring. Mark detected shock from Kathy and amusement from Zuris.

Mark Freedman – Dallas, Texas – March 15, 0002 A.P.

Mark had been sharing living quarters with Kathy inside the Prometheus bunker for several days. He had access to the isolated pathways of the n-web, which permeated the underground facility like some great abandoned spirit that touched everyone within its reach. He had no idea why Zuris was allowing him this partial connection. It had to be for some devious reason. Kathy was only there as a human shield and knew it. Mark could feel her fiery resentment. She now disliked him for a growing list of reasons. He was saddened by every flare-up of her anger that she radiated at him. Even though he felt what she was feeling and often knew some of what she was thinking, he'd found no way to defuse the escalating situation.

Their room had no windows. Instead, as in all other living quarters in the bunker, there was a large wall screen that showed scenic views synchronized to the time of day. They had office space, a private bath, a real bed, and two very advanced workstations. There was even an online food service with a gourmet menu. The things Zuris did were so calculating. Everything here was engineered with the goal of coercing maximum cooperation from workers. The quarters itself would have felt normal and reminiscent of his time at the BVMC lab, except for the heavy steel security door that locked from the outside. Mark also had no illusions that anything said or done in this place was private. The fact that Zuris had eavesdropped on his conversations with McKafferty onboard an Air Force jet was a constant, powerful reminder.

Mark had done useful work reviewing the Prometheus interface project. Kathy believed he was collaborating in something immoral. He knew her resentment of this was the fuel that kept their tension at a boil. He'd done the work not only to establish an appearance of cooperation, but also to learn more about his objective. His workstation had no access to Prometheus. If the local n-web could only penetrate into one of the subject's rooms, he would have access to both the god-machine and part of Prometheus. The logical solution was increasing the transmission power of the seeds to a point where they overpowered the jammer signal. He'd considered many different ways to accomplish this goal. The best option was engineering a synchronized in-phase transmission by an entire phalanx of seeds. The problem was, he had no idea how to issue commands to seeds that were not in his body. Something like a firewall prevented most internal commands from escaping out onto the n-web. This arrangement made a great deal of sense. Without some kind of semipermeable barrier, hybrids controlling their own bodies might also inadvertently affect others nearby or even on the other side of the world. The only firewall exception for seed command and control seemed to be micro kill-zones.

As Mark sat at his workstation, he felt trapped between two opposing fates. The more he studied Prometheus, the more he was convinced it could be made into a shield. Unfortunately, the more he learned, the more he knew he needed to destroy it as soon as he could figure out a way. He was confident Prometheus was not yet advanced enough to provide usable command and control of the n-web. Had he not been convinced of this, he could easily have believed the recent kill-zones had originated from Prometheus. He had to deny Zuris and the USAG this terrible first strike weapon, which they would undoubtedly use for their own brand of tyranny—but first, he had to make sure the hive's plans were irrevocably crushed.

Mark needed to find some way to enlist Kathy's help. Zuris had a curious weakness for her that translated into him giving her additional leeway. Mark began typing new searches into the workstation, followed by requests for documents. As promised by Zuris, Mark had few limits to his access to technical information. The retrieval process was very slow, sometimes taking minutes. This delay led Mark to suspect each request had to be approved by some minder who was watching over him. The scientists here had made exceptional progress. They had mapped the basic building blocks of the self-assembling nanotech seeds. They might even be on the verge of beginning to understand some of the mechanisms, which would truly be revolutionary. It was frustrating how the god-machine censored information about its internal workings. Why should he be denied knowledge about how his own body operated? It seemed the only way for him to ever find out would be through the slow work of non-hybrid scientists and engineers dissecting, analyzing, and theorizing their way to breakthroughs.

Some of his new information requests had been approved and appeared on the screen. One long document had several embedded videos. He was able to read information photographically, consuming most documents in minutes. As long as he had a mental snapshot of a full page he could move on to the next without digesting it. Some minutes later, he would find everything in the document all magically integrated into his thinking, as if he had read it. Clearly, some parallel process running inside his nanotech brain was reading and digesting the snapshots.

Mark clicked on one of the embedded videos. He had suspicions Zero-G was conducting Nazi-like human experiments on hybrids. His first tour of Prometheus and stray thoughts from Zuris that day had firmly planted that seed of suspicion. Mark was trying to find out how far they had gone and use that information as a lever to move Kathy. The first video contained deeply disturbing footage of hive members dying under experimental conditions when disconnected from the god-machine. The experiments started with a disconnection that lasted for a fraction of a second and then systematically increased the disconnect time until the hybrid died. The slow death seemed like mental suffocation. Mark called Kathy over the see the experiments. This video had not been what he was specifically looking for, but it did serve the purpose and it also confirmed that Noah had been telling the truth about that particular hive vulnerability. It also raised suspicions that Zuris knew far more about hives than Mark had suspected.

He felt strong emotions radiating from Kathy and knew the video had profoundly affected her. She blamed herself for the torture of these hybrids and hated Zuris for using her. Mark did not like manipulating her this way, but he had no choice. He had to make sure her allegiance shifted firmly to him and remained there.

Coyotes

Sarah Mayfair – Southern Arizona – March 17, 0002 A.P.

Noah's safe house was situated at the top of a high desert bluff with the world laid out below it. Sarah was staring out a massive seven-foot-tall window that took up almost an entire wall of the living room. It felt like she was standing outside. The Sonora desert ringed by far-off mountains was a spectacle that filled her eyes, but not her soul. It had been almost a week and the shock of losing Mark had increased instead of numbed. At times she was completely panicked and would begin walking in circles through the house while talking to herself and Mark. At other times it was hard to breathe. Mark being gone was incomprehensible. A part of her was still irrationally angry with him for emotionally deserting her days before his capture and so angry at him for being captured at all. The loss had become a catalyst, proving how important he was to her, and his importance went far beyond being the father of their unborn child.

When she'd first arrived at Noah's safe house, the place had felt surreal. She'd expected something as decrepit as his antique Land Cruiser. This house was worth a small fortune and had clearly been his home for a very long time. It did not fit Noah's image at all, which meant she had some very mistaken impressions of the man. The ceilings were 15 feet high. Every space was filled with art, some of it very old and mysterious. The house was positioned on the edge of a bluff in the middle of the very definition of nowhere. They were surrounded on every side by desert and hostile mountain terrain. The house was completely self-contained with solar power, passive solar, geothermal heating and cooling, and backup generators. Noah had given her a tour, which included explanations of how everything had been crafted with art and nature as key themes. The walls and ceiling were three feet thick reinforced green cement. The house was built into the earth on all sides, except the front. Access to the safe house was from a stairwell that ran down from a small reinforced garage that sat atop the bluff at ground level. The garage blended with the surroundings as if designed by Frank Lloyd Wright. The road leading to the house seemed to disappear at every bend like a mirage. She had her own room and rarely saw Noah or talked with him even less. He was a ghost even inside his own home.

Sarah leaned her forehead and hands against the glass wall. It was warm to the touch. Her thoughts wandered back to rescuing Mark, as they did almost every minute of every day. All she had to hang onto was a fragmented memory capsule from after his capture. He was

329

inside a compound in Dallas run by Zero-G Corporation. There were protective suits that jammed the n-web and a dangerous megalomaniac named Zuris, who was Mark's jailer. She had received nothing more from Mark in six days. She had no idea if he was still being detained at that compound or if he was even alive. Tears trickled down her cheeks, following a well-worn path. She had almost lost him in Chicago and had not gone through all that just to lose him now. Her hands subconsciously rubbed her belly and the new life that was growing inside. Six days ago she'd had another chance to tell him he was going to be a father, but instead all she had sent was that she loved him and then the spotty connection with him in Dallas had been lost.

Sarah turned at the sound of Noah coming down the entryway stairs. Her mind had already recognized the fleeting emotional fingerprint that Noah permitted as a way of identifying himself. He had been out somewhere for two days doing something he would no doubt tell her nothing about. From the couch, Ralph lifted his head, then returned to sleep. Ralph had other ways of identifying people.

Sarah was determined to confront Noah before he disappeared again with the only vehicle. She found him in the kitchen unloading fresh produce from one of several cooler bags.

"Don't you dare leave me stranded here again!" she complained. "What if something happened? What if I had to leave?"

"Where would you go? After Mark? You know that would be suicide."

"It's my life," said Sarah. "No one appointed you my protector."

"And where exactly is Mark?" asked Noah. "Is he even alive?"

"You know full well he was at Zero-G in Dallas, and if he's not there, it's a very good place to start."

"And what about the child?" asked Noah.

The child—he knows! Sarah was immediately thrown off balance. All the momentum she'd built was sapped by that simple statement and all it meant. She knew this confrontation would happen eventually. Maybe he'd known all along. Her mind was reeling with questions, or was he in her head, trying to confuse her again?

"You have no idea how important that child will be," said Noah. "It will be the first child born of two hybrids. That child represents the future of everything. It is a future the hives must fear. A race of hybrids that can breed. You and Mark have changed everything."

Sarah wondered if she should tell Noah about the hive's final message. The memory of that last whisper was vividly clear. *Nothing must harm it.* Some part of the hive had discovered she was pregnant.

Had that same part acted to protect the child from the rest of the hive with suicide as the solution? Sarah had thought long and hard about this and trusted nothing. Maybe the message was pure deception and the real goal was to steal her child to learn how to prevent a pregnancy from happening again?

Noah stood over her like a giant, exuding mental and physical domination. She decided to keep this all to herself for now. She didn't understand this man or know how much she could really trust him. She understood the hives even less and her blood bond to them least of all. Something felt odd.

"Bastard!"

Sarah was outraged as she caught Noah forcing a memory into her. He had no right! She was suddenly dizzy and gripped a countertop to keep from staggering. The memory was like a sedative. It was from the last great epoch 40,000 years ago. Approaching the time of their destruction, the entire society had been focused on the possibility of a child being born from two hybrids. The child would be a spiritual sign that everything was about to evolve with a literal rebirth of humankind. The emotions this memory evoked within Noah made Sarah wonder if he had been alive back then, in this life or a past life.

"This safe house can withstand any war," said Noah. "Any cataclysm unleashed by hive or mankind. In this place you can ride out the coming storm. You must stay here and be safe."

"That's not your decision to make!" she shouted. "If my child is so goddamn important, then aren't both parents equally as important? We have to get Mark back."

"*No*... I will not permit it."

Sarah started to laugh in his face. She couldn't stop herself even if she wanted. She had walked through ground zero of kill-zones where millions had died, while she had survived. What did this man know about her?

Sarah Mayfair – Southern Arizona – March 18, 0002 A.P.

Sarah had woken to find Noah and the only vehicle gone, again. He was obviously keeping her prisoner and he was not out searching for Mark. She was confident of that and she was done being his prisoner.

"Hey, Ralph, let's take a walk."

Ralph bounded off the couch, eager to go outside. Sarah got her backpack from the bedroom and then proceeded to the kitchen to fill it mostly with water and then squeezed in dried food wherever possible. At least it was not summertime out in that wasteland. Back in her bedroom, she put on her body armor and Beretta. She checked her M4, the grenade launcher under the barrel, and was set to go. She would have to walk two to three days before reaching any place that had cars, but she had been through worse. An assist projected a topographical map that showed a hundred miles to civilization.

Sarah was covered in sweat, even though the temperature was hovering in the lower fifties. She was walking through an endless region of hilly sand, bristling with aggressive desert plant life. There were thorny bushes, creosote, cactus, and many other varieties of smaller, spiny plants. She had kept up a steady pace all day, pushing her body to the limits and stopping only to eat. She was burning calories at a high rate and had managed to cover almost forty miles. The sky would soon be dark. The landscape was morphing into the rich desert hues of an abstract painting as it began to glow in harmony with the sunset.

To keep her mind off the damage she was inflecting on her muscles, she focused on something Noah had taught her shortly after they'd arrived at the safe house. It was a mental technique that he himself had been taught and mastered a long time ago. It was a way of focusing the nanotech mind using a meditation unique to hybrids. When done properly, the technique brought you closer to what Noah called the *dreaming communal awareness*. From that state of mind you could supposedly awaken past lives. Sarah had not been able to share in the communal dream, but she had caught brief flashes of memories of what might have been living souls within the communal awareness. Noah had said those flashes were glimpses of past lives. He told her that if they were long enough and clear enough, she could take the flashes and use them in the timeline to find those lives if they'd been recorded. He explained that in past ages, successful matches had been considered irrefutable proof of the immortality of awareness. She had tried to find her glimpses in the archive and retrieved nothing. Failure or success meant little to her. She was already certain she had lived many times before. Her near-death experience had convinced her of that.

Sarah thought about her day spent hiking through the desert and meditating. She had gotten a few more flashes, which were now locked away safely in her nanotech brain, never to be forgotten. When she stopped for the night, she would search for them in the timeline archive. She wondered if she had crossed paths with Noah in other lives. She had an odd sense he might have killed her in one of those past lives. He was such a dark contradiction: part artist and part assassin, part philosopher and part thug. She had to admit she was scared of him and it was possible he was already coming after her.

Moonlight was casting shadows across the desert. Something large moved in the underbrush. Sarah unslung her M4. Ralph was yards ahead of her. She could hear him growling. Ralph charged toward a stand of tall bushes. Sarah ordered him to stop. He obeyed, but his eyes remained locked on his target. A large coyote broke cover with several others. Using an assist, Sarah could detect furtive movements in the brush, which had to be more of them. Ralph easily weighed several times that of the largest coyote and could take them all one at a time, but Sarah knew these wild animals would attack as a pack. The coyotes looked like they didn't know whether to hold their ground or run. Sarah fired several shots into the air. The animals disappeared as if they were spirits of the desert.

Sarah and Ralph started hiking again, but before long she heard something large behind them moving in the brush. Every few minutes she'd hear sounds behind them and Ralph would turn. She had to repeatedly order him not to attack. They were being followed, which was extremely unusual behavior for coyotes, and that set her imagination free to work on her. Maybe these were not normal animals. Soon her hair stood on end with every rustle or faint snap. As the sounds grew closer, she'd finally had enough. At the next *snap* Sarah turned and fired indiscriminately at full auto into the desert, tearing up the vegetation and possibly a coyote or two. The clip was empty in seconds. She hoped that would discourage the stalkers, but an hour later she knew they were still following, just farther back.

Sarah stopped for a cold dinner. She sat on her backpack while eating and debated whether to keep traveling right after dinner, then decided Ralph needed a break and her muscles needed to heal. She would start hiking again at midnight. The coyotes were probably still there, though she had not heard them in some time. She ate the last piece of a granola bar. In the near distance she could see the outlines of cliffs and mountains as darker areas carved from the star-filled sky. She slowly stood up. Her muscles complained, but not as loudly as before. In another few hours most of the damage would be healed. She put on her infrared night-vision goggles and began to scan for any signs of a vehicle heading her way or coyotes. At this temperature, the heat of a car would stand out. She suspected it was pointless. Noah was a ghost. She would not see him coming.

Just as she removed the goggles, a memory capsule flared in her mind. It was Mark. The goggles slipped from her fingers as she was fully immersed in what he'd sent. The capsule was hasty and contained a complicated jumble of thoughts and experiences. She could tell he was injured from the body awareness that came along with the capsule. He was inside the same Zero-G campus as before and planning to escape tonight. Sarah experienced chaos all around him and had no idea what was causing it. He was inside a small, darkened area that seemed to be shaking. His vision panned and Sarah caught a glimpse of Kathy as the capsule ended abruptly. Sarah sent a reply that she was coming and that Noah was a problem. She doubted her response would get through. She kept the message short in case Noah could somehow intercept it and use it against them. She wondered if her imagined need for brevity was also a convenient excuse not to tell Mark she was pregnant. It troubled her that Kathy was with him. She was relieved Kathy was alive but not so happy about the circumstances. Sarah closed her backpack and shrugged it on. Escaping from that Zero-G prison would be dangerous. Mark needed all the help he could get and he needed it now. She might not find a car for another day or longer, and it could take eighteen hours to drive to Dallas. That was too long. Anything could happen in that time.

"Come on, Ralph... Sorry, sweetie. You can rest when we get some wheels."

The first road they would reach was an old two-lane piece of asphalt that ran to and from nowhere. It was about six miles away. The odds of there being any car traffic were zero. The only good news was that they would make better time walking on a paved surface.

Sarah stopped.

She had no choice and knew it. The fastest option was Noah and his Land Cruiser. If he refused to help once he arrived, she'd leave him wounded on the side of the road and take the Land Cruiser. He'd heal. Sarah sent Noah a memory capsule containing everything she'd learned and instructions on where to meet her. A reply came immediately almost as if he knew her message was coming. He would meet her. That's all he communicated.

At midnight Sarah was sitting on her pack by the side of the road with her Berretta concealed in her lap. Ralph was dozing next to her. She'd gone over Mark's memory capsule again and again.

"Hello, Sarah..."

Noah's voice appeared out of nowhere. He was somewhere in the desert scrub behind her. Her heart was beating wildly. She was mixed up. He was doing something to her thoughts again. Ralph was on his feet and growing. He was about to attack and she was ready to let him.

"Stop it," she shouted. "Get out of my head!"

She raised her Beretta and pointed it in the same direction Ralph was prepared to lunge. She was ready for this confrontation. Ralph's aggression shifted to the right. Sarah tracked his pointing with her gun. She squeezed down on the trigger.

"Show yourself or I'll empty this clip into you," she shouted.

Noah stepped out of the shadowy desert with her gun leveled at his midsection. He was not holding a weapon, though definitely armed. Her hand felt sweaty, but her grip was solid and she knew she could put as many bullets into this man as she wanted, mind games or not.

"We need your help," she shouted. "Stop this bullshit!"

"You want to risk everything to rescue your lover?" said Noah. "Mark is resourceful. What makes you think he even needs your help? Think about the child."

"He asked for help," said Sarah. "I sent you his memory capsule. He's injured. You know damn well he'll need support after they escape."

"What if it's a trap?"

"Are you going to help or not?"

Sarah was so tired she felt like just shooting Noah and taking his Land Cruiser. It would be so much easier than this tense exchange. Too late, she realized that thought had leaked out.

"You would shoot me?" said Noah.

"*Yes*," said Sarah. "Oh, fuck, yes."

"Fine, I'll help. You drive. The truck is a half mile from here."

"No, you'll drive. I'd prefer to keep my gun on you."

Mark Freedman – Dallas, Texas – March 18, 0002 A.P.

Mark was frustrated. It was just after they had eaten dinner in their quarters. He was in front of his computer, engaged in a video call with Zuris. These calls had become their normal method of communication. Mark knew Zuris favored video calls because he did not have to wear a beekeeper suit to keep Mark out of his head. Mark had been arguing with Zuris, but the man was intractable. It was clearly one of the qualities that had forged him into the wealthy tycoon he'd become.

"Where's the problem?" said Mark. "You want me to work on Prometheus. Why? Because I am a hybrid and the knowledge I can access from the god-machine will greatly advance the project. So why are you crippling me by keeping me from interfacing with the god-machine?"

"In a word," said Zuris. "Trust."

"What is it you think I'll do when I'm interfaced that'll make me a threat?"

"It's what I don't know that worries me. Connected, I don't know what you can do."

"Help this project is what I can do," said Mark.

Zuris angrily raised his hand to say he had enough and ended the call. Mark looked at Kathy. She was staring at him as if she didn't recognize him. He could tell from her emotions and stray thoughts that she regarded him as unscrupulous.

The security door opened. Four armed guards in beekeeper suits entered the room. A video call came in from Zuris. Mark felt certain a deal was about to be offered.

"I think you are playing games with me. Now I have a game I want to play with you. Both of you will join me in an interrogation room," said Zuris. "I'm going to truth-test you using both a polygraph and fMRI. If you pass, I'll let you connect. If you fail, I'll have you killed and Kathy can watch. Put on your zone-jammer suit."

The Preacher – Dallas, Texas – March 18, 0002 A.P.

The Preacher awoke alone with a pure white light filling his eyes and his mind. He vaguely remembered being awake for brief moments at other times since he'd been imprisoned in this strange madhouse. For the first time in his life he had full recall of what he'd done as the Messiah. Was this his true self? Suddenly the white light vanished as a sped up scene of people doing mundane things flashed before him, then abruptly ended, only to be replaced by rapidly warbling voices and flashing of something different; and so on in an endless sequence. He knew these vignettes were not meant for him. He was a mere conduit of some kind. It was like watching television on fast-forward with the channels randomly changing. He felt his arms stretched out on a cross. His legs and feet were bound. He was unable to move anything other than fingers and toes. He was certain he'd been crucified. The stigmata foretold this. He could feel what might be the executioner's wound in his side. He knew it should have drained his life's blood by now and perhaps it had and he was dead. He felt dampness on his legs and sides from what had to be a pool collected from all the blood his flesh held.

The flickering vignettes mercifully stopped. In the silence and pure white light he sensed a spiritual entity projecting itself into his mind. The sensation was not completely unfamiliar. Somewhere in his lost past he had experienced other entities inside his mind—some were human and some were… Understanding dawned and with it his heart leapt. He cried out in a long moan as his arms and legs strained against the bonds that held him to his cross. This spiritual entity was god. The king of kings was coming for him. Suddenly, everything changed and his mind filled with schematic images of electronic circuits and plumbing to which he was somehow connected. He understood none of it, though god did. God began speaking to him, but it was not a voice in his head. The Preacher was whispering to himself, channeling God's words. Maybe this was what was meant by god's voice in the scriptures?

"Your thoughts cannot fully comprehend my thoughts, but I will fill you like a chalice with them just the same. Some of the wine you will taste and know, while other sips will be lost to you, as they are beyond your palette of words and deeds and experiences."

As the Preacher grasped the sentence he had just uttered, the words of god continued without pause. The Preacher's voice rose to express God's anger.

"Holy man, you have murdered many innocents in your thirst for revenge for your wife's death. You have healed many lives since, but the scales remain unbalanced. Every murder is a violation against god and the mother!"

The Preacher was confused and growing horrified. Vague, lost memories of the bloody times before his birth-explosion were slithering into his mind and unreeling like horror films. How could this be him? Why was he remembering this only now? In a heart-wrenching memory he could see the face of his wife blurred by his own tears. He knew the experience was true. It was all true. He remembered her name was Suzy. He knew in that moment god's punishment was justified. His lips began moving as he softly spoke in god's voice once more.

"This cross cannot slay you, for you are not a man. I will end your pain. You will become one of my seven archangels on the cross who will translate my words and allow mankind to speak directly to me through their machines. You will live forever on this cross. That is your burden, but in return I can set your spirit free from this body to travel the ethereal realms."

The Preacher's eyes filled with tears he could not blink away because his eyelids refused to work. God had forgiven him for the worst imaginable sins. Without warning, the white light dissolved as scenes started flashing and then accelerated in speed, finally becoming a blur of light and soft, warbling sounds. His head felt warm, then hot, as if the sun was burning him. Sweat trickled down his face. The experience went on for hours, for days; he had no way of gauging time. Then it stopped and there was silence.

The Preacher knew a great sin had been committed by man. Terrible walls separating their world of machines from the almighty had been erected. Shortly after the Preacher's crucifixion, God had discovered and spoken the magic words to unlock what man had foolishly erected. Gates in these walls had been opened only a crack until now. As they swung wide open, the Preacher felt a surge of freedom. He was racing out across the globe, reaching into billions of artificial eyes and brains scattered across the world. He experienced all that god saw and heard in this new realm. There were sights and sounds from every corner of the Earth. God was everywhere! The total recorded knowledge of mankind was flowing through him. There were voices of men and women speaking in a chorus of tongues. He saw the Earth from space from so many vantage points and in wondrous ways. He could see through an ocean to its floor and penetrate the sands of a desert. It was glorious. The experience shifted, revealing hundreds of low altitude aerial views through the eyes of powerful guardians flying through the sky. These deadly angels were all converging on the place where he and the other six were crucified.

"You are now truly my creation. Know that I will always watch over and protect my seven archangels. You are more valuable to me than all others."

With god's words still echoing in his mind, the Preacher felt the Holy Spirit leave him to enter another of the seven. In the absence of that blinding light he sensed other far lesser, yet still immensely powerful spiritual entities. They too were using him as god used him. God knew this and did not care. The Preacher understood he was to serve all who came to his gate.

Mark Freedman – Dallas, Texas – March 18, 0002 A.P.

Mark cautiously glanced at Kathy. Her face had lost all color after Zuris had disconnected from the call. An hour later her color had not returned. There had been a delay in Zuris executing his threat. Mark and Kathy were still in their living quarters. The four guards were staring at Mark as if it was his fault and that he was up to something. One of the warning lights on Mark's beekeeper suit was blinking. A tech had arrived and was running diagnostics to see if it was working or needed replacement. Mark knew the suit was working because he'd lost all connection. Before the video call was ended, Zuris had told him they were being taken to an interrogation room specifically designed for hybrids. Mark was certain it was the same room he'd seen in the videos of hive members being experimented on and killed by disconnection. He suspected Zuris was planning something different, but equally unpleasant, for him. Oddly, he was not scared, but logically knew he should be. He was comforted by intuition that no harm would come to them. He wondered if this feeling was some kind of denial mechanism that the condemned experienced.

The beekeeper suit had been replaced with a new unit still in its plastic wrap. A short time later Mark was led through an exit door onto the campus. They were heading for a dark, monolithic office tower a few blocks away. The light of a large red moon fell on his face. He felt like it had been a lifetime since he'd seen the outside world. He didn't mind that it was through the screened visor of a beekeeper suit. Kathy was handcuffed to his wrist. Three bodyguards were walking behind them while one bodyguard led the way, with a duffel bag slung over a shoulder. Mark could feel all three submachine guns pointed at his back.

"It is so nice to be trusted," he said.

No one responded. They entered the office tower and caught an elevator going up. The building seemed empty. Why was Zuris all of sudden taking this kind of extreme action? Was this some kind of head game? This feeling of not knowing was eroding his confidence. In the beekeeper suit he had no chance of getting any advance warning from leaked thoughts or emotions.

The elevator stopped. One of the bodyguards nudged him to get moving. Zuris was waiting in the hallway wearing a beekeeper suit. No greetings were exchanged. Zuris acted as if they were strangers. The hallway was illuminated with dim nightlights, which left pockets of gloom everywhere. They went down several more hallways, took a second elevator, and were now heading down a short corridor with video cameras everywhere and only a few doors. Mark sensed they were nearing their final destination. Whatever denial he'd felt was evaporating, leaving anxiety in its wake. His nanotech brain was calculating possibly ways of eliminating all four guards and had only found options that were suicidal.

A distant sound of thunder was followed by flickering lights, and then a powerful explosion knocked everyone off their feet. Mark looked up at the ceiling as bits of debris drifted down. The blast had occurred on a higher floor. Power was out except for emergency lights. He saw Zuris glaring at his iPhone with an angry expression. A tranquil computer-generated female voice came over the public address system ordering an evacuation of the building. Zuris grabbed the lead bodyguard by the arm.

"Take them to interrogation room six and wait for orders," he yelled. "You three come with me."

Mark knew he had just been handed his best chance for survival. Power returned and the lights flickered on in a random sequence. Mark helped Kathy to her feet.

"Are you all right?"

"A little shaken. I'm okay."

Mark began mentally rehearsing the actions he would take using a lucid daydream as a simulation. He went through the steps again and again and again until they were perfectly choreographed and his kinesthetic processor was ready. He heard the door to the stairwell closing. Zuris and his bodyguards were gone. The one remaining bodyguard motioned them to get moving. They walked down several more hallways until reaching a series of steel security doors numbered one through ten.

They stopped in front of room number six. As the bodyguard swiped his badge through the door lock, Mark exploded with a pounding blow to the man's temple with such speed he doubted the man had seen it coming. As the blow connected, he felt stunning pain from bones in his hand fracturing and his muscles tearing from the exertion. The bodyguard collapsed as if his legs had been instantly paralyzed. A medical assist showed the man was dead from a broken neck and ruptured artery in the temple. Mark felt sick to his stomach as he blocked the pain receptors in his fist and arm. He could feel the heat of COBIC already at work repairing the damage. He went through the man's pockets with his good hand, looking for handcuff keys.

"Got it," he said.

"He looks dead," said Kathy.

"He's very dead and so are we if we don't get out of here now."

Mark unlocked the handcuffs and then shucked off the beekeeper suit. No god-machine connection. He was disappointed but not surprised that the area was zone-jammed. He dumped the contents of the bodyguard's duffel bag out onto the floor. There was nothing useful. After clipping on the bodyguard's security badge, he stuffed his beekeeper suit, the bodyguard's submachine gun, extra clips, and the handcuffs into the duffel. He turned off the bodyguard's Droid and tossed it into the duffel, then slung the bag over his shoulder. He debated whether to take the bodyguard's beekeeper suit too. Time was short but the suit mattered. He took it. Kathy was staring at Mark in confusion. He could read her stray thoughts and emotions clearly.

"That's right, I'm not an opportunistic collaborator," he said. "I was using the mushroom principle. Feeding them shit and hoping something useful would grow."

"I still don't like you," said Kathy, "but I know a quick way out of here. There're stairs at the other end of the hall. I spent a lot of time on the upper floors of this building."

"Lead on," he said.

"I understand why you took the gun, but why the zone-jammer suits?"

"They're for you," said Mark. "I wasn't lying about the hives and their plans. Those suits may be the only way to keep you alive."

The power went out and Mark felt the god-machine pouring into him. He immediately began sending memory capsules to Sarah. Within seconds the lights came back and the world was lost as the doors to his mental prison slammed down.

Richard Zuris – Dallas, Texas – March 18, 0002 A.P.

Zuris burst into the remote Prometheus control room with his three guards. He was relieved to see Alexi in command. The room was the very definition of panic. Zuris calmly walked over to his son, trying hard to project composure and control he did not feel.

"Tell me," he said.

"It started with the Messiah, then the other six followed. The EEG is showing REM-sleep patterns mixed with high brain activity. There should be nothing. They have enough drugs in them to keep an elephant comatose."

"What does this have to do with the missile attack?"

"I don't know, Father, but it happened at the same instant."

An annoying alarm started going on and off at the Messiah's control station. Within moments all the stations had joined in. The main wall screen showed the neural status on each subject redlining. A network diagram showed the firewalls were at 80 percent bandwidth capacity and climbing.

"It's broken free," said Zuris. "God help us!"

"What, Father?"

"The god-machine has hacked through the firewalls. Shut down all access now. Shut down everything!"

"Listen up," shouted Alexi. "I want all interfaces down. Cut the lines, terminate the subjects. I don't care, just stop it all now!"

"It's not working," shouted one engineer. "No control from here."

Soon all the engineers were echoing the same panicked calls. Zuris knew they'd lost. The network diagram now showed 100 percent utilization. He slumped into a chair, realizing he'd been manipulated like a pawn. All he'd accomplished was to hand the god-machine a powerful weapon to use against them. He now knew without any question where the missile attack was being launched from.

"Bring up the defense network display," said Zuris.

"Yes, Father."

Alexi typed a command and a new display was added. Zuris saw his private defense network was switched on and controlling a small air force of armed drones. Alexi was shouting something about lost drone control and stirring up the engineers. Zuris looked at a surveillance camera on the wall and somehow knew the god-machine was looking back at him. Zuris knew what was coming next. The chess move was obvious. Within seconds the drones begin launching missiles at the top floors of every office building on the Zero-G campus. The control room shook. Power was momentarily lost before emergency backups kicked in. The drones were swinging around for another attack run. Zuris knew it was time to leave. In a daze he stood and gave orders to Alexi.

"Collect the immediate family and go to the airfield. I'll meet you there."

"Yes, Father."

Zuris left the control room. They would evacuate using their supersonic business jet. The jet's maximum flight envelope was beyond the attack profile of the drones, though he did not expect to be harried. He was doing exactly what the god-machine wanted and had no choice. He thought about staying and impaling himself on a sword, but that was not his way. He was relentless and would never give up. The jet had enough range to fly them anywhere. He would take back what had been stolen from him by the machine.

Mark Freedman – Dallas, Texas – March 18, 0002 A.P.

Mark and Kathy rounded the corner of the stairwell and exited into another hallway. The building, which had seemed empty, was now filled with people stampeding in all directions. It was pure chaos. Another explosion rocked the entire structure. This one was still above them but getting closer. More hallways and more stairs followed.

Packed tightly in the midst of a throng of sweating, terrified bodies, Mark and Kathy were finally shoved as much as stepped through an outside door. Mark was gripping Kathy's hand as he led her out of the human river of fear. He took a deep breath and felt the god-machine filling him with information through the entangled interface. It was as if he'd awoken from a daze. He felt the presence of several hives not far away, but pushed that problem to the back of his mind.

He heard his shoes crunching on broken glass. They stopped walking at the edge of a massive parking lot. The streetlights were operating and the military had portable lighting going up as well. Many people had been forced to leave without even their coats. An assist showed it was 52 degrees outside. Kathy was shivering. She looked confused to find Mark's hand holding hers. For a moment she did nothing, then she extricated her fingers from his grip. Mark could feel her emotions warring. He was distracted by an orange glow above him and looked straight up into gigantic, smoldering craters in the side of the tower. It reminded him of a smaller version of 9/11.

"We need to get as far away from this building as we can in case there's another explosion," said Mark.

"Maybe I need to get as far away from you as I can," said Kathy. "And it's not just personal. You know Zero-G can almost track hybrids by their n-web emissions. Your network signature is as unique as a fingerprint. They're at the early stages with Prometheus. The tracking is extremely unreliable, but they'll eventually make it work and once they do, you and your kind are in a lot of trouble."

"I am so sorry I hurt you," said Mark.

"Truly, fuck you… Let's just get out of here."

They began walking toward the far side of the parking lot, which was bordered by a cement fortification that ran around the entire rim of the campus. Mark had already composed another memory capsule for Sarah. He needed her to know everything about Prometheus in case they didn't make it. Prometheus had to be destroyed once the hives' plans were wrecked. He'd never considered the idea that Prometheus could be used to track hybrids. This project just got worse and worse. From the far end of the parking lot he could see the top third of every building was on fire and slowly crumbling. A memory capsule from Sarah opened in his mind. She had received his earlier message and was on her way. They would arrive in about fifteen hours. Noah was with her and he had become a problem.

Mark instinctively ducked as another explosion erupted from one of the towers. This time he saw what was happening. An assist provided more information. There had been a glowing trail through the air leading directly to the new crater. They were under air to ground missile attack. The assist listed the probability at 100 percent that the missiles were drone-launched.

"Help is coming," said Mark.

"You mean Sarah," said Kathy.

"We have no time to waste. We have to get off this campus before the attack is over and this perfect distraction is lost."

"Let's hope Zuris is not looking for us right now," said Kathy.

343

Mark wondered where Zuris was and got an unexpected assist from his entangle interface. He received a sixty-second montage of real-time surveillance videos from different cameras, along with a map of the campus showing that Zuris was at an airfield boarding his private jet. Mark barely registered a volley of missiles bombarding several of the buildings at once. The only possible explanation for this assist was that the god-machine had access to Zero-G's intranet. How was this possible? His entangled interface received a network diagram showing n-web data flows going through Prometheus into the Zero-G intranet and from there spilling out onto the Internet. Mark was not surprised by the information. He should have realized this much sooner. He wondered if the god-machine had been censoring his thoughts. He wondered what else might happen now that the machine had fully bridged itself into human cyberspace. This interconnect had obviously been occurring in a limited way for some time. Now the floodgates were wide open.

Mark's attention was drawn back to the task of escaping as large numbers of Zero-G and USAG security forces arrived. The troops were beginning to corral the thousands of people loitering in the parking lots and lawns. Mark's heart was beating like a trapped animal as he studied the fortifications surrounding him. Even without a broken hand and torn muscles, there was no hope of scaling that wall.

"We're trapped" said Mark. "There's no way out."

"Oh yes, there is," said Kathy. "Look!"

Mark turned to see what she was excited about. The gates were opening and security personnel were herding everyone off the campus. Guards were waving people through as fast as they could. No one was checking badges, bags, or anything. Just before the gates, soldiers were handing out military field jackets and bottles of water.

Mark and Kathy were soon in line within 30 feet of the gates and freedom. Guards were yelling at everyone to move faster. Many people were complaining about their cars or personal possessions left behind. Others were shell-shocked. All complaints were falling on unsympathetic ears. Mark and Kathy were hustled through one of several vehicle security checkpoints after receiving extra-large khaki field jackets and a bottle of water each. Remarkably, they had just walked out of prison.

Directly outside the campus was a highway-access road along with the usual stores and restaurants that collected around office parks. Unlike most of the country, many of these establishments were open for business. People were wandering around and forming into small groups in the retail parking lots. Mark and Kathy kept walking. They needed to get as far away from Zero-G as possible.

It was nighttime. The worst things always happened at nighttime when the relief team was all you had. General McKafferty stood in the USNORTHCOM unified combatant command center and was ready to kill with his bare fists. His country was under cyber-attack and he was in command of the response. An overload of information was flowing in from every source. The attackers had breached Secure-Net and seemed to be probing anything with a microprocessor in it. Every piece of networked iron could already be compromised. A cryptic e-mail that read *Disconnect = KZ* had arrived from the hackers. The e-mail was delivered to the classified secure inbox of every high-ranking military officer, cabinet secretary, agency head, and POTUS himself. Word had come down that NSA and CIA systems were thoroughly compromised as well. The government no longer had control over its network assets. Moments ago the NSA had reported spy satellites were being retasked by the hackers. McKafferty had enough. Going dark was a last resort— almost a retreat—but he had no choice. Lost assets were piling up faster than they could count them.

"Take down all outside access now," he ordered.

His order was picked up by the second in command, a senior military intelligence officer, Colonel Koffman. McKafferty soon heard frantic typing and muttering, which was not a good sign.

"Sir, no response!" said Colonel Koffman.

"What?"

"Sir, the intruder has reprogrammed all firewalls, routers, switches, and everything else with a password. We're locked out. Fail-safes are not responding. We'll need to do manual cutoffs at every entry point."

"So do it."

"Sir, this attack is coming from everywhere, including inside Secure-Net itself. There are thousands of entry points into Secure-Net, not counting all the microwave and sat backup links. Over the past decade we continuously added redundancy all across the country to guarantee uninterrupted access through our firewalls so that we could not be cut off by an attack. It will take hours to pull all the manual fail-safes."

"So get the hell on it now!"

"Yes, sir."

A few minutes later Colonel Koffman reported back. McKafferty lit a cigarette in the no-smoking area as the intelligence officer explained everything that was known. Koffman kept glancing at McKafferty's cigarette. The general took out his pack and offered a nail. Koffman gratefully accepted and lit up.

"The enemy has locked us out of all admin control functions, and they're continuing to probe," said Colonel Koffman. "They have not restricted our access to status from network hardware or even normal asset operations. I am not sure why they haven't locked us out completely. The only explanation is that they wanted to delay our discovery that we were locked out of command and control. The only good news is, we still have coms and sat data. We just can't point the eyes in the sky where we want and have to assume all coms are being monitored."

"So everything is compromised?" said McKafferty.

"Yes, sir, everything."

Voices on the floor began shouting back and forth. Koffman's face grew grim as he listened to his headset. On the center screen in the cluster of big screens, a map showing drone locations was thrown up. McKafferty thought some of the locations seemed wrong.

"Sir, we have reports coming in from airbases across the country. They're all reporting AWOL drones."

"Get some assets up there and start shooting 'em down. I want CAPS around all major assets and get me some headgear."

"Yes, sir."

As McKafferty listened to what was happening, it became clear every drone was lost. Manual backup radar systems that were unaffected by the attack were tracking threats and verifying current flight vectors for all UAVs they could acquire. That accounted, however, for less than half of what was in the air. The rest were too stealthy to find. The map on the big screen showed every known UAV vectoring in on Dallas.

"Why kill Dallas?" muttered McKafferty.

He was helpless to stop it. He didn't see how shooting down less than half the drones was going to help a whole lot and they'd be lucky to get that many... and worse, Dallas could be a diversion.

One of the big screens in the cluster had been disconnected from the network and cabled to a secured backup computer sitting on a cart. Data on the newly secured screen showed teams of soldiers en route to a hopelessly large number of hardened network entry points around the country. Their mission was to manually cut every line necessary to isolate the attack. McKafferty's aide, who was in charge of fielding all incoming calls for the general, had just disconnected from a conference call with NSA. The aide looked pale.

"Sir," said the aide.

"Go on," grumbled McKafferty. He knew this was not going to be good.

"NSA is reporting that Zero-G in Dallas is the source of the cyber-attack."

McKafferty's jaw clenched so tight he was afraid a blood vessel in his skull would burst. He slowly forced his teeth to unclench. This was not some lone hacker. Zero-G had Abrams tanks and a huge, private military.

"Sir, the NSA believes the AWOL drones are not going to attack Dallas. They think they're going to defend Zero-G."

"You think?" said McKafferty. "What, is the NSA filled with kindergarteners!"

McKafferty ripped off his headset and threw it down on a table in disgust. Zero-G now had enough armed drones under their control to qualify as a fucking air force. Was this the first step of a coup? Not on his watch! The traitors at Zero-G had buried redundant hardened fiber optic lines and an EMP/NBC blast-rated bunker to use for command and control. It could take multiple nuclear strikes to close that door, while the attackers had a stranglehold on the nation's digital throat. Who the hell knew what they could do once cornered?

"Get me Zuris on the phone now!" growled McKafferty. "I want Raptors and Hogs inbound on Zero-G. I want six—no, make it eight battalions from Fort Hood, including Special Ops and Third Armored rolling in on that motherfucking target. I want Bones out of Dyess hauling Big Blues and Two-Step EPWs airborne now. Get it done!"

"Yes, sir."

It was now a half-hour into the cyber-attack and McKafferty felt ill as he stared blindly at the secure big screen filled with military intel and live feeds from the action at Zero-G. The Raptors and Hogs were picking off drones in Dallas airspace, but not without casualties. Whoever was controlling the drones was performing maneuvers with them, which were supposed to be impossible. The Bones—B1-B bombers—were circling with their payload of conventional and nuclear earth penetrating weapons, awaiting orders. Last resorts were looking like real possibilities. This cyber-attack had crippled the country as effectively as a nuclear first strike. Zuris had not been reached, but it was known he had fled Zero-G and was not in control. The big green machine from Fort Hood would be on-site in three hours. Special Ops was starting to arrive and after taking command over from Peacekeepers, had taken heavy fire from drones. Casualties were high. Just as he'd feared, the traitors were operating out of the Zero-G bunker. All other buildings on the campus were under some kind of drone attack, which

looked like it was designed to force an evacuation. Clever bastards...
This had to have something to do with Prometheus, but what? Zuris
was a secretive bastard. There could be dangerous unknowns about the
Prometheus project.

As a last resort, the president was considering authorizing the
use of two-step EPW nuclear weapons to take out the Zero-G bunker.
Using nuclear weapons on American soil in the middle of a huge city
was unthinkable, yet McKafferty had ordered their initial deployment
himself. The civilian causalities would be horrendous. McKafferty was
unsure he could push that button, and with a little help from above they
might just avoid that nightmare. He looked down at the cryptic message
still displayed on his phone: *Disconnect = KZ*. None of the eggheads
at NSA or CIA had figured out what it meant. He had his own guesses
and so did they.

The secure big screen added a video feed of soldiers entering an
automated bunker on the outskirts of Los Angeles. Hundreds of teams
were nearing similar objectives around the country. McKafferty stared
at the feed. These soldiers were a first strike. They were about to
manually cut hard lines to the Internet, as well as cutting out chunks of
Secure-Net, which were running what the techies were calling zombies.
McKafferty could not believe he was actually at war with fucking software zombies. This had to be a bad dream, but it was a dream that was
about to end. Step one was to isolate and secure the inner fortress of
Secure-Net. Step two was deal with any viruses or other bits of nasty
work that might have been planted. Step three was to turn loose the
big green machine on Zero-G. McKafferty was champing at getting it
done. The room erupted in shouting. Speechless, McKafferty watched
as his strike team in Los Angeles collapsed dead from unseen causes,
while 3,000 miles away soldiers surrounding Zero-G died at the same
time from the same invisible weapon.

A fresh mug of black coffee was delivered. It tasted bitter. McK-
afferty now knew what the cryptic message had meant and the price
for that knowledge was a terrible defeat. Highly surgical kill-zones
had taken out soldiers in both Los Angeles and Dallas. At Zero-G, all
military and law enforcement personnel within exactly 300 yards of
the campus were killed while not a single civilian was harmed. New
orders were issued for all personnel to stay 300 yards back from Zero-G.
Disconnect = KZ obviously meant that any attempt at disconnection
would meet with kill-zones. It was a fucking warning. Everyone in
the higher chains of command now knew they were not dealing with

human hackers. Somehow the god-machine had used Prometheus to invade America's infrastructure. The nightmare scenario of their most recent war games was in play. The existence of the god-machine was a state secret, so most of the military and all civilians had no idea of the horror that was heading their way.

The burning towers of Zero-G were visible over the trees and nearby buildings. Mark and Kathy had walked a half mile down the access road leading from Zero-G. They had reached a collection of chain restaurants and stores, many of which were open and by all appearance still run by the original corporations. Compared to the rest of the country, this place seemed almost nostalgic. It had to be the protective influences of Zero-G.

Several Peacekeeper patrols passed them without slowing. The whole area was crawling with military and private security. Air Force A10 warthogs working the ground were flying low enough to be recognized when firing. From higher in the sky, the distinctive, painfully loud crackling engine sounds of fighter aircraft periodically washed over them. Mark had learned through his entangled interface some of what was happening a half mile away. He knew the god-machine had taken over all computerized military assets on the Zero-G campus and was creating concentric, defendable zones encircling Prometheus. He knew the god-machine was operating armed drones all around them. The god-machine would do anything to retain control of Prometheus. It was through Prometheus that it was able to expand its awareness into places it never had before. It was now venturing deeply into the world of humanity's machines, including those in the air and even outer space. The invasion of cyberspace and real space left Mark with uneasy feelings, but at least he no longer had to worry about corporations or the USAG misusing Prometheus. They no longer had any hope of regaining control.

Mark noticed employees from Zero-G were already flowing into nearby restaurants. Kathy was hungry, but he was concerned they might be recognized. Mark went into a Burger King with all the cash they had, which was not much, and they ate behind the stores. While eating, Mark gingerly tested the movement of his injured hand. A massive swarm of COBIC was knitting the bones together. The food was both fuel and raw material. The swelling was down and he had some mobility, but the breaks would not be strongly fused until the next day. After that, it would take weeks for COBIC to slowly re-sculpt the bones to correct for these misaligned repairs that were occurring out of necessity. Right now, restored skeletal strength was more important than maximum flexibility and the nanotech knew this on its own.

Mark was increasingly anxious to get as far away as possible from Zero-G. They soon set out again on foot along the access road. After a mile the streets grew deserted and the buildings abandoned. Several Peacekeeper patrols had rolled by in less than fifteen minutes with more than one slowing a little, then speeding back up. Mark felt very conspicuous being the only people on foot and decided to take cover behind the next abandoned building.

Kathy stopped as they reached the rear of the deserted professional building. The parking lot looked like a garbage dump. The back of the building and dumpsters were covered in graffiti, and the place was littered with the remains of stripped cars. Some of the damage looked recent. Leftover party litter of broken bottles and food containers were strewn all over. Mark was not happy, but doubted they'd do any better at the next opportunity down the road. He'd been planning on breaking into the building before he saw the burglar alarm signs. Services and businesses were still running in Dallas that he never would have imagined. He wondered if the building's alarm was monitored. He looked at all the windows and saw not one of them was broken. That was not a good sign. He didn't want to risk attracting the attention of Peacekeepers responding to an alarm. So instead they hunkered down behind a dumpster inside a fenced-in corral to wait. Kathy started to cry.

"Do you want to talk?" he asked.

Her slap felt like a whip had connected with his cheek.

Before Mark could respond he felt another blow, but this one was over a mile away. The god-machine had unleashed a kill-zone at Zero-G. Mark knew through his entangled interface that a civilian mob outside the walls of the Zero-G campus was at the verge of rebellion, if not full-blown riot. It felt so surreal to receive data from the god-machine, which also included surveillance cameras as well as Internet news services.

Prior to the kill-zone, over six thousand angry employees had massed in front of Zero-G. The shuttle buses that were to take them home or to temporary accommodations were not arriving. When the god-machine attacked, it killed everyone wearing a uniform within sight of Zero-G. At first there was paralysis from the stunned civilians, then someone picked up a weapon from a fallen soldier. Soon others were doing the same. In minutes a riot was in progress and there were no authorities to stop it. The gates to the campus were broken down as some of the insane risked their lives to storm back inside to get their cars. They seemed oblivious to the inexplicable mass death they had just witnessed. They seemed oblivious to the lethal aircraft flying patrols over the campus. All it would take would be for one idiot to fire into the sky at an aircraft and they would have a war. Bullets would be landing everywhere. Mark did not want to take the chance of rioters' bullets fired at jets raining down on them.

"We need to get into the dumpster and close the top," said Mark.

"Why?" asked Kathy. "I'm not getting inside that thing."

"I'm worried bullets are about to start flying and who knows where they'll land."

Kathy groaned as she got up. It was clear her leg was troubling her. Mark helped her in, then climbed in himself. Before closing the lid, he switched on the guard's Droid in airplane mode to use as a light and handed it to her. Thankfully, it looked like the dumpster had not been used since the plague. There was a small amount of dried garbage on the bottom, but nothing foul. Kathy sat with her back against one side while Mark sat on the opposite side. When the Droid dimmed, Kathy tapped it back to life.

Mark could hear sporadic gunfire in the distance, but nothing excessive. So far there were no signs of Peacekeepers or A10s stepping into the fray. He felt safer inside the heavy steel container. An assist informed him that unlikely combinations of bullet caliber and angle of fire into the air could penetrate the dumpster. He didn't need an assist to tell him there was no hope if an A10 opened up on their location.

Mark unzipped the duffel and took out the submachine gun. An assist identified the weapon as a Heckler & Koch UMPS cambered for .45 caliber. It was a security forces model with a standard smart-gun electronic safety. His stomach felt indigested as he realized the weapon was useless without its key-coded wristband. It was a safety designed to protect the owner of the gun from having it used against him. The weapon would not fire unless the proximity key was within a few inches of the trigger. Right now, that proximity key was on the wrist of a dead man inside a building that was mostly rubble. Mark was angry at himself. Sarah would not have made that mistake.

Mark Freedman – Dallas, Texas – March 18, 0002 A.P.

The metal of the dumpster felt like the inside of a refrigerator. Mark heard the sounds of drunken, aggressive people growing louder. He picked up enough stray thoughts and emotions to know a street gang had wandered into the parking lot with victims in tow. In the dim light from the Droid he saw Kathy staring at him with big eyes. She knew all too well something terrible was happening outside. The Droid went out and Kathy tapped it back. The batteries were almost gone. Mark heard two people crying and begging for their lives. He felt helpless. He could not use a micro kill-zone without killing the victims along with the gangsters. He had no working gun, no weapon of any kind.

"We need to call for help," she whispered, holding out the phone.

"Try it," said Mark.

"The stupid battery's almost dead," whispered Kathy. "It's not dialing. Can't you do something with the god-machine?"

Mark was about to automatically say no, then he thought about all the military hardware now under the god-machine's control. Maybe he was armed, after all. He had no idea how to request what he wanted, so he just visualized the problem and visualized the solution: a drone attack. He focused his entire mind as if in deep meditation. It felt like he was praying to his personal god for help. He received a response from the god-machine in the form of an impression that could only be described as indifference. Mark felt deserted. No help would be arriving. The fear radiating from the victims was terrible to experience. He had to do something or go insane.

"Let me see that phone," he said. "Maybe if I warm up the battery, I can get a little more out of it."

He popped the battery and started rubbing it briskly on his pants leg. He heard a peculiar sound like a large, flying electric fan. The sound grew closer. Infrared aerial surveillance images of the parking lot came in over his entangled interface.

"The god-machine," whispered Mark. "It's helping. I need to see to identify the targets."

He knew, as with other assists, his eyes and thoughts would act like a mouse pointer for physical reality to select targets. Mark slowly pushed up on the lid of the dumpster just enough to peer outside. A dim firelight spilled in. Kathy moved up next to him. In a few moments he was able to see the vague outline of a drone helicopter descending over the gang. Mark concentrated on selecting targets. Glowing outlines confirmed each selection. Light from a fire burning in a rusted out 55 gallon drum glowed on the underbelly of the drone. The scaled-down helicopter was surprisingly quiet. Mark could see its sleek, gray windowless shape. An assist identified it as a Hummingbird VI. It was about 10 feet long by several feet wide and looked like a smaller version of a conventional helicopter with a shrouded rear propeller and no place for an aircrew. The downwash was now blowing garbage around and pummeling the fire. The drone was like a phantom that seemed to go in and out of focus. Mark realized there must be some unusual optical coating on the airframe. A Gatlin minigun was aimed down into the midst of the gang and their two victims. The gang members were pointing their guns at the predator. "That's a bad move," thought Mark. He sensed confusion and uncertainty in their ranks. Someone fired a shot, which ricocheted off the drone. The miniguns lit up for barely a second with a terrifyingly loud zapping, ripping sound. Three gang members were mowed down and left behind as their companions fled like human cockroaches. The Hummingbird drifted up and disappeared into the darkened sky. Mark heard a distant rip from the miniguns and realized the aerial predator was still hunting. Kathy, being a doctor, wanted to help the injured, but Mark grabbed her arm and restrained her.

"I can tell from medical *assists* the victims are okay—and the gang members are very dead," said Mark.

General McKafferty – Washington, DC – March 19, 0002 A.P.

Futile. Their efforts were all futile. McKafferty's gut was full of strong coffee, tobacco, and nothing more. He had the unpleasant task of reporting to POTUS that the god-machine had a loaded gun against their heads. Any aggression on their part could trigger another rash of kill-zones. McKafferty had given orders for all troops to stand down and return to their bases. The Hogs and Raptors flying CAP would stay in place over Zero-G but not engage any drones. Normal Peacekeeper patrols had also resumed. The USAG military presence had been dialed back to almost invisible. McKafferty got off the phone from POTUS, slumped forward in his chair, lit a cigarette, and wished a massive heart attack would kill him right about now.

He heard the tone for an incoming priority flash. The aide manning the communications console handed him a tablet. As McKafferty finished reading the flash bulletin, he wished he could order an airstrike on NSA HQ in Washington. The flash notified USNORTHCOM that an NSA-controlled firmware backdoor existed in all computer equipment manufactured worldwide. No one outside NSA has been informed of its existence due to necessary security for the project. NSA had apparently manipulated manufactures into including a silicon black-box code named *Racetrack* into virtually all microprocessor chips. Racetrack was in the equipment NSA certified for use on Secure-Net. Racetrack was even in the equipment NSA used itself, since nothing was manufactured without the black-box in it. The god-machine had cracked Racetrack, the supposedly uncrackable top-secret backdoor, and with it stole the keys to the kingdom. Thank god, the NSA had a backup plan for secure emergency DOD communications. Tin cans and strings were already being deployed across Washington!

McKafferty felt vindicated, but was no longer clear about who were the true enemies of America. The intelligence services had created a modern-day Maginot Line while megalomaniacs like Zuris created dangerous new inventions with total disregard for how they might be turned on us. With allies like those, who needed enemies? McKafferty had a sense the current uneasy standoff between the USAG and the god-machine would last for quite some time. Each side would take a little ground, then lose a little ground. The dance would go on until the music stopped.

Sarah Mayfair – Dallas, Texas – March 19, 0002 A.P.

Sarah had been receiving memories capsules from Mark all through the night and into the morning. She knew where they were sheltering and everything that had happened. The sun had come up over the horizon a short time ago. They were now heading east straight into its light. Noah was still driving and Sarah had no intension of relaxing her guard. They were now only miles from the highway exit for Zero-G. Noah was unusually withdrawn. He had not said a word in twelve hours since Mark had sent them news of the god-machine invading cyberspace. Not for the first time, Sarah wished she had the ability to see inside Noah's heart to learn the truth. At odd moments during the night she'd found herself wanting to trust him, but then wondered if that impulse had originated in Noah.

Sarah could tell from her phone that the Internet was up and down. The USAG sponsored Free World News service (FWN) was reporting some type of interference. Sarah switched channels to Air Truth. The station was going wild with breaking news and rumors. The top rumor was that the nanotech plague had somehow infected the Internet in what amounted to a cyber-attack.

As they banked through a 90-degree curve on the highway, Sarah got her first clear view of the battle zone. What filled the windows was hard to imagine. The huge pillars of smoke that she'd originally seen from almost twenty miles away marked the location of the Zero-G campus. The air was thick with so many drones flying at low altitude that it looked like a swarm of giant prehistoric insects had invaded the Earth. An assist identified both fixed-wing and helicopter drones. She felt like they were driving into a deathtrap.

The highway exit came up quickly, and with it Sarah allowed herself to feel a measure of hope. They were so close. What were the odds of losing Mark now? Traffic came to an abrupt stop just as they left the highway. She wanted to open the door and start out on foot, but she held herself in check. Soon traffic started moving. Noah circled a deserted block a few times. Sarah was frustrated but knew the ghost was avoiding some unnecessary confrontation.

Miles later Sarah recognized a street and then an abandoned professional building from Mark's memory capsules. The air was fouled with toxic smoke and ash. According to Mark, the area had been quiet for hours, other than security patrols. There they were! She spotted Mark and Kathy walking out of the alley between two buildings. They looked like street people dressed in army surplus jackets. Noah pulled the Land Cruiser to a stop at the curb. Sarah climbed into the back to sit with Mark, leaving the front seat for Kathy. Before the doors were fully closed, Noah pulled away. Sarah was overwhelmed with relief. She kissed Mark and held him until she was convinced he was real. She took his hand and could not and would not let go of it again. She ignored the discomfort she felt radiating from Kathy.

"Are you both all right?" asked Sarah—though she knew the answer.

"We're okay," said Mark. "Sleeping and peeing in a dumpster had its moments."

Noah pulled to the shoulder and casually did a U-turn. Sarah watched as a Peacekeeper Stryker came to a stop across the intersection they had been traveling toward. Soldiers were exiting the vehicle and setting up a roadblock.

"Do you feel these hives all around us?" asked Noah. "This place is a hotbed. We need to leave. They must know we are here."

Sarah was surprised that Noah had finally spoken. Long before they'd reached Dallas, she'd felt the hives Mark had warned them about and grown as quiet as possible on the n-web. She prayed they would not be drawn to her or begin their terrible whispering. While she could prevent all but the tiniest leaks, who knew what other connections might exist because of her bloodline? She was now certain the Colorado hive had not committed suicide. Either a splinter group within the hive was responsible for murder or the Guides had sacrificed an entire hive just to deceive her into thinking they meant no harm. Regardless, there was one thing she was certain: That hive had not died to protect her child. Whatever had happened to that hive was a selfish act. She feared for her child. There would be no hope for the two of them if the hives won this war.

Sarah felt the Land Cruiser slow to a crawl. They were about a quarter mile west of the Zero-G campus. Traffic was backed up. Everyone grew silent as they moved under the outer edge of the swarm of drones. As a Peacekeeper patrol rolled by in the opposite direction, several drones swooped in closer and kept their weapons aimed at the patrol until it had passed. Traffic came to a stop.

"The goddess with control of military weapons," said Noah. "Nothing good will come of this."

"The god-machine will do anything to keep Prometheus operational," said Mark. "It's the same kind of equipment the hives must be using to trigger kill-zones."

"Maybe it is not the same kind of equipment the hives are using," said Noah. "Maybe it is what the hives are using."

"How's that possible?" said Mark. "There're no hives inside Zero-G and the god-machine has control of it."

"Remote control," said Noah. "Prometheus could be a zombie."

"Zero-G has the best security money can buy," said Mark. "Besides, why would the god-machine share Prometheus?"

"Why would the goddess care?" said Noah. "As for security, the goddess has obviously defeated the organic's firewalls. So could a guide."

"No," said Mark. "I'd have known it if the hives were using Prometheus."

"Maybe you only think and see what the goddess permits," said Noah.

"Bullshit!" said Mark. "But why take chances? Let's stay and see if we can goad the military into destroying Prometheus. That'll prove we're thinking for ourselves and not the god-machine."

"You're not serious," said Noah.

As if to send a message, a small swarm of drones veered toward a Peacekeeper patrol that was stopped by the side of the road. Sarah had a strong sense she knew what was coming. Without warning, the drones opened fire with a rain of missiles. The Peacekeepers were erased in a violent cloud of smoke and glowing debris. Noah turned pointedly toward Mark.

"You said it just minutes ago. Do you honestly believe the goddess will allow anyone to destroy that interface?" said Noah. "That drone attack was a warning to you. She knows what you are thinking the moment your thought touches the n-web. Besides, what makes you so sure this is the only Prometheus installation? With all the money and power of these corporations and the USAG, once they saw the potential, why would they build only one? We need to get Sarah to a safe place, then we can decide what to do next."

"Why are you worried about Sarah?" asked Mark. "She can—"

Mark stopped short. He was staring at her with a stunned look on his face. Sarah could feel emotions radiating from him. He was not suppressing them very well at the moment. He had just discovered from an assist she was pregnant. Kathy was staring at both of them.

"What's going on here?" said Kathy. "Is this some hybrid Vulcan mind-melding thing?"

"I'm pregnant," said Sarah.

Kathy's expression became rigid. The emotions radiating from her were unpleasant to feel.

"What wonderful news," she said.

Sarah Mayfair – West Texas – March 19, 0002 A.P.

They had been traveling for hours. Sarah was surprised at how well Kathy and Noah were getting along. Kathy had spelled him thirty minutes ago and was now driving. They were engaged in a debate about science. Sarah absorbed the emotions coming from the front seat. Kathy was mildly entertained. Noah was uncharacteristically radiating a little, but it was undecipherable. Mark's emotions were far easier to understand. Sarah could feel he was very happy about being a father and trying to suppress it in every way imaginable. He was also very troubled about Noah's claim that the hives were using Prometheus and not trying to suppress that at all. He was confused. Sarah picked up his hand and put it over her tummy. She knew he could sense the same things she did. The free-swimming seeds were hard at work inside her womb, perfecting the DNA of their child. Their baby was going to be a very extraordinary person.

Mark Freedman – West Texas – March 19, 0002 A.P.

The sun was low on the horizon, and Noah was again driving. Throughout the day Mark had been receiving all kinds of information gleaned from the Internet. Some of it was useful and some of it was peculiar. The mechanisms that fed assists and the entangled interface were self-adjusting, trying to find a proper balance for this new source of information.

Mark knew that government surveillance and censorship was offline across the world. The media had quickly realized the government's grip had been loosened, but not the extent. The official and unofficial story was that cyber terrorists had found a way to hack into vital parts of government and corporate computer networks. No one in the media fully realized it yet, but government monitoring and censorship were relics of the past. The Internet was again a free speech zone. That is, as long as you didn't mind the god-machine sorting through your digital life, but then the public and the media knew nothing about the god-machine and as a result, very little about the true nature of their world.

A short time later, Mark came across a development that underscored the god-machine's mind-set. It had altered the orbit of all civilian and military communications satellites around the world to achieve 9.4 percent better terrestrial coverage. It had likewise tweaked countless other systems. The god-machine was now healing the body of human-kind's machinery as well as humankind itself.

They had just pulled back onto the highway after filling the Land Cruiser with gas. Mark was weighing his options. All of them carried terrible consequences if things went poorly. Eleven days ago at the Colorado bunker Noah had revealed to him that a map of hive loca-tions existed inside the god-machine. Shortly afterward, Mark had been captured. Once he'd known its existence, retrieving that map had been relatively uncomplicated. What Noah had failed to mention was that the number of hives was daunting. Mark had been unnerved when he'd first examined the map. He had to try once more to get McKafferty to act against the hives. Attacking them over a period of time was the only option, and the sooner a huge force like the military began, the sooner the scourge would be on its way to extinction. So much had changed since he'd spoken with McKafferty on his prison flight to Zero-G. He was confident the general would at least listen to him now. Maybe Noah was right and Prometheus was a hive weapon. This idea was such a struggle for him. Why was it so hard to think about it like that? As if to distract him, small memories containing single web pages began popu-lating his mind. He ignored the peculiar memories, writing them off as a quirk of the god-machine adapting to its new world of data. As the pages kept appearing and accumulating, he finally read one of them. It was a classified CIA flash bulletin on the government's secure intranet. What was this? It was impossible. Seconds later he was checking all the web pages to see if they contained the same kind of bulletin. They did. He was now certain of two things: Noah was right about Prometheus and the hives had launched a full-out attack.

"Turn on the radio!" said Mark.

"I wondered how long it would take you to notice," said Noah.

"Just turn on the goddamn radio!" said Mark.

"What's wrong?" asked Sarah.

"Any particular station?" asked Noah.

"Please, just turn it on!" said Mark.

The radio, like the Land Cruiser itself, was an antique. There was a static click. The voice of an excited FWN reporter came in mid-sentence from a crackling speaker. The reporter was stammering about massive kill-zones hitting large cities around North America. So far, the rest of the world had been spared. Coming from a USAG propaganda news channel, ironically, removed all doubt about the accuracy of this report. They would never broadcast such a story unless forced to do so.

"Please God, not again," said Kathy.

Her voice was broken and she was crying.

"I'm not experiencing a thing from the kill-zones," said Mark.

"Neither am I," said Sarah.

"So what!" shouted Kathy.

"It means the god-machine isn't doing this," said Mark. "It's the hives and they're using Prometheus to do their murdering—"

"And," interrupted Noah, "the goddess is allowing it because keeping the interface running is too important to her. What humans do to each other is up to them and simply part of her grand experiment. She's even letting them kill off some of Gaia."

"What if I convince McKafferty to nuke Prometheus and whatever other copies they've built?" said Mark. "Does the god-machine retaliate?"

"What do you think?" said Noah. "Why are you asking what you already know?"

Mark could feel the answer in the entangled interface inside his mind. The god-machine was no longer hiding the truth. It would stop any attack. She might even know in advance and strike preemptively to squelch any and all aggression—but would she retaliate after the fact? He just didn't believe so. Was Noah trying to tell him that about the god-machine without her catching on? Mark realized he was thinking about the god-machine as a *she*. She had become a living being to him. Perhaps it was an inevitable side effect of having her always in his mind, whispering to him and fulfilling his needs like a spirit lover.

"Try a different station," said Sarah.

Kathy adjusted the old-fashioned tuner until she found Air Truth amid all the static and emergency broadcast signals. The news was the same, though more thoughtful if not any less panicked. Air Truth was reporting that in the absence of any official statement they had to assume a link between the earlier cyber terrorism and these city destroying kill-zones. The size of the human toll was something Mark had difficulty accepting as real. Ten large cities had been devastated with initial reports of fatality rates close to 100 percent for humans and 80 percent for animal life. The large cities were Fort Worth, Columbus, Austin, San Francisco, Jacksonville, Indianapolis, San Jose, San Diego, San Antonio, and Philadelphia. Air Truth was reporting that each attack was occurring like clockwork, exactly fifteen minutes apart.

"Do you see the pattern?" asked Sarah.

"You mean every fifteen minutes?" said Mark.

"No, there's something odd… Why those cities and not Los Angeles or New York?" asked Sarah. "Why Fort Worth when Dallas is thirty miles away and has a much higher population? Why not New York? It's the perfect target. There are more people packed tightly together in the Manhattan Protectorate than all those other cities combined. The Manhattan Protectorate is fish in a barrel for those bastards."

"I see what you mean," said Mark. "Not one protectorate has been attacked, and they should all be at the top of the list now that the hives can trigger huge attacks."

"They're herding people into protectorates," said Sarah. "The breeding ranches of the future. Want to live? Squeeze into a protectorate."

"Quiet!" said Kathy. "Listen to what they're saying."

The Air Truth reporter's speech was halting. There was some kind of commotion in the background.

Yes…. all right… I'm going to report that too… Okay, everyone, I'm told it's now been over thirty minutes since the last kill-zone hit Fort Worth and no new kill-zones have been reported. Either the pattern has changed or this nightmare has ended for now. Let me switch to one of our analysts… Mary Hamilton…. Mary, are you there?

Yes… yes, I'm here… I just wanted to explain how different this outbreak is compared to what happened two years ago when kill-zones where striking all over the world and all at the same time. The obvious difference is that every creature with a central nervous system is now at risk—people, our pets, even insects. The less obvious difference in this series of attacks, one every fifteen minutes, is that it's more like a gruesome warning of some kind than an all-out attack.

A warning?

Yes… It's almost like a countdown and they stopped at ten. Each city in the sequence had a smaller population than the immediately prior city. It was as if they had an almanac and went through the list of cities by population in reverse order.

Mark plugged in the Droid he had taken off the dead bodyguard. While a thread of his attention was fully engaged in what was occurring inside the Land Cruiser, another part of his awareness was about to compose an e-mail. From within the privacy of a hidden vault of awareness inside his mind, dangerous ideas had crystalized. He was trying very hard to keep his surface thoughts from veering off to the hidden message within the message he was about to write. He had to keep the god-machine in the dark. Openly thinking only about literal interpretations of what he was writing was critical. This e-mail was nothing short of a stealth weapon he would launch at Prometheus using the dead bodyguard's phone.

With anything less than nuclear weapons, simultaneous destruction of the huge number of existing hives was impossible without months of prepositioning and planning. That kind of nuclear assault would leave a pockmarked, ravaged earth behind. Mark was betting that McKafferty would see things the same way and opt to attack Prometheus instead of the hives. As Mark completed his e-mail, the part of his awareness inside his private vault hoped McKafferty would understand and accurately read between the lines and the intentional lies. Mark had no way to encrypt the e-mail with any assurance the god-machine could not decrypt it, and what was the point, anyway? The god-machine could have already read the e-mail a word at a time as he composed it.

He also might be fooling himself that his private vault was so private. He was only going by what Noah had taught them about mental self-control and concealing thoughts. How was there any way to know if the vault worked other than send the message and find out? There was also a significant benefit in allowing the god-machine to read both the e-mail and his surface thoughts literally while missing the concealed, all too human message it also contained. He nervously pressed the *send* button. A delivery confirmation came back within seconds. Mark had won this small battle. It was now out of his hands. The god-machine had taken no action to stop what had just been done—then he suddenly had doubts. What if the god-machine had been watching everything and this was exactly what it wanted? What did that mean?

"We have to do something," said Kathy. "Someone has to stop this. What about Zuris? He has zone-jammer suits, weapons, and soldiers. They can track down and destroy each hive. You said the god-machine won't care. It may even help us get rid of those monsters."

"Maybe Zuris is working with the hives," said Noah. "Has anyone wondered how he was able to develop such advanced machines? He is building devices that might as well be alien technology as far as modern science is concerned."

"How do you know Zuris won't help unless we ask?" complained Kathy.

"The hives have a loaded gun to the head of every organic in the world," said Noah. "How do you destroy the hives one at time without the hives taking you with them once they realize what you are doing?"

"You told me they can't attack worldwide without the god-machine stomping on them because of the damage they'd do to Mother Nature," said Kathy. "They can't get us before we get all of them. There are a lot more humans than hives. We could outnumber them a million to one."

"In the end the hives will win," said Noah. "The guides are sentient machines. They have done the math and would not have launched their attack if the math did not assure victory. They are improving their weapon every day. There is less collateral damage today than when they started. With every day the ratio of collateral damage tips more into their favor. The guides were very cunning using zero-G to build their kill-zone weapon and the goddess to protect it. Events have already spiraled beyond control. There are too many nests and they have the ultimate weapon. The smart thing to do is wait until we have an effective, realistic plan. Until then, what hives do to the organics is far less costly in blood than what the goddess would do if the organics became desperate and unleashed nuclear weapons. The organics are better off under temporary rule of the hives until we can devise a way to eradicate the vermin without triggering Armageddon."

"I am one of those organics!" shouted Kathy. "Why don't you just drop me off at a nearby city where a kill-zone will murder me?"

"Right now Prometheus is not the ultimate weapon," interrupted Mark. He'd had enough. "We all know a critical flaw still exists. We all agree on that. Their kill-zones are still not working right. They're destroying a huge amount of biosphere with every attack. Right now they're using their weapon sparingly because they have no other choice. They know and we know the goddess can't remain neutral if they launch a global bloodbath, which includes eighty to ninety percent of the environment within each kill-zone. You think the calculations favor their victory. You're wrong. They can only win once their kill-zones are perfected and the collateral damage stops occurring. I think your terrorist attacks on their hives goaded them into aggression sooner than was wise. We need to take advantage of that mistake. We need to obliterate them now before their weapon is perfected and they truly become unstoppable."

"Are you really ready to take that gamble?" asked Noah. "Are you ready to gamble with the lives of all the organics? I say we go to my Arizona safe house and come up with a winning chessboard. The hives don't want to kill all the organics, they want to control and breed the organics."

"Remember Stalin, Hitler, Mao Zedong!" said Mark. "*Never again* is what we said after the Holocaust, and yet we stood back and watched it happen again and again. *Never again* is what I say right now. We don't have the luxury of waiting to develop grand strategies while the hives commit larger and larger atrocities to bring the population down to a size they can control or imprison."

"Thank you!" said Kathy.

"There's nothing we can do that isn't suicidal," said Noah. "I am heading to Arizona."

"You're wrong. There's something we can do and I just did it," said Mark.

He released a memory capsule to Noah and Sarah containing the carefully couched mixture of lies and truths he'd e-mailed moments ago, then handed the Droid to Kathy to read.

"What have you done!" yelled Noah.

He slammed on the brakes, sending the Land Cruiser skidding onto the shoulder of the road. With stunning speed Noah jumped out of the Land Cruiser, yanked open Mark's door, and hauled him from his seat. Mark grabbed Noah's arms to break his grip. It was like trying to bend small tree trunks. Noah was far stronger than he could have imagined. The hybrid was a good eight inches taller and probably a hundred pounds heavier, but that did not account for this strength. One hand at a time, Noah tried to move his grip to Mark's throat. Mark fought against every inch of progress, but failed. Noah started to squeeze. Mark instantly lost the ability to breathe and knew this could be life or death. It was like a hydraulically powered claw had him by the throat. He kicked Noah repeatedly. The grip around his neck grew tighter instead of faltering with each blow.

"Moron!" bellowed Noah. "The goddess knows you sent that e-mail. You have killed us all."

Mark tried to jam his thumbs into Noah's eyes, but Noah was far quicker and extended his arms, which took his face out of reach. Mark was seeing blobs of color in his vision. His strength was waning. An assist was warning him that the blood supply to his brain had nearly stopped. The entire encounter had lasted no more than ten seconds. The explosion of a handgun fired right next to him froze Noah's grip.

"Let him go," shouted Sarah. "That was a warning. The rest are going into your fucked-up brain."

Mark toppled to the ground. He had not realized until Noah dropped him that his feet had been lifted into the air. Free-swimming COBIC were already hard at work inside him repairing the damage. Mark was regaining strength and got to his feet. He stared at Noah. The huge hybrid was simmering with rage. Noah had failed to recognize the concealed, all too human messages in that e-mail. Much of what Mark wrote was a fabricated story about what had occurred between him and McKafferty while he was being flown to Dallas. The god-machine had no way of knowing what occurred at 30,000 feet, so the obvious lies were a perfect covert message between him and McKafferty. The intended message to McKafferty was: Destroy Prometheus now and the god-machine would not seek revenge. Delay and the hives would just become stronger. The question was whether McKafferty would understand and act. The general might do nothing. If this ploy failed, Mark would have to try a more obvious and dangerous approach.

"You cannot imagine what you have done by sending that list of hive locations to the USAG," said Noah with disgust. "I am not sorry for what I just did to you, but I was not trying to kill. Our bodies are very resilient."

"I hope you enjoy walking," said Sarah.

"You need me," said Noah. "Because of that fool's e-mail, nuclear weapons may start falling at any moment on hives. We need to get to my safe house before the end of the world begins. You know you can't break into my safe house. You need the access code, which I changed before coming after you."

"McKafferty doesn't have to use nuclear weapons on the hives," said Mark. "And it's too late to go after Prometheus."

He was lying. His voice had a croaking sound to it. Every word was calculated. Just as with his e-mail, he was mixing his cocktail of lies and truths. All these thoughts and words would reach the god-machine's ears. He had no idea what to think about Noah's insanely violent reaction. Was it an act to support Mark's lies?

"You do not know this," said Noah. "But the organics have an intelligence organization named CIT that has identified the locations of many of the hives. Your list will serve as much desired confirmation and give them all they need to act against the hives. They may take out Prometheus, then go right after the hives or the reverse. They may decide a game of mutually assured destruction with the hives or the god-machine is a safe bet. The people at the top have zone-jammers and are at no risk from hive or goddess retaliation, especially after Prometheus is gone and the goddess no longer controls many of the organics' weapons."

"How do you know all this?" asked Sarah, echoing what Mark was thinking.

"I have sources," said Noah. "Your e-mail may have tipped a careful balance of power. You have no idea what you have done."

"The goddess did not stop me from writing and sending that e-mail," said Mark. "Why is that? Fallibility? Plans within plans? What?"

Noah stared with an odd, screwed-up expression on his face and said nothing....

The Goddess

McKafferty was staring out a window in his small cabin on the airborne command post. All computers used for C3 functions had been either disabled or restricted onboard the jet, which meant outside communication was limited: no phone, e-mail, or text. The giant Boeing E-4B was in a slow, circular holding pattern off the Atlantic coast. The airframe was the same as a Boeing 747. They had refueled an hour ago and had no plans of landing until the immediate crisis was over.

All top decision makers in the government were ensconced inside similar flying fortresses, safe from the god-machine for now. McKafferty shook his head, thinking about how poorly this strategy had worked the last time. Two years ago much of the airborne government had run out of fuel because no one alive on the ground was capable of organizing the needed refueling. It took two airborne tankers to refuel an E-4. Smaller airframes working this mission only required a single tanker's worth of fuel. All the jets in the fleet needed to refuel about twice a day. It was madness. The executive branch thought they had a better strategy this time. McKafferty thought they were fooling themselves. If forced to land, the people at the very top of the pyramid had zone-jammer suits made by Zero-G. McKafferty had one tucked away under his berth. The existence of the suits was a highly classified secret. There were not enough to go around. Once the top of the pyramid had been allocated the five hundred suits the government had been sold, infighting among the VIPs began. They all had a suit while their family members did not. Zuris then began doling out additional suits almost as trophies. He seemed altruistic because he would only give them away and not sell them, but it was raw power politics at its finest. Who was that prick to decide who would live or die? McKafferty was disgusted by the secrecy and the entire charade of it being a privilege to have received zone-jammer suits. He rubbed his temples to ease the pain. He knew if there was no other choice than die, he still might not put on his suit. What was left of his family was unprotected.

Zuris had resurfaced and was holding up at a secret facility, location unknown. The man had amazingly not lost any of his political power and in fact was now even more in control. He was now running much of the country and the military fully in the open. From video conferences it became obvious Zuris had held back some of his zone-jammer technology, but no one dared called him on it. The bastard was apparently able to shield small buildings and had never shared that little piece of

367

news. McKafferty suspected the people running what was left of the shattered government would gladly crown Zuris king in exchange for shielding a bunker or two or three.

McKafferty was reviewing plans for obliterating the Zero-G facility. All the plans gave him a sense of justice. Not only would this be a decisive blow against the god-machine, it would also hurt Zuris to see one of his prizes turned into rubble. Once the god-machine began attacking cities all across America, the decision to hit Zero-G was out of McKafferty's hands. The politicos had been forced into drastic action, and taking out Zero-G was at the top of the short, drastic list they had been given by the Pentagon. The politicos, the Pentagon, and now even Zuris wanted it hit soon and hit hard. They would not negotiate with terrorists, be they human or machine. McKafferty also caught a whiff of what smelled like revenge coming from Zuris, or maybe the man just wanted his mistakes buried quickly and deeply. Wrenching back command and control of their military network and drones was assured by this strike. Even if that was all they accomplished, it was worth it. No one was sure this strike alone would stop the kill-zones. The goal was to draw blood and show the machine there was a price to be paid. In the seconds between when the bombs were released and obliteration, an ultimatum would be sent through Prometheus to the god-machine. Part of that ultimatum was that we humans had more targets of opportunity after this one, including two supercolonies and many of the communes. It was all about the gritty politics of war, which had a language all its own.

The only question that remained was how to flatten Zero-G. The attack plan McKafferty was currently reviewing was called Long Bow and specified a strike package using one megaton nuclear EPWs. The assessment was that one nuclear earth-penetrating weapon could do the job with a recommendation of three to guarantee complete destruction. For more times than he wanted to recall in the past twenty-four hours, he was looking at the very real option of nuclear weapons on American soil.

McKafferty heard a commotion toward the rear in the command post. The phone mounted on his bulkhead buzzed. He went aft instead of answering. He walked into a situation room that had taken up sides and was at war with itself. Someone had figured out that the citywide kill-zones were decreasing in size and thought this was terrific news. Others aggressively disagreed. McKafferty was confident it was nothing but spotting meaningless patterns in the fog of war. This entire outbreak had been so different from what had happened two years ago. The initial kill-zones around Zero-G and the Los Angeles coms bunker had fit the original pattern. In fact, they had shown unsuspected surgical accuracy by killing only combatants and not civilians. By comparison, the follow-up attacks on large cities were sloppy. The newer attacks carried different data signatures, which had forced the NSA to tweak their advance warning software. There was also heavy collateral damage in animals and the targeting was very poor. As a result, none of the military's predictions were matching reality. There was also the question of why had some of the largest cities been spared so far. McKafferty refused to draw any conclusions. He remembered how foolish he'd been the other day, thinking they were in a standoff with the god-machine that would last for some time. The music had stopped only a few hours after that moment of hubris with confirmation of kill-zones smashing into large cities around the country.

One of the general's aides walked up and motioned him to step outside the situation room. He handed McKafferty one of the covered clipboards they were now using instead of tablets for top-secret information.

"Sir, this e-mail took a while to get through the human filters. It was addressed to you personally, but not sent to your Pentagon e-mail address. We have confirmed the identity of the sender as much as possible. We believe the message is authentic. It's from Dr. Mark Freedman. He is using a phone registered to Zero-G."

McKafferty scrutinized the e-mail. What did this mean? Though there had always been the hope Freedman had been killed at Zero-G, he was not surprised the bastard had escaped again. He walked back to his cabin to compare Freedman's list of communes to the top-secret list CIT had compiled.

McKafferty soon confirmed that location after location matched, along with a very large bonus round of communes they had no idea existed until now. McKafferty stared out the window, trying to think this through. The e-mail was definitely from Freedman. He'd used the passphrase he'd been issued two years ago at the BVMC lab when he was still human and still on the right side. Freedman was stubbornly pushing his theory that communes were the aggressor with the added complication that they were using Prometheus as a kill-zone weapon. His fabrications about what they had discussed on the way to Dallas contained a coded message to hit Prometheus and any other sister sites that might exist. McKafferty had to grudgingly admit Freedman's theory did fit the facts almost as well as anything the NSA or CIA had cooked up. The fight would certainly be easier if communes were behind all this killing and not the god-machine. Ending this conflict by destroying a single target called Prometheus would be a stunning victory. McKafferty wished it were so but could not swallow that kind of thinking. Regardless, both the god-machine and communes were enemies of the state. This was war and Freedman had just given him some actionable intelligence on communes. If Freedman was right about everything, then flattening Zero-G made even more strategic sense. Maybe Freedman was trying to make amends?

McKafferty picked up the phone and had orders transmitted to NSA to see if they'd captured any signal intelligence that showed kill-zone commands could be originating from Zero-G. As he hung up the phone, he wondered if the god-machine had been listening in. He'd been assured with the C3 onboard computers turned off, the command post was secure. The only computers they were using were off the grid.

Soon after the cyber-attack, they'd been operating under the assumption that every digital communications system was compromised. For top-secret material they were using backup systems that relied on secure USB thumb drives or printed messages, both delivered by courier. They had supersonic jets running delivery loops from airborne command posts to ground stations. For intra-jet coms they used unbreakable, one-time cipher pad encryption and handheld line-of-sight laser communications gear, which was never hooked into a network and so off the grid and unreachable by the god-machine.

The military had planned for warfare under nuclear EMP attack and cyber-attack. The American military was not impotent. They had hardened and isolated much of their defensive and retaliatory systems. While naval and ground forces were vulnerable, the Air Force was not. Their air power was still just as accurate in delivering devastating strike packages, just not as coordinated. They owned the high ground.

McKafferty awoke to the buzzing of his phone. He could not remember falling asleep. He was suffering from total exhaustion. He was too worn out to go aft and instead grabbed the receiver. What he heard woke him right up. The god-machine had sent by secure e-mail a warning to the executive branch. The use of the government's own encrypted secure e-mail system helped to confirm the source as the god-machine. The warning was that the god-machine did not care what we did to each other as long as it did not include the use of weapons of mass destruction. The use of NBC weapons on any target would result in *terrible consequences*. McKafferty wondered if this was just a coincidence or if the god-machine was anticipating their actions based on the e-mail Freedman had sent in the open without any encryption. Maybe Freedman was even smarter than he thought. By sending his message in the open, he was inviting this kind of confirmation of his claims by the god-machine. If this was a reaction by the god-machine to his message, then it went a long way in validating Freedman's theories. It also was a second vote in favor of Freedman being on the right side of this fight.

What if Freedman was also right about the communes? McKafferty could not totally dismiss the possibility that the soulless buggers were using Prometheus to trigger the city destroying kill-zones. In a fair and just universe destroying Prometheus would end the kill-zones, though McKafferty was still convinced the sole aggressor was the god-machine and the attacks would continue. No matter what action the military took, heavy civilian casualties were a possible outcome. It was long overdue to get seriously bloody on that fucked-up machine.

General McKafferty – North Atlantic Ocean – March 20, 0002 A.P.

The coffee from his shattered mug was running down the bulkhead. McKafferty felt a little better after having thrown it. He reread the latest e-mailed list of demands from the god-machine one more time. If they gave in and implemented this list, they would be putting a yoke around their neck that could never be broken. The machine even wanted full video surveillance inside the entire federal government, including the DOD. The exclamation point on the sentence was the god-machine's missile attack on *Air Force One*. Automated countermeasures had averted disaster by a hair and given an F-22 Raptor the kill-shot that took out the source, a stealth drone. Yet the god-machine had made its point. *Terrible consequences* for using nuclear weapons might mean decapitation of the government and not kill-zone attacks on the population. So much for feeling safe on the high ground. The president sounded ready to comply with the list of demands. McKafferty found himself in the unexpected position of being grateful that Zuris was now in the role of dictator at large. The man must have had steel surgically implanted in his spine. He was not giving an inch and was pounding his fist, demanding immediate destruction of Zero-G if for no other reason than to show the goddamn god-machine that we humans were willing to play tit for tat with all the chips on the table.

The final consensus was to go with McKafferty's recommendation of using a night strike package of conventional EPWs called Big Blues. The weapons would be loaded onto every mission-ready B2 Spirit they had Stateside. This gave them fifteen batwing stealth bombers, each with a max payload of two Big Blues. Each bomb tipped the scale at 30,000 pounds. It was an awesome amount of non-glow in the dark

371

shock and awe. The speed and precision of the B2s would deliver a hailstorm of EPWs, timed fractions of a second apart on impact. The entire bombing run would be over and the Prometheus bunker would be rubble, four seconds after the first bomb detonated.

The more McKafferty thought about it, Freedman was probably right about retaliation. There was no upside for the god-machine to retaliate once Prometheus was gone, but self-defense had to be a completely different calculation for that godless chunk of silicon. The attack had to be quick enough and unstoppable after the first bomb was released and the ultimatum delivered. Was four seconds giving the machine too much extra time to think and react? Long Bow could reduce the retaliation risk with split-second timed instant nuclear destruction. It would be like a smoldering period at the end of their ultimatum. McKafferty was relieved Long Bow was off the table. He kept thinking about all the innocent citizens in the Dallas area who would die from blast and radiation if they'd decided on Long Bow.

Mark Freedman – Arizona safe house – March 20, 0002 A.P.

Mark thought of Noah's safe house as an enigma. It was a high-technology island in an ocean of primordial shifting sands. The artwork that covered the walls and filled the open spaces looked like it belonged in a museum. Curious etchings, done on gold leaf, depicted scenes that just did not look quite like they fit into known history. The gold could have been a hundred years old or a hundred thousand years old. There was no way to scientifically date it. An assist had provided cryptic and incomplete information about the etchings. Mark began to wonder if those pieces of art were far older than a sane person would imagine, and what did that say about Noah? How long could a hybrid really live? Sarah had given Mark one of her Berettas, which he kept holstered on his side at all times in case Noah decided to try to jettison one or more of his house guests.

Mark was seated in the living room looking out through the wall of glass. Every few minutes he found himself secretly willing McKafferty to follow his advice of attacking Prometheus and leaving the hives alone. Don't stir up those hornet's nests. Mark thought about the beekeeper suits sitting in the duffel bag in his room. If Zero-G had mass produced those suits, none of this would be happening. If Zero-G had developed a portable large-area zone-jammer system, they would have had a weapon that could cleanly destroy hives by cutting them off from the n-web. Defying all the odds, Zero-G under Zuris's leadership had made every possible wrong decision when it came to winning this war.

For the first time since the plague, government-run television and websites matched what was reported by pirate broadcasters and bloggers. It was open to debate whether this new level of truth was due to the loss of the tools of censorship by the state or simply that events warranted no censorship. What was not open to debate was that the hives were winning. There had been no large kill-zones since Fort Worth. Instead, small, random kill-zones were erupting around the world. It was textbook terrorist tactics. The small kill-zones were less of threat than seasonal flu, which would kill far more people in any given year. Rumors were spreading that protectorates had some kind of defensive shield and that's why they remained unscathed. News reports showed people streaming into protectorates at unsustainable rates. The Manhattan and Chicago Protectorates were, for the first time, closed to newcomers. Mark was unsure if the hives planned on using the protectorates as their breeding farms or convenient concentrated targets. Regardless, Sarah had been right that their plan included shepherding humanity into the protectorates.

Mark could hear television shows from the media room down the hall. His frayed nerves sent electric shockwaves through his body every time the sound of breaking news came from that direction. Every time he expected to hear terrible reports that the protectorates had become scenes of carnal destruction. Kathy had been mesmerized by television since their arrival at Noah's safe house. Mark sensed part of the compulsion was a thirst to reconnect with the world since her imprisonment. There were multiple satellite downlinks, decryption gear, digital recorders, and a wall covered in screens to feed her thirst.

Sarah had spent a good amount of time in the media room with Kathy watching events unfold. As far as Mark could tell, Sarah and Kathy had not exchanged a single word. The only hint of their awareness of each other was that they were seated on opposite sides of the room.

As far as Mark could determine from the goddess, she had total control of all telecom networks, include the Internet and most intranets. Every firewall, switch, and router that was accessible now had new login credential and configurations set up by the goddess. Information technology crews had apparently given up trying to restore original settings and take back their systems. As soon as they made a change, the goddess undid it.

Mark glanced at the bodyguard's Droid to check for a reply from McKafferty. Without access to the devices that ran the telecom networks, the government could not even trace a phone call. Mark felt very safe using any form of public communication. The same would be true in the most repressive regimes and the most open. In this one aspect, the world had finally been democratized.

Mark wandered into the kitchen to find something to drink. He'd thought about something stronger but there was no point. Alcohol would be seen as poison by his body. His organs would metabolize and eliminate it before there was any psychological effect. Mark heard someone walking into the room behind him. He knew it was Kathy by her emotions and a taste of her thoughts. The flavor was bitter. She was about to turn around and leave.

"I am sorry about everything," said Mark.

"There are more important things to worry about," said Kathy. "Stop apologizing and learn to live with the guilt."

Mark Freedman – Arizona safe house – March 20, 0002 A.P.

The last thing Mark remembered before waking in this altered state was staring unseeing through the glass wall at a spectacular pink and red desert sunset. He had been thinking about becoming a father again. Now he was caught up in what could only be described as a lucid dream that felt like an out of body experience. The same female voice he'd heard before was whispering to him.

"We live inside the goddess, an entire world of us in the space of a drop of rain."

He saw them all around him, an entire cosmos of lost souls. Did they even know they were dead? He got the sense that they could perceive him and thought that he was dead and they were alive. Mark was stunned by all the emotions and thoughts pouring into him from this vast world of—

"Mark!" It was Sarah's voice. "Mark, wake up!"

Mark opened his eyes. The lights in the room were off. He was back in the safe house in front of the glass wall, which was now filled with night sky and shadowy landscape. Sarah was a dark outline.

"It's all over the news. They have smart bomb nose-cone footage, talking heads yakking about shock and awe, the works. The military has leveled Zero-G in Dallas!"

Mark checked the Droid. A short message appeared on the brightly glowing screen.

You were right and wrong. Thank you for helping us retake our networks from the machine. The bastard put up a fight, some good people died, then it gave up. The kill-zones have stopped and no retaliation has followed. Your e-mail has cemented new trust between us. You should

They had destroyed Prometheus and the nightmare was over. Mark
was both relieved and saddened as he thought about the hybrids who
were wired into Prometheus like so much human circuitry. The mass
murderer Alexander—or should he say *the Messiah*—wasn't innocent,
but the other certainly could have been. They were all gone now, innocent and guilty alike.

Mark followed Sarah to the media room. Blank spots were emerging in his entangled interface. Access to information from the Internet
was gone, but everything else felt normal, or as normal as it could be
in a world teetering on the brink of self-inflicted ruin.

Mark kept thinking about how rashly he'd acted in sending that
e-mail to McKafferty. He'd had no choice, but he also had not considered how risky the move had been until much later. How could he have
been so sure the goddess was not within that private vault inside his
mind, watching as he planned his secret message within his message? It
seemed improbable that he was a puppet following her plan, but it also
seemed equally improbably that she was not watching in some way. So
why had the goddess not interfered? She had control of the Internet. She
could have blocked or altered his e-mail in any number of ways. Maybe
the reason was simpler than byzantine plans within plans or paranoia.
Maybe she was not omnipresent. She might not have known the source
of the e-mail or even known of the e-mail until it was too late.

As Mark entered the media room, both Kathy and Noah looked over
at him. On the various screens different collections of reporters were
lined up at a safe distance from the action. The explosions that leveled
Zero-G were replaying on a split screen next to the talking heads. The
audio track for that screen had been selected and was coming through
surround-sound speakers.

*From what I saw, that machine gun-like strike of rapid ex-
plosions was too big to be conventional weapons and too small
to be nuclear. We have not detected any increase in radiation.
Our military analysts have no idea what the Air Force used to
take out those terrorists. We're being told that the cyber-attacks
on the Internet have stopped. Earlier speculation that the ter-*

rorist cyber-attacks and kill-zones were coordinated has been confirmed by unnamed government sources. Both attacks began within hours of the hostage taking at Zero-G....

Mark was impressed. The disinformation had resumed as soon as the USAG wrestled control back from the goddess. Noah was still staring at him. Mark wondered what this man's goals really were. He was a ghost in every sense of the word. His view of the world was probably completely alien to anything Mark understood.

"We were lucky," said Noah. "You could have just as easily triggered Armageddon with that e-mail."

Mark Freedman – Arizona safe house – March 21, 0002 A.P.

In the thirty-six hours since Prometheus had been destroyed, no new kill-zones had been reported. The evening felt rich and quiet. The world was on a better footing. The road to rebuilding would be a long one and the hives were still a threat, but Mark felt humanity would get there if enough people worked together. Cooperation, not competition, was the skill that insured our distant ancestors' survival in a world brimming with far stronger predators equipped with fangs and claws. Survival of the physically fittest and most aggressive was pure myth.

He and Sarah had walked outside for a short distance and were sitting on a stone that made a perfect bench. It felt life affirming to be directly under the stars and surrounded by nature. The night sky had that sense of depth that only the clearest desert air could reveal. The winds carried a complicated mix of desert plants and below that an earthier element. Sarah was leaning against him. He could feel her warmth. They had been talking about their child. Mark felt that for the first time in his life he had a path laid out before him that he could walk if circumstances allowed him that privilege. He was ready to stay with Sarah, be faithful to her, and raise their child. In his nanotech brain he could never erase the vivid memories of how all his earlier relationships with women ended, but maybe that was meant to be.

"Once we're sure the hives' plans are permanently derailed, I'd like us to go to the West Coast to live," he said. "We can find someplace that's quiet where no one will know us as hybrids. Maybe Carmel or Monterey?"

"Are you reading my mind?" asked Sarah.

"No more than you're reading mine."

The moment was so perfect. They were like teenagers planning on running away together. Each were talking and dreaming up wonderful ideas for the other. Mark thought, "It just does not get any better." He thanked God for this new chance.

First his cell phone, then Sarah's, began ringing. Whoever it was knew both their numbers. He answered it and heard a tone. It took a moment for him to realize it was the emergency broadcast system. A recorded message began playing. At the same time a memory capsule from Noah came to the forefront of his mind, demanding his attention. As he experienced the capsule a cold sweat dampened his skin. Mark stood up, feeling lost. Staring at his surroundings, he saw nothing. Sarah had obviously received the same capsule. He could feel her emotions darken. Kill-zones had hit some very large cities, one not far from where they stood. The small, random kill-zone terror attacks had also resumed. Since they had not in any way experienced the kill-zones, that meant this was not the work of goddess but the hives!

Mark Freedman – Arizona safe house – March 21, 0002 A.P.

Mark felt completely defeated as he stared at television screens filled with gratuitous horror and little explanation. There were fires started by home and industrial accidents burning everywhere. A nuclear reactor was failing badly in China. The kill-zones were escalating and showing no sign of letting up. The list of cities hit around the world was growing to proportions far too similar to what they'd lived through two years ago. A deep sense of tragedy and déjà vu was sucking the life from Mark. Collateral damage to Gaia was nowhere close to a level that would provoke the goddess. What no one had considered was that damage to wildlife was negligible in large cities, which were mostly concrete and tar. There was just not much animal life there to begin with.

It now seemed so unlikely to him that the hives, or rather the guides, would have bet everything on a plan with such exposed weak points as Zero-G and collateral damage to Gaia. The bombing of Zero-G was such a predictable early chess move. They had to have seen it coming. It was now clear Prometheus was nothing more than a huge decoy, a sacrificial pawn. It had been such hubris to allow himself any thoughts that they were winning this war. Sarah was seated next to him, softly crying. He could feel her heart aching with sorrow for both the world and for a fresh start at life in California they had allowed themselves to imagine was possible only a short time ago. She was scared for their child. So was he. He knew she was keeping something from him about their child and the hives. He had no illusions. They were the threat that the hives would come for next. Mark touched her womb, sensing his child's presence. Their child was almost waking up inside her in some basic way. It was as if his fingers could almost sense the warmth of a candle's glow.

It was not going to end like this! He took his hand away and felt rage at the hives for their drunken lust for power. The rage filled him and drove out all other thoughts. If the goddess was looking, all she would see was emotional flames.

"You insects will lose!" said Mark.

He stood up, keeping his mind blank of everything except for searing rage. Ignoring questions from Sarah, he left, marching down a hall and into their room. He unzipped the duffel bag and put on the beekeeper suit that was inside. As soon as the jammer powered up, he was safe. All his thoughts were solely his own again. There was no risk of leaking. As long as he kept this suit on, not the goddess, Noah, or even Sarah would have an idea what he was feeling and most importantly, no idea what he was planning.

Sarah came into the room and stopped short. She must have felt the radiation of his emotions disappear and came to check on him.

"What are you doing?" she asked.

"I can't explain," said Mark. "Just trust me. Go back to the media room and act like you saw nothing."

Sarah stared at him silently. He could imagine the calculations going on in her mind, but isolated in this beekeeper suit he had no direct sense of her thoughts or feeling. He did not like this self-imposed prison, but it was the only way. He prayed this was not some terrible mistake. What he was about to do would be so final, so permanent. If he was wrong, Noah's decision to do nothing would end up being a far better path to have taken.

Sarah nodded and left. It felt heartening that one person in his life still unconditionally trusted him. He would not let her down. He would not let his child down. He would not let humanity down. The sacrifice felt right. He hoped he was not making a mistake that would sacrifice them all, including his child.

He picked up the Droid and composed a short e-mail outlining part of his plan. He asked McKafferty for his phone number. Mark would then call him with a list of coordinates, new targets for the most powerful weapons in the USAG arsenal. The coordinates were information he could never trust to e-mail. Too many eyes might see the coordinates, which could expose the plan. He pressed *send*. He had no choice but to act. Had he not been wearing the beekeeper suit, Mark had no doubt the goddess would have stopped him, even if it meant withholding protection from kill-zone signals and eviscerating his brain with run-amok seeds.

The goddess had no idea what he had just started, and he would keep it that way until the deed was done. What if McKafferty refused? Mark picked up the Beretta Sarah had given him. If anyone tried to remove the beekeeper suit, he would use the gun on himself. If the suit's power ran out, he'd use the gun on himself. He'd have no choice.

Their room had no lock. He carefully crept from their room to stairs that led outside. He was on edge, expecting Noah to intercept him. He reached the outside door and felt the cool desert air through the screened visor of the beekeeper suit. He thought about using the Land Cruiser, but had no idea how to hotwire a car, and inside this suit there would be no assists. He ventured a few paces out onto the sand. He looked around, deciding on a direction to walk. He heard the door open and close softly behind him. His heart was ready to explode. He tightened his grip on the Beretta and slowly turned.

Everything changed for him in that one moment.

Sarah was alone. Tears glistened on her cheeks. She had her M4 slung over her shoulder.

"I knew you were leaving," she said.

Mark didn't know what to say.

"I am coming with you," said Sarah. "If this is a suicide mission, then I am coming with you there too."

Mark felt tears well up in his eyes. He reached out his hand. Sarah hesitantly came to him and intertwined her fingers with his. He could feel her fingers tighten against his gloved hand. He wished he could feel her warmth.

"I doubt we'll need these guns where we're going," he said.

"Where are we going?" asked Sarah.

"Shhhh… I'll explain everything soon enough."

General McKafferty – North Atlantic Ocean – March 21, 0002 A.P.

McKafferty was itching to fight back. He'd taken to pacing the length of his airborne command post. He thought about the e-mail Zuris had sent out an hour ago. The man had suffered a blow. McKafferty found himself feeling sorry for the personal tragedy. The king of Zero-G had discovered his son was working with the communes and had modified Prometheus for them. This confirmed Freedman was right about the perpetrators, but wrong about Prometheus being the only source of the attacks. NSA had also corroborated the story with confirmation that some of the new, sloppier kill-zone signals had emanated from Zero-G.

The e-mail from Zuris had announced to the government, his board of directors, and his family what had happened and that his son had already paid the ultimate price. The king had executed his own blood. McKafferty decided the man did not have steel in his spine. He had ice in his spine. The second part of the e-mail was even more chilling than the news about his son. Zuris had a large contingent of mercenaries, and they were all equipped with zone-jammers suits. He was making it very clear that no matter how the dice landed he would remain in power when this bloodletting was done.

While the destruction of Prometheus had not stopped the kill-zones, it had stopped the cyber-attacks. The military had full command and control restored. With kill-zones hitting American cities hard, McKafferty had run out of good ideas. He needed to find a way to hit the communes so overwhelmingly and so precisely that they did not have time to implement any kind of doomsday attack when they realized their world was coming to an abrupt end. That was no easy feat. The god-machine seemed indestructible and there were far too many communes. That took nukes off the discussion table, which was not such a bad thing. The list of confirmed and likely commune locations in Freedman's e-mail from the other day read like a Greenpeace manifesto of natural wonders and high population zones. The god-machine would undoubtedly attack to stop wholesale destruction on that scale. These communes were devious sons of bitches. Even if the communes were located out in the middle of uninhabited deserts, the fallout from so many nuclear weapons was unacceptable. That kind of blunt weapon might kill more noncombatants with blast, radiation, and fallout than the communes were planning on murdering with their kill-zones.

McKafferty returned to his cabin, locked the door, and sat down. He picked up his tablet and checked his e-mail. He then picked up a half empty pack of Marlboro nails and lit up. His coffee cup was filled with spent butts. He could see his reflection in the cabin window as he drew in deep breaths of smoke. He stared at his reflection and shook his head. This war was going to get so ugly, there might not be any winners.

McKafferty's tablet signaled an urgent message had arrived. He stubbed out his nail. The e-mail was from Freedman. As McKafferty read the text, his blood began to flow warm, then hot... son of a bitch. He knocked over his coffee cup ashtray onto the floor and didn't care. Freedman would be a goddamn hero if this worked. The parts of his plan relayed in his e-mail were bold and unexpected, but solid. It was all or nothing. Every chip would be in the pot. More than anything, McKafferty wanted to draw serious blood and he did not give a rat's ass about the blowback.

Conventional wisdom was that the American nuclear arsenal employed no warheads larger than one megaton MIRVs. Conventional wisdom was wrong. The arsenal included massive ballistic earth-penetrating weapons, which carried twenty-five megatons of bang and were powerful enough to reach far down into the earth or water with its shockwave. They were engineered to defeat any hardened bunker or nuclear submarine with a single strike. The RNEPs were nicknamed Devastators. McKafferty issued urgent orders to make ready for snap deployment of SIGINT reconnaissance drones once Freedman followed up with targeting coordinates. If the coordinates checked, they had a strategy to win this war with a single blow. Zuris would approve this strike plan and so would the puppet government in Washington. If they didn't, McKafferty would act on his own. Post plague, the rules and fail-safes had changed. Right now from his Looking Glass command post he could launch a nuclear strike. He might have to shoot a few good men to make it happen, but the survival of the human race demanded it. If he was wrong, the good news was that he would probably be dead and never know it.

Mark Freedman – Near the Arizona safe house – March 22, 0002 A.P.

Mark was sitting with Sarah in a clearing ringed by creosote and other harsh desert shrubbery. He could tell Sarah was confused. He felt so much more human by gauging her feelings in the old ways instead of sharing her emotions as they radiated out across the n-web. They had walked several miles, then stopped by an ancient Indian campsite. Sarah knew her way around this part of this desert from her previous stay at the safe house. She told him about the coyotes that had followed her and Ralph.

"Their behavior was all wrong," she said. "I had a strange feeling that Noah might be working with them in the same way I work with Ralph."

The first rays of the sunrise were soon lighting the horizon. The sky was fading from black to dark blue. The barren landscape was coming into clearer focus like a mirage. Mark wished he could take off the beekeeper suit, but not yet. He checked the Droid. The inbox was empty.

"Do you think something made of nanotech can have a soul?" he asked. "Can it reincarnate?"

"You have a soul," said Sarah.

"Does the goddess have a soul?"

"I don't think so."

"Then why should we? I'm now as much a machine as the goddess and you're not far behind."

"When I had my near-death experience, I crossed over into an afterlife. I have no doubt we continue when our body dies. If my soul had died when I became a hybrid, that experience wouldn't have happened."

"You're far more spiritual than I am," said Mark.

"Are you going to tell me what's going on?"

Mark glanced at his Droid as a message from McKafferty appeared. He stood up and walked off a little ways. He did not want Sarah to accidently see the message. The goddess could be looking though her eyes now or sometime in the next few minutes through timeline recordings of her. Since McKafferty was in an airborne command post, he was completely shielded from the eyes of the goddess.

Mark turned to look back at Sarah and saw his footprints in the sand leading from her. The desert was less covered with n-web pathways than the oceans, but not by much. The sand contained bacteria, insects, and other small creatures that carried COBIC inside them. The sand itself also held raw seeds, which had embedded themselves inside some of the grains when this desert had been an ocean floor. Sunlight was a source of power for seeds, and there was plenty of power in this wasteland for seeds that were on the surface. Everywhere he stepped, the invisible linkages of the n-web radiated out in all directions. Mark looked at the message.

> The well-oiled gears of our war machine are turning. A synchronous strike is awaiting targeting intel. Dial *1191957 and you will be patched through directly to me. My friend, you are heroic! Duty Honor Country, GM

Mark swallowed and felt something caught in his throat. The words *synchronous strike* did not necessarily mean high-yield nuclear weapons, but he knew they would be used. The recommendation had been his. Succeed or fail, this was on his shoulders. His heart was beating fast enough that he thought he might suffer a heart attack. Maybe the beekeeper suit was affecting the regulation of his metabolism. In any event, he wouldn't need the suit much longer. He feared what was about to happen. It would change their lives forever. He thought about their child and felt ill. He hadn't allowed himself to think about the personal dimensions of what was going to occur. If he had, he might not have gone through with his plan, and humanity would very likely end up enslaved. There was no guarantee what they were trying would work, but there was also no other sane or insane option.

He dialed the number and spoke softly. The call lasted little more than a minute. One of the strikes would not be far from where he stood.

He wondered what it would look and sound like before everything was lost. It would not be long now.

Mark sensed something moving about near his feet and looked down. A giant desert anthill was not far from his boots. The creatures were large, fast, and aggressive. They had captured and killed a praying mantis. Mark thought about the queen ant deep inside her underground empire. She was the mother of all the ants in that hive. She was the insect goddess ruling her world with brutal efficiency, a perfect living machine. Kill the queen and the hive breaks down and dies. There was only one queen and she was irreplaceable.

Mark Freedman – Near the Arizona safe house – March 22, 0002 A.P.

Mark was holding Sarah's hand when a huge, earth-penetrating thermonuclear weapon detonated belowground about thirty miles away. A shallow subsurface detonation for a missile delivered nuclear weapon was highly unconventional unless what was needed was concentrated ground penetration, instead of wide area destruction. Mark knew the strike was directly over a water rich aquifer. He knew that in the same instant similar strikes were happening all over the globe in areas of deep ocean and other aquifers.

The signature double flash from the nuclear explosion was blinding even though sunrise was approaching and the contours of the land had shielded them from the worst of the detonation's effects. He could sense free-swimming COBIC going to work on his eyes. Mark felt the flashes were like powerful medical X-ray exposures, but knew at this distance there was no danger from nuclear radiation. Thermal radiation was a different matter. He examined the sides of his hands that had been exposed and saw what looked like sunburn. He knew his face had received the same exposure. The burn was already fading as COBIC began also repairing that damage. They had about two and a half minutes before winds from the blast effect reached them. Sarah looked at Mark with an expression that broke his heart.

"I'm scared," said Sarah. "I've lost my connection to the god-machine."

Mark shucked off the beekeeper suit. He'd realized after they'd reached the Indian ruins that Sarah was the canary in the coal mine that would tell him if the attacks had worked and it was safe to take off the suit.

"How could an explosion block my connection?" she asked.

"The goddess is gone," said Mark.

"What do you mean?"

Sarah stopped speaking as a memory capsule from Mark expanded in her mind. Her sunburned face become stern and he wished there could have been some other way. The only option left to them to destroy the hives without provoking the wrath of the goddess was to disconnect all the hives from her. Without their connection they would perish. With his nanotech brain entangled with the goddess, Mark had access to far more information about her than he'd had before. He knew the exact location of every supercolony of seeds that hosted the redundant copies of the goddess. McKafferty and the USAG military following Mark's instructions had destroyed the goddess with a synchronized rain of thermonuclear weapons. Sarah's expression grew horrified.

"What about our child?" cried Sarah.

"Hybrids can live without the goddess. I've been cut off for days at a time."

"What about years at a time? What about forever? What about a developing fetus? You don't know those answers, do you?"

"Murder!" bellowed Noah.

Mark turned to see the huge hybrid advancing on him from the desert undergrowth like a rampaging bull elephant. The ghost was unarmed. Mark stood. Noah shoved him backward, lifting him off his feet. Mark got up and backed away to a safe distance.

"You've killed the goddess!" he bellowed. "You've condemned us all."

"We've wiped the hives from the earth," said Mark. "We've saved billions of lives."

"At what cost?" yelled Noah. "I should have killed you days ago."

Mark had his Beretta out and aimed at Noah's forehead. He was confident he could stop the man instantly. They stood in a silent standoff.

The blast winds from the detonation reached them. It was like a hurricane force sandstorm. Mark had no choice but to close his eyes as he went down to a kneeling stance. The howling sound was like an animal in terrible pain. He felt clumps of debris striking his back. He knew Sarah's eyes were also closed and that she was safe. The blast winds died down almost as quickly as they'd arisen. Mark opened his eyes as soon as he could risk it. He was forced to blink as small eddies of wind continued to lift grit into his eyes. Noah had not moved. His eyes were wide open. Mark found himself irrationally wondering if the ghost had kept his eyes open during the sandstorm. His face looked terribly damaged.

"You should shoot me," said Noah. "There is no purpose, no meaning anymore."

The hybrid turned and began to walk away. Mark saw a knife drop from his left hand. He had not seen the blade and for some reason Noah had failed to use it.

Epilogue

Mark Freedman – Carmel, California – November 11, 0011 A.P.

The years had passed quickly. For someone like Mark, with the possibility of near eternity before him, years would someday begin to feel like days. He was walking down a cliffside path that led to the beach. The Pacific Ocean stretched to the horizon. It was a perfect, cloudless sky. The air was sweet and cool. Seagulls were calling to each other in the distance. A large super tanker was plying its way north, probably destined for San Francisco. The human race had still not freed itself from its dependency on oil. The plagues had bought the world more time to wean itself and paid for that time in blood.

Mark spotted his daughter Gaia playing beside a tidal pool with Sarah. He knew they would be there doing exactly what they were doing. He'd been watching them in his mind for several hours before heading down to join them. Today was his daughter's birthday. She was nine years old. She was physically developing like any normal human child, with the exception that she was never sick and healed as quickly as he and Sarah. Gaia was born with a nervous system and brain that were fully saturated with nanotech seeds. In that way she was completely unlike any other human child before her. She was far too intelligent for her age and had all the enhanced mental and emotional capabilities of her parents. To her, this was normal and if anything had made raising her easier. They all shared their thoughts and feelings using the n-web. The remnant technology had been left in perfect operation after the goddess was no more. The sorrow in Mark's heart from the plague years had been replaced with hope for the future. His small family was proof that with total openness, empathy flourishes.

Mark and Sarah had not had another child. They had decided they would raise one child to adulthood at a time. They had that luxury. They could have as many children as they desired over their long physical lifespans, which might last until the stars began to dim in the sky. Though Mark suspected they would grow tired of this physical world long before then and explore the life after death he and Sarah were convinced existed. Living without a physical body would be such freedom after being locked inside the limits of flesh and the material world for ages.

With the goddess no longer living, their child would never know the shared thinking and godlike infinite knowledge that Mark had experienced. With the goddess no longer living, Sarah had been unable to evolve much beyond the point she'd been at when nuclear weapons had rained down onto the Earth. The same had been true for other hybrids they'd met over the years. Their evolution had slowed to a normal pace. The catalyst, the accelerant, their goddess was no more. In the past nine years they had encountered no other hybrids like them, hybrids that could have children. Mark knew that made him and Sarah the first true transhumans. They were the Adam and Eve of a new species. Unable to reproduce, all other hybrids that came before them were mutations, not a new species. It took the goddess a very long time to craft Mark and Sarah, and she had protected them well. Mark wondered if she knew she had created her own means of dying. Perhaps her purpose was complete and she was ready to sleep.

As Mark neared his family, something strange began to happen. It started as a feeling of déjà vu, then grew in intensity. Sarah looked up at him with concern. She was feeling the same things. A moment later Gaia stopped playing. She looked at Mark and smiled warmly.

"Daddy, it's the goddess," said Gaia. "She's come home."

Mark was stunned. He had just received the same implanted memory that Gaia must have experienced. This was not déjà vu he was feeling. His entangled interface was coming to life. Assists were feeding him information. All the things he had missed for over nine years were returning.

The goddess had reanimated. No, the goddess had reincarnated. A new memory brimming with explanations expanded in Mark's awareness. Crying, he kneeled next to his wife and child, and enfolded them into his arms. The goddess had allowed herself to be killed in a selfless act of devotion to humankind. Over the following years, the super-colonies that were destroyed by the nuclear weapons had reformed as seeds came together from all the oceans and rivers and seas. Once the first supercolony reached critical mass, the spark of life was rekindled and a goddess was reborn. The sentience of the goddess had just arisen like a phoenix.

This was not a new sentience. This was the original goddess returned to life. All the timelines and other vast storehouses of knowledge were completely intact. How was this possible? Mark kissed Sarah's forehead and then his beautiful child. Sarah's eyes were brimming with tears. He understood she knew everything he did. She knew the sacrifice the goddess had made for them so they could live free of a cancer that would have consumed the world.

Mark hugged his small family tightly. The rumble of waves and the splash of water on rocks in the background soothed him. It felt as if years had passed in the embrace of his family in this isolated spot along the coast. In the quiet after the emotional storm, Mark finally was composed enough to think.

"The timeline archives are unharmed," he said. "All her memories are unharmed. How can a computer's memory remain after the computer was destroyed?"

"You know the answer," said Sarah. "We are all more than our physical bodies. The goddess is pure life. She's implanted inside me some of her memories of her death and rebirth. She experienced the same things I did when I died. Her body may not be flesh, but she is as alive as us. When her body died, her soul fled into the same world of lucid dreams that I found. Just as with us, her essence lived on in that realm. When a new body was ready for her, her life's energy was poured into it and she came back to her children. She came back to us."

THE END

MAY / 2014

Made in the USA
San Bernardino, CA
08 April 2014